Amanda Addison writes and illustrates both adult and children's fiction. A common theme to her work is the world of art, craft and design; Amanda is a graduate of Chelsea School of Art. She lives in a small village in Norfolk with her husband and two children.

For more information on Amanda's writing and designs, visit her website at www.amandaaddison.com.

Turn to the back of this book for quick, fun and easy patterns to make and sew at home.

Laura's
Handmade
Life

Amanda Addison

SPHERE

First published in Great Britain in 2011 by Sphere

A CIP catalogue record for this book
is available from the British Library.

ISBN 978-0-7515-4534-0

Typeset in Caslon by M Rules
Printed and bound in Great Britain by
Clays Ltd, St Ives plc

Sphere
An imprint of
Little, Brown Book Group
100 Victoria Embankment
London EC4Y 0DY

An Hachette UK Company
www.hachette.co.uk

www.littlebrown.co.uk

To Joyce, who really can sew!

Acknowledgements

Heartfelt thanks to everyone who helped bring this book to life. Special thanks to Sonia and all at Sheil Land and to my wonderful editor Caroline Hogg at Little, Brown, whose interest in all things 'crafty' have helped bring *Laura's Handmade Life* to print. Jan Miller and Jennifer Sharpley for patiently teaching me the joys and sorrows of sewing in the first place. Cathy Terry and the staff at Carrow House for filling in the gaps. Fashion and textile friends and colleagues for sharing their own stories. And finally to my husband and family for letting me get on with my writing.

Methinks it is a token of healthy and gentle characteristics, when women of high thoughts and accomplishments love to sew; especially as they are never more at home with their own hearts than while so occupied.

Nathaniel Hawthorne, *The Marble Faun*, 1859

Part 1

Part 1

Chapter 1

Arrowhead stitch consists of a pair of straight stitches worked at right angles to each other.

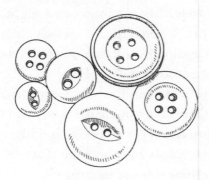

Keep calm! Keep calm! Breathe deeply!

I open the door to our first guests.

'Hello Mrs Stark. So kind of you to invite us,' our neighbour shouts in my face over the chimes of the church clock. She's standing expectantly in her tightly buttoned up jacket and matching green wellies. She doesn't look dressed for a party. How punctual, I think, as the last bell rings through my ears. I look at her silver-haired husband who's laden down with a Waitrose platter of salmon canapés and a bottle of burgundy. Here it's not just the thatched cottages; everything is upmarket. The credit crunch hasn't hit the good villagers of Reedby!

'Heather and Kurt Weatheral,' she says on behalf of them both. They grin and nod their neatly cropped heads in unison.

Something about them reminds me of those little wooden couples who precisely on the hour, every hour, come out of cuckoo clocks.

'Call me Laura,' I say, placing the burgundy next to the other bottles of white wine lining our doorstep. 'Make-do fridge,' I add, trying to justify having so many bottles of alcohol half buried in the snow.

They brush the snowflakes off their waxed jackets, take off their boots and Heather rummages in a gigantic carrier bag. Out come the his 'n' hers slippers. I watch them slip into their comfy sheepskin slippers and for a moment I wonder, will Adi and I be like them some day?

I neglect to add that I'm not Laura Stark. I'm Laura Lovegrove. I thought about changing my name when I married Adi, but just never got around to it. I like the alliteration of Laura Lovegrove, as I live in hope that one day my fabric designs will become a household name.

'Do you think my footless tights are OK?' I ask Heather Weatherall. 'I wasn't sure about the electric blue with the ballet pumps.'

'What I do like is the fact you're not wearing your outdoor shoes. It's very Japanese, changing into house shoes,' says Heather, giving me a knowing look.

'Are you into Japanese design?' I add, trying to make some polite chit-chat.

'They do know a lot. I've Feng Shuied our house several times. Kurt nearly did himself an injury the last time. He came home and without looking he went to sit in his favourite chair. I'd replaced it with a big bowl of stones,' says Heather, chortling a big horsey laugh.

I smile politely.

She then stares at my dress. 'Not really the weather for bare arms. I've got thermals on under these,' she says smoothing down her velvet trousers.

'I'd never have guessed.'

'You can't be too careful when you reach a certain age.' Heather steps closer, 'You watch out for cold and damp in Reedby.' She then mouths, 'Urinary tract infections.'

I nod, saying, 'I'll stock up on the cranberry juice.'

'Oh silly me, I get it now. I know why you've got a summer dress on – it's fancy dress,' she says, looking really worried at first and then breaking into another loud laugh. 'I'm sure my mother had a frock just like yours,' she adds.

'Oh she always dresses like that,' butts in Adi, coming out of the bathroom with two freshly scrubbed little girls. He looks the perfect dad, with Daisy holding one hand and Lilly clutching the other. The girls don't really resemble me or Adi. Although looking at them now, Lilly is starting to take on Adi's gangliness and Daisy is more soft and curvy like me. They've still got blonde hair, but at age seven, Lilly's is starting to turn mousy, or dark blonde, the more flattering term hairdressers use for my boring hair colour.

'Laura's big passion – clothes.' Adi winks at Heather and brings me back to the here and now. She blushes. So much for my attempt at girl talk. Adi's pulled. It's Adi's grin that does it – well, it always has for me.

'Watch your head,' says Heather, helpfully lifting the stair door latch. Adi swiftly follows the girls up the stairs, ducking just in time to miss the door frame. She looks at me. 'These cottages weren't made for men as tall as your husband.'

'Adi,' I call. 'The girls promised to put themselves to bed tonight.' I know what he's doing. He's trying to avoid socialising and leaving the hostess bit all to me. I'm certain that for each year we've been married Adi has withdrawn further into his own little world of designing other people's homes and offices on a computer screen. He hardly ever suggests going out and I have to confess that this party was all my idea.

'I've got this for you,' calls Kurt Weatherall, halting Adi's escape upstairs. He holds up one of those brown jute supermarket bags which everybody seems to carry so proudly, and announces, 'It's a torch. A present for all newcomers to Reedby.'

Adi comes back down. 'Lilly, Daisy,' he calls, 'get yourselves into bed and I'll be up in a minute.'

'Can't we stay up a bit longer?' pleads Lilly.

'Go on, it's late enough already.'

'May I present it on behalf of the parish council,' Kurt says thrusting the bag into Adi's hand. 'You can't have too many torches in Reedby,' he says, proudly.

'Thanks,' mumbles Adi. He always goes quiet and mumbly when he's feeling shy and embarrassed. He hands the torch to me as if we're playing Pass the Parcel.

'Men today, they are so helpful around the house. So good with the children,' Heather muses. I don't reply, I'm thinking that Adi is always more helpful when other people are around.

Heather carries on talking. 'Oh I always wondered what it was like inside Marsh Cottage,' she says, leading me around my own house. 'Mrs Jones, your predecessor, wasn't one for inviting you in,' she adds. 'Kept herself to herself once all those children left.' Mrs Jones couldn't wait to get us in, I remember. Only Londoners would fall for a hard-to-insure thatched cottage, close to a river and of course the sound of the less-quaint-by-the-day chimes which ring out day and night from the oh-so-picturesque flint church across the Green. That's what happens when you relocate in a rush. But even Adi, a fully fledged modern architect of glass and metal, had fallen in love with the natural materials: flint, thatch, stone.

'What a lovely fireplace – and a woodburner too. Just the place for a dog to curl up and get cosy in the winter,' says Heather.

'We don't have a dog. I'm not really a dog person,' I say.

'Just you wait,' says Heather with an enormous grin. 'A house isn't a home without a dog I've seen it all before, in my line of business.'

'What is your line of business?' I ask, genuinely intrigued.

'All things dog really. Paws and Claws, that's the dog grooming part of the business. Then there's the training: K9 Capers. You see, people move to Reedby and after a few months they're out walking, or to be honest tugging, a puppy around the village,' she chortles 'And the third strand,' she says, moving closer, 'is under wraps at the moment. But just between you and me,' she whispers, 'I'm working on a dog training book.'

'That's impressive,' I say. 'I've always wanted to have my own business. But I don't know what I'd do.'

'Anyway, where is the lavatory?' asks Heather, changing the subject as she notices Kurt coming towards us. 'I don't need it at the moment, but one doesn't want to be caught short. Does one?'

I point Heather in the direction of the loo.

'You need some logs for that fire,' says Kurt. 'I'll give Adi the logman's details.' Why can't he give me the details? I wonder.

Kurt Weatherall escapes from his wife into the conservatory. I follow him. He sits down and makes himself at home in the cane rocking chair.

'You look smashing. That dress – it's so exotic!' he says, fondling my cheese plant. I smile. I always fall for it. Any flattery is appreciated once you're past thirty. Mind you, not that I'm much past thirty!

'It's hand-painted, watercolour on silk,' I say. He isn't listening. He looks up at my cleavage. The bodice bones dig into my ribs if I bend forward. 'You coordinate. Your dress and that bowl of fruit. So ripe.'

'How observant,' I say in my schoolteacher voice. Well, I'm a college lecturer, but close enough. I spot the fruit bowl, next to him. Just don't move anything, I almost shout. There's no time to explain that I'll need the pineapple in the morning, and I don't relish the idea of finding another pineapple on a Sunday, in February, in Reedby. They are my still-life collection, my work tools. I've got one more design for the Tropicana collection to finish in the morning. With a magician's sleight of hand I remove the fruit bowl and replace it with a bowl of crisps. Well not just any crisps. I bought the deep-fried root vegetable variety. I see Kurt put his hand in the bowl and retract it again. I wonder if I made the right decision with the crisps. I so wanted to create the right impression. Perhaps I should have put Hula Hoops out after all.

'Almost ate your pot-pourri,' he laughs. 'Heather has a bowl in the bedroom. It's something to do with creating good vibes,' he says.

I cringe, wondering just where this conversation is leading.

'These don't smell of much. They need a splash of perfume.'

I munch a beetroot crisp and notice how cold the conservatory is. I know any sensible person would put a jumper on; but I can't bring myself to ruin my outfit. I'm as bad as the 'midriff girls', my teenage art students who show their midriff (decorated with tattoos and piercings) all year round.

Kurt talks about the village allotment group, which he is chair of. I tune in and out of his gardening tips. To avoid slugs: '. . . you can go down the organic route, copper tape or coffee grounds; it dehydrates them.'

I feel anxious and pick up my supersize glass of bubbly. Without getting too close, I manage to glance at his chrome watch. I never wear one myself. Watches just confirm how late I always am. This time I see that it's early. It's only 8.30 p.m. Someone else please come to our party, I pray. I begin to wish the snow hadn't come. If it hadn't friends from London would be stepping into our new home any minute now.

'Thanks for the torch,' I say, trying to re-enter the conversation.

'It's no ordinary torch.'

'Really?'

'It's a wind-up one. No need for batteries or electricity. You'd survive a siege with that,' he says, starting to wind the blue plastic handle.

Is there trouble in Reedby? I want to say.

'The Neighbourhood Watch is ever vigilant. Did you know that rural crime has doubled in just the last year?'

'No, I didn't,' I answer in all honesty. I then say something that I know Adi will kill me for. After all it was his idea that we uprooted (or 'streamlined' as the architectural partnership called it) to Norfolk.

'I'm sure Adi would be interested in joining the Neighbourhood Watch. Shall we go and find him?' I suggest, walking towards the door, noting how settled Kurt looks in the rocking chair. He takes the hint and gets up. It's hard to imagine any crime other than the Miss Marple kind in Reedby. The village isn't on the way to anywhere, other than the Broad. Just as we head out of the conservatory the doorbell rings and I make a quick exit from Kurt.

Adi's work colleagues, or rent-a-party, as they're known, fill the empty rooms. It's strange to think that it was only at Christmas that we last saw Adi's motley group of architects; not in the wilds of Reedby, but in the suburbia of Ealing – my natural environment. I'm still surprised that they all moved en masse from London, but then again, 'a job's a job,' as Adi said at the time, secretly relishing the opportunity to get out of the city.

Then come the school-run mums and dads. I hardly know these people, but they still give cause for me to breathe a sigh of relief. Perhaps it's the resemblance to the Ealing mums and dads. They all dress in the same brightly coloured natural fabrics: polka dots, stripes and stylised florals. This sounds as though I'm judging them by what they wear, and I suppose in a way I am. But as a fashion and textile designer I'm pretty much entitled to, you might say.

Then I realise that the real reason they seem so familiar is that one of them is wearing one of my designs. The red and white stylised tulips are definitely mine. It's not often that one of my surface pattern designs actually makes it past my agent, the shops and the buyers into an actual real piece of clothing. The tulip repeat around the bottom of the satin tunic works really well, especially as this woman is slim enough round the hips to carry it off. Feeling much more confident I walk up to the pale, black curly-haired woman, whose name I can't remember, and say, 'Hi, Laura Lovegrove. Can I get you a drink? By the way, I do like your top.'

'Thank you. I didn't think it was my sort of thing,' she laughs. 'Not the design – the price. I couldn't afford anything like this,' she whispers. 'It was a Christmas present from the mother-in-law,' she says, failing to tell me her name.

'Oh,' I say. I go off the idea of getting her a drink and we're soon diverted by a crowd which is gathering at the bottom of the stairs. All I need now is for the girls to be up.

David, Adi's right-hand man and a brilliant, yet unconventional, architect (Adi's words, not mine), is standing with his fingers on the stair door latch. Do you like my suit, Laura? Got it yesterday for seven pounds in a charity shop.'

This is a real sharp-intake-of-breath moment. David was always Mr Savile Row, looking every bit the hero from *Brideshead Revisited*. He is the blonde-haired blue-eyed boy. I can't stop myself from staring at the outsized polyester suit, thinking that he should be in linen.

'Look what's in here,' he says holding up a worn leather rucksack. Before I can look inside, he undoes the bag and pulls out a pair of paisley pyjamas.

Their bright red and green fabric brings a smile to my face. There's something joyful about the design. I wish Adi would sleep in brightly patterned pyjamas, rather than his black Y-fronts. Adi is a plain (or 'block' colour as we say in the industry) dresser. But don't get me wrong, he probably spends more than me on getting the right jeans and T-shirts, sufficiently distressed not to look new, or make him look middle-aged.

'I told the old dear in the charity shop that I was going to a sleepover and usually slept in my birthday suit, but didn't want to embarrass my hosts. I also told her how the word pyjama in the original Persian means clothes to go outside in, and how the word pyjama had got lost in translation. She said I was a mine of information and decided I could have them for free.'

'You're too charming for your own good,' I say, punching him on the arm. 'And how do you know these Trivial Pursuit facts?'

'You know my dad, genius scientist, master of ten Middle Eastern languages, fluent in another five …' He then looks serious and says, 'It's a bit weird being in Reedby actually.'

I want to say, yes, it feels a bit weird to me too; but I'm too scared to say that as I'll probably offend someone.

'What do you mean?' I ask, intrigued.

'Mum and Dad live just down the road. Dear little house. Not that I'm living with them. I'm too old for all that. They wouldn't approve of my decadent ways,' laughs David. 'They moved up here when I was at Cambridge.

'So Laura, a question for you.'

I wonder what on earth David is going to say. Please don't ask me what I think about living in Reedby, miles away from my friends.

'What's the origin of the paisley motif?'

'I know this one! It was the shape of little children's crooked thumbprints.'

'No, urban myth,' says David.

'So what's the answer?'

'Must dash,' he says with a wink.

'You can't do that! I need to know the answer.'

'As with the pyjamas, we have to go back to Persia. That's where the motif originated.'

'Paisley doesn't sound Persian,' I say, sceptically.

'It's a textile odyssey. The motif went to India, Kashmir to be precise, and then to Paisley.'

'You mean Paisley in Scotland?' I say, smiling and shaking my head at David. He's such a mine of information.

'Of course. It could have just as easily been Norwich – with their big textile industry.'

'David, you should be on Mastermind,' I laugh.

'You're not the first person to have said that.'

Kurt passes me with Adi following closely behind. 'He wants to see the cellar,' Adi whispers, 'he thinks it's a security risk.'

I try not to laugh out loud, Adi always says things to give me the giggles. I watch Adi, Kurt's head disappearing down the steps. 'Shouldn't he be following *you*?' I mouth back.

'Ladies and gentlemen, our cabaret for the evening,' announces David.

I look up at Danny, another of Adi's colleagues. *How could he?* His hairy chest peeks over my brocade corset. The silk organza flowers balance on his wiry hair. Like one of the Ugly Sisters, he totters precariously on the landing. He grabs the stair rail, unsure how to negotiate the narrow cottage steps in my fur mules. I hear laughter.

'Looks like they were made for him!' laughs Heather Weatherall, downing another glass of pink champagne.

I can't breathe. All sound drops away. My temples bang. I see Danny descend the staircase. His dark hairy, yet shapely, legs strut down the narrow stairs. I'm going to pass out. The woman in my tulip design top takes my hand and leads me into the kitchen.

'You're not all right with that, are you?' she asks. 'Your face. You look like you've seen a ghost.'

'Oh I'm fine. He does look funny in my clothes, doesn't he?' I say, forcing a laugh.

'Well, burlesque is supposed to be back in fashion,' she smiles.

'The corset's original Art Nouveau, with swirly leaf patterns on the brocade. I found it in a charity shop in Tooting. I can't believe it, that he'd, that someone could rummage through my collection,' I mutter, pouring myself a very full glass of wine. 'If Adi put him up to it, I'll kill him.'

'That's a bit strong.'

'No, I wouldn't kill him, I'd just cut up his clothes – he might not have many jeans and shirts – but the ones he's got cost a fortune.'

'I can see your husband's not a Primark kind of man.'

'How do you know that?' I ask.

'It's the little details,' she says with a knowing smile. 'And the visible labels,' she confesses.

We both snigger as if we've known each other for ages.

'But the chap on the stairs could have put the right decades together, at least. A 1920s corset with the 1970s housewife mules: it just doesn't go! I'm Liz by the way. It's like mixing up my mum's and great-granny's wardrobes.'

I laugh and am impressed that she knows her fashion.

'I guess the 1950s woman who first wore my dress is turning in her grave, seeing as I'm wearing it with footless tights and ballet pumps!' I say, taking a big gulp of wine. I don't tell her the whole story, how it was my mother's favourite dress. Now isn't the time to go into all that.

We stay in the kitchen. I wonder what Liz thinks of the colour scheme. I did my best – a low-wattage ivory bedroom lamp is perched on the Formica unit. The chocolate brown walls don't look too bad in the subdued party lighting. I'm still in mourning for my sparkly granite worktops and butler sink from the London house, though Mrs Jones' kitchen hasn't had a makeover since the late '60s. It's only vintage clothes that I collect, though if I'm honest perhaps the odd leopardskin bowl or Clarice Cliff cake stand (Adi would say I'm hopelessly underestimating here) makes it into the house. My furnishing tastes have grown more like Adi's. He's a minimalist. Gone are my days of painting bedrooms red and draping exotic fabrics from the ceiling. Now we have natural, neutral colours and materials.

Except for this kitchen – whose rebelliousness I'm starting to enjoy. The bright orange Formica worktops and yellow unfitted units have kind of grown on me. They're neither contemporary or countrified. And the truth is we can't afford to replace them.

As if reading my mind, Liz says, 'A good time to move out of London and lose your mortgage.'

'Our friends in London are amazed that we've moved to a brick and flint thatched cottage. Adi's architectural designs have always been ultra modern, as much glass and steel as he could get his clients to pay for.'

I decide not to tell her how we ended up selling our Ealing house in a great hurry for far less than the white 1930s semi was worth. But at least Adi has a job. I realise as we talk that long gone are my days of searching for the most eligible man at a party. Now I just enjoy being able to chat to another adult female! I mean to really chat about clothes – the fabric, the stitch work, the colours. It turns out Liz studied journalism at the London College of Fashion. It feels so good that someone in the village is on my wavelength! I love sharing my vintage fashion bargain-hunting stories with someone who really understands.

The church chimes midnight and I feel like Cinderella. The time has gone all too quickly this evening. 'I haven't been up this late since I can't remember when,' I say.

'Me neither. Late nights and young kids don't mix. Kate never slept much. She still doesn't – and she's seven now!'

I give her a sympathetic smile.

'Although things have improved since Jack started school,' says Liz. 'He's slept a full twelve hours a night since September.'

'I can't imagine that,' I say with a mixture of envy and hopefulness.

I pour myself another glass of what is now lukewarm wine. 'You know I met Adi in a kitchen at a housewarming party in Tooting. Our eyes met over a bowl of Bombay mix.'

Liz laughs and almost chokes on her white wine.

'I didn't even know whose house it was. Those were the days. He'd moved to London for his first job, at Lutyens and Foster, the place to be. I didn't know at the time how much we were leading the good life. We both worked full-time and there was an endless round of gallery private views, parties and weekends away.'

It all seems like another life. Somebody else's life.

After Liz and her husband Mark (also a journalist) leave I've had enough of my own party. When I was younger I always wanted to be the last to leave a party. Now with two children and an enormous mess to clear away I want to make an announcement: 'The party is formally over and the hostess is retiring to bed. And if you want to stay, fill a bin bag or better still put on some rubber gloves – we don't have a dishwasher.' Yet I'm too much of a coward to say anything. Instead I count how many hours' sleep I'm going to get. Tonight looks like four, and that is if David decides to finally crash out. I do understand that they were sent up to Norfolk en masse, or relocated, as they say. I know they're all as lonely as we are, with that same 'fish out of water' feeling. Except there are two big differences: they're all younger than us *and* none of them have any kids, so they can sleep in all day tomorrow!

I toss and turn and am desperate to get to sleep. The damn church clock now strikes two. Can't they turn it off at night-time? It's always the same after a party. I need some wind-down time before going to bed. But if I were to do that, Daisy, who amazingly has slept through all this furore and will be up at six on the dot – would wake just as I was finally falling asleep.

Chapter 2

Back stitch is an old and very adaptable stitch which can be used as a delicate outline or as a foundation in composite stitches.

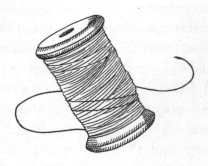

I can hear her feet running across the landing.

'Mummy, is it going to snow again today?' shouts Daisy, right into my ear, and as well as deafening me she almost smothers me with something damp and furry.

I push the furry something out of the way and squint at the alarm clock. 6.30 a.m.

'Mummy, Mummy,' says Daisy nuzzling her face into mine and now in bed next to me. Why isn't she climbing into Adi's side of the bed? 'Patch wants to make a snow dog,' she says, tucking the toy dog into bed as well.

It's pitch dark through the gap in the curtains. One of the estate agent's selling points was the starry skies.

'Look, the moon and the stars are up,' I say, trying to sound like the country wife and mother I feel I should become.

'Why's the moon up in the day?' asks Daisy. I want to hide under the covers and tell her to go back to bed. But I can't resist her plump dimpled face and neat fringe of golden hair.

'I don't think the moon ever goes to bed,' I say. It's just like being a mother. Does the moon feel as knackered as I do? I wonder.

'Come on then,' I say, taking Daisy downstairs. I hope Adi is awake and aware that I'm letting *him* have a lie in. I'm so competitive about childcare points. Sometimes I think that rather than the kids, maybe the parents of young children should have a star chart. And if you get, say, fifty, you get a day off.

Daisy and I finish breakfast and I survey the damage. Daisy's Rice Krispy-covered table, chair and carpet sweep into insignificance against a backdrop of half-empty wine glasses and trails of crisps and nibbles. I spot a note under one of the glasses.

Dear A, L, L & D (5 a.m.)
    Decided to walk to Norwich train station. Too risky to drive (the roads – not just my alcohol consumption!). Must get the 8.30 train to London.
    Great party.
    David
    P.S. Will collect the car later.

'Uncle David's walking to the city. Isn't he brave?'

'He's not our real uncle? Is he?' asks Daisy, oblivious to the fact that David is out in freezing temperatures.

'No, but he's one of Mummy and Daddy's best friends. And when I was little I called all my mum and dad's friends aunty or uncle.'

I feel slightly nauseous as I notice ivory lumps smudged into our chocolate coloured carpet. What was I thinking of with cream cheese canapés?

Can someone please tell me why we have housewarmings after we've cleaned and decorated our new homes? I'm not a killjoy or anything, but what's the point? I check the conservatory and am hit by a blast of icy air. It's survived the party relatively unscathed; just as well, as it doubles up as my studio.

I smile like a madwoman at the conservatory blinds. I handpainted the design on those blinds in twenty minutes flat. 'My blinds are completely unique,' I say, as if selling them to myself. Swirls of crimson and turquoise dotted petals still make me smile.

I take the fruit bowl out from the cupboard – my own still-life cupboard of objects which Adi finds too 'unaesthetic' to be allowed into the rest of the house. It's all there ready to inspire me: to paint, collage, draw over the top of in my recognisable Laura Lovegrove style. I blot out the chaos (after all, the house *always* needs cleaning and tidying).

I look at the pineapple, mangoes and kiwis perched on the leopardskin plate and before I even begin, I hear, 'Mummy.' Daisy is hovering by the door. 'Can I have a piece of that pineapple?' How do I explain to a three-year-old that it's a still life, a tool of my trade, and not for eating? Not yet anyway.

I do love being a textile designer. I might moan about working evenings and weekends. No such things as Sundays off for the freelance worker! But the adrenalin rush I get when I go into one of the chain stores and see my designs on a dress, duvet cover or curtains; I get a real buzz out of it, making everyone's world my vision of beauty and getting paid for it.

That is the fantasy image of Laura Lovegrove that I tell others – my fellow college staff, old school friends, Adi's colleagues. I don't tell them the truth that only very occasionally do I sell any designs and that if I didn't teach I wouldn't really be earning anything.

Perhaps I'll check my e-mails and then start work. I'm always hopeful that I can design something that will sell. I'm always hopeful that the big break is just around the corner. Although I'm a long time out of art school and sometimes I wonder if I'm deluding myself that one day I'll be a top selling designer. There are moments when I think I should just go and work in an office and forget about it all. Except I know I couldn't do it, I would die of boredom. Being creative is a human right. I relent and go into the kitchen and bring back a plastic bowl and take away a few pieces of fruit from the still life. I hand Daisy the Postman Pat bowl. I know I'm procrastinating; I'm just like one of my textile students putting off that moment of getting started.

Thank God for the wonders of e-mail. I tell Gill, my agent, that it's best to e-mail me, as I don't like stopping to answer the phone when I'm mid-design, mid-painting. Of course there is some truth in that, but the real reason is nobody knows that I manage to type and send attachments of my designs amidst squabbling kids, or while breastfeeding (well not now of course – Daisy is three!) or making dinner. I can still convince the world and myself that I am a professional designer!

21

to: lauralovegrove@virgin.net
from: gilldavison.co.uk
subject: Tropicana designs

Hiya Laura,
just a tincy wincey change with one of your designs. Do
say that you can do it today. You know how it is, if not
I'll have to ask one of those eager beaver girls at St
Martin's School of Art. But they just don't have your
experience, darling. The pineapple one you're sending
today. You are sending it today? Aren't you Laura? Just
could you add some lime green hues to the background?

Well that's easy, I think, we'll just fiddle with the colour filters
in Photoshop. Or rather Adi can, if he ever gets up. It's then I
read the next bit.

It's the summer 2010 series. Ice cream pick 'n' mix. I'm
sure I sent it with the others. Anyway we need four
designs for this. I've attached the colour palette. Rather
not my colours. It all reminds me of British seaside
holidays: candy floss and beach huts. So just think of
pick 'n' mix sweets and candy floss by the sea.
Apparently we'll all be holidaying in the UK by the
seaside for years to come! I'll be waiting for them.

Yours Gill

Part of me thinks, can't I have Sunday off for once? Another
part of me relishes the buzz of a deadline and being forced to

come up with four designs on a Sunday morning when most people are still in bed.

Of course there's no guarantee that she'll sell any of these and if I counted the hours I work and the designs I actually sell I'm sure that my designs don't even earn me the minimum wage.

I look out at the snow. It is falling in great white flakes. They really look like the paper cut-out snowflakes we stick to the windows every Christmas. I am in a picture postcard village. The frozen pond, with the snow-covered church, its thatched roof and the round flint tower hidden under white, all makes for a backdrop as charming as a Brueghel painting. Except, where are the skaters? Skating is probably not allowed, health and safety ... Why aren't I designing Christmas cards?

I think of sunny days on the beach eating pastel-coloured ice cream and sweets. I can't think of anything further away from winter in Reedby. What I really need is some visual reference of sunny, summer colours. Images of Liquorice Allsorts flash across my mind. Suddenly my head is throbbing and my stomach lurches. How many glasses of wine did Liz and I drink? I load up the three-wheeler. If anyone still sells liquorice Phyllis at the village shop will.

'Laura! What are you doing? You're not going out in this, are you?' says Adi – finally up. This is a strange comment, as Adi has been known to go for a five-mile run in the snow – and that's before breakfast!

'Don't worry, I'm not planning on walking to Norwich. David may think he's Ray Mears but I know my limitations,' I say, playfully.

'He's more Doctor Livingstone. And he's tougher than he

looks. He's used to roughing it. He had quite a childhood trailing through various wildernesses with his parents. I just hope he's put on more than his paisley pyjamas,' says Adi in all seriousness.

I laugh, imagining David trudging through the snow in nothing but his pyjamas. The eccentric English explorer. Before Adi can get a word in, I say, 'I'd rather wear paisley pyjamas than a windcheater.' Immediately I feel good that someone as intelligent as David will champion style over substance. Just like me.

'So where are you off to?'

'Just popping to the shop.'

'You can't possibly need to go shopping.' Usually I don't mind Adi's hatred of shopping. My theory is it's a manifestation of extreme maleness and now he's an internet shopper no one loses out – birthdays and Christmases are well provided for.

But what I do mind is the fact that Adi doesn't always see my textile designs as real work. I suppose in some ways he's right, in as far as it isn't nine-to-five every day with a regular income – but it helps. It buys us all the little extras.

'I just need a few things for my designs.'

'Don't drive. The road's a death trap. And anyway you'll be there and back by the time you've got into your car,' says Adi, always the sensible one.

I don't tell him that he'll need to clear up and mind Lilly. That's easy enough though: she not only takes after her father with her willowy looks, like him she could sleep for England.

I push the buggy up our road, the Green, which today is snow white. I daydream about walking onwards through the icy

24

wilderness to Norwich and taking the train home – to London. Here in the country the houses are an odd assortment of styles: an old ochre-painted farmhouse, bungalows from the 1960s and '70s replete with stone cladding and big, uPVC windows. Somehow these homes look impermanent, as though they might set sail along the Broad and out into the North Sea.

Finally a pretty terracotta pantiled cottage, with a misleading metal plaque calling it *The Thatched Cottage*, comes into view, and next to it the safe haven of the village shop.

All ideas of walking through snowy wildernesses and escaping to civilisation dissolve. I'm trapped in Reedby. I have cabin fever. I know that in London the Tubes and buses will be running taking you wherever you need to get to.

I hold open the heavy door with one frozen hand and manoeuvre the buggy onto the worn brown carpet and into the shop. I feel like one of those little people in a shaken-up snow storm dome. Three-wheelers weren't designed for the Aladdin's cave that is the village shop – a place that doubles up as the dry cleaners, post office and hub of village gossip.

'Shut that door. There's nothing between here and Siberia when that east wind blows,' calls Phyllis from behind the counter. I almost knock over the carousel of washing up gloves and half price Christmas decorations. Daisy comes to life and makes a grab for the crisps – conveniently located at toddler height. It's not my fault that I've got a buggy and there's a real snow storm outside. Buggy drivers, it seems, are always in the wrong.

Phyllis looks in a better state than me. Her black hair is definitely out of the bottle. She's wearing a full face of makeup, including gold painted nails accompanied by gold chains round her wrist. My blonde/mousy hair is dripping sleet and my feet are soaked through. I look sadly at my vintage cream suede platform boots. They've survived since the 1970s and now Laura Lovegrove has ruined them.

'You need a pair of wellingtons. I've got a few in the corner.' I make a mental note to go to Boden online and order some floral wellies. I draw the line at Phyllis' green ones. I'm not joining the green wellie brigade. I'm an individual. But the fact is that another outing in the snow and my suede boots will be no good for anyone.

Phyllis really does seem to sell everything. I survey the Aladdin's cave for Liquorice Allsorts. There are big plastic jars of sweets and penny chews. They remind me of the jars of buttons, buckles, brooches and bows in Alderton's, the haberdashers I used to visit with Mum. My treat was a fancy button, some ribbons or if Mum was in a really good mood, a brooch. According to Mum, when we visited my infant school the headmistress asked the children if they had any questions. No one said a word, except for me, who asked, 'Where are the dressing up clothes?' Will my girls remember Phyllis' shop? Will they have a lifelong love of sweets?

I still find it hard not having Mum around. She passed away three weeks before I had Lilly. It came as no surprise, but made me feel different to all my London antenatal group friends. They had their mums virtually move in after their babies were born. My old neighbour Lotte had her mother fly in from Copenhagen and she stayed for three months! But, to their credit, my friends all rallied round and just about filled in any spare moment with a helping hand. Life was easier in London, with friends a few minutes away.

I make myself focus on the girls and being a good mum to them.

I can't believe how well behaved Daisy is being, that is until she starts yelling.

'Sweeties. Sweeties!' screams Daisy, undoing her straps and jumping out of the buggy, causing it to tumble backwards into the newspaper rack. It is going to be a difficult one to get out of the shop with enough sweets for my work and to pacify both Daisy and Phyllis.

'Don't worry about that,' says Phyllis. 'Oh look at her. She's the spitting image of you.'

This isn't true, although I wish *I* was the spitting image of Daisy, with her thick blonde (controllable) hair and smooth blemish- and wrinkle-free complexion.

I smile on auto-pilot. Inside I'm tired and annoyed. I grab handfuls of pastel sweets without thinking too much about my choice. Just a range of colours and shapes. I don't care what they taste like. Then the guilt. Am I a bad mum? Buying sweets to draw and not bothering to get any for her girls to eat. I sneak in a packet of Maltesers for Lilly. Does Adi have these guilt trips in the middle of a working morning? I think not. I add one of the snow storm domes. Next Christmas' stocking filler for Adi. Am I mean? I've compromised for so many years with all white decorations, Christmas according to Adi. It's time for a bit of kitsch in our lives.

'Just jump in the buggy and you can have them,' I say, resorting to bribery – the lowest form of parenting. But needs must.

I hold onto the buggy and we slip and slide down the road. In a flash I see a car sliding across the snow towards us, I ram the buggy into the nearest driveway. So much for it being safer bringing children up in the country! Why doesn't Reedby have pavements? I think, realising that my whole body is shaking not from the cold, but shock.

Back at Marsh Cottage I don't mention the incident. I know that Adi doesn't want to hear any of my complaints about living in the country. I've tried to keep my thoughts to myself. I know he couldn't have lasted much longer living in the city. I grab my printout of Pantone colours and I retreat to my studio and take out pots of Brusho, tubes of acrylic, water-colours and oil pastels. I'd always thought of their bright colours as almost edible. My sort of sweets. Nil calories! I paint sheets of paper with pick 'n' mix colours. Candy floss pink, limes, yellows and a dash of mauve. I pin the sheets up to dry and suddenly notice that I am frozen. Smells of fried garlic seep through the cottage.

I need my coffee fix. Now coffee is something Adi and I have come to worship. Not your Starbucks' lattes but a thick treacle of filter coffee. Sleep deprivation slips away. I stand in the kitchen and sip while Adi stirs the pot.

'Good party,' he says. 'I've got a good feeling about us being in Reedby. A proper country childhood for the girls.'

I nod and smile, but say nothing. I resort to my usual solution in times of trouble and in seconds my head buzzes with shapes and colours of sherbet lemons and Liquorice Allsorts. I feel my hands and feet coming back to life as I wander around the cottage in a design daze.

I hear singing coming from the studio. I left the door open!

'Twinkle twinkle little star . . .

'My God, Daisy! What are you doing?' I scream. I watch her lick my sheets of pastel papers as if they were ice lollies. She sticks out her bright orange watercolour-stained tongue. *Act! Act! Do something!* I pick Daisy up, she feels as light as a feather as I sprint with her to the kitchen.

'Don't swallow!' I shout, crashing about in the cupboard looking for a clean mug. 'Just swirl it in your mouth,' I say, pushing the mug of water against her lips.

Daisy's lips are stuck firmly shut as if I'm trying to force-feed her Brussels sprouts.

'Daisy, please drink it,' I plead. 'Good girl. Spit it out, like when you're cleaning your teeth.'

Daisy's little heart-shaped face looks terrified. Her big brown eyes are welling up with tears.

'Sweetheart, you'll be all right.' I say cuddling her. 'You're lucky Mummy was painting with watercolours, some of the other paints have really nasty chemicals in them.'

'Laura, stop it, you're frightening her,' says Adi, stepping into the kitchen.

'I thought you were minding the girls?' I yell.

'Mummy, don't shout,' whimpers Daisy.

'Multitasking. Clearing up. Making their lunch,' answers Adi.

'Multitasking is keeping an eye out for them and making lunch,' I snap, forcing another cup of water down Daisy.

'You need a proper studio, with a lock,' says Adi, not taking any responsibility for what's just happened. 'Working in a conservatory with a carpeted floor is not a proper option. Either it's a family room or a work room. You can't mix the two,' he says, as if architectural design is the solution to any problem. I don't say anything, knowing what is coming next. Adi begins.

'If you didn't have two spare rooms clogged up with all those smelly old clothes, you'd have room for a studio.'

Before I can say that they're not smelly, they're just old, or rather should I say they are antiques, an idea hits me. 'Lollipops, gobstoppers,' I shout.

I run back into the conservatory almost as speedily as I left it. Daisy thought the colours were lollipops. I think of big circular ones, stripy-edged ones on sticks. Lollipops are much more summery than sweets.

I carefully cut out my coloured sheets of paper. I always pride myself on being the queen of collage. The handmade look, which is currently so fashionable. I rip a few edges for a soft focused line and carefully cut the sticks with my artist's scalpel and glue them down onto some light card. Ready. They are all set to scan. Adi knocks on the door.

'Lunch in two minutes,' he says, looking at my designs. 'Why don't you use a ruler and cutting mat? You'd get nice straight edges then. In fact, thinking about it why don't you Photoshop your designs? You could add different colours and repeat the motif.'

'I want rough lines and I haven't got time to learn a whole computer program,' I say, contradicting my teacher-self who's always telling students to cut, paste and change colours on the computer. 'My designs are wanted for their handmade look,' I tell Adi, not wholly believing that my designs are wanted at all. In fact since everyone can scan, colour, cut and paste on the computer now anyone can be a textile designer.

I attach, send and wait. I don't dare leave the dial-up connection. Well done Laura, you got your designs in on time, I congratulate myself.

'Lunch is ready,' calls Adi.

'I won't be a minute.' I watch the sending green shape fill up.

'Come on Laura, it'll go cold in this weather,' shouts Adi.

'Daddy. Daddy, can we go sledging? There must be enough snow now,' shouts Lilly We bolt down our second bowlfuls of pasta in record breaking time. That is Adi, Daisy and myself. Lilly is still moving twirls and red pepper round and round.

'Come on Lilly, another couple of mouthfuls and we'll all get out of Mum's hair for a bit,' says Adi.

'Have fun!' I call as they trundle out of the house, looking ready for a polar expedition. I know that Adi is probably more desperate to get outside in the fresh air than the girls. Peace at last! I sip a cup of tea from my red polka dot mug. There's something very cheerful about spotted things. You can't be miserable if you're having a cup of tea out of a spotted mug, can you? Maybe I should be designing more polka dot prints? It would cheer everyone, much needed with all the doom and gloom in the news. Except there's no free will in print design. I'm always a year or two ahead and working to someone's colour palette and theme. Two years ago we didn't know that people would be living on a shoestring and in need of cheering up.

I'm already distracted and thinking how nice it would be if the kitchen was all white, not a sterile hospital white, but a homely whitewash, instead of dark chocolate, a colour I'd never use for decorating a kitchen – not even in my wildest moments. I even have a tin of traditional English white emulsion in the conservatory – what self-respecting woman doesn't? I joke to myself, at once building up the momentum to decorate. (Actually, the truth is it makes a great ground for my print designs.) I could complement the white with some of my design off cuts. I can see it in my mind's eye, the perfect country kitchen. I'm almost preferring it to my old mass-produced granite and butler sink version in London.

Before I know it I'm standing on the kitchen stool with 'Once in a Lifetime' by Talking Heads blasting out on my now paint splattered CD player. I add a second coat of paint (chocolate brown must be the worst colour in the world to cover up!).

I keep one foot on the old wooden stool and there's no choice for it, my other foot rests in the wet kitchen sink. I see the last patch of pale brown wall. 'I'm going to get you! You will be pure old English white,' I talk to the wall. I stretch up to the side of the cupboard. I can feel the stool begin to wobble. Just paint that last piece, I foolishly tell myself just before something hard and metallic digs into my forehead. The kitchen spins round and round and I know I should jump down. Then I am on the floor. I stand up, feeling fine. I can't feel any bumps. I wipe my hand across my face and when I look it is covered in blood. The blood keeps coming and coming.

From the ambulance window I can see Adi and the girls dragging the sledge up the road. I wave, but I don't think they recognise the woman with a green bathroom towel turban waving frantically at them.

'Mummy! Mummy!' call the girls arriving in A & E. 'Daddy says you've been a bit silly.'

The nurse turns to Adi and shakes his head. 'The amount of DIY accidents we get here – you wouldn't believe it.' Adi rolls his eyes in some kind of male conspiracy when what I really need is a big hug. But after all these years, eleven to be exact, Adi's still too shy to display any public affection.

The nurse continues to ignore me and turns to the girls.

Daisy is now crying. 'Is Mummy all right?' she whimpers.

'Unlike Humpty Dumpty, your mummy has been stuck back together again.' Finally he turns to me. 'Just sign here and you can go.'

We walk down the corridor.

'Laura, what on earth were you thinking of? Why do you always act so impulsively? I could have painted it. You only had to ask,' Adi says, putting his arm around me.

'I'd only just had the idea.'

'And you had to do it there and then?' scolds Adi, as if I'm a child.

I shrug my shoulders.

'You're like Molly Dolly,' says Daisy.

'Molly Dolly?'

'You stuck her back together when all her filling came out.'

'Yes, I'm a bit like Molly Dolly,' I say, feeling quite light-headed. 'When I was little we used to have toy hospitals.'

'We could set up a toy hospital,' says Lilly.

'I don't know about that,' says Adi. 'These days people don't repair things, they just buy a new one, made in China.'

'Some toys can't be replaced,' says Lilly, in her best grown-up voice.

That's my girl.

Chapter 3

Barb stitch creates an ornamental line with a ridge down the centre. It is an easy stitch which makes it an ideal choice for children and beginners as they will be able to sew projects quickly and gain a sense of achievement and satisfaction.

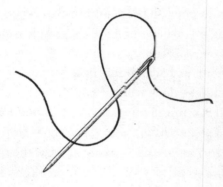

'Mummy, did you pack a duvet and hot drinks? Daddy said you should,' calls Daisy from the back seat as we slip down Walnut Hill (which must be the steepest hill in The Broads) and out of Reedby.

'Do you think Lilly's school will shut?' asks Daisy.

'Let's hope not. Anyway Daddy dropped her off at Breakfast Club, so he'll have to sort out collecting her,' I say, feeling guilty that I can't be in all places at all times.

For a girl who isn't going to be four until the summer Daisy sounds so grown up – so sensible, just like her father. 'No more questions now. Mummy needs to concentrate.'

We slide across the icy roads and I hear a bump. 'Ouch!' shouts Daisy. I check her in the driver's mirror and am reminded of the enormous plaster across my forehead. I see Daisy rummaging through my new Cath Kidston holdall, which is now on her lap.

Just when I think I can't concentrate on the road any longer, and the whole contents of my bag are strewn across the back seat, I turn into Town and Country College. I look in my rear-view mirror and see my lesson plan covered in red biro swirls, my blue geometric tablecloth strewn across the seat and Daisy clutching my fox and hen milk jug. At least my work bag is interesting.

For a moment, as I search for somewhere to park, I mourn my single, childless days when I commuted to Old Street. I long to be 'carless' and to travel on the London Underground. It now seems the height of indulgence to sit sipping a coffee, flicking through a magazine, looking at what the other passengers are wearing – and all on the way to work. So what if I was employed by some back-street textile company rather than a designer label. I was paid to sit and draw and colour in ideas for the latest trends.

Mum was still alive then and I'd go home at the weekend to our cold fenland bungalow, with its icy metal-framed windows that never defrosted, and we'd soon warm up on a proper nut roast, with all the trimmings – just for the two of us. We both became veggie after Dad died. It all happened so suddenly. He'd had a heart attack at work, was rushed to hospital – but it was all too late. I was fifteen, and looking back becoming a vegetarian was a bit like us taking up a new religion.

The conversation would always come round to Mum saying, 'Laura, if you're colouring in pictures all day, when do you go to work and earn some money?' She lived in another world. Perhaps I'm living in another world, wishing that I could still spend my days designing – and getting paid for it. Sometimes I so wish that I could take the girls to Mum's for the weekend; but the house, like Mum, isn't there any more – it was snapped up by developers and turned into three houses with all mod cons.

I step out of the overheated car and realise that I don't have a coat. Today, I feel as if I've done a day's work already. I could have rung in sick and been grilled by the call-centre nurses that we have to ring. They then decide if we really are sick enough to have a day's paid sick leave. Also, with Adi's company threatening another round of redundancies I can't be ill. Even if I look like I've just crept out of a car crash. And of course I'm late.

It was all such a rush, getting into the car, getting the engine running, while finishing getting everyone dressed, de-icing the car, packing Daisy's bag, packing my bags. There was no time to think about myself.

I plead with the nursery staff to give Daisy some Rice Krispies. They look up at the clock gravely. I feel as if it is me, not Daisy, who is the child, unable to make a decision for myself. Am I imagining it? Or are all these young girls without kids of their own looking at me disapprovingly? Is it my lack of a coat, or are they thinking, Why didn't she feed her child before taking her out in the cold? Bad mother. Why do I care what they think? It's just however much I deny it, their opinion matters. I need to be tougher. I am after all paying a fortune for childcare.

I sprint back to the car and see that the Micra's no longer purple, she's wearing what looks like a white fur coat. Oh why does it have to keep snowing! I'm late enough as it is! I'm tempted to leave the car in the nursery drop off, or park in a disabled space. By the time I clear the snow and drive round to the staff car park I'll be *really* late. And what's more the door to the art department is a tempting thirty-second sprint from the nursery drop-off. I look around as though I'm about to commit some terrible crime and open the boot. I grab my wicker basket, refill my holdall, pick up my carrier bags (as I never have enough posh bags) and somehow carry all of these in two hands across the ice and through the double doors.

I feel a proper teacher barging my way down the corridor with a heap of bags and then ducking into the staffroom. Teachers, male or female, are the real bag people of the world. There's always marking, books, resources and if you're an art teacher there are all those bits and pieces for a still life. When I think about getting run over I don't think about my mother's warning to 'always wear clean knickers, just in case.' Instead, I wonder what they would think of my bag full of dried flowers, milk jugs, off-cuts of fabric, a tin tray with orange and chocolate brown repeat patterns (from the same era as my kitchen) and a rosebud cake stand, among other things.

I go back outside and peep through the windows of the mobile, or as it is more grandly called, the mobile studio. Already the students are all there, my audience. Waiting. All waiting for me. Who let them in? I don't want to do this. As well as teachers being bag people, they're also consummate actors. I certainly remember that mine were. I don't want to go on stage today. I want a duvet day!

For a moment I think, how did I end up here, doing this job? It was that fateful telephone call. 'You can teach textiles? You've worked in the industry?' Curtis Lampard had drooled down the phone in November when I was sitting comfortably in our Ealing semi.

'Of course. Of course I can,' I said, remembering rule number one with part-time work and the deepening recession – you can't say no. They may never ask you again. Yet today feels as difficult as my first day back in January, even though I've known these kids for almost half a term.

I just don't want to do this today. Of course I like the dressing up, looking the art teacher. What other job would celebrate me turning up in my vintage prints? I love seeing what the students make. It's just all the other bits 'n' pieces which dominate the day.

Poor Adi, since our move to Norfolk he's been issued with a dress code. They wouldn't have dared to do it in London. Now he has to wear shirts (ironed) and a suit jacket, although a blazer is acceptable. So gone are his jeans-and-T-shirt London days. He's stepped back in history and is dressing up for work like my dad did – and he hates it.

Here in the creative arts department, I can wear whatever I want for work. Nobody will blink an eyelid at my 1950s skirt (with a repeat teapot and cake print) and woolly tights.

I take a deep breath and change into teacher mode. What will my audience's mood be today? Mondays and Fridays are the worst days to teach. And I do Mondays. Monday is my long work day. At the end of it I usually feel as if I've actually done a whole week's work already and am longing for Tuesday – my home day. Let's see if they are still recovering from their hangovers. Speaking of hangovers I still don't quite feel back to normal. It takes me a long time to recover these days. Maybe it's an age thing? When I cut my finger on my best brocade corset, built with real whale bone, it took two weeks to even start to heal; Daisy on the other hand has cuts and grazes which seem to disappear overnight. 'What have you done to your head, miss?' says one of the boys as I place the bags under the table.

'Morning Leon. It's Laura,' I correct him.

'That was quick. Our last teacher still didn't know anyone's name by Christmas.'

I notice that Leon not only doesn't have a coat on (just like me), he's come to college in a T-shirt and it's still snowing outside! As usual he's constantly jiggling up and down on his chair.

Maybe we'll all have to jiggle about? I think, switching on the sole fan heater and looking around for a board marker. My hands are so cold that I can hardly write *pattern and decoration* on the whiteboard.

Everyone else files in noisily. I'm supposed to tell them to take off their coats now, but I don't have the heart to. So what if their hoodies and hats are a health and safety risk. Today hypothermia is a bigger threat to their health.

'What's in the bags, miss?' asks another.

I sidestep the question. 'You're all budding designers,' I say, beginning my script. 'All objects tell us something about their owner, their place in the world. Designers also get much of their inspiration from everyday objects.' I see their faces glaze over. This isn't a good start. I need some action.

I pick the bags up off the floor and bang them down on the table and as if I'm a cross between a magician and a door-to-door salesman I pull out a piece of stripy cloth, a teapot covered in blue and green repeat patterns resembling a spirograph picture, then the rosebud cake stand. Soon the objects begin to make up a very colourful and patterned still life.

'The college has stuff like this in the props cupboard,' says Leon. 'Shall I go and get some more things?' he asks, already out of his seat and by the door.

'They're not nice like this, they're all broken and hideous,' says Amy, with her arms folded and glaring at Leon. She looks scary in her obscenely short tartan skirt and thigh-high clunky boots. He returns to his seat and rocks from side to side.

'Let's use some descriptive language,' I say, pointing to my teapot.

'Do we really have to do this?' moans Lizzy, twisting her blonde dreadlocks. 'It's supposed to be an art lesson.'

Keep going Laura, I say to myself. Don't get into an argument as to why most of your students can hardly read or write. You're the adult, you're the teacher, you know best.

'Shut up Lizzy,' says Amy on my behalf. Lizzy pouts theatrically just like a toddler; she then pushes her numerous Indian bangles up and down her arm. Amy, a girl with more piercings than I ever thought possible, wants to learn and the others are scared of her. Thank God for Amy, my class policewoman.

'But first,' I say, deciding to abandon my script, I can hardly read it anyway through the red biro. 'Give me a word for this,' I say, holding up my 1960s teapot.

'It's pretty wild, miss, all those circles make your eyes go funny,' says Leon.

I hold up the cake stand. 'What about this? How's it different?'

'It's romantic with all the rosebuds and hearts,' says Lizzy, not noticing one of the boys behind her miming a gag.

'Don't be so wet,' shouts Amy.

'What do you like then?' I challenge her.

'The milk jug's all right. All those greens and ovals, it looks natural.'

Just as I seem to have them all hooked, Leon shouts, 'He's behind you,' as if we're all in a pantomime. Before I can say, let's focus on the still life, I am face to face with Jim, our learning support lecturer.

'You're late,' shouts Amy. Jim's normally flushed face turns a deeper shade of pink.

'Snow, caught in the traffic. A bit nippy in here,' he says, rubbing his hands together theatrically.

The students all glare at him. I found out when I joined, almost by accident, that Jim had been shunted around from department to department like an unwanted Christmas present. And like pack animals the students want him out from our class.

I turn back to the group and see Leon holding a perfect handstand on the work bench.

'You need eyes in the back of your head with him,' mutters Jim.

'Can I have everybody sitting in their seats and looking at the still life,' I say in as calm and unphased a voice as possible.

'Which object would you choose to draw?' I ask. Before I can finish the question they make a mad dash for the objects. 'Now you've chosen your subject,' I shout over the rabble, 'what I'd like you to do is to choose a section and enlarge it using pastels and coloured pencils.'

'Laura,' says Amy. 'What are we going to do after that? Have we got to draw these things all day?'

'Of course not,' I lie. 'It's a surprise what we're doing after break,' I say, realising that my plan of doing a large A1 repeat design for the rest of the day isn't that exciting.

The studio door flings opens and reveals a man wearing a green fluorescent jacket. He is as broad as he's tall, more suited to being a night-club bouncer than a college security guard. He booms, 'Laura Lovegrove?' I nod. 'Is that your purple Micra parked at the nursery drop-off?'

'Yes, I couldn't get it to start,' I lie, thinking on my feet. Yet my face feels as if it's burning up. Why can't I even tell a simple white lie?

'It's strictly no parking in the drop-off. You'll have to move it, luv,' he says. Amazingly the class is quiet, absorbed in this little drama.

Go for the simple injured woman bit, I think.

'I bet I can get it to start, miss,' offers Leon.

'That's OK, I'm sure this kind man here . . .' I say, looking at the security man, who still has his arms folded.

'If I give you the keys could you try and move it?' I smile pleadingly. 'I've got a class here.' He takes the keys. 'It's more than my job's worth,' he mutters on his way out.

'Miss, he fancies you!' giggles Leon.

'Now, where was I? Leon, perhaps you could recap for us?'

'We're drawing these weird things,' says Leon, holding up my teapot.

'It's perfectly hideous,' says Jon, looking up from his list of birds. Jon is the only student who hasn't chosen anything to draw. I know he is autistic and finds decisions hard so I pick up a remnant of teapot and tulip curtain fabric. 'What about this?' I ask, putting it literally under Jon's nose.

'It's hideous,' he says for the second time. This is the most he's ever said in one of my classes, although to tell the truth it's hard for most of them (the other fourteen students) to get a word in with the likes of Leon and Amy in the group. He then gets up and walks over to the still-life table and picks up a spotted green and white mug. Without a further word, he sits down and begins to draw.

'I bet he'll draw every dot,' shouts Lizzy, as if Jon isn't in the room.

'It's 10.31. It's break,' says Jon.

'Snowball fight, Leon,' says Amy. Leon looks a bit scared of her as she stomps across the room in her black buckled boots; nevertheless he follows her. They're all out of the door before I have a chance to say, 'Go to break now.'

'Fancy a cuppa in the cafe?' asks Jim.

'Sorry, I've got too much work to do,' I say, heading toward the staffroom, realising that I've got a week's worth of e-mails to plough through.

'Why did I take on a class halfway through the year?' I say to Sue, the senior lecturer, in the staffroom. She just smiles, keeps her head down and continues clicking through her e-mails, as if I should know better.

'Sorry, Laura. I was in the middle of something,' says Sue

a moment later, looking up at me with her elfin smile. She's so tiny it's hard to believe that teenage boys are petrified of her.

'Nothing, it's just been a long day already,' I say, immediately feeling guilty as we all know that Sue is the first to arrive and last to leave – every day.

I sip my black coffee and begin to defrost. I hate black coffee! 'Doesn't anyone bring milk in?' I mutter. This falls on deaf ears. Everyone is printing endless profiles and lesson plans for the inspection.

I pick up the phone and put it down again. I should ring Aaron, he's absent again. I feel so sorry for him having to look after his dad. A boy of seventeen shouldn't be rushing home to clean and cook. I ought to report Leon to the child protection officer for coming to college inappropriately dressed. It's supposed to be a tell-tale sign of child neglect. But he's seventeen, not seven, and I believe him when he swears he never feels the cold.

I open my e-mails and find more forms to complete. I really do need an administrator, I think as I type another complaint to campus services about the lack of heating in the mobile studio. If only it was truly mobile and we could take it to the south of France, I daydream.

I begin to think of pre-email days, when there was a secretary to type up project briefs and write letters to students. Now I'm a lecturer, administrator, typist, and sometime counsellor. I look at my 1950s skirt, all homely with teapots and slices of Victoria sandwich printed on it. Those were the days when people had proper tea breaks. I wish I was back in those times, not that I was even born then. Surely life would have been easier. But then again I probably wouldn't have had a job at all. I'd have been like my mum, packing up a lunchbox of grisly meat sandwiches and cake to deliver to Dad's office. No wonder I turned vegetarian at fifteen.

'So Laura, what are we doing today?' asks Jim, peering round into the staffroom. Jim, you should have a project brief. You should have looked at it. Even some of the students read the brief, I think. Instead I say, completely off the top of my head, 'We're going to be screen printing. Could you go and get all the screens out of the store cupboard? And the inks and squeegees.'

'Yes, ma'am,' says Jim, with a mock salute.

Sue gives me a worried look.

'I'm going to get them to do some repeat patterns and then print them up onto paper and fabric,' I say, feeling really excited.

'Are you sure? I wouldn't do something that messy, that unpredictable. You'll never be able to keep an eye on them all. And what if Curtis comes in to inspect your lesson?'

'He can have a go at a print too,' I say, sounding far more blasé than I'm really feeling.

The security man peeps round the staffroom door. I'd completely forgotten about the car.

'Couldn't find you. Left it up by the field. It started first time,' winks the security man, as he hands back my keys.

'Thank you,' I say.

'All in a day's work,' he replies.

'Could I ask you one more favour?'

'Ask away.'

Chapter 4

Basque stitch is also known as twisted daisy border stitch. As the name suggests, this stitch is found on old embroideries from the Basque area of northern Spain. Embroideries from Portugal and southern France also make use of this stitch.

It's 4 p.m. and I've had the best teaching day ever. 'Come on Amy, it's home time,' I say.

'Can't I just print one more design?'

'Next time. They're all washed up now,' I say, looking at the pile of screens stacked precariously by the sink.

'Bye Laura,' she says with a big smile as she goes out of the studio door.

'I did enjoy that lesson,' says Jim. 'Just like the old days. That's the sign of a good class – when they don't want to go home.'

'Or go home wearing what was a white T-shirt, now printed in retro geometric spirals,' I say, thinking of Leon.

I look at Jim, who has streaks of yellow and crimson across his face. The 'war paint' is a tell-tale sign that he's enjoyed himself too.

The work benches are strewn with colourful screen prints in a mock-retro style of the still life. 'They're good,' I say. 'We could put up a display in the corridors.'

'It would certainly brighten the place up. Blast!' shouts Jim, 'we should be in the staff meeting.'

We rush into the big, warm meeting room. Everyone looks up. We sit down next to Sue and she passes us the register.

'I haven't got a pen,' I whisper.

'Sign it in blood,' whispers Jim.

'Or screen-printing ink,' I giggle.

'You're just in time to not be marked late,' says Curtis, his chubby fingers clicking on his Powerpoint. I look at Curtis and shrug my shoulders, as if to say, 'Is it my fault that I was busy teaching?' and sit down at the back.

When I first started at the college I always felt that Curtis didn't look quite real. As if he was a soft-sculpture puppet and pretending to be Head of School. I still think his rotund body really does look as if it's stuffed with cushion wadding and his straight, silver-blonde hair would pass as a wig.

'Tonight's theme is health and safety. This is one of the things that Mrs Parker and I will be looking at when we come and inspect, I mean observe, your lessons. At Town and Country we take health and safety very seriously,' says Curtis facing us full-on with his hands on his hips.

'Laura,' whispers Sue, 'there are rumours that you're on Curtis's naughty list.'

'What?' I'm not sure whether to laugh or cry.

'It's to do with your complaints about the heating, well I think it is. You know this place, everything is communicated by rumour.'

'How come it's *my* fault?' I ask.

'Everyone come and collect a camera,' says Curtis, standing at the front with a big box of expensive digital cameras.

'Could you just recap what we're doing?' I ask.

'We're doing an audit swap. I want you all to photograph any health and safety dangers in the department. And I think you should swap with Nathan here from digital media.' Nathan waves a hand. I smile weakly.

'Can I have your keys?' Nathan asks.

'Of course,' I say, already wondering whether or not Jim and I locked the room in our rush to get here on time.

'We don't have keys. Here's my swipe card,' says Nathan.

'Twenty minutes, then back with your evidence,' calls Curtis.

Once I get into the IT room I struggle to find any evidence of danger. After some time I notice the printer is on. I take a photo and switch it off. In the rubbish bin I spot a screwed up paper cup. Some naughty person has been eating and drinking in here. I return to the meeting room with my measly two photos.

'Just in time,' says Curtis. 'Nathan, would you like to tell us what you found in the mobile studio?'

Nathan looks around nervously. 'Firstly the door wasn't locked.' Jim and I sneak a glance at each other. 'I then tripped on the cables of a fan heater and rested my arm on the work-top and look …' He lifts up his arm and reveals a lovely blue and green spotted pattern permanently printed onto his crisp, white cotton shirt.

'That was Jon's,' whispers Jim. 'I helped hold the screen, while he printed. I've never seen him work so hard.'

'Do you have something you wish to share with us?' asks Curtis.

Jim shakes his head. His face flushes and almost matches the colour of his red hair.

'Thank you, Nathan,' says Curtis, scribbling in his little notebook.

'I haven't finished. It looked like a tea shop. There were half-eaten cupcakes on a cake stand,' continues Nathan, looking completely baffled.

'That was our "carrot" for getting three prints finished,' whispers Jim.

'The security man was really sweet to go over to the hotel school bakery and get those.' I look at the clock and see it's 5 p.m.

'Excuse me, I'm sorry, I have to go now,' I say, standing up. I decide not to say that the nursery closes at 5 p.m. and for each five minutes you're late you get charged five pounds.

'Sit down,' says Curtis.

Something comes over me and I stay standing. 'The nursery is now shut. The college nursery that is. And for each five minutes I'm late I'll receive a fine,' I say.

'Laura, I don't believe I'm hearing this. My wife takes the children to the nursery and she manages.'

'But *you* don't take your children, do you? You have no

50

idea.' All this comes out of my mouth before I realise what I'm saying. I'm one of the least radical people I know and now I've said something I'm not going to be able to retract. I feel a sinking feeling in my stomach. Then, open-mouthed and wishing that the ground would swallow me whole, I see everyone else get up and put their coats on to leave.

As I move to go I feel a whole host of mixed emotions. I'm proud that I've stood up for working mums; but equally annoyed with myself for being seen as a troublemaker. We need my little part-time income. My name is going to be at the top of the naughty list.

Chapter 5

Wave stitch is used as a filling stitch or border. Begin by making a series of diagonal stitches in a series of 'V' shapes. To work subsequent rows, turn the fabric and begin in the same hole as the base, or point of each 'V'.

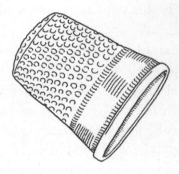

It's Tuesday already. My home day. My home alone day with Daisy. My real full-time mother day. And after yesterday's events, my best teaching day ever ending in a health and safety scandal and the unintended start of a mini-revolt, every day might be my home day very soon.

Daisy is up before the sun and together we prepare a veggie lasagne for tonight's dinner. I chop real vegetables while she moves around plastic carrots and tomatoes in her home cooker. My former self, my pre-children self, could never have imagined chopping onions and carrots at 6.30 a.m. when it was dark outside. Since having children I am on duty

24/7. At the moment I feel like I'm completing a night shift, except my shift work never comes to an end.

We walk up to school through the grey slush. In London the pavements had been swamped with parents and buggies like a happy crowd leaving a busy football match. Here, the walk is a lonely affair. We take our lives in our hands and like some army officer, I shout, 'Keep on the verge! Lilly, keep on the verge!' while we battle the parents in their four by fours, who blatantly ignore the 30mph speed limit. Nobody on our road in Ealing would have dreamt of driving such a short distance, I seethe. Is this what real country life is going to be like?'

'Great party,' says Liz, looking really good in a pastel Fair Isle tank-top that peeps through the gap in her black wool coat. Liz is definitely one of those women who successfully tread the difficult line between looking smart and looking stuffy. She ushers her daughter Kate up the steps of Reedby Primary. Our party seems far more than a couple of days ago. 'Very brave of you to invite so many of us new people.'

I smile, noting it wasn't brave at all. We don't really know many people here, so we didn't have a choice. And who'd drive up from London in February for a housewarming? Our London friends are waiting for balmy summer weekends before they'll come out to the country and inspect us. I don't actually say any of this, especially as Liz is my only friend at the moment. I must try to make more friends in the village. It's me, not Lilly, who seems to feel like the new girl! Am I sounding like a schoolgirl? The answer is probably yes. I did always think school was for making friends, rather than learning.

'I heard about your fall,' she says, staring at the plaster. 'You were lucky it wasn't your eye.'

I smile, not really knowing what to say. And wondering how she heard. I haven't spoken to anyone in the village.

'But are you all right? Do you need anything? You only have to ask, you know.'

'I'm feeling much better now. Thanks for asking,' I say, transfixed by Mrs Palmer, the headteacher, or headmistress as she still likes to be called.

'She's always that smart,' says Liz, as if reading my mind. 'She has something of the Queen about her in that well-fitted yellow woollen jacket, don't you think?'

I laugh. It feels good to have a laugh with an adult. 'The pearls are a bit Sloane Ranger aren't they? And I can't imagine her running after the reception children,' I chuckle. I look down at my vintage black cotton dress and see cooking stains and Daisy handprints around the embroidered hem. I look as messy as a reception child and what's more, Mum must be turning in her grave at the sight of her once-classy '60s dinner-dance dress now being worn as a pinafore (I don't have sufficient bosoms to wear it without a thick jumper underneath).

'Yeah, but we're lucky to have her,' says Liz, looking over at Mrs Palmer. 'Apparently when she took over a few years ago the school was really run down. It was way down in the league tables – not that I bother too much about those,' she adds, hastily. 'Mark always says that she's turned it into her own little prep school. Except it's free! So he doesn't have to wrestle with his conscience to send Kate here.'

'Adi's always too busy with work to think much about the girls' education,' I say, immediately feeling a bit disloyal.

As if reading my mind, Liz adds, 'Mark doesn't have much to say about his own children's education. It's the principle of it all that he likes to battle out at dinner parties. Anyway, I must go. See you later.'

It's 9.30 a.m. and Daisy and I have a whole grey February day before us. If I take the long way back down the bridleway she might just nod off and give me an hour to plan next Monday's lesson.

By the time I push the buggy into the porch Daisy is sound asleep under the patchwork blanket Adi's mum Pam proudly presented to us after her birth. I love the multicoloured knitted squares, probably as much as Adi loathes them!

I head for the conservatory and take out all my bits and pieces. I then start having thoughts about child-snatchers and begin to push the buggy indoors making tyre prints over the carpet. She begins to rumble. I'm sure she's the same as me and can't stand being in the cottage. It's dark and dingy. We always need the lights on, even on a rare sunny day, and for Adi with his Seasonal Affective Disorder (SAD), this makes it a bad place to live. Daylight never seems to really come.

I remember those rainy days with Lilly in London, when I could escape into a cafe, a shop or a gallery. It suddenly all seems a lifetime ago. Here there's no escape from these long lonely winter days. I feel trapped. I've got to get out of the house, away from here, anywhere.

I reverse Daisy back through the porch and head down Ferry Road past muddy fields towards the river. I know Reedby is beautiful. The big open skies are like a Constable painting. The marsh is romantic in a way. It's just sad there's no one grown-up to share it with.

One interesting, loneliness-quenching thing about Reedby is that there are odd, unexplained pairs of men who walk around the village. I see a couple coming towards me, and as usual they nod and smile at me and I reply, Morning. I must ask Liz who they are. Soon my mood lifts. I've always been a bit of a fickle depressive. I'm easily upset and then just as easily cured. Maybe I'm just a shallow person?

Are these men bird spotters? We're close to the RSPB reserve. They'd actually mentioned this in our house details, as if someone might want to move near to a bird reserve. Of course Adi was quick off the mark, saying. 'That means there's a whole stretch of Reedby they won't be able to develop. We'll be living in a proper village, no suburbia for us.'

But where are their binoculars? I think, looking at these men. There is something very unReedby about them. They're slightly grungier, more urban looking and kitted out as if a walk around Reedby was a survival course. They appear to belong to the same tribe. I begin to list the characteristics: thick jumpers visible beneath sensible windcheaters, tan hiking boots and unkempt hair attempting to escape from rainbow-coloured woollen hats.

I think up a tribe task for my students. They could choose someone, friend, family or celebrity, and list clothes, accessories and hair in order to find their tribe. Are they a rebel? A hippy? Middle of the road? Fashionista? That's a great task for my fashion and textile students – they'll like that, I think. They could look at themselves, their family, their own tribe. Or they could go people spotting. A good example of personalised learning. Curtis Lampard would like it. Maybe that will be enough to get me back into his good books.

Lesson plan done. But not really. It's not enough to think what I'm going to do. I've got to prove I've thought about it. I've got to be prepared for all eventualities. I'll write it down later. Slog, slog, slog. Type it all up. And then it is real. Work is neverending, it's as if it's me not the students who has tonnes of homework.

I don't believe it! In the distance, climbing over a wooden stile, I spot one of the men in pairs, a very tall man wearing a multicoloured shirt. He's definitely not one of the usual 'tribe'. He must be freezing. But it's not the fact that someone is out in a shirt that's caught my attention, it's the shirt itself: red and turquoise paisley.

I dart up the track to the marsh. From my vantage point the shirt is just as I thought, vintage Liberty paisley in crimson and pale turquoise – almost duck egg (one of my favourite colours) cotton. Since I was a student, Liberty's, seemingly tucked away off Carnaby Street, has been my all-time favourite store. For me, London's big players, the likes of Harrods, Harvey Nichols and Peter Jones can't compete with Liberty's top floor of fabrics and trimmings, a feast of colour and texture.

I know that there's only one man in the whole of England who would wear a shirt like that. I peek through the hedge. Daisy, just don't cry now. It is him. I know it is. It's Chris Taylor. I haven't thought of him for ten years or so. I remember the day we searched all the shops on the King's Road for that perfect shirt – and he's still wearing it! Just seeing him makes me feel all kind of normal again. The old me, and not on the outside in the middle of nowhere.

When I come to think about it I was a worse student than most of the kids I teach. We often skipped lectures. It wasn't our fault that Chelsea School of Art was located just off the King's Road, a short stroll to the most amazing set of clothes shops, was it? Well – that used to be our excuse.

The day of the paisley shirt we didn't make it to college at all. We hadn't intended to miss a whole day. It was just that each little boutique was like Dr Who's tardis. Once inside it was another world of fabrics, colours, textures that were different from the chain stores. It was the uniqueness of each item, as if everything had been custom-made. We felt heady, intoxicated on beautiful things. I'd never been shopping with a *man* before. Where I came from boys just didn't go clothes shopping. The boys of my youth spent all day loitering in music shops, flipping through record sleeves. None of them would ever dream of venturing into a boutique.

Chris and I had such a laugh trying clothes on, items we couldn't really afford. Even the second-hand clothes were almost out of the reach of our student grants. It was me who'd spotted the paisley shirt. Chris followed me into the miniature changing room. We'd only been dating a few weeks and hadn't progressed far beyond a snog in the college bar. I felt very exposed in front of the full-length mirror and rather like one of the ugly sisters, praying that the shirt would fit. The long sleeves came down past my fingertips.

Chris said, 'I want it.' I thought he was joking, but was secretly relieved that he'd focused on the shirt, rather than me, my pale ordinary figure embarrassingly revealed to him under the dressing room spotlights. He grabbed the shirt, and like Cinderella and the glass slipper, the shirt was the perfect fit.

The sales assistant carefully wrapped the shirt in tissue paper and nestled it in a little paper carrier bag. Chris immediately put it on and the rest of the day we spent darting in and out of the rain from clothes shops, to interior designers and the tile shops of Fulham Road. It was my perfect shopping day, helped by the fact that the sales assistants' eyes would follow Chris around the shops, each vying to serve him. But he was spoken for. He was with me. Laura Lovegrove was finally one of the in-people! It was also that day that a very well-groomed woman in her fifties accosted Chris just as we headed out of one of the shops, Chris still wearing the paisley shirt over his T-shirt.

'I'm a scout for Models One,' she explained. 'Here's my card, come and drop by if you're interested.' Of course that was the beginning of the end for me and Chris. He moved on to another league – surrounded by other models in Paris and Milan.

I push Daisy back down to the Green, my mind still on Chris and the shops of the King's Road. We used to look down on anyone who bought their clothes from chain stores on the high street. We were awful snobs! Yet part of me hasn't changed that much; I still hate the conformity of the high street.

I slip into teenage mode and wonder: what would my life be like if I'd stayed with Chris? Would he love my rails of vintage clothes? Would we have tall, beautiful blue-eyed children who took after their father? Would I be living in some cosmopolitan city, Paris or Rome, rather than Reedby? I arrive at the front door and wonder how we got back to Marsh Cottage so quickly.

I can't quite call the place home. The old house really felt like home. It was right for us. Sometimes I can't quite believe that I can't just go back there, that the house really does belong to what we thought were a lovely couple. They seemed so nice, her being pregnant and desperate for a house ready to move into. They were suitably impressed by the catchment area. Then there had been the threats to pull out of the sale unless we renegotiated a better price. So much for seeming nice.

I hear a lorry grind to a stop outside the cottage. In London there was so much traffic going up and down our road I never noticed any of it. In Reedby it's different. Here, I notice the slightest noise. I hear footsteps on the gravel and there's a loud knocking on the door, which immediately wakes Daisy up with a moan and then a cry. I open the door.

'Delivery for Mr A Stark,' says the burly man in overalls. 'Sign here please,' he adds, handing me a pen with his stubby fingers. For a moment I'm distracted – I think of how Chris had such elegant hands, piano playing hands.

I can't remember us ordering anything, yet in front of this stranger I don't want to sound stupid.

'Just leave it by the door, will you,' I say wondering what *it* is.

'Can't do that ma'am. I'm only insured to get it out of the lorry. You'll have to take it from there. Health and safety, you see.' I don't see and follow him to the lorry door, where I take charge of a shiny blue bicycle.

'Don't forget your receipt,' says the man. 'Can't return it without one.'

I actually have plenty to chat to Adi about today. For once Lilly's fiddling and moving her lasagne around her plate isn't irritating him. That is until Adi says, 'Maybe she just needs some meat.'

I don't rise to the occasion. Instead I say, 'That's fine, you bring some meat home *and* cook it.' Adi is too excited and too happy to respond. It's amazing how excited a bicycle can make someone feel.

I casually mention the 'men in pairs' thing to Adi, carefully avoiding the fact that I saw Chris. Adi knows a bit about past boyfriends. I've still got photos and letters stashed away in a box somewhere.

I guess dating is all different nowadays – and I suddenly feel really old. Nobody sends love letters, just texts, perhaps an e-mail. No real photos, perhaps a disk somewhere. There's nothing that your past love has touched. Will today's past be lost?

'It's a gay commune!' he jokes, jolting me forward into the here and now. For a split second I am prepared to believe this. Why am I always the gullible one? 'Oh I don't know who they are. I'm at work all day and don't seem to see anything of Reedby, or the Norfolk countryside. I just sit in front of a screen all day.'

'Can't you sit in front of your funny lamp?' asks Daisy.

'It's not a lamp, it's a light box for Daddy's disorder,' says Lilly.

'Just all discuss me as if I'm not here. I would,' he snaps back at me. What is it with Adi? He's constantly uptight, ready to burst at any moment! And *I* haven't said anything!

Then, moving as quickly from one mood to another as Daisy does, Adi adds, 'Hence buying the bike. I'm going to cycle to work.'

'But you've got a bike already,' I chip in.

'A racer's no good for roads around here. I'd have a puncture every few minutes. Did you know there's a cycle track all the way from here into town? It'll save money too, no petrol to pay for,' says Adi, carrying the dishes into the kitchen and almost bumping his mop of brown hair on the door frame.

'It's like Daddy is living in a hobbit house,' says Lilly. 'He doesn't fit in.'

'Shush!' I whisper, 'I don't think Daddy is in the mood for jokes.' I should add that even Mummy doesn't know quite what it is that's stressing him out so much. I flit from thinking, is it the job? Is it the new house? to, worst of all, is it our marriage?

Chapter 6

Buttonhole stitch is also known as blanket stitch because it was often used as an edging on blankets.

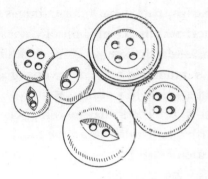

The working week goes by and I keep expecting a formal summons from the college. Maybe my rant about the stresses of being a working mother has been brushed under the carpet. Every time the phone rings I wonder if it is Curtis, or else the HR department.

I resort to walking Daisy endlessly round the village hoping for another glimpse of Chris and to take my mind off things and back to the time when art and design was so full of promise. Part of me knows that if I wasn't so in need of company, excitement and a break from myself I wouldn't be doing this. It's a little lift, like a coffee, a chocolate bar, a cigarette – not that I smoke, unlike my mother-in-law on her forty a day.

That reminds me, when Adi and I get a minute to speak I'm going to broach the smoking in the house issue. There's no way his mother is coming to stay with us and lighting up in the cottage. It was bad enough in Ealing forcing her out into our minuscule garden, as if I were the wicked daughter-in-law. Does Pam want to bring on my asthma? Give me an asthma attack? I wouldn't put it past her. That way she'd have Adi to herself again! Oh I'm sounding mean now. But I can't stand the way she takes over and what's worse, I can't stand the way Adi defers to her, not me. It's my house!

At least here at Marsh Cottage we've an enormous garden. And as the estate agent told us, 'There's enough land with the cottage to build a whole row of houses – if you get planning permission that is.' It's the Friday morning school run, at last I'll be able to ask Liz Randall about the men. It isn't exactly the sort of question I could nip over the road and ask Heather Weatherall. 'Why are there all these men wandering around the village?' She'd have an answer, I'm sure. The estate agent never mentioned Heather's mine of information as a selling point. He should have done.

We walk up to school and are first at the big old Victorian school gates. I swear it's quicker to walk to school rather than circling round and round the pond, almost vulture-like, in the hope of securing a parking space. I still feel so much the new girl. I ought to go up and pass the time of day with the mums in their little groups. But all I can think about is Park Royal Infant School in Ealing and how I knew almost all the other mums. We'd been friends since our post-natal group and had met every week for coffee and cake at each other's houses. Park Royal Infants seems a very long time ago. A lot of the mums here are still the shabby bohemian type of my Ealing set, with ripped jeans, clogs and fresh discreetly made-up faces. Though there are more well groomed mums here than in Ealing, with a full face of make-up and carefully pressed clothes ready for a day at the office, or working out at the gym.

'Hi Laura,' says Liz, breaking my daydream.

'Our days don't seem to overlap. I'm never here on a Monday, my work day,' I gabble, excited that somebody is talking to me.

'Oh yes, at the college. Well I'm going to be back to work, now Jack is settled into reception class. I've just rented an office in town,' she says.

'For your journalism?' I venture.

'Yup, Liz Randall: public relations and journalism,' she laughs, rather tongue in cheek. 'I'm just starting to get some good slots now. Mostly fashion, interiors, a few profiles on artists and if I'm lucky I'll get to interview a few art and design celebs for the Sunday papers. You know, people like Laurence Llewellyn-Bowen, the interior designer in his white suit and pink floral shirts,' she smiles, her lipstick-red lips, pale skin and dark hair giving her an almost Snow White look – or perhaps I haven't been reading enough adult books lately!

The talk of patterned shirts reminds me of Chris, and my sighting of him with the men – Adi's gay commune men!

'Liz, have you seen these pairs of men who wander around the village? Who are they?' I whisper.

She giggles. 'No need to whisper. It's nothing odd. Everybody knows they're visiting Trishna, the Buddhist retreat. It's usually a male-only retreat. My Mark used to go down there for yoga classes. But he hasn't made it to Trishna for ages. I wish he would. He was a lot less stressed out when he did go there.

'By the way, is Lilly free for tea tonight? Kate and Lilly are the best of friends already,' says Liz. At least the children are making friends!

It seems that all the world is usefully occupied at school or work. I somehow find myself pushing the buggy down the little track towards the Buddhist retreat. I feel like some kind of prowler. I spot some of the men in the garden amidst the crocuses. Then, there he is, Chris Taylor, well what looks like the back of him. He is wearing his Liberty-print shirt again, the green stylised leaves almost merging into the garden. Good for him, I think. I remember the saying that people dress in the clothes from the time they were happiest. Was Chris happiest when he was at art school? When he was with me? Men are usually so conservative with their fabrics and colours. Chris is the exception that proves the rule. Every time I'm asked to design a male fabric collection, it's always a washed-out version of the women's wear. Or rather, a muddy version, as if all I need to do is spill tea or coffee over my women's wear range and they'd – or should I say Gill would – be happy with it. Laura, what a good idea, I almost say out loud. I'm going to go home and try that. I do need to design something that she could sell after all. It's strange this design business, for it's always when I'm thinking of something else, seemingly un-related, that I come up with my ideas.

'You were miles away,' says a familiar voice. 'Fancy seeing you here.' I look up at Chris Taylor. He sees my face drop.

I was hoping that when he finally saw me I'd be on one of my good days: freshly washed hair (instead of my greasy mane scraped into a ponytail), wearing a bit of make-up (any remnants of this morning's lipstick are gone) and most importantly without a plaster across my forehead. I'm not quite sure why I wanted to impress. Why had I wanted to prove that the years had treated me well? Perhaps I want to prove to Chris that he shouldn't have ditched me, that it was him – not me – who missed out on an opportunity?

'It is Laura, Laura Lovegrove? Isn't it?'

'Yes. It's me,' I smile.

'You've hardly changed. In fact you haven't changed a bit. It must be fifteen years or so since our degree show. That must have been the last time I saw you.' I feel a bit better about my hair and face. Unless of course he means I looked a bit of a mess then as well as now.

On closer inspection Chris looks as if it's been twenty, twenty-five years since we graduated. His face is saggy, worn and has a grey kind of look to it. He's clearly overdone it on the good life. Yet he's still handsome, his blue eyes like gemstones piercing me. On closer inspection his nose is a bit red and bumpy. Is that a drinker's nose? I wonder, already feeling better about my own inadequacies.

'Well, Laura, I have to say you're the last person I expected to meet in darkest Norfolk.'

'Why?' I snap, thrusting my head backwards in order to look up at him, my head in line with his shoulders. 'It's not dark. The biggest skies are here,' I say, suddenly very defensive of my new home. I don't say that you need a clear, dry day to have the big skies Norfolk is so famous for.

'Just a joke. And since when have you been so serious? You haven't forgotten Laura Lovegrove, the girl who'd prop up the wine bars and cafes of the King's Road? Remember "My Old Dutch"?'

'Pancake heaven.' I smile. I feel myself visibly relax. Maybe the spell of the retreat is getting to me.

'I'm just so tired all the time. You know,' (or maybe you don't, I think) 'juggling work, kids.' A night out at a wine bar, things like that happen to other people.

'So who did you marry? Was it Mikey or was it Carlos, the Spanish boy? He was very handsome.'

I shake my head, hardly able to remember who Carlos was.

'Wrong on both counts. I met this guy, Adi, a friend of a friend kind of thing,' I say, feeling as if I've undersold my husband. I don't say that when we met at a housewarming party (which neither of us had been invited to) it was just like in romance novels when the tall, dark and handsome man appears and the heroine immediately knows he's Mr Right. Although it took Adi somewhat longer to realise I was his Ms Right.

'So what about you?' I say, part of me hoping that he's not living happily ever after.

'Married and divorced. Twice.'

'Oh! Is that why you're into this stuff then?' I say, looking up at the manor house.

'You mean Buddhism.'

I nod, feeling a little embarrassed by my own directness.

'I wouldn't say that I'm a Buddhist, but the time has come to think about these things.' As if on cue Daisy wakes up, mumbles and falls back to sleep.

'I think I'd better walk on. I'll ruin your peaceful retreat.'

'See you anon,' he says, with a gentle stroke to my arm.

I walk on feeling as if I've been let out of a cage and I could fly; which I know sounds corny. But somehow seeing Chris has been like a great weight being lifted. I gaze up at the sky. Norfolk's skies are as big as the fens, and I begin to feel at home. The fields of horizontal stripes of green, magenta, blue and grey, still dusted with a sprinkling of snow, are beautiful.

Once upon a time a view such as this would have made me pull in at the nearest lay-by and churn out watercolour after watercolour, some of which I'd later develop into abstract fabric designs. Now it's a snatched moment. Maybe I could lean a little sketch book on top of the buggy, I wonder. The horizontal stripes could make really nice fabric designs.

I rummage in the bottom of the buggy, feeling my way between a water bottle, a Tupperware box of rice cakes, wipes, a bicycle pump (in case of a flat tyre) and finally I find what I'm after. Like a girl guide I'm always prepared, I always carry a sketch book – just in case. I place it on the buggy hood, take a pencil out of Daisy's pencil case and begin. I lose myself in stripes of green and white.

There's a rustling from under the hood. Then a few cries. Even now she's three she still wakes up from her naps with a cry. Please sleep, just one more minute. Arms push up through the hood and knock my sketch book off into the muddy, slushy verge. I pick it up and want to join Daisy with a loud scream. Except I can't. I'm the grown-up and I'm supposed to cope with it all.

I walk into the hall. The red light on the phone is hard to miss flashing in a hall as dingy as ours. For a moment I'm too scared to pick up the receiver. Will it be college? I pick it up and hear that strange, robotic woman say, 'You have one new message.' Until this week I was always excited by the prospect of messages. I don't get texts any more, as our side of Reedby has no mobile reception, so it's land line only. Will it be a new design commission from some competition I've forgotten I've entered? Or maybe the offer of an exhibition? How long will it take to really get my textile career going? I've stopped and started ever since I left art school. A foolish part of me hopes that the call is from Chris – even though I haven't given him my phone number!

Instead I hear Adi's quiet deep tone. 'Hey, Laura, just ringing to say I'm really sorry I've been a bit snappy this week. Let's talk when I get back. I'll pick up a bottle of pink bubbly.' My first thought is: He's remembered what my favourite is. Then I think, What has he done? Why does he want to talk when he gets back?

I set Daisy up with her train set. It was Adi's only toy to survive his childhood. Lilly never got to play with it. Somehow I think he gave up on a son after Daisy was born and gave her his train set. I now know that I'm too unambitious to have a boy. That is according to some professor on *Women's Hour*. Apparently highly stressed and ambitious women have boys; and when it's the man who is ambitious and stressed they have daughters. Adi's always been our little family's conscientious breadwinner.

I watch Daisy through the glass conservatory door as I paint up some modifications to my floral designs. I untangle the hairdryer and Daisy makes a dash for the conservatory. I alternate between pretending to play hairdressers and drying Daisy's dry hair, and drying my wet paintings – which as any textile designer will tell you is the real function of a hairdryer.

I make two cups of coffee, one for me and one for the designs – for the men's 'muddy' design range. This is the bit I love. I don't know if this will work, but who cares? I sponge over the paintings with the brown liquid. Already I can see Adi wearing a shirt in this print. It's his colour scheme: brown, fawn, tan, khaki, and would match his green/hazel eyes perfectly. If only he'd let himself go and wear a print instead of sticking to block colours. I sip my coffee and realise I've taken a great gulp of khaki water. My automatic reflex takes control and I spit it out over my camouflage-style leaf designs.

'Wow! Come and look at this Daisy!' I call into the lounge. She doesn't look up from her world of Thomas the Tank Engine. Why is it that children will happily play when you want their attention? And then as soon as you want to get on, you suddenly become so much more interesting than Thomas? I make the most of Daisy's 'flow' time and grab a couple of the iris and daisy designs. I rinse them under the tap. Yes. Almost washed out, but not quite. Perfect. I replay the rigmarole with the hairdryer, scan them and e-mail them off to Gill.

I look up at the clock. I've been working for nearly two hours, non-stop. Guilt takes over. I need to properly play with Daisy. I sit on the carpet next to her and rebuild the track and decide where to put the station. I'm not enjoying playing trains. Why is it that Daisy and Adi can happily play trains all morning?

Daisy looks up at me and gives me a big dimply grin. I pull her to me and give her a big kiss. A big, spontaneous kiss which Lilly is almost too old for.

The phone rings; as usual Daisy sprints across the room and into the hall and shouts into the receiver. 'Who is it?'

I wrestle with Daisy and the receiver and shout equally loudly, 'Just speak to her and then she'll lose interest.' This is always a useful tool with cold callers who usually hang up at this point. Although not so good if it's someone that I'm trying to impress.

'Hello!' I say, to whoever it is, 'sorry about that.'

'Hello Laura,' says Gill. My heart sinks on hearing her forever upbeat tone. Gill only rings when something is wrong: a hard to chase client, last minute amendments.

'What a glorious spring day and made even better when I got your pictures, Laura.'

'You like them?' I say, impressed with Gill's quick response. What I want to say is, Will you actually be able to sell these?

'Like? Like isn't the word. They're absolutely fabulous. A stroke of genius. They're what the market's missing. We've had all these bright floral shirts. But do they sell? Well, not enough. Men can't wear them for work, unless they're an interior designer or the like. They're party gear. But these white on white, neutral, coffee-coloured florals and leaves. Brilliant! I'm on the case for selling them.'

Gill sounds almost out of breath. And then adds, 'Of course, in the current climate I can't promise anything.'

Chapter 7

Bullion knot is a versatile stitch which can be used as an accent or massed together to create a dense texture. The weight of the thread used determines the size of the finished knot. You can create interesting effects by threading two or three contrasting fine threads through the needle at the same time.

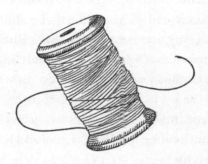

I'm really excited as I pull up in front of Liz's grand house. This is the first time any of us have actually been invited to someone else's home in the village. I park next to her shiny Toyota four by four, and I can't help but think that in comparison my Micra looks like a toy-town car in need of a good clean.

We stand on the doorstep and look up at the Randalls' house. It's enormous. Our cottage would fit into Birch House several times over. Daisy knocks about ten times on the solid wooden door.

'Stop knocking. It probably takes a while to get to the door.'

'Come on in,' says Liz. Over her black leggings she's wearing a thigh-length red, black and white tunic with Russian dolls repeated around the hem. Red, black and white really are her trademark colours, I think.

And as if wanting to make a good impression and reflect Liz's dress code, my own turquoise, black and white tunic coordinates with hers brilliantly. Except for one big difference, my tunic is pure 1960s Crimplene, rather than a polyester elastine mix, which even though it's man-made fabric still lets your skin breathe. I feel like I'm wearing nylon.

I look around the big, light hall which is full of wood. The staircase, the ceiling, the floor – everything is wooden. It's like a Scandinavian or Frank Lloyd Wright house merging into the landscape. It's certainly worthy of a spread in an interiors magazine.

'What a lovely house,' I say. 'Adi would love it.'

Rather than looking pleased, Liz looks slightly embarrassed and quickly says, 'Mark and I both lost our dads a couple of years ago, otherwise we'd never have bought it.'

'I lost my dad when I was still at school and then my mum too, nearly eight years ago.'

'Poor you,' says Liz, putting her hand on my shoulder.

'In fact this tunic was my mum's,' I say, pulling on the turquoise flower patterns.

'It's nice to have a more personal heirloom. Our house is far too littered with Mark's Great Aunt Nester's outsize furniture,' says Liz, lowering her voice – even though no one is eavesdropping.

'It's not just this tunic,' I confess. 'I've got rails and rails of clothes. I guess an interest in clothes was what Mum and I had in common.'

'I didn't have any similar interests to my mum,' says Liz with a smirk. 'It wasn't until Kate came along that things improved. You see we had something in common at last.'

I nod.

'Fancy a cuppa?' she asks, changing the subject.

Daisy runs off into the playroom and Liz and I sit up at the big wooden kitchen table drinking Earl Grey tea and eating homemade flapjacks – and I feel normal again. The old London Laura.

'How are you doing?'

I'm so surprised that anyone is actually asking about my life. I begin to ramble on about college.

'Sounds like you should jump before you are pushed,' says Liz, sensibly.

'Oh don't say that. It's all so scary. The thing is I really enjoy teaching art.'

'What about selling your own designs?'

'I'd love to be able to just sell my work directly. But I'm reliant on an agent.'

'Couldn't you make one-off designs to sell, bypass your agent? I don't know, on the internet perhaps?'

'But what would people do with them? My designs are for factories to print on to your clothes and duvets.'

'Good point. They could just put them on the wall like paintings,' says Liz. 'We've got lots of empty wall space – I'd buy one.'

'That's really sweet of you. But I want to create things that people use, touch, remember – every day.'

'I wish I was creative,' says Liz. 'I can't even sew a button on,' she says laughing.

I smile, too scared to admit that I can't sew very well either. When I was at art school it was all about ideas and concepts. It didn't matter if you couldn't make something yourself. And now, well just look at Damien Hirst – he has a whole team of assistants.

'I'm more likely to put a button on with a glue gun,' I joke, not letting it show how close to the truth that is.

We manage to spend the next hour discussing Reedby life. I finally round up the girls.

'So, I'll let you know when the Reedby Ladies' Book Club meets next.'

I let out an anxious smile.

'Don't worry, Laura, it's quite informal.'

'I haven't read anything written for adults for quite some time.'

'All the more reason you should come,' adds Liz.

'Everyone's got a pet. Kate has a cat, dog, guinea pig and chickens. Why can't we have one?' says Lilly in her most embarrassingly spoilt voice the moment we get in the car.

'Let's see what Daddy says,' I say, trying to avoid being the 'bad' parent. We pull up at the cottage. There's no sign of Adi or the bottle of bubbly.

'Did you have a pet when you were little?' says Lilly, following me around the house.

'I did have a dog.'

'What sort? What sort? What was it called?'

'It was a little dog, a Yorkshire terrier. He was called Pepper and was very highly strung.'

'What's highly strung?'

'He didn't like to be left alone and would try and claw and chew through the door. He almost escaped once. You see pets take a lot of looking after. I'm not an animal person,' I say honestly. 'What about a virtual pet?' I suggest. 'Or as we're in the country now, we could walk to see the sheep and horses.'

Lilly folds her arms and doesn't look at all impressed.

'Do you really need your own animal?' I say.

'Yes we do, Mummy. I'm going to ask Daddy the moment he comes in. He said he might be getting some chickens.'

'What!' I shout. I feel mean and secretly wouldn't mind having a cat. But chickens? Dogs are bad enough. You always know the houses with dogs, they have that awful doggy smell, which their owners deny. How do you explain your worries about doggy smells and a fear of birds to a young child? It doesn't enter the equation.

I fiddle about in the kitchen. We need to do a proper shop. There are still some good bottles of wine and beer, packets of vegetable crisps (they weren't too popular) and boxes of chocolates from the housewarming. I open and shut the cupboards. It'll be pasta again. Lotte, former neighbour and chair of the PTA in Ealing, once said that pasta is the middle class's version of egg and chips. Lately I've been thinking she was right.

The house is completely quiet. What's more there's no noise coming from the girls. And no noise is often bad news. My alarm bells are ringing – I call it mother's intuition. I rush into the study. I see two pairs of eyes fixed on a monitor full of pictures of glamorous scantily clad girls and kittens.

I stand between the girls and the screen (students really hate it when I do this), then switch off the monitor. 'How do you know how to do all this?' I ask, immediately feeling a very old-fashioned parent. Why hasn't Adi, (the family computer expert) thought about his own children and put some sort of block on inappropriate sites? He's like the builder whose own house is falling down.

'School, we use the internet at school. You signed a letter saying I could.' I have no recollection of any letter; we seem to get letters every other day about this, that and the other.

'Did I? Anyway, computers are such a time waster. My art students waste hours surfing the net when they could open a book and find exactly what they want, and with better quality pictures.'

'Well, I'm not one of your students,' says Lilly, sounding every bit as stroppy as one of my teenagers. 'But, Mum. You said I should get a virtual pet. I'm only doing what you told me to do. I googled kitten and cute. Loads of sites came up. I can't get a virtual pet in a book,' she moans. Laura, you're in charge, I think. Do something. Discipline your daughter. 'Daisy and I want to join the "Pussy Club".'

'Maybe a real pet would be less dangerous, darling,' I say. At least then I'd see what the girls were getting up to. 'I have an idea. We're going up to Phyllis'.'

I march the girls up the Green to the village shop. Not only is the shop an Aladdin's cave of bits 'n' bobs, she also has a notice board selling anything and everything. I gaze longingly at it. I forget I'm supposed to be looking for a dog and scan the board for jobs, any job. Several people want cleaners. For a moment I think seriously about taking up a few cleaning jobs. I calculate how much I'd earn cleaning while the girls are at school and playgroup and what we'd save by not having to pay nursery bills.

78

But I know Adi, he would never call himself a snob, but neither would he ever approve of his wife cleaning for other people. He would love it if I cleaned the cottage more often, though.

'Mummy, look there's rabbits, guinea pigs, even stick insects and snails for sale,' shouts Lilly. I ignore all talk of what I consider very strange choices for a pet.

'Listen to this, Lilly,' I say. 'Poodle for free to the right home.'

'I thought you didn't like dogs,' says Lilly.

'Well, a poodle is neat. It hasn't got a long coat which moults. And they're little, a bit like an accessory. You know when Daddy and I went to Paris lots of ladies used to take their miniature dogs out shopping and to cafes. Perhaps I'll even design a poodle print fabric,' I say, excitedly.

'Well I'll feed her,' says Lilly. 'Because you haven't thought about that, have you Mummy?'

'I'm going to ring the number now.' I can't believe our luck. I make one of those split-second decisions. I switch my phone on, not completely expecting to get any coverage.

'We're not near any of those there masts.' says Phyllis. 'If you go out into the middle of the road, you can usually get a reception.'

I stand in the middle of the road with half my attention on the passing cars.

'You've still got it, wonderful,' I say, thinking there's something very familiar about the crackly voice at the other end of the line. I feel as excited as when I'm bidding for a must-have vintage dress on eBay, or suddenly rushing into a hairdresser's, with the knowledge that my hair must be cut there and then, regardless of the stylist's talents.

'You'll need my address,' says the voice.

'Of course,' I splutter.

I begin to write it down but realise there's no need.

'You'll never believe it,' I say to the girls. 'Mummy's got you a dog and we don't have very far to go to get it.'

'Where's the dog then?' asks Lilly impatiently as we walk back down the Green.

I take the girls' hands, cross over the road and ring the doorbell.

'What did I tell you?' says Heather, opening the door carrying a miniature white poodle. 'Everyone in Reedby has a dog. Good job really. It keeps me in business.'

The girls immediately start to stroke and cuddle the dog.

'She belonged to a friend of one of my Paws and Claws clients, the dog grooming branch of my business. I never know whether it's the dogs or the owners who are my clients. It's a sad story,' begins Heather. The girls settle themselves down on Heather's big squashy pink velvet sofa. 'Snowball was a Christmas present. Then both the owners lost their jobs and couldn't afford to feed her.'

I look at the girls. They've both got tears welling up in their eyes and I hope the dog isn't going to be a bad omen about Adi's precarious job situation.

'Well, it's best we say our goodbyes,' says Heather, standing up abruptly.

'Dogs are for life,' says Lilly as only an hour after the 'Pussy Club' incident we walk away with a small poodle. The 'a dog is for life' slogan makes me feel very uneasy. Why have I taken on a new commitment?

'About the dog's name. It needs to have a name I'm happy with – as I'll be mostly looking after her until you girls are bigger,' I say, suddenly noticing a lump in my throat and a fear of the future.

'I don't like it anyway,' says Lilly. 'Snowball's a cat's name.'

What a relief! 'What do you think of Chanel or Ascher?'

'What, Mum? Who's Shannelorasher?'

'Designers. I just thought it would be nice to name her after a fashion designer. You know, the way people call their dogs after footballers: Ronaldo or Beckham . . . '

'She needs something to rhyme or go with poodle.'

'What about Prada?'

'Prada the poodle! That's really cool, Mum. But isn't she too old for a change of name?' says Lilly, forever the sensible girl.

'New home. New name. She'll love it.'

'Mummy, why did her owners give her away? I didn't really understand.' Lilly asks, concerned.

'They couldn't afford to feed her,' I say, wondering if we really live in the twenty-first century. 'Heather said that thirty dogs have been abandoned every day since this recession started.'

'What's a recession?'

'When there isn't much money about,' I reply, deciding to keep it simple. 'Shall we take Prada for her first walk,' I say, as we turn into the drive.

'Mummy, it's nearly dark,' says Lilly.

Prada walks in stops and starts and makes a long stop outside our neighbours'. I see Heather looking out through her blinds at us. I try to avoid eye contact as Prada squats down on the verge.

I realise that we don't have any dog equipment, except for her lead.

Heather bangs on the window and makes a beckoning sign. Oh no, she's going to tell me off. I've seen people with pooper scoopers and bags but have no idea where they buy such things.

We go back up the path. Heather stands at the door holding a basket, travel cage and bowl. 'Here we are. A starter pack.'

We walk over the road and up the drive with all our paraphernalia. I see Adi's bike upside down on the lawn.

I remember that dinner got no further than an unopened packet of pasta and a can of tomatoes. Maybe he's made dinner as well as bringing the promised bubbly home? But in my heart I know that won't have happened. I'm still reeling from last summer when I took the girls to stay with Louise (my best friend from Chelsea) and Adi called me two hundred miles away to let me know he had nothing for dinner. Although he had found some really strange looking bean burgers in the freezer. I don't know how I stayed calm when I suggested that he could get in the car and go to the supermarket.

I can't believe it; as we go inside I can smell food! I follow my nose and see the dining table set with a tablecloth (that I don't recognise), candles, an enormous bowl of pasta (Adi always cooks supersize portions). One thing is missing. There's no sign of Adi.

'Mummy! It's a celebration for Prada,' Lilly squeals excitedly spotting our mid-week feast.

'I don't think so. Remember Daddy doesn't know about Prada yet.'

Adi walks in all smiles carrying the bottle of bubbly.

'I had to stick it in the freezer,' he announces.

'We do have loads of bottles of wine from the party,' I say, feeling an ungrateful killjoy the moment I utter the words.

'Not the same as a few bubbles. Hello old chap,' says Adi giving Prada a stroke. 'Are we dogsitting?'

'It's a girl, not a boy,' says Lilly, lifting Prada up and away from Adi.

'Do you want to tell your dad or shall I?'

'Daddy, this is Prada. Our very own dog.'

I wait, thinking Adi is going to go mad. But instead he says, 'Well, I got the bubbly as I wanted us to celebrate the good news. It's a double celebration, then.'

'Good news?' I ask, suddenly feeling rather anxious.

'Kurt rang me at work today. He's really excited, my name's come up on the allotment list.'

'Allotment list? I didn't even know your name was on the allotment list. We've got a huge garden.' For a moment I have a vision of our new neighbours organising our whole life. With the Weatheralls it feels like having your parents living next door. 'Why do we need an allotment?'

'Kurt's going to give me a hand to get started,' says Adi, giving us all a big smile as he dishes up the pasta.

'Delicious,' I say.

'Pasta Napolitana,' says Adi proudly, 'if that's how you pronounce the recipe.'

I can't help but smile to myself. Only Adi would need to follow a recipe when making veggie pasta. I can't believe that he is being so easy-going about the dog. And then he says, 'I've been thinking we could get some chickens.'

'What do you know about chickens?'

'Well, I can find out,' he says opening the bubbly.

Everything seems a bit better after a glass or two.

But then Adi says, 'We need to think about economising. We're all going to be doing a four-day week starting on Monday.'

'What? How can they do that after getting you all to relocate from London?' I say.

'They can do whatever they want. At least they're not sacking anyone. And look on the bright side, with the allotment we'll save money on our food shop.'

'You could mind Daisy while I'm at work on Mondays. That would save our nursery bill.'

'I don't know what day or hours I'll be at work. And if things look up we'll be back to five days. In fact David's offered to drop down to two days a week.'

'Why? Don't tell me he's off on his travels,' I say, enviously.

'No. he's got some business idea to do with tents.'

'Tents? He's a fully trained architect.'

'People do live in tents. I was thinking we could get a tent,' says Adi. 'Laura, you'd love a tent. It'll be part of our economy drive. We'll still go on holiday, we can explore England and save money. The girls would love it. You'd love it – it's made of fabric. It's a textile thing,' says Adi.

'Yes, we would love it,' say the girls almost in unison.

'OK, I'm outnumbered.' I smile. Adi's obviously been planning this speech about the tent all day. It's just I'm not a camping sort of girl.

'Perhaps you could get some more hours at the college?' suggests Adi, 'if you want a proper holiday.'

I don't answer. I haven't confided in Adi about my college 'misdemeanours'. I'm half afraid he'll take Curtis' side and tell me to stop being so impetuous and messy.

'Anyway it's another early start tomorrow.'

'How early?'

'4 a.m. Breakfast meeting in the Midlands.'

Chapter 8

Cast on stitch is used to create raised loops of thread in textured needlework techniques. It is often used today to create raised flower petals and leaves in highly textured work such as Brazilian embroidery.

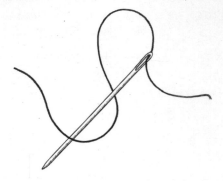

I sleep in fits and starts. I've now been into Daisy's room four times to settle her back to sleep. I slip in and out of dreaming about my lesson inspection. It's even colder than usual, with Adi having left in what seemed the middle of the night for a long drive to the Midlands. I keep thinking about Kurt's news reports of rural crime. It's so quiet in Reedby that the slightest noise has me sitting bolt upright in bed.

In Ealing I was often home alone with the girls. I felt safe there, with street lights and neighbours who I knew really well. The shop by the Tube station was open at the crack of dawn till late and the petrol station was open 24/7 and satisfied all my premenstrual and pregnancy cravings. Towards the end of Lilly's pregnancy the petrol station attendant only needed to see me crossing the concourse and he would already have wrapped up my fresh cream doughnut with chocolate sprinkles. And people say big cities are unfriendly!

'Mummy! Mummy!' calls Daisy for the fifth time – and I know if I was a better mother I wouldn't be counting. I fill her beaker again and feel my head throbbing. Perhaps we're both coming down with something. How many glasses of Cava did I drink? I pray that she'll get back to sleep. I add a P.S. to the prayer. Please, please don't really be ill. I have to go to work. I'm tempted to give her another dose of Calpol, but restrain myself. I get back into the frozen bed and then the guilt comes. Why aren't I worried about Daisy being off-colour? You've got your priorities wrong. Your mother wouldn't have begrudged looking after you.

Each time I wake I remember something else I should have put on my lesson plan. Have I written something for diversity? This is madness. My group is the most diverse group of students I've ever taught. Do I really have to prove it? This week is the third and final week of the college observation cycle – our mock Ofsted – and I haven't been inspected – not yet. Today has to be the day. Will today be the day that Curtis gets back at me for my rant? Will he write a nasty report about my teaching methods?

Curtis Lampard is even paying for a real inspector to join his team of observers. I could re-stock the textile cupboard with the money this consultant is being paid for five minutes. Curtis has bought artwork from 'real' artists to cover the walls. He looked baffled when I tried to suggest we frame my class's screen prints to brighten up the corridors.

I can't stop thinking of little flourishes I could add to my lesson plan. I begin to doubt the plan completely. Have I put enough differentiation in there? Oh this is ridiculous! All art has different outcomes, doesn't it? Unless my class is made up of clones all their work will be different. They're all selecting their own materials and themes and each student's work, like their handwriting, is different.

I'm finally distracted by a noise in the kitchen. My first reaction is to stick my head under the covers. What if it is an intruder? I play games with myself, saying things like, Nobody drives to Reedby in the middle of the night. Reedby, nestled in the bend in the river, is the end of the line. The luminous numbers on the clock say 4.33 a.m. Why did Adi have to leave so early for a meeting in the Midlands? Why did we choose to live in a backwater miles from anywhere? Wouldn't it be cheaper for Adi's company to use a webcam?

I put on my fur mules and pick up my Chinese paper parasol (as a weapon) from my clothes room. It's so cold in there that I stop and switch on the little fan heater. My vintage dresses are going to end up going mouldy in this house. Why am I living in a damp, marsh ridden house? I can hear my heart beating and my hands trembling as I step down the stairs. I slide on the stair carpet and quickly descend the dark, narrow staircase.

I can feel carpet burns on my legs as I enter the kitchen. It's freezing cold. What happened to our brief glimpse of spring? Prada is whimpering in her basket. Of course it was Prada, not one of Kurt's 'burglars', whimpering in the kitchen.

'You poor girl.' I'm about to pick her up and take her back to bed with me when she scratches my face. That's gratitude!

'You silly dog. I'm only trying to help you. Oh, hang on, you poor thing, there's blood on your leg,' I say, immediately feeling guilty.

I'm living in a house of invalids, I think, washing her leg. Perhaps I should have been a nurse. I soon change my mind when I realise how empty my first aid box is. I was sure we had bandages. I neatly stick on a plaster which Prada immediately pulls off. There's nothing for it. I rummage through my scarf drawer and wrap Prada's leg in a red and purple patterned scarf. 'You pampered girl!' This dog business is just like having another child, something I've sworn not to do. I get little enough sleep as it is. I then spot the broken wine glass on the floor in the corner. Did I really leave my last glass of Cava there? It's all my fault!

It's 8 a.m. I've already woken up the Weatheralls, needing a dog carrier and the name of a vet. I've dropped Lilly at the breakfast club and driven to Norwich. Prada, Daisy and myself are sitting in the vet's. It doesn't look like a vet's. I look around at what must have been the sitting room in Georgian times, with its big proportioned windows (letting in loads of light), a ceiling rose and wrought-iron fireplace. And what's more it's slap bang next to the shops and cafes. If this place didn't smell so bad I'd be moving in.

'Prada, why did you have to do this today of all days?' She replies with a whimper.

'Mummy, I don't feel well,' says Daisy.

'You're in sympathy for Prada. And you're probably tired,' I say, hoping that's the case. 'Do you want me to get the vet to have a look at you?' I joke. Daisy nestles into my arm and clearly doesn't think that Mummy is being funny.

'It smells in here,' says Daisy, wedging her face further into my velvet coat. 'It smells like London Zoo.' I don't answer, but think maybe this is how my kitchen would smell if I was one of those super housewives who squirted bleach onto every surface. Why is it that Adi is away when I really need him? Why is it that I am here with a dog and a toddler? These thoughts race around in my mind.

I try to distract myself by flicking through the uninspiring pile of *What Car?* and *Vet Monthly* magazines. When I think that I can't look at another article for treating pet fleas or neutering your tomcat I spot a very different sort of magazine. I pick it up and turn the thick, textured pages and admire the brightly printed dresses, shirts and rugs. Even the tea towels are beautiful – and probably all I could afford to buy from this designer. The models are in exotic locations: smiling beside snowy cabins wearing multicoloured knitwear, standing in billowy dresses in front of Rajasthani palaces. I love the bold colour combinations. I turn another page and see the watercolour design studies and handwritten notes. This whole collection is created by somebody called Annika, who appears to be Scandinavia's queen of fashion and textile design. I want to be Annika.

'I think it's your coat that smells, Mummy,' says Daisy, breaking my designer dreams.

'Thanks!' I say, sniffing the sleeve of my velvet coat. I know it's fifty years old, but this is the first time I've noticed the damp, mouldy (slightly studenty – if I remember rightly) smell of the cottage on my clothes.

A nurse calls out,

'Prada Stark.' My worst fears are realised. This dog *is* my third child.

'Well, Miss Prada, what can I do for you?' winks the young vet, looking and sounding like some beach boy from an Australian soap.

'I think she's got something in her paw,' I say.

'Is this some trendy dog outfit?' he says, pointing to the scarf wrapped around her leg. 'We see all sorts here.'

'I couldn't find a bandage.'

'Use a paler scarf next time. It's hard to see how much blood she's lost,' he says earnestly. I half smile, unsure whether he is joking or not. He then does the unthinkable and sticks a thermometer up her bottom. Daisy screams, yet Prada is unperturbed.

'I'll need you to hold her now,' he says, tying his slightly matted sandy hair into a ponytail with an elastic band. I step into action and hold Prada in place. He then positions a magnifying glass over her paw and with a tweezer pulls out a shard of wine glass.

I suddenly notice just how close I'm standing to 'surf boy' as I'm now thinking of the vet with his golden skin. He looks so well, so healthy, and I feel so pale and tired.

'You'll need to keep an eye on her for the rest of the day, just in case there's any more glass in her paw,' says the vet.

I nod, wondering how on earth I'm going to be able to keep an eye on her for the rest of the day.

Back in reception I loiter around for a moment by the coffee table. I pick up the *Annika* magazine and stuff it through the bars of Prada's cage. I'm about to struggle through the double doors when the nurse comes running up to me.

'Mrs Stark.'

I freeze for a moment and grab Daisy's hand tightly. Is it

really a crime to steal a magazine? I always know it's bad news when I'm called Mrs Stark. It's usually used by telesales people trying to sell double glazing. 'You need to pay the bill.' We move over to the counter and I'm handed a bill for £185. I can't believe it. There must be some mistake. It doesn't even cost this much at the dentist. I look at the clock and decide there's no time for quibbling and hand over my credit card. So much for our economy drive. I key in my pin number and realise that half of this month's wages will be paying for the vet bill.

'You might like to think about taking out pet insurance,' she says, handing me a leaflet with my receipt. Very briefly I consider leaving Prada at the RSPCA, although I'd never, ever admit this to anyone in the whole world. I toy with the idea of taking her home, yet there isn't time to drop Daisy at nursery and get to Reedby and back through the rush hour.

I open the mobile-classroom door expecting the usual blast of cold air. To my amazement I'm met with a waft of warm air. All around the room are brand new wall heaters. I put Prada's cage in the corner. An alarm bell rings in my head: 'never work with children or animals'. I wonder whether to drape some cloth over the cage. She might just go unnoticed, she could almost be a still-life object. Or maybe she could be added to my lesson plan as an enrichment activity.

I do it, I cover the sleeping dog with an old 1950s curtain print. I look at the pink blancmanges on the fabric and smile. It was my kitchen curtain fabric in my first ever flat. I took it with me when I moved from house share to house share. Well, I guess I stole it. I couldn't bear to be parted from it. Adi won't have it anywhere in the cottage. He says it's too pink and too kitsch. I say, what's wrong with kitsch? – it's just a bit of playfulness. So here it is in the still-life cupboard – an old friend. A good luck omen? Today's going to be OK after all. I rummage in the still-life cupboard and find a broken jug, floral plates and a couple of dried giant sunflowers. A perfect still-life setting. If I get the sack I could always go into window dressing, I muse.

Prada lets out a few little whimpers. There's nothing for it, I take out my bribe for Curtis, a pack of chocolate Buttons, lift the curtain and feed them to Prada. I can see Heather shaking her head at me right now and hear her admonishment. 'You shouldn't resort to bribes. The dog has to learn. And chocolate is bad for dogs, you know.'

'I don't care. Heather will never know. It's our secret,' I whisper to Prada, who is finally asleep.

I see my face in the window. I can't teach them looking like this – I look like I've been in a fight! I've finally been able to take the plaster off my forehead, only to now have to raid the first aid box and stick a plaster over my scratch from Prada.

The students come in and I realise I was so busy with my still life and my scratch that I haven't written the aims of the lesson on the whiteboard. I write Retro Fashion. In brackets, a recycling fashion and textile project.

I stand with my back to the door and check the register. I don't call out names, just have a quick look around, after all they're too old for this kind of formality. Everyone's here.

There's a clatter of chairs and doors as Jim rushes in.

'Awful traffic,' he mouths, his face bright red once again.

Suddenly the low level chatter stops and I see Curtis

Lampard has followed Jim into the studio. Behind Curtis, our own in-house inspector, is a lady in a suit. Her carefully manicured nails and immaculate outfit reminds me of my mother-in-law. Curtis struggles to hoist his extensive rear onto a dressmaking stool. The woman, who I realise must be the 'mock inspector', prefers to stand. I wonder if they'll make a note of my injuries, for if I was a pupil they'd definitely raise some suspicions.

I feel like an actor at the beginning of a play. The thought flits through my mind that out-of-work actors would make very good teachers – especially when an inspector calls.

Lizzy Buck begins to giggle and twirl her dreadlocks. I stare her out fighting to control myself as Curtis shuffles about, unable to get both his wide bottom cheeks on the stool. He looks as if his polyester trousers are lined with cushion wadding.

'I'm being standardised by Mrs Parker,' says Curtis. I want to say, 'Oh that sounds painful, Curtis,' instead, I breathe deeply and force a laugh into a theatrical cough.

I soon feel as if I'm on red alert when Curtis beckons me over. 'I'll be observing your lesson and writing a full length report,' he whispers.

'I see,' I say. Keep focused, Laura. He'll have to do this fairly, after all Mrs Parker is watching him. Then I start to panic. This really is Big Brother gone mad! This is no time for lateral thinking. Yet, something reminds me of my wedding day. Not knowing whether to laugh or cry. Is this my reaction in the face of authority?

This is it, Laura. Keep calm. It'll be over with by morning break. My stomach lurches, I feel sick. I hand him my scheme of work and handwritten lesson plan, covered in crossings-out, which he places on his clipboard. Curtis proudly strokes his identity badge. I look at Jim, also wearing his ID. Where is mine? I never want to wear it. I know who I am and so does everybody else, it makes me feel like a prisoner. And worse still the thick corporate ribbon doesn't match any of my clothes!

A tall auburn-haired girl walks in. I have no idea who she is. She's too young to be part of the inspection team, I think, I hope. The students look at her and tut a bit, as if they know who she is.

'Take a seat, I'll speak to you later,' I say.

Now I'm in full flow, acting my part. I always loved dressing up. I'm on my stage doing my bit.

'So, who can tell me what Retro fashion is?'

'It's to do with the past,' says Leon, bouncing up and down in his seat. 'And what have you done to your face *this time*?'

'The dog attacked me,' I say.

'What sort of dog have you got?' continues Leon, now sharpening pencils with a craft knife in double quick time.

'Let's stick to Retro fashion. Anyone got a definition of Retro fashion?' I ask again, writing it up on the board. I get them to take out the old garments they've brought in. One point to Laura. I've checked their 'prior learning', as Curtis would say.

'That's hideous!' says Jon, as Lizzy holds up a purple polyester shirt. Lizzy goes pink.

'It's supposed to be hideous,' snaps Amy. 'Don't you get it?'

Before I know it they've embarked on World War Three. How am I going to get onto constructing a garment? Curtis keeps raising his eyebrows and shuffling on the stool. I wish I'd brought an extra packet of chocolate Buttons. They'd give him something else to focus on. His accomplice Mrs Parker stands to attention. All I need now is for him to fall off his stool.

I change tack and abandon my lesson plan.

'OK guys, let's discuss this. This is an important issue in art and design. How do we define a beautiful piece of design?' I say, thinking of the *Annika* magazine. But now isn't the time to rummage in Prada's cage for it.

'Beauty is in the eye of the beholder,' says Lizzy, twiddling her dreadlocks. I notice Mrs Parker glance at her nails.

'What this all means,' says Amy, catching Curtis' eye, 'is that it's about being right for a particular time or place.'

'It's so you can fit in,' says the auburn-haired girl in a thick, probably eastern European, accent.

'Thank you,' I say, in the vague hope that she'll say her name.

Leon is desperately waving his arm and about to get up. 'Go on then, Leon,' I say, hoping to avoid him getting up and performing some of his acrobatics – especially as he has an audience.

'I saw this TV programme about the way fashion goes in cycles ...' I watch Leon, trying not to feel dizzy as he continuously bobs up and down while talking.

They are doing me proud. They may not have more than a handful of GCSEs between them but can they think laterally and discuss things. Curtis is scribbling hard. Mrs Parker seems to only have eyes for Jim. Thank God. At least Jim's behaving today.

We finally get onto the practical part of the lesson.

'So what are the ways you can join fabric?'

'Stitch,' says Lizzy.

'Is that it?'

Then comes the brainstorming.

'Buttons.'

'Safety pins. You could go punk.'

'Lace. Like a corset, miss.'

'Glue, pins, Velcro,' shouts Leon, clearly becoming very excited.

I divide them into threes. This leaves Leon and a quiet boy called Adam as an odd pair. Well, I can't solve everything. Jim joins the odd pair and the foreign girl insists on working on her own.

Then they're up on their feet grabbing fabric from their bags and the fabric bins. Their enthusiasm is reminiscent of shoppers at the January sales. The studio resembles a jumble sale for adolescents.

'But miss – you still haven't told us what we've got to do,' says Amy, on the ball as usual. I can't believe I've done this. Now I have to ad-lib.

'Well,' I say. 'The question is what can you make from this?'

'I'm going to make a bandanna for skateboarding,' says Leon.

'I'm making a fairy dress with wings,' shouts Lizzy.

'You've got to the end of the session,' I say. 'Off you go.' I look at the clock. Curtis has been here for an hour and a half. These observations are supposed to only be for an hour. I don't know how much longer I can keep this up. I see Mrs

Parker get up to leave, dusting some flecks of pastel off her black suit.

She goes over to Jim. 'I recognise you from somewhere. I just can't place you.'

'Widow Twanky in last year's production. You probably don't recognise me without my make-up.'

'Of course!' she exclaims.

I'm feeling tenser by the minute. Let her leave! I think.

But her eyes are following Jim as he moves across the room. 'Can I use this?' calls Jim, standing near Prada's cage. 'I love blancmange! My nan used to make us blancmange every Saturday night – no one makes it any more,' says Jim looking wistful.

'My question is why don't designers make fabrics like this any more?' I ask, realising that I'm getting distracted from managing the group. It is, however, a useful snippet of social history.

Before I can say, 'Don't move the fabric!', he's lifted up the cover, knocking the jug off to reveal Prada. Mrs Parker is at the door about to leave. Go! Go now! Follow Curtis and standardise him! She turns to me and says, 'I like the recycling, that was good.' Miraculously, she hasn't spotted Prada. I want to punch the air, but instead I open the door and hope they'll leave. They obey my thoughts and step onto the top rung of the metal steps. I hear Mrs Parker say, 'These steps really should be gritted.' I dread to think what she'd say if she had seen Prada. I turn the radio up to full blast and close the door.

'Can the dog join our team?' asks Leon. I'm past caring now Curtis and his accomplice are gone. 'We could make a designer dog jacket? I was really good while they were here. I wouldn't be that good for any other teacher.'

'Why not?' I reply, watching him run across the room and do a somersault.

'Their lessons are all boring,' he shouts back.

'Great lesson, Laura,' enthuses Jim. 'By the way, our auburn-haired beauty is Andrea Lasky. She's on my support list.'

'But not on my register,' I say, raising my eyebrows as if I'm impersonating Mrs Parker. 'Break time, everyone,' I call.

The morning is finally over. I check the coast is clear and carry Prada into the office. What a day! I bet Annika doesn't have to teach to supplement her design income by jumping through Ofsted hoops. Why can't I sell enough designs to pay the bills?

'There's a message for you to ring the nursery,' says Sue. My heart sinks. Daisy! How could I have forgotten about her? I'm a terrible mother!

'Do you know when they rang?' I ask.

'An hour or so ago, I think. With all those observers and inspectors roaming around no one dared to take a break or come and tell you.'

My heart is pounding as I ring the nursery extension.

'It's Daisy's mum,' I say, images of Daisy falling off the slide, escaping out of the play area, an unexpected bump on her head, all run through my mind.

'We've got her in a room on her own. She's come out in spots. It looks like chickenpox. Can you come and get her?'

'Of course. Of course. I only just got the message,' I say.

'We did call some time ago,' says the voice.

I look down at Sue, who's standing next to me with a concerned look. She's as dainty as a ballerina and is actually wearing red ballet pumps. But it's no time for discussing shoes.

'Daisy's not well. I'm going to have to cancel this afternoon's class. Adi is away at a meeting and won't be back until tonight,' I say. I feel doubly guilty that I've got a sick child who I should have picked up an hour ago and that I'm leaving work early.

'You just go,' says Sue. 'I'll try and keep it quiet,' she whispers, 'if not HR will deduct your pay.'

'Isn't there any sort of compassionate leave?' I venture.

'Education isn't compassionate any more. It's all about keeping costs down.'

I pick up my bags and Prada's cage and walk down the corridor. When I first started teaching everything was so different. Lecturers were special; experts in their field. Now I'm just a cog in a wheel churning out designers who tick a few government dreamt-up boxes. I don't know how much longer I can do this.

For a moment I wonder whether to take Prada into the nursery. The children would love her (even if she doesn't have a CRB check, I laugh to myself, overcome by the day's officialdom). I do the sensible thing and place her on the back seat of the car before making my way through three different security gates. After all, she did scratch me this morning. I finally enter the farmyard room, Daisy's room. There's no sign of her. I feel a horrible tight feeling in the pit of my stomach. Where is she? They haven't taken her to hospital, have they?

'Daisy's in the side room,' says one of the teenage nursery

nurses with her midriff on show. She points to a door behind the home corner. 'We had to segregate her,' she adds, unsympathetically, as if Daisy has got the plague.

I open the side door and see Daisy and the nursery manager sitting happily colouring in at a miniature table.

'Mummy! Mummy!' She runs over and snuggles into my skirt. 'Look at my picture. It's Prada.' I look at the drawing of a very big-eyed dog with long eyelashes.

'It's lovely.' There seems to be nothing wrong with Daisy. The nursery manager stands up and says, 'Daisy, show Mummy your rash.'

She obediently pulls up the Fair Isle jumper (which doesn't belong to her) and reveals a bright red rash.

I rub her tummy and then feel the jumper. 'Is this wool?' I ask.

The manager shrugs her shoulders.

I check the care label: lambswool. 'We're both allergic to wool. It should be in her notes. Is it?'

Before the manager can answer she's talking to someone on her walkie-talkie.

'Please excuse me. I have to attend to something.'

'Come on Daisy. It's time to go home. Prada's waiting in the car.'

'Can I sit next to her?'

'Of course you can.'

I take Daisy into the cloakroom, rummage in her change of clothes bag and put her in a cotton sweatshirt. I finally get her into her coat, hat, mittens and shoes and we leave.

When I thought that work couldn't get any worse, I've really outdone myself: a few hours' sleep, a sick dog and having every movement observed and written about. If there was an award for the worst day at work ever – I'd be the first in line. Rather than bursting into tears, I find myself laughing out loud. I'm so tired I feel as if I've got jet lag – if only!

Chapter 9

Cross stitch is also known as sampler stitch, Berlin stitch and point de marquee. It is one of the oldest stitches in the history of textiles and is still used worldwide today as it has been in the past.

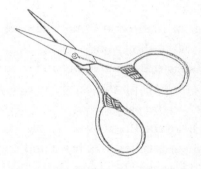

The guilt pangs are wearing off and I'm enjoying being at home when I should be teaching this afternoon. Having survived this morning's lesson inspection I feel as if I've worked a whole day anyway.

'What do you want to do this afternoon?' I ask Daisy, who looks perfectly happy playing trains on the dining room floor. 'We've got all afternoon. Lilly's going to after-school club.'

'I want to draw Prada.'

'What a good idea.'

'I want to use your special art things,' says Daisy, looking up at me with her big eyes. 'Have you got white paint?'

At this point I should be really pleased that my pre-school daughter wants to paint a picture. But all I can think about is the mess.

'We'll have to work in the kitchen. I know what would be better than paint,' I say in an exaggerated nursery-nurse voice. 'You sit up at the table and I'll go and get the surprise.'

I cover the kitchen table with old newspapers saved for the wood burner. I plonk a stack of printer paper and boxes of wax crayons on the kitchen table. Daisy picks up a white crayon and begins to furiously scribble Prada's fur.

'Mummy! Look!'

'Ah, it's Prada in a snowstorm. Wait a minute, Mummy's got something magical to show you.'

I raid my stash in the conservatory and return with brushes and little pots of ink. I dip the brush in a light grey ink and make a wash across the paper.

'It's magic! I can see Prada now.'

'This technique is called wax resist and makes really nice swirly designs.' Daisy isn't listening, she's busy making washes of inks.

'Daisy, you've given me an idea for the men's floral range! And for next week's lesson. This is called multi-tasking.'

I rummage in the kitchen cupboard for a saucepan. I'm sure we had some old pans. Perhaps Adi threw them out when we moved. I take out the main vegetable pan. I go to the linen cupboard and pull out the nearest white cotton sheet and finally I take out our box of emergency candles (which of course we no longer need now we have a wind-up torch). I rip up the white sheet into handkerchief sized pieces. I love the rip sound of fabric. It reminds me of being a kid and going with Mum to buy dress fabric. The shop assistant would pull the material through some measuring machine and make a snip. Then miraculously they'd rip the fabric in a perfect line. I chop up the candles and place them in the pan. Soon the smell of hot wax permeates the kitchen.

Daisy is in her element drawing Prada. She has big smudges of red and blue on her cheeks. I'm glad she's as messy as me – I have an ally in the house. I too am in my element as I plunge the metal tjanting into the melted-wax pot. I hold the cool wooden handle and through the tjanting's little hole I drip hot wax swirls and dots. Soon the wax begins to resemble flowers on the white cotton.

'Is it teatime yet? I'm hungry,' says Daisy, still drawing. 'What time is it on the clock?'

'I can't believe it. It's quarter to six. Not only do we need to collect Lilly, Prada needs her walk.'

'But she's poorly.'

'Come on Daisy, let's go.' I pick up Kurt's torch and we start off up the Green for school. Prada gives up after a few minutes and I'm left holding Daisy in one hand, trying to shine the torch on the road and carrying Prada in my other hand.

'There's Daddy's car,' shouts Daisy. We walk into the school club with a minute to go. Luckily we're not the only 'just in time' parents. A handful of children gather around Prada, just like the mums do with a newborn. The children compete to stroke and cuddle her.

'Laura,' says Adi, as if I've intruded on his surprise for the girls.

'I didn't think you'd be back yet,' I say, immediately

105

realising that I don't sound too pleased to see him either – which isn't the case.

'The meeting wasn't much fun. Lately architecture doesn't seem to have anything to do with designing beautiful and functional buildings. It's all about the cheapest option. They might as well get a builder to design for them,' huffs Adi. 'And Lilly's wanted me to collect her for weeks,' he says, giving her a cuddle. 'What on earth is that dog wearing?' asks Adi, looking down at Prada.

'It's a long story. I was observed today,' I say. 'And as Prada couldn't be left at home she made up one of the design teams. The kids made her coat.'

'Why couldn't Prada be left at home? She's not a baby.' Adi looks at me, the same raised eyebrows I had from Mrs Parker, the inspector.

'She hurt her leg. Anyway that wasn't the worst of it. Jim joined in the lesson and managed to lift up the fabric covering her cage.'

'Mummy! Mummy! Prada's got a leopardskin coat,' squeals Lilly.

'Yes, Mummy's oh-so-helpful colleague Jim made it.'

'It must be the first bit of work he's ever done,' says Adi. 'That dog will have an identity crisis,' he adds. I burst out laughing.

'Can we go home,' I say. 'It's been a long day.'

We stand outside the school hall. It's cold and damp.

'Can Prada sit on my lap in the car?' pleads Lilly, cradling Prada.

'In my car?' says Adi. 'OK, there aren't any policemen about. Are her paws clean?'

'Of course she's clean. Thank you Daddy!' says Lilly.

It smells like Bonfire Night,' says Lilly, sniffing the air, almost impersonating Prada.

'Probably someone burning weeds on their allotment,' says Adi, knowledgeably.

Then I hear the sirens.

'Nee nah, nee nah,' joins in Daisy pretending to be a whole fleet of fire engines. The real fire engines race past us. I have an awful feeling in the pit of my stomach. I can't remember if I turned the wax off. From the top of the Green I can't see Marsh Cottage. It looks like it's wrapped in a thick veil of fog. As Adi drives closer the sirens scream past us and stop at *our* house.

We stand by the car, our arms linked together, all hypnotised by the fire. None of us move, except Prada who jumps down onto the gravel. I watch the firemen rushing around as if I'm at the cinema and this isn't really my house that's on fire.

'Where's Prada?' screams Lilly, frantically looking around. Before we can stop her she's running towards the house. I grab Daisy's hand and see Adi chasing after Lilly. Then their silhouettes are swallowed up by the smoke.

'Don't go in the house!' I scream. And as if on auto pilot, I disobey my own instructions and begin to run towards the house, dragging Daisy along. A fireman grabs me by the tail of my velvet coat. I hear a ripping noise. I'm paralysed. The only sound is the roaring of the flames.

A figure runs out of the house, looking like a patchwork ghost with its head covered in my prized Amish quilt. The multicoloured ghost wrestles it off to reveal Adi, with Lilly in one arm and Prada in the other.

107

'Lilly!' I yell, running up to her and prodding and pulling on her to make sure she's OK.

'Mum! Stop it!' complains Lilly.

'I think she's going to live,' says Adi with a wry grin.

I then look at Prada, who is as still as a toy dog. 'She's not moving! She's all floppy,' I yell to anyone and everyone. In desperation I begin to poke her. She doesn't respond.

The fireman rushes over, takes one look at her and goes back to the fire engine. He runs back and holds a mask over her face, while Adi cradles her.

'Is she going to die?' cries Daisy.

'She'll be fine. I'm giving her some extra oxygen,' says the fireman.

Just like Sleeping Beauty Prada sits up, but then begins to wrestle with the mask and jumps up.

'That's a good sign. We could take her to the vet's. It's your call,' says the fireman.

I can't bring myself to tell him that we've already been to the vet's today. He'll start to wonder about us. We'll end up being reported to the RSPCA at this rate, I start to think, victim to my own over-active imagination.

Adi steps in, 'She'll be fine. I'll keep an eye on her.'

With Adi, the girls (and I have to confess Prada, now really part of our family) safe and sound, I think about where I am going to begin with owning up to the fire being my fault. Then another thought flashes across my mind – what about my clothes? They're in the bedroom above the kitchen.

Before I had the girls the clothes really were my babies, as much as any of my fabric designs or paintings. I'm not being materialistic, I don't even have an iPod. In my prouder moments I think of them like a museum collection. They're part of all of our pasts – not just mine. Each item is unique, an irreplaceable one-off. A bit like people really. Right now moving to Reedby feels like my biggest mistake ever. I don't really feel anything for Marsh Cottage – other than a bit numb. Maybe we should just move back to London, everything felt safe and familiar there. My collection has suffered so much since moving from dry as a bone Ealing to damp Marsh Cottage.

'Are you OK?' says the fireman. 'You look very pale. Do you want one of the medics to have a look at you?'

'I'm fine,' I say, which of course I'm not.

'We've got the worst of it under control. Chip pan left on, was it?'

'The amount of chip pan fires we're called to,' says the other fireman, the one who ripped my coat. 'And it doesn't help that the house is thatched.'

'Were you cooking chips? asks Adi.

'I think so,' I mutter. I can't tell him. I can't tell Adi who is now a hero, more like Bruce Willis in *Die Hard* than my husband; I can't tell the man who ran into a house with a raging fire to save our daughter, and the dog, that I left a pan of wax heating up on the cooker. But another part of me just can't lie.

I find the main fireman again and say, 'It wasn't a chip pan.'

He gives me a puzzled look. 'You could have fooled me, love. Perhaps you're in shock.'

'It was a pan. It didn't have chips in it,' I try to explain. 'It had wax in it.'

'I think you're a bit confused,' he says, putting his arm around me.

'She's not confused,' says Adi. 'Were you doing batik?' he says, looking at me as if he's my dad.

'It's my work,' I answer.

'Laura, I'm not angry. We're all safe.'

'We usually do a mail out,' says the fireman.

'A mail out?' Adi and I ask in unison.

'Part of the firefighter's job nowadays. Not only do we put out fires. After each incident we mail out the neighbourhood. If something's happened to you, the likelihood is that it will happen to one of your neighbours.'

I nod obligingly.

'I don't think anyone else in the village will be heating up wax, my wife is a one-off,' says Adi, giving me a squeeze on the shoulders.

Adi rushes over to Kurt. I follow him. 'If it hadn't been for Kurt ringing the fire brigade the whole house might have burnt down,' says Adi, gazing up at Kurt, who seems to permanently be dressed in a blue boiler suit.

'It could be arson, you know,' says Kurt, sounding knowledgeable.

'Why would anyone want to burn our house down? We haven't got any enemies,' I say incredulously – except of course my boss, but even Curtis has his limits.

'Theft. To cover up a theft,' he says. 'They weren't after your new bike. That's a relief,' says Kurt.

I look at Adi. Are you going to tell Kurt the cause of the fire?

'It was the cooker,' says Adi, unprepared to enlighten Kurt any further.

'Things can be replaced on the insurance,' says Adi casually. 'As long as we're all safe.'

The thing that is really upsetting me now, which I can't tell anyone, is that I won't be able to get another vintage clothes collection on the insurance. These clothes aren't replaceable. And I don't have the right to complain because the fire was all my fault.

'You might have to camp out on the allotment,' says Kurt. It's got a nice little summerhouse. A bit nippy this time of year though. Surely with your skills you could design your own summerhouse,' suggests Kurt.

'Do you have somewhere to stay tonight, friends, family?' asks the coat-ripping fireman.

It hits me that we don't have any friends or family within fifty, or more realistically a hundred, miles, except that is for Adi's parents, who are a good forty-five minutes' drive away on the coast. Please, please let's not go there. If we have to go to Adi's parents' we'll all die of second-hand smoke inhalation from his mother's Silk Cuts. If only we were in Ealing we could have gone next door to my friend Lotte's, or round the corner to Matt and Emma's. But here? Here I feel stranded.

'You see, we should have bought a tent from David,' says Adi, with a wink. I want to say this is no laughing matter. But I know Adi, he's just trying to make us all feel a bit better.

'Mummy, we could go to Kate's house,' shouts Lilly. 'Her mum said I could have a sleepover soon.'

'I bet she wasn't expecting all of us … and a dog, so soon,' says Adi.

Chapter 10

Chain stitch is simple to work. Bring the needle up through the fabric and loop the thread beneath the needle. Insert the needle back into the same place as before. Take the needle through the fabric bringing the point of the needle out a short space along the line to be stitched. With the thread beneath the needle as before, pull the needle through the fabric.

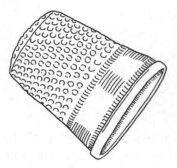

I return from a night at Liz's house and plan to go inside to survey the damage. I stand on the doorstep and can't quite make myself open the door. I realise that I don't really know anyone here, bar Heather and Kurt and the Randalls. They've been so kind I don't dare ring them and ask any more favours.

I still can't quite believe it that Adi is at work. 'I can't take time off over something like this,' he said. 'Not how things are going at the moment with this proposed four-day week.' All of which is highly ironic. It was Adi who was so keen to buy a traditional thatched cottage. Back then I'd have had visions of him up on a ladder with the thatcher discussing all the ins and outs of the craft.

What I really want to do is to dial a friend. But my friends are miles away. I'm stuck in the middle of nowhere and as on my own as I've ever felt. If I could wind back time like they do in the movies I would be back in Ealing in a matter of seconds. But I can't. I've got to go inside.

I turn the door handle and step onto the porch, almost expecting something to jump out at me. Nothing does. The firemen said the damage was only in the kitchen, the bedroom above it and the thatch, which is wet and burnt.

I don't even attempt to go in the kitchen. Instead I lift the stair door latch somehow hoping that everything will be OK as I go along the landing. Everything is black, covered in soot as if Mount Vesuvius had erupted in the middle of Reedby and Marsh Cottage was the epicentre. The charred wood smells rotten.

What I really want to do is go and check my clothes collection. But I divert myself with my to-do list, which today is a long list of phone numbers. I go downstairs and pick up the phone. The line is dead.

I rummage in my bag for my mobile and go out onto the Green. It's a long time since I'd wished I was model-height but today I need to be a whole foot taller than my measly five foot two inches. I can only get reception if I hold my arm up in the air; which then means I can't actually speak into the phone. There's nothing for it, I heave out one of the dining room chairs. Why do we have such heavy ones, like something from a posh restaurant? I climb on the white canvas cushion. Everything begins to wobble just as I tell the thatcher our address.

Ah! I don't believe it! 'Damn!' Everything is moving.

I'm sitting on the grass nursing a grazed elbow. And the seat is covered with a large sooty footprint. What's more Heather is twitching her blinds at me. She's coming over now. And there's no escape!

'Mrs Stark.'

'Laura,' I whine.

'Come and use our phone. I'll make you a nice cup of tea,' she says firmly, as if I'm a wayward dog who needs taking in hand.

I hover in the lounge. I look around at the fluffy carpets and dressers full of crystal and feel comforted by the kitschness of the house: Adi would call it 'Doily City'. Adi was always joking around when we lived in London. The thought makes me smile. It feels like the jokes have been a bit few and far between lately.

'Sit!' commands Heather. I immediately sink into the well-upholstered pink sofa, thinking that Heather could come and do a bit of behavioural management with my wayward students.

Heather carries in a floral plastic tray. She places it on the glass coffee table. I look at the two mugs and matching biscuit barrel, all covered with repeat patterns of Scottie dogs and finished off with tartan trim. There's no evidence of her interest in Japanese design, apart from the carefully arranged stones on the coffee table and a black vase with a single (unidentifiable) flower in it.

'Help yourself to the custard creams,' she says, taking a handful for herself. 'And how is little Snowball getting on?'

'Fine, the girls love her. She's really part of the family.' I

114

leave out telling Heather that she's called Prada, about her injuries, her day at the college and nearly causing the death of Adi and Lilly by running into a house on fire.

'If you want to go on my waiting list for dog-training lessons, let me know. No pressure. But dogs are like children; they need taking in hand.'

'I'll think about it,' I say.

'I'll leave you in peace. The phone's on the buffet.' She goes into her study, calling 'I'm not being anti-social but I'm writing a book about dog training and I'm trying to do a thousand words a day.'

I'm beginning to like Heather. She seems to have her life pretty well sorted. I nestle into the velvet armchair. I ring the thatcher back, omitting to tell him the reason for cutting him off. I simply apologise. I then ring the insurance company. They promise to send a surveyor straight away.

I can't believe how helpful they are being until they begin to ask probing questions: 'Was it an accident? Could it have been arson? Have you spoken to the police? Did you know that rural crime is rocketing?' I try to say as little as possible. I'm not in the mood for explaining the finer details of heating up batik wax. I cross off each phone call and begin to feel I've achieved something today.

I knock on the study door. 'Thank you for the phone loan.'

'No trouble – anytime. But where are you going to live while the builders are in?'

'I don't know,' I say, starting to get a bit tearful. 'I guess we'll get put up in a hotel or something.'

'There isn't a hotel around here. You're not in London now. Leave it with me,' says Heather.

I return to the cottage, unsure of what Heather has in mind, but knowing that the moment I've been dreading is going to have to happen.

I peep my head around the stair door and make my way past the soot-coloured walls to my dressing room. The smell of burnt plastic makes me want to retch. I pull my skinny rib jumper up higher over my nose and mouth and must look like some cartoon robber. I bet the designer of the skinny rib never thought that the long polo neck would have such a practical use. I don't think there are many smells worse than burnt plastic.

Why did I leave the cooker on? I've brought this all on myself. If Curtis ever finds out I'll never be trusted to teach again. The far corner of the room looks like the remains of a bonfire. Like a mad woman trying to find a particular bargain at Selfridges' January sale I pull coathangers backwards and forwards. Only a handful of things are left unscathed – I hug my Paris skirt, with repeated images of the Eiffel Tower and a flower stall that cover the whole skirt. Can you love an inanimate object? Or am I just so lonely here that I'm beginning to think of my clothes as old friends?

I sit surrounded by scraps of my fabrics. I don't seem to be able to move. I am a fraud. I call myself a textile designer, yet my own attempts at sewing wouldn't help me pass a GCSE in needlework. That is if they even still teach sewing these days? I paint and print my ideas, which is fine. I tell myself that surface pattern design is a valid area of textile design.

I look at my beautiful fabrics, which I fell in love with, though not because they were in fashion. Almost the opposite, they are all one-offs. Bespoke. I don't really care about high street fashion. I just love the chase of finding that special item. A dress or skirt which carries with it a whole history, or should I say usually a *her-story*. That is if I was feeling in a radical mood.

I hold up a piece of dress fabric covered in a strawberry-pink blancmange print. It's very similar to my curtain fabric, same hand-drawn style motif, same colourway, what's different though is that these blancmanges are tiny, discreet and not actual blancmange size (as they are on the curtains). Come to think about it that was probably why Adi found the curtains too much to handle.

Like Jim at the college I too remember eating blancmange, usually for school dinners. Mum actually had an apron covered with prints of blancmanges and jugs of homemade lemonade. I'd love to see that apron again. In fact I'd give anything to have Mum here right now. You're never too old to need your mum.

I wipe my eyes on the blancmange fabric and begin to fold what is left of my vintage clothes collection and put it in a suitcase. I'm packing up my past. It brings back memories of a well meant INSET day recently. The day we had to put ourselves in the shoes of refugees and asylum seekers. The task was to list what you'd put in a suitcase, if you had thirty minutes to pack. I can't believe how I'd laughed and joked inappropriately, saying things like 'How many handbags can you fit in a suitcase?' Now, apart from a few garments, I'm only left with scraps.

I still remember when I bought my first vintage piece almost by accident when I was eighteen, my coming-of-age purchase. A girl called Wanda, who lived opposite me in my halls of residence, took me on a shopping trip. I haven't thought of Wanda for years. Where is she now? Does she still wear vintage, or has she moved on? She never dressed like any of us. She never wore jeans. Wanda dressed like an Edwardian lady, revealing a pale bit of ivory ankle flesh. Her translucent skin matched the pale, delicate, lacy fabrics she wore. Wanda hustled me out of the charity shop, as if we were on some mission, and might get caught.

On the bus home I flung on my proud purchase – an ocean liner scarf. I loved the feel of silk, and the look of the blue and crimson stripes and sails. Wanda revealed that I had found a real collector's item – an Ascher scarf. 'A wonder of post-war design,' she called it. 'Laura, it's worth far more than the two pounds you paid for it.' I, on the other hand, didn't really care, I just liked the scarf.

Then there were Mum's dresses, which I kept after she died. I couldn't throw them out, I couldn't give them away, and for a long time I couldn't wear them. They lived in a no-man's land. Wanda wouldn't have understood the bright psychedelic shirts in nylon and Crimplene, or the ethnic embroidered kaftans. They were 1960s and 1970s, far too recent, and crime of all crimes (in her eyes) were made from synthetic fabrics.

Yet after a few years Mum's clothes came out of mourning and found their way into my vintage clothes collection. I'd inherited a wardrobe of clothes the way other people are left jewellery, ornaments or even a painting.

I run my hand across the coarse Crimplene. I can still see Mum in her green and purple tunic with the swirly print. Now there is only an oblong with a singed border left.

I run down to the kitchen and tip everything out of the drawer in the search for a pair of scissors, then rush back upstairs with the faint realisation that I'm glad I'm here alone, committing this act of almost-madness. I begin to cut and salvage a piece of Mum's tunic.

'Damn. This always happens!' I mutter to myself. I need some left-handed scissors. Horrible memories of 'awkward' Laura at high school come to mind. 'What a mess, you're so untidy,' Mrs Dawson, my old art teacher, used to say. Her name and images of her in long brown cord skirts, her pudding basin haircut and clogs which you could hear a mile off, are still etched on my mind. I think I became an artist not because of her, but in spite of her.

In a split second I know that I'm going to conquer sewing at long last and do something with my fabrics. I grandly think it would be a fitting memorial to Mum to make something from my inheritance. What is it that poets and musicians compose in memorial to a loved one? Is it a eulogy? You can even write with stitching. I think of Tracey Emin's stitched tent with the names of all her lovers. Textile work is very personal.

I think of Chris and know that if Mum was still around she wouldn't approve of such dreamy thoughts. She met him once when she made the trip down to London for our degree show. She didn't know what to make of any of the artworks. But she did know what to make of Chris. I can still remember her words: 'Laura, it's not just his good looks that concern me, they're merely an extra. There's something about him. You'll never be the only one.' Mum had said all that with an enigmatic look in her eye.

Now, the only problem with sewing is that I can't really

sew. There are rumours that Tracey Emin and the Brit Art brigade get other people to make up their work, but if I'm going to make constructed textiles I want to make them myself.

I go downstairs and cross over the barrier tape into the kitchen. Somewhere in one of the kitchen drawers is the parish magazine. And I'm sure I saw an advert for a sewing class. How can there be so many piles of papers? We've only been in Reedby a month. I tip the mostly ashen contents of the drawer on the floor. It's the best way to find things. I always do this when I can't find something in my handbag. I hear a great commotion coming up the Green. The noises are louder than a tractor and coming my way. There's a sudden screech of brakes.

I peep out of the kitchen window and spot my visitors.

'This is it,' shouts Heather to the woman driving an open-top sports car, leading the convoy. Behind her, clutching the wheel of a pickup truck, is a fuchsia-faced Kurt dripping with sweat. He looks far less cool than he did last night, as he steers a caravan into our drive.

Heather rushes over.

'This is my sister, Charlotte.'

'And you must be Laura,' says Charlotte in a clipped BBC-type of voice – just like we used to get on the television all the time when I was a child. 'We've all heard about the awful fire. Heather told me that you've got nowhere to live. So I thought of Harriet,' she says, taking her hands out of her waxed jacket pocket and revealing a set of keys.

'Harriet?' I ask. 'Who is Harriet?'

'The caravan. We lived in her while we built River Cottage.

120

Then I couldn't bear to get rid of her – having no children of my own,' she laughs very loudly. 'She's yours for as long as you want her.'

'Thank you. Thank you so much,' I say, and at the generosity of this complete stranger I feel my eyes begin to well up with tears again.

'There's just one catch,' says Charlotte, completely ignoring Kurt as he struggles to put the wheel brake on. 'I need you to join the Midsummer Fayre committee. We need someone for the arty things. Heather tells me you're an art teacher. It's going to be at Trishna, the Buddhist retreat, this year. Such a lovely venue in that old Georgian house and those Buddhist boys are adorable. Don't you think?' she says, not stopping for breath.

I nod, suddenly remembering Chris Taylor in his paisley shirt. That's the second time he's found his way into my mind today.

'It's a done deal then. Come along Kurt,' she calls. 'I'll let you know when the next meeting is. Bring all your ideas. There's nothing like a bit of hard work to take your mind off things.'

'Heather,' I call.

'Yes, dear?'

'Could I come back and make a couple more phone calls?'

'Of course.'

Excited, I ring Adi with a news report.

'We have a caravan. Heather's sister brought it round.'

'I'm not living in a bloody caravan. Can't stand them!' he snaps. 'Didn't it occur to you that a caravan isn't suitable for someone who is six foot tall *and* an architect?'

'Some caravans are design classics,' I mumble, aware that I'm on uncertain ground.

'Why didn't you tell me? I've sorted everything out. You just wait and see tomorrow,' he says in a more excited voice than I've heard in ages. 'I'll be a bit late tonight, I'm going to pick up some clothes for the girls on the way home. I've managed to re-stock my wardrobe online, without stepping into one shop. Isn't that brilliant?'

'Yes, aren't you lucky,' I say, flatly.

'What about you, do you need anything?'

'What do you mean?'

'Clothes from the supermarket. Anyway, I can't talk now. Ring me back if you want anything,' he says, hanging up.

Since when did Adi buy clothes from a supermarket? I think not. And he expects *me* to wear supermarket clothes! He'd better have been joking. He may be able to replace his wardrobe in a few minutes with just the click of a mouse at some select online boutique. But my clothes collection took fifteen years to put together. Each piece was unique, that's what I loved about them. I can't just throw them out. I notice that my hands are shaking. I stand up and take a couple of deep breaths and feel a little bit better.

The study door is ajar and I wonder whether to knock, when Heather calls, 'All sorted?'

'Getting there. By the way, do you have a copy of the parish newsletter?'

'Certainly.' She stands and reaches up for one of the big box files. 'A place for everything,' she says taking out the February edition of *On the Broads*. I'm glad Adi isn't here watching Heather's efficiency. It would give him too many ideas.

'This is a mine of information, look: yoga classes, sewing, bee-keeping ... all of life is in Reedby.' It's impossible to tell if Heather is being sarcastic or blindingly honest. 'How's Snowball getting on?'

'Who? Oh fine. The girls love her,' I say. I've got to tell her. 'Actually the girls have given her another name, a nickname,' I add, trying to water down the information. 'Snowball is now Prada,' I say very quickly. Heather doesn't blink an eyelid. I think that there's something very Old English Sheepdog about Heather, with her thick, shaggy greying hair. It was newly cropped at our housewarming. I wish my hair grew as quickly as hers.

Heather gives out a funny snorty laugh. 'I've heard much worse than that. In fact I make a point of not discussing dog names.'

I walk over the road and back into our house, feeling both excited and scared about the prospect of going to a sewing class. Perhaps the college will pay my fees? After all it is CPD, or continuing professional development, as HR like to call it. I've also got a number for a yoga and meditation class, it would do Adi good. But I'm not sure yet how I'll persuade him to go. He'll think yoga isn't manly enough for him. If it was a martial arts class he'd be there in no time. Yoga can't be that different, can it? Then I suddenly remember Prada. Where is she?

'Prada! Prada!' I yell, sounding like some madwoman who's lost her handbag, or worse, her child. I search the garden and go back upstairs. I go into the girls' room and am hit again by the smell of melted plastic. There are a few singed clothes which look more like Cinderella rags than bright patterned children's clothing. All that's left of one of their tops is half of

123

a pink appliqué heart. I love the girls' clothes. I would wear the lot of them with their bright colours and lovely prints deemed too much for grown-up taste. If only they went up into adult sizes. 'Prada! Come on girl!' I call.

I go into the utility room and see Prada nestled in the wash basket. 'You're Mummy's third daughter,' I say. In reality she is another child who I keep forgetting about. Prada just carries on sleeping. I fill a bowl with her chunks and biscuits, and she immediately bounds out of the basket and begins eating, completely ignoring me. In the basket I spy an enormous squashed pile of clothes. Thank goodness I'm not a capable housekeeper I think, seeing a few of mine and the girls' clothes – saved. My disorganisation has won the day!

'Prada, look, my electric blue shirt from when I was a student,' I say stroking her. She completely ignores me and keeps her head firmly in the bowl. Aren't dogs supposed to be loving, affectionate companions? She ignores me just like Adi. Lately I've sometimes found myself thinking that the partnership Adi and I have is solely a business partnership – and the house and kids are our business. We never seem to get any time together these days. There's no time or money to go out. It wasn't always like that. Before the girls we used to go off for weekends away. That seems a lifetime ago now. Even after the girls came along we were in a babysitting circle and used to get out – just the two of us.

I go outside and into the caravan. It smells of Charlotte's perfume – sweet geranium, perhaps? Everything is in miniature. I laugh out loud thinking of my boss (or Head of School, as he likes to be called) Curtis Lampard, who would probably be unable to get through the door, let alone squeeze on to the foam seats. The seats are upholstered in an orange and brown floral print straight out of the 1970s. The covers are stuck together w th Velcro. I love it. Adi will hate this, I think. I fiddle about moving the seats into a bed and back into mini sofas. I feel as if I am playing house. I've reverted to being like Daisy in her beloved home corner at playgroup.

I hear a whimper and look out the window. 'Prada! Prada! My baby girl,' I shout. Prada scratches on the door. 'You like it, don't you,' I say.

'Daisy!' I exclaim, looking at the old fashioned clock. If Charlotte's clock is right I'm late. Very late.

I screech into the car park and note that there's only a couple of cars parked outside the playgroup, which means I'm either incredibly early or incredibly late. Through the glass doors I spot Daisy, the only child still at playgroup, pushing a fire engine round and round the room.

'Nee nah. Don't worry firemen, Daisy is here,' she says to the teddy bears.

'Linda, I'm so sorry I'm late,' I apologise to the playgroup leader. 'It's been a bit of a nightmare getting everything sorted.'

'Quite all right,' she says, not looking as if it is all right. I get Daisy in her coat and out of the playgroup as quickly as I can.

'Why were you late, Mummy?'

'Sorry, sweetheart. It's all been a bit traumatic, hasn't it?' I say, feeling absolutely awful watching her little face in the car mirror. 'I've got a big surprise for you, though.'

'Is it a present? Is it new dressing up clothes, or wings?'

'Bigger than that.'

We play this guessing game all the way home. I feel slightly

125

mean as I know she'll never guess, but she's enjoying the game.

'Close your eyes until we're on the Green.' The car comes to a halt.

'Can I open my eyes now?'

'Course you can.'

'I love the caravan!' she says instantly. 'Can we go inside?' I unlock the door and we climb in.

'It's like the home corner at playgroup!' she exclaims.

I love the look on Daisy's little cherub face, it's still podgy and not yet growing into a proper girl's like Lilly's is. It's as if Christmas has arrived in the form of an enormous and very well kitted-out doll's house.

Daisy occupies herself all afternoon organising the caravan. I lose count of the number of times she's moved the cushions around and 'cooked' dinner.

We walk up to school. Daisy shouts through the bars of the school gate.

'Lilly! Lilly! We've got a Harriet to live in.'

'Daisy, you're not making any sense,' replies Lilly in her grown-up voice. Daisy's going at such a pace that we almost run home. Within minutes Lilly joins Daisy and for once they are playing together without squabbling.

'Mummy, what an adventure,' squeals Lilly. 'Do you think we'll be able to take Harriet to the seaside for a little holiday?'

'When the weather picks up.'

'Daddy's back,' shouts an eagle eyed Daisy. 'Let's ask him about going to the seaside!'

'Why have you got your cross face?' demands Daisy, as Adi gazes up at the caravan.

'What's in the bags?' asks Lilly never one to miss anything.

'New clothes – this one is for you, and this one is for Daisy,' he says as if they're visiting Santa in his grotto. They squeeze down to the far end of the caravan and begin to try clothes on which are too small for Daisy and too big for Lilly. Part of me gloats in the selfish pleasure that only I, the mother, know the exact size of my children. My gloating is soon put to a stop when a tearful Lilly says, 'I want my pink top with the heart on.'

'Me too, I want my pink top with the heart on.' says Daisy in parrot fashion.

'We'll just have to manage. It's not the end of the world,' says Adi.

'Daddy, can we take Harriet to the seaside?'

Adi pretends not to hear. But I could answer on his behalf. I would say I don't think that will happen. Daddy was brought up at the seaside, not a million miles from here on the east coast, and he *never* went on holiday. When we visit Adi's dad, Dennis, he still says, 'Why would we ever have wanted to take the kids on holiday when we live at the seaside?' But according to Adi's mother Pam, Dennis never wants to go anywhere. I vividly remember her telling me years ago that even the most outward-bound of men become reclusive, like Dennis, once they're married. I didn't pay it any heed at the time. I never thought that Adi and I would end up never going anywhere together. But lately I'm starting to wonder if Pam was right after all.

'I used to live on these at uni,' confesses Adi, scraping the plastic bottom of his Pot Noodle dinner.

'It's only the kitchen and bedrooms that are damaged,' I say. 'Apart from the electrics that is.'

'You haven't been trying to use things, have you? We have to have a structural engineer's report before you step inside.' Instead of rising to the bait, and saying I'm *not* one of his clients, I keep quiet and don't mention my bags of salvaged fabrics from the bedroom I apparently wasn't supposed to go in.

'It's not a crime scene. It's our house.'

'And costing the earth to get fixed up,' says Adi. 'Anyway, let's not talk about money.'

'I didn't even know you could still buy these,' he says, emptying out and clearly enjoying the Pot Noodles.'

'Phyllis sells everything.'

Adi turns the carton upside down.

'What on earth are you doing?' I say. 'You don't want to get Pot Noodle on your new T-shirt.'

'Not bad for two pounds,' he laughs, tugging on his white T-shirt. 'Anyway, you know what she's like. That loaf of bread I bought from her was well past it. Maybe these Pot Noodles are from the 1980s!'

I want to run to Phyllis' defence. After all, she's the supplier of my illicit little treats. If it wasn't for her shop I'd never be able to buy the odd chocolate bar – well, it's more than the odd chocolate bar really, especially when I hit my low premenstrual sugar craving days.

Instead I say, 'If it wasn't for the post office I'd be driving miles to the nearest supermarket. I need Phyllis!'

'It was just a joke, Laura. Sometimes it seems like you've lost your sense of humour since we moved to Reedby. Try to lighten up a bit. You'll feel better,' says Adi, as if talking to one of the girls.

I feign speechlessness and immediately realise that a caravan is too small a home to have a row in. I change tack.

'They're running a yoga class down at the Buddhist retreat.'

'Go for it,' says Adi. 'You ought to take up some exercise. We're not as young as we were. Look at me,' he says, tapping his tummy.

'I was thinking that maybe you would like to go. It would complement your cycling, you know, getting fit plus stress relief and all that.'

'Are you saying I'm fat?' laughs Adi.

Before I can say anything the girls get up from colouring in on the mini table and are immediately there in front of us.

'Daddy! Daddy! Can we have *Wind in the Willows* tonight?' says Lilly, with Daisy echoing her.

'I'm needed here, not at a yoga class,' he says.

'I don't know what day the class is on. You'll have to ring them.'

I hear Adi doing the voices. Adi's version of Toad sounds particularly hyper and Moley has a very stuffed up Midlands drawl. He ought to be a mimic, I think.

I then hear him explain to the girls that Harriet isn't big enough for us. I fall asleep and try to distract myself from thinking about my vintage clothes. Focus on the positive, I tell myself. I wonder what Adi has planned. I think of holiday home rentals (a barn conversion, a windmill) or maybe a few days, weeks or months in a hotel. The girls would love a hotel. I love hotels. I love the fluffy white towels and all the miniature luxuries: soaps, shampoos, a chocolate placed on a freshly laundered white pillowcase. Even just one night away would make a difference. Why did I take all those freebie trips to hotels and country houses for granted? While Adi talked shop about extensions and renovations, I'd swim in the pool or relax in the sauna. At this very moment I'd gladly go to any of them – even the ones we complained about!

Chapter 11

*Rows of **chevron stitch** worked closely together produce a lattice effect, which makes a good patterned filling for larger areas since this creates a grid of diamond shapes.*

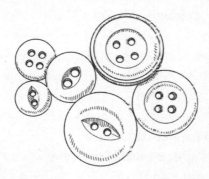

I wake up to peace and quiet. Where am I? Have I died and gone back to some child-free long lie-in heaven? I look out through the little curved-cornered window and soon remember where I am. Outside I see a tall figure pacing around our garden. The man turns round and I breathe a sigh of relief.

'Adi, what's David doing here? It's Saturday morning.'

There's no answer. I look around the caravan – there's no sign of Adi or the girls. David sees me. Laughing and waving he walks over and knocks on the door. There's going to be no privacy from now on, I think. I search for a comb and end up brushing my knotted hair with one of the girls' miniature dolly hairbrushes.

I suppose my white long-sleeved cotton nightie covers up more of me than most people's daywear so I open the caravan door.

'Good morning, Laura,' says David, purposefully looking in the other direction. He's always the perfect gentleman.

'Hi, I've got no idea where anyone is,' I say, catching his eye.

'They'll be out the back making sure there's enough space,' he says, now looking me in the eye. 'Hey, you look like someone from *Pride and Prejudice*,' he says, pointing at my nightgown.

'It's Victorian, actually,' I say with a smile, not wanting to let on that I haven't got a clue as to what is happening 'out the back'.

'I'll go and find them. A cuppa wouldn't go amiss. I hope you've stocked up on builder's tea.'

'Builders?' I mutter quietly, reluctant to let on that I have no idea what's going on.

'But with any luck we should get it erected in a day.'

I do like David, there's something so comfortingly and time-lessly English about him. I still find it hard to imagine him designing enormous glass and steel constructions; he seems more suited to classical architecture. He always says that a Georgian country house epitomises the golden section proportions so loved by the Ancient Greeks. I still haven't dared to ask why.

I go out barefoot and stand behind the conifers, and, as if spying in my own garden, I see lots of trellises being carried around to the back. I know it's spring but it seems a bit early to be doing the garden. Adi's really taking this country living to heart.

'Laura, you're up,' says Adi. 'You were dog tired and Daisy was making a fuss about the Portaloo, so I had to take her over the road to Heather's.

'She must love us, always popping over to use the loo.' I don't tell Adi that I sneak under the barrier tape and use the house loo (occasionally).

'I thought I'd get ahead with the surprise. I've also invited David's parents over for afternoon tea – to thank them. They only live just down the road. We should be all sorted by then.'

'What are we thanking them for?'

'It'll ruin the surprise. You'll just have to wait. But I do think you should go and get dressed.'

Adi doesn't normally talk in terms of afternoon tea. Adi doesn't normally do surprises, he's more the sort to avoid them; the kind of man who prefers to key in an Amazon wish list so that he doesn't get unexpected gifts cluttering up the house.

'Why don't you pop into town and get some new clothes? That way we'll be all sorted by the time you get back.'

I decide not to tell Adi that it will take more than a few hours to buy a new set of clothes. Vintage shopping is for the one-off, the unique item of clothing that no one else in the world has. And a new set could take months to find. But I could do with some new underwear, I suppose, for there are limits to what I'll wear second hand.

I drive back along the Green wondering whether to wear the black lacy briefs (which are only effective when you're not wearing any other clothes) or the big support knickers, which even after two pregnancies make me look svelte (but only with clothes on top).

I feel the shiny Marks and Spencer carrier bags and wonder if new lingerie is really enough to rekindle Adi's interest in me. When we first moved from London I thought he was tired with the new job; now there's no privacy with all of us in the caravan. Perhaps he's booked a night away, just for the two of us? And that's why good old David is there – to babysit.

I look at the time and remember afternoon tea. Nobody will have made or bought a cake. They'll have hoped that a nice slice of Victoria sandwich will have arrived by magic. How am I going to rustle up a homemade cake in a caravan? There's nothing for it. I pull up at the post office and browse the shelves of French fancies and Viennese whirls – all of which bear the promise of being exceedingly good – but in my experience are usually exceedingly dry. Then I spot the McVitie's ginger cake. I'll get that. It appeals to the child in me. I always used to model the squidgy cake into little figures. Perhaps if the talked-about cuts come to Town and Country we could use McVitie's ginger cake instead of clay? *Edible artworks!* I laugh out loud. Then I wonder if other people's minds drift in and out of such random thoughts.

I walk into what looks like a garden party in my own house – except it isn't quite the time of year.

Sat on one of our fold-up chairs, with a blood red metallic Sergio Rossi bag at her feet, is a smart blonde woman. Who is she? She looks scary.

'You've seen Mummy,' says David sidling up to me. 'What do you think of the yurt? Your little home from home.'

Before I can say, What? What are you talking about? I

thought you were probably putting up a shed to humour Adi and this newfound gardening interest, David signals to the blonde lady, who at a distance doesn't look old enough to be his mother.

'You see it's portable architecture,' says David's mother, in what sounds like an indefinable *Mitteleuropa* accent. But who am I to know where's she's from? I'm hopeless at accents and often can't identify even close friends on the phone. And curiously David, for all his trivia knowledge, has never mentioned whether his mother is Polish or Hungarian or whatever. It's as though there's a family secret – and we've left it too late to ask.

'I'm Hannelore and I know who you are,' she says, proudly pointing at what looks like a marquee in *my* garden. She strokes the stole, or should I say dead fox, draped around her cashmere coat. We shake hands and the moment is gone for me to say I love marquees for weddings, May balls, even the Chelsea Flower Show. But not for sleeping in.

'I'm Laura,' I say, almost catching my fingers on one of her many jewel-encrusted rings.

'Everyone seems to be enjoying themselves,' says Adi, joining us. 'What do you think of the yurt? We can stay in it until the house is sorted. Exciting isn't it?'

'Excellent cake,' says David's dad, who looks every inch the English gentleman in his chocolate-coloured corduroys and tweed jacket. Except that he's rolling the ginger cake into little models as if it were play-dough. 'This little yurt is one of the most recent in our collection. It's David's really – his inheritance.'

'Sorry? I say, feeling puzzled.

'David will inherit the yurt, rather than our house.'

Hannelore gives her husband a steely stare with her cool, grey-blue eyes.

For a moment I'm taken back to thinking about strange inheritances – such as my mother's vintage clothes, and I feel comforted.

'Do you run your own yurt company or something?' I ask.

'Goodness no! I'm a scientist. For forty years I've been studying soil types, especially those in desert regions. It's taken us to all corners of the world and the yurts we've seen have rather piqued my wife's interest. She is fascinated by all fabric techniques and constructions.'

'Peter, give Laura one of my business cards,' says Hannelore. I should have bought some of my books. I wrote a guide to Uzbek embroidery and now my latest work, *Material World*, is going to print.'

I sit there unable to say anything. A real textile expert in my midst – a published author – and I'm struck dumb in awe. I try to think of something intelligent to say, desperately wanting to impress them.

'Is the *Material World* book about people like Christo and Jeanne-Claude? The wrapped buildings – the Reichstag in Berlin and those islands all looked fabulous in fabric,' I say.

'No no. Real material worlds, such as homes made of fabric,' she says. 'I'll show you, you haven't even looked at the yurt. Come with me.'

We wander over and I now see the trellis and realise it's the tent frame and I am standing beside it as if modelling it.

'The tent is measured out by parts of the body. Waist, shoulder,' she says, touching my waist and shoulders in a way that seems very familiar given that we've just met.

'Aren't they traditionally covered in felt? I do a bit of felt-making at college.' I don't add that I'm allergic to wool, she doesn't look the sympathetic type.

'The felt is to keep out snakes and scorpions. You probably only get grass snakes here,' she says, looking out across the lawn towards Adi. This is just the sort of talk that puts me off camping.

'Laura, what's going on? It looks like a festival,' says Liz, peering over the hedge.

'Come on in, well into the garden,' I say.

Liz squeezes past the vans and cars now parked outside Marsh Cottage.

'This is Adi's yurt,' I say, unable to refrain myself from pulling a face.

'I always wanted to live in a yurt,' says Liz.

'You're joking!'

'But Mark was having nothing of it.'

I shrug my shoulders and think that perhaps we could do a wife swap. I have to admit that after a night at Birch House I've rather fallen in love with it. 'Um,' I say. 'Adi seems very excited about erecting this yurt. I haven't seen him enjoy himself this much for ages,' I giggle. 'I think I'll stay in the caravan, though,' I whisper. 'And I've got a plan for my old vintage clothes.'

'What? What plans?' says Liz giving me a curious look.

'All in good time.'

Chapter 12

Cretan stitch is also known as Persian stitch and long-armed feather stitch. When worked in a straight vertical line it is also referred to as quill stitch. For centuries women on the island of Crete have used this stitch to decorate clothing.

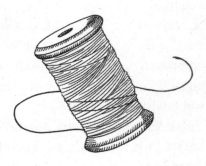

I take the scrumpled-up cutting out of my handbag and double check. Yes, I've got the right time and the right place. Except that Kirby St Mary village hall doesn't really look like the Embroiderers' Guild's regional centre. Neither does it look like any art or craft school I've ever been to. It certainly doesn't look like my old college, Chelsea (now proudly positioned on the Thames embankment). In mine and Chris' time Chelsea Art School was a curious collection of rented buildings all over West London. Why am I thinking about my student days and Chris again? For years I hardly gave those days a thought. I'm too young for a mid-life crisis!

The setting definitely looks more uplifting than the studios at Town and Country, where you have the pleasure of looking out onto a concrete car park. I smile as I look up at the roof. It has three ducks following each other across the thatch. They remind me of the three flying ducks (or was it birds?) which Mum used to have over the fireplace. Since my house fire it's not just been Chris and my student days, it's also Mum who keeps coming to mind. I long to be able to go back in time and go home to Mum's for Sunday lunch.

I peep through the windows at a sea of silver-haired women. Is this really where I'll learn to sew? And another thing, will I make a friend or two here? One of the women looks up and beckons for me to come inside. I've been spotted, I have to go in. I feel every inch the new girl as I walk into the freezing cold hall.

A familiar smell wafts around the room. For a moment I can't quite place the rich, sweet aroma. Then I'm taken back in time to being ten or eleven and buying all my friends and Mum lavender bath cubes for Christmas. I don't think anywhere sells bath cubes any more – but the lavender smells just the same. I really do feel ten years old in a room full of ladies, mostly old enough to be my mother. This is a complete contrast to being surrounded by a studio full of teenagers young enough to be my children. Silver heads turn around and smile.

'We meet again. Laura isn't it?' says a very smart Hannelore Lawrence, making her way towards me.

Today she's dressed in what looks like a wool and silk mix

olive green suit. She shakes my hand and I feel welcomed, if a little unused to such a gesture.

'So, how are you enjoying the yurt?' she asks.

'The girls and Adi absolutely love it,' I say, which is the honest truth.

'They are the homes of princes,' she says.

I'm not sure if she's alluding to the fact that I think I'm too good for the yurt. I'm also not sure what I expected when I saw the advert in the parish newsletter, where the sewing teacher called herself Mrs H Lawrence. I thought it oddly formal that she didn't give her first name. What I never expected was for it to be taught by David's mother.

The noise of the wall heaters eventually subsides and the hall slowly warms up. I spot a Japanese girl in the corner, she's wearing jeans and a patterned T-shirt and has a whole head of jet black hair. Perhaps she's my age? Maybe I could sit with her? It is so hard to tell with oriental people though, with their clear, unwrinkled skin. Laura, are you being racist?

'Come and sit here,' says Hannelore. I obey like a reception-class kid and take my seat between two ladies who are already busily sewing.

'René and Joyce,' says Hannelore. They look up briefly, smile and carry on sewing. They look as different as chalk and cheese. René has neatly bobbed hair and is wearing a linen trouser suit in neutral colours (probably from Marks and Spencer). Joyce, on the other hand, has mostly silver/grey cropped hair, except for her fringe which is dyed pink and blue in streaks. Her hand-knitted pullover in rainbow stripes complements her quirky hair.

There are a couple of notices about must-visit exhibitions,

such as the Art of the Stitch at the Barbican, and the best thread shop, which is miles away from here in the heart of the Cotswolds. These ladies certainly seem to be the *silver pound*, jetting off here, there and everywhere. Credit crunch or no credit crunch.

Everyone begins sewing. If only my students came in and started work without endless mollycoddling. If I left them to their own devices it would be breaktime before they even got a pencil out.

I take everything out of my bag and cover the Formica table with patches of fabric, my sketches of bags, necklaces and cushion covers and cuttings from the *Annika* magazine. I move everything around, desperately trying to make sense of it all, as if it's a jigsaw puzzle; except with this puzzle there are so many possible answers.

I sit and stare at my assortment of fabrics. I've even divided them up into theme colourways: reds, pinks and oranges; blues, greens and turquoises; and neutrals: blacks, greys, whites, creams. I change my mind though and decide to look at the remnants by subject: florals, geometrics and household objects seem to be the main motifs when it comes to vintage fabrics.

I look around and everyone is busy sewing. Everyone that is except for me. I'm hypnotised by the ladies rhythmically stitching away. I enjoy just watching them and for once not having to do anything. Hannelore comes over and looks at my table of fabrics.

'I've got lots of ideas for handbags, purses, necklaces, cup-cakes,' I say meekly.

'Cupcakes?' quizzes Hannelore. 'What is the point of

having a cake made out of fabric?' she says, her steely eyes glaring at me.

'Nil calories,' calls Joyce. 'And they're never past their sell-by date,' she adds with a wink. I like Joyce.

'I love these designs,' I carry on. I show Hannelore Annika's Scandinavian rose patterns.

'Roses are my all-time favourite,' says Hannelore, looking at the plump, stylised flowers on the cutting. 'Did you know that different types of roses can be found in most textiles?'

I nod and hope I save face. I had no idea that roses could be found in most textiles. And I'm supposed to be a textile teacher!

'At least in central Europe and Asia they are,' she continues knowledgeably. 'Did you know that almost identical roses can be found in Scandinavia, Central Europe, India, China, Mongolia, Tibet and Uzbekistan? In China the roses are absolutely perfect. Here, in Europe our roses are more naïve in form.'

'They look nice though, don't you think?' I ask, always preferring art that isn't quite perfect.

She sighs. 'They do look attractive, but you need to know your history, your motif, and materials and functions, otherwise you'll end up with watered-down work.'

I nod and feel as if I'm in an MA seminar rather than a village sewing class. And what's more, for once I'm really enjoying not being the teacher and being able to learn something new for myself.

'What do you think of these?' asks Hannelore, pointing at the swirly shapes.

'I think it's good to take inspiration from where you find it,' I say, tentatively.

Hannelore is looking scary, so I quickly add, 'But I know what you mean about knowing the basics, how things work. It's like learning to mix a colour wheel before tackling a landscape painting.'

'Or walking before you can run,' chips in Joyce, who immediately returns to her sewing.

'How do you feel about starting at the beginning?' asks Hannelore.

I pull a face. 'I've got so many ideas. So many things I want to make.'

'The problem is, you're one of the lost girls.'

'Lost what?' I say. What have I lost? 'Actually I want to use all these fabrics to make things,' I say, wondering if she's heard me correctly.

She completely ignores my comment and continues with her own agenda.

'The lost girls is my term for all these girls who can't sew. You've lost out. Tell me. No, let me guess. Were you from some *academische* school that thought girls no longer needed to sew and cook?'

I nod, saying, 'I did make a skirt at primary school though.' I remember all the girls made a skirt. We'd all driven our mums crazy to buy us Laura Ashley fabric. I still remember the tiny white floral prints on blue, green and brown backgrounds. Except my mum, a regular at Thodays fabric shop, decided to differ. My fabric wasn't like the others. It was a swirl of orange and purple to which Dad had said, with a big smile on his face, 'You'll see her coming a mile off in that.'

'In the old days girls needed to be able to stitch by hand to make their clothes and textiles for the family. Then with the introduction of sewing machines stitching was mainly used for mending and darning,' says Hannelore.

'I remember Mum darning my socks. They always felt really uncomfortable. The stitches used to push against my school shoes.'

'You didn't darn your own?' asks Hannelore with mock outrage.

I shake my head sheepishly. Please don't ask me what I do with socks with holes in. I don't want to confess to buying the girls new socks. It's just that they're so cheap. It would cost more to buy needles and wool.

I watch Hannelore. She takes a square of calico and her nimble fingers stitch a perfect line. 'This is called running stitch. That is step one, let's see how you get on. When you have mastered it we can move on to whipped running stitch, laced running stitch, Holbein stitch, back stitch, split stitch ...'

'You'll frighten her off like that,' laughs Joyce, who must have seen the worried look on my face. Hannelore leaves her sampler on my desk and goes over to see the others.

I struggle to copy Hannelore's sample. How can anyone do a line of running stitch with all the stitches exactly the same length? Already I want to rebel and do different lengths. As usual being left-handed makes me feel as if I'm working upside down and back to front all in one. I begin to wonder why all these able, capable sewers who bring all their own materials, come here at all. They know it all already. I'm sure they could do what they're doing now at home.

'We sew better when we're all at it,' says René, as if reading my mind. She flicks her neat bobbed brown hair out of her eyes. 'We're a collective. We're a bit like my husband's bees.'

'Bees?'

'He's a beekeeper. He took early retirement, bought the bees and I hardly see or hear of him,' she laughs.

'Just as well really,' says Joyce. 'She's highly allergic to them.'

I continually unpick threads as fast as I self-consciously sew them back again. Immediately I am transported years back to being the clumsy child in the art room who couldn't cut neatly with right-handed scissors, and who struggled with a sewing machine, as of course, well, as far as I know, they've yet to invent a left-handed sewing machine. Knitting was no better, Mum finally taught me to knit by watching her in a mirror.

'Come and sit over here, by the window,' says Hannelore. 'Just look at the window and do the same as me,' she commands.

For a moment this coincidence sends a shiver down my spine. It's almost as if Mum is here watching and guiding me.

It seems strange watching this immaculately dressed woman sitting on a dusty black plastic stackable chair. I watch Hannelore's nimble and confident fingers work away.

'You know, there's a proven link between the tip-tapping of your fingertips and keeping your brain active. We don't need sudoku here. And of course with sewing you have something to show for it at the end. Far better to have a work of art than a sheet of newsprint scribbled with numbers.'

I nod. 'So what made you take up sewing?'

She lets out a guttural laugh and all eyes are suddenly on us. The ladies soon settle back to work.

'I *had* to make my own clothes. My Veritas sewing machine was the world's best seller. The East Germans had their own fashion designers, they did some good designs and rumour has it a few were sold to a C&A department store in West Berlin. They were always desperate for some hard currency. I was tempted to do a course at the Mode Institut but couldn't bear to design something which would never come to life the way I planned. The fabric, the raw ingredients, were too expensive, you see.'

I sew quietly for a while. All this talk of Communist times makes me think of spy films and James Bond. I never ever thought of it having anything to do with fashion and textiles.

'Now my turn for a question. How long have you been in Reedby?'

'A couple of months.'

'Ah, that explains much. When humans move house they're thrown into turmoil. The muddle of the unfamiliar.'

'But what about all the nomadic tribes you met on your travels? They were always on the move, weren't they?'

Hannelore shakes her head. 'A popular misconception. The nomads, and migratory birds for that matter, are a triumph of the familiar over vast, often hostile places. The nomad knows exactly where to stop for water, where to set up summer camp. You've traded everything for a blank canvas. There is no inherited knowledge to light up your path.'

I feel as if a weight has been lifted as I listen to her poetic way of speaking.

'What I'm saying is, go easy on yourself. It may take a year to recover.'

One by one the sewing ladies come and look at what I'm

making. They seem more interested in my vintage remnants than the purse they will become.

'I remember green patterned curtains just like that,' says René, picking up one of my remnants. 'You'll have to come and see my studio.'

'Your studio?'

'It's my pride and joy. You should come and see all my fabrics. I'm a terrible hoarder. One day Derek had finally had enough of my loom, spinning wheel and carrier bags of threads in the sitting room. Three months later the studio was built. It's as much my bolthole as my studio. It's even got a bed and a kettle, so I could hold out for days,' she finishes with a whisper.

I smile and think how these ladies are nothing like what I expected. René sounds like a modern-day Virginia Woolf with a room of her own. I'm jealous!

I keep sewing amidst the chatter. I'm feeling very proud of my first sewing project – a purse. I've sewn a cut strip from an old bodice so that instead of a zip it shuts with a row of tiny pearl buttons. I put a few coins inside and close the buttons. I then try and open it and realise it's not going to be a purse for quickly finding change in the supermarket; but it would certainly be a challenge for any pickpocket to open it.

'That's not bad,' says Hannelore. 'I like the way you're using conservation stitch across this,' she says, pointing to the purple running stitches.

I finish the class feeling really proud and having completely forgotten about all the house jobs I'll be returning to.

'Ladies!' announces Hannelore. 'Before anyone leaves can

I remind you that next week we're meeting at the Textile Study Centre,' she says, handing out glossy leaflets. 'And we'll be having an extra class member.'

'Is that nice young man coming out with us again?' asks Joyce.

Hannelore smiles and taps her nose.

'I've never heard of a textile study centre in Norwich,' I whisper to René.

'Norwich was the centre of the textile industry. It started in medieval times and went right up to the 1860s and '70s with their very popular woven shawls. The place is a gem. With your interest in vintage fabrics, you'll love it there,' says René, packing away her sewing basket.

I nip into the loo. I've become quite obsessed about loo stops since the fire. Any loo is better than the bright blue Portaloo in our garden.

I jump into the Micra, clutching my receipt for Curtis, and feel a new lease of life. Change is as good as a rest, they say. I feel that I've had a good rest from myself and my worries.

I drive home obsessing about sewing. Hand stitching is certainly not for the time-poor among us. My students ought to have a sewing day, I think. A handmade day. They spend most of their lives getting immediate results using the computer, yet there's something unreal about all the digital art. You can't touch it or feel it. You always have to be plugged in, and usually online stealing, or should I say *manipulating*, somebody else's work.

Handmade art can be created anywhere. And something about the 'realness' and repetitiveness of stitching has calmed my nerves. Sewing is a kind of meditation. Which reminds me, I must speak to Adi again about the yoga class. It's not that I want to organise his life or anything. But he is still tetchy, so it would do us *all* good if he went to yoga!

Chapter 13

Lazy daisy stitch is often worked in a circle to form a flower motif.

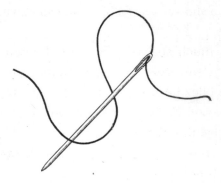

I sit on the brown and orange floral couch and listen to the rhythmic tap-tapping of the rain on the caravan roof. After finally conquering running stitch I've moved on from my purse sampler to making a doorstop. There's no one looking over my shoulder like at college – I'm free! This isn't just any doorstop, but one for living in the country – a chicken doorstop. Well, that's what I have in mind. I'm using my nail scissors to carefully cut out vintage shapes and colours and struggling to make it look chicken-like. Chick doorstops are going to be an Easter surprise for Adi and the girls.

I used to buy them big chocolate eggs and a present. I even used to buy new dresses for the girls, it was a family tradition. Mum always bought me a new dress at Easter, just as her mother before her had. This year my wages aren't for treats, they're for the bills – especially vet's bills.

Sewing in the caravan is like sewing in a straitjacket. I want to get all my pieces out and spread them around the caravan. But I can't let Daisy stand on a pin again and give Adi more reasons for sleeping in the yurt.

I stuff all my scrap fabrics into a couple of carrier bags and peep out of the door. I run through the light shower to the yurt. How can a shower sound like a monsoon when you're in a caravan?

There's so much space in the yurt. It seems positively magisterial. The sun is coming out and shining in through the top onto a neat pile of Adi's clothes. I feel guilty that I'm sleeping in the caravan. Perhaps I should get over my camping phobia and move into the yurt.

I turn the handle of Adi's wind-up radio (another gift from Kurt) and listen to it for company. I feel like my old student self. The friendly voices bring back memories of working all-nighters. I always listened to LBC, although I'm not sure now what LBC stands for, something to do with London. From midnight onwards people would phone in with their problems. I loved listening to that show – it made me feel so grown up.

Then, without realising it, I'm no longer listening to the radio. I'm off somewhere else completely engrossed by the cutting and stitching. I've abandoned the step-by-step design process altogether and my doorstop's looking like a chicken. Will I ever confess to my students that I'm a complete hypocrite? I have no plans, no real design drawings, no colour tests. I dive in at the final piece. *Don't do as I do, do as I say, that's me!* I let the colours and patterns guide me into a chickenish shape. I like the materials being more important than my ideas. This is true liberation – well for an artist, if no one else!

Is this what meditation is like? A break from oneself – the best kind of holiday. I've managed a whole two hours without thinking about Town and Country's inspection and my debrief, which is tomorrow. Why am I jumping through all these teaching hoops? I once had such high hopes of being a real designer, that is a successful designer – not just a hobbyist.

Perhaps I could offer private patchwork meditation classes? It could become the latest celebrity craze. There's plenty of knitting circles, and even actresses knitting on film sets. Women everywhere could be making patchwork. And it's green! Everything is being re-used, recycled. There must be something more worthwhile that I could do. Teaching doesn't have any meaning when it's all about ticking boxes.

I'm soon distracted from feeling sorry for myself by a practical problem. Design is good like that. It takes you away from yourself. What's going to be heavy enough to fill the chicken? I look out at Daisy's sandpit and decide against wet sand.

I hear footsteps crunch over the gravel. It'll be one of the workmen – a real house builder, not a yurt maker. I'm not very good at dealing with these men. I've lost confidence in so many things since moving here, including chit-chat. Lately, I've been spending most of the time hiding in the caravan.

There's a tapping on the louvre door. It still seems really strange having wooden doors on a tent. I mean yurt. I open them.

'Chris! I exclaim. 'How did you know?' I say, feeling very excited at having a visitor. A house isn't a home without visitors.

'How did I know you were here?' says Chris, answering my question with a question. 'The whole of Reedby knows about the yurt. The news has even reached us down at Trishna. Are you going to invite me in?'

'Of course. Come into my yurt. Watch your head!'

Chris makes a beeline for my pieces of fabric. 'You know I had a stint in textiles.'

'Textiles?'

'Remember, I did visual studies. I'm a jack of all trades and master of none. After college I was given a bursary to make knitted sculptures.'

I can't help but laugh. 'I remember the bursary but not what you made. I think we all started to lose touch then,' I lie. Of course I do remember what Chris made. His sculpture of knitted wires and cables was exhibited in the Glisson Gallery. The rest of us would have given our right arm to get an exhibition there.

Chris picks up the chick doorstop. I'm feeling really nervous as to what he's going to say.

'This is beautiful. The little silk stitches are so tactile,' he says, pulling on each loop. 'You know I think the future of art is with the handmade. Are you going to make more of these? I'd buy one.'

'If I didn't have to spend most of my free time planning perfect lessons and then delivering perfect lessons,' I blurt out, feeling my eyes welling up.

Chris puts his arm round me.

For once I feel looked after, rather than looking after everyone else. And I like it.

'Don't lose sight of what's important. I've learnt the hard

way. I think you've got something good and real with your sewing.'

I nod, desperately trying not to snivel and look a mess. It's just so good to have someone to talk to. I've thought of ringing Lotte or Emma in London, but it's not the same as talking face to face. And they've never even been to Reedby.

'Mrs Stark,' says Robbie, our lead builder, suddenly standing right in front of me. 'Sorry to disturb you.'

Guiltily, Chris moves his arm away and starts fiddling with my scraps, pairing crimson stripes with rosebud florals.

'We're going to take down the tape barrier. But you're not to go upstairs. We're ready to start painting,' says Robbie.

He hands me a wad of colour charts and I'm feeling really excited. The little flat squares of colour are so yummy; I feel they're almost edible. Part of me wants to go mad and make the cottage a rainbow of colours. Although that would probably finish Adi off.

'I'll have to talk this over with my husband,' I say, swallowing deeply. 'And by the way, do you have any spare sand?'

'Never been asked that before,' he says laughing. 'Is it for the kids, a sandpit?'

'Oh no,' I answer, feeling slightly guilty.

'Well I'll see what I can do, anyway. A cuppa would be great. The electrics are up and running in the kitchen.'

'Of course,' I say, jumping up immediately, leaving Chris looking at the colour charts.

Chris finally gets up. 'I'll be off, now. See you anon.'

I wave, unsure how to say goodbye, and chase after Robbie. 'Does that mean that we can use the loo?' I ask.

'The loo doesn't run on electricity, Mrs Stark.'

'I know. It's just there isn't a window. The loo's more like a cupboard. As soon as you shut the door you're plunged into darkness and the girls are scared of the dark …'

'Yeah, that poor little girl of yours, she'll be happy now. I've never seen anyone cry at the sight of a Portaloo.'

I'm beginning to think that Daisy is taking after Adi's mum, Pam, who I bet would also cry if she had to use a Portaloo.

'Kettle's working too,' adds Robbie, looking at me expectantly.

I take the hint and make a big pot of tea. I then tip out a plate of chocolate chip cookies.

'There you go Robbie,' I say (the other builders come over – but never seem to speak).

'Thanks for the biscuits,' says Robbie, giving me a wink.

Finally, I go back into the yurt and to my sewing. For a moment I consider putting a big Do Not Disturb sign up on the louvre doors.

Chapter 14

Drizzle stitch is used in Brazilian embroidery with rayon thread but you can use any thread with a good twist such as cotton pearl. This version of double cross stitch is a canvas stitch but it is also a pleasure to work this stitch as a filling on linen or any even count fabric in a fine thread. As a hand embroidery stitch it has much potential.

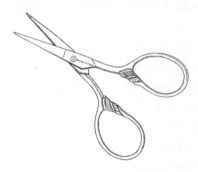

I watch Curtis park his shiny black Mercedes. There is something 'Mr Bean' about the way he straightens up, reverses, straightens up again. Am I being like my students in thinking this? Or am I trying to belittle the man who seems to hold my teaching career in his hands?

Curtis is still creeping backwards and forwards by millimetres. He doesn't know I'm watching and I like looking down on him from the second floor studio. The view of the car park has never been so interesting. He steps out carrying a leather briefcase with a combination lock. I know that my report is in there and he is expecting to see me in his office at 4 p.m. I've got to get through a whole day before I get the results of my observation. I feel like a student expecting their GCSE grades. It's been almost as long a wait – over three weeks since the fateful day I took Prada to work and, of course, the fire. Why is it that nothing happens for ages and then everything seems to happen at once?

At 4.30 p.m. I'm still sitting outside Curtis Lampard's office, watching the second hand click round on the wall clock. He's doing this deliberately so that I'm late for the nursery again. I try to distract myself by thinking about my visit from Chris. Like a mantra I tell myself, 'You need to know what's important, make more handmade things.' I'm feeling stronger. I can do this, I tell myself. I cross my legs and feel very smart, feminine with a dash of the military, in my grey 1940s pencil skirt. Have I subconsciously dressed for battle? There's no sign of my colleague Sue coming out of his office. How long does it take to debrief someone? If I have to wait much longer I'm going to have to cancel my appointment and go and pick up Lilly from the after-school club.

Just then he opens his door and lets Sue Latimer out. I feel my resolve begin to crumble. Sue turns to me and is smiling. Maybe it's not going to be so bad after all. But then Sue teaches mostly art history, and her lessons will be far more 'normal', more appreciated than my practical attempts at exploring fashion and textiles.

'If you don't get a one, if you aren't Outstanding, my advice is to put him on the spot and ask him why,' says Sue, standing on tiptoes to whisper in my ear. 'Good luck!'

'Come in. Sorry to keep you waiting,' he says in his insincere transatlantic drawl. 'So how do you think you got on?'

'I thought you were going to tell me that,' I say. His smile vanishes and I realise I've been too honest – again.

'It's on here, in my reflection form,' I say, handing it over. I wonder if I should have wrapped it round a packet of milk chocolate Buttons. I then notice Mrs Parker sitting in the darkest corner of the office. I smile and let out a little wave, in return she raises one eyebrow as she gives a lopsided smile.

'Mrs Parker is just a fly on the wall,' he says.

Or a praying mantis, I think.

'And it's all confidential. This isn't personal – about you, Laura. It's about the provision you're delivering,' he says with a cheesy grin. Really, I think, it sounds as if I'm selling soap powder, not teaching art.

'Let's begin with your strengths.' There were some, then, I think to myself. 'They all bought in some old clothes. But not exactly a demanding piece of homework.'

'That depends,' I say, defensively.

'And where was your differentiation?' Instead of saying, 'You tell me,' something assertive takes over and I go on for some time about the fact that they all chose different garments to bring in (they would have had to – but that isn't the point when you're discussing the latest education jargon) and they all worked together. 'They were all engaged in the session,' I find myself saying. 'Engaged' is one of Curtis' latest buzz words. I then wished I hadn't said it.

'Well, the levels of engagement varied considerably from what I could see. Did you know that Jon – I think his name is – was acting out a scene from *Psycho* with a pair of scissors while you had your back turned to write on the board?' I almost say that I should have eyes in the back of my head, but let that one go. I feel as if I've been caught on *You've Been Framed*. 'It was very good work on the part of Jim, your support tutor, to go over and work with Jon and his friends.' If you really knew the group, I think, you'd know that Jon doesn't have any friends. 'He sat between Jon and the boy with the very short hair and modelled the correct responses. You've got a good bit of support there.' I don't believe I'm hearing this. Curtis has just dropped to an all-time low in my estimation.

'Then there are the high noise levels. A radio. Whatever next?' he says, banging his chubby hand on the desk, as if having a radio was a criminal offence.

'It's common practice to listen to a radio in a design studio. It creates a productive environment,' I say, feeling pleased with my defence.

'Yes, but we're an educational institution.'

'And I'm teaching on a vocational course, it isn't academic like A levels,' I say catching Mrs Farker's glare.

'And then the deviation from the lesson plan. If *all* the group need to deviate then I think it is OK.'

I'm surprised at this. Before I can say that I think most of them did need to deviate from my plan, he adds, with a big sympathetic grin, which unfortunately reveals his triple chin, 'All in all the lesson felt a bit rushed.'

At this point I give up. What's the point in explaining that working to deadlines is obligatory in the design industry? In design there aren't many rules, except if you miss a deadline you've lost your client – for good. Curtis' mind is made up anyway. So why bother?

Mrs Parker then decides to chip in, 'One thing that didn't add up was your numbers.'

I'm not sure what she's talking about. Is she alluding to the small bit of numeracy they did measuring each other? Or is she thinking of *my* poor maths skills?

'You had one extra student there,' she says, almost triumphantly, as if her goal in life is to catch others out.

'That makes my attendance over 100% then. Isn't that good?' I say, no longer caring. 'The registers are generated by the admin office, not me,' I add, glaring at Curtis. I think through the draft of a resignation letter, while Mrs Parker writes something down. I can't do this job any more.

Curtis coughs theatrically.

This is it, I think, the result. This is worse than being on *The X Factor*.

'I was going to give you a three, for satisfactory. I can't say that the student behaviour was good. But I can say it was satisfactory.' My heart sinks. This will mean being observed all over again next term. 'But in light of your explanations I think I'll give you a two – for good.'

Laura Lovegrove, I say to myself, you've just kept your head above water. You're part of the 'in-group' of lecturers who survive the inspection process, get top marks and keep their jobs. However, I can't help but feel so much is down to luck that it doesn't really mean very much. After all, what would they have said if Leon had decided to do a somersault halfway through the observation lesson? It would have been a serious breach of health and safety – and deemed my fault. And it would have meant the immediate failure of my lesson. Nobody is interested in the fact that Leon attends all my lessons and never attended school. Well, I've got a job for the time being. You may need to find yourself another job soon, though, I think. I do like teaching fashion and textiles and I like my quirky students. But as Chris says *I* need to be creative too.

In my head is Sue's voice saying, Aren't you going to ask why you didn't get a one, for Outstanding? If it was a Hollywood movie wouldn't I get a one for effort? For turning up against all the odds, when I'd got a husband away on business, a sleepless daughter with a high temperature, a dog with an injured foot and had had three hours' sleep at the most. I should be collecting a superwoman medal. Instead I get up and shake hands with Curtis and Mrs Parker.

'Thank you,' I say. I'm not sure for what, but I was brought up to always be polite and do what was expected of me. 'And I've got something to ask,' I say, thinking this will earn me some more Brownie points and safeguard my job. 'Would you be able to sign this?' I hold out my fee waiver form for the sewing class. I smile.

Curtis shakes his head. 'I'm afraid you've really missed the point here. Sewing is not staff development.' He goes over to his computer and prints something off. 'Take this away with you. This is the approved list.' He begins to read: Electronic register training, numeracy in the curriculum, the perfect lesson plan, literacy in the curriculum, remote tutorials, health and safety on field trips. I'd be very happy for you to do any or all of these. But in these harsh times we would expect you to do the training as part of your general duties.'

I want to say, 'You mean you want me to do all this training in my own time?' But I don't. With my head held high I make for the door.

'Curtis, we need to talk about the validity of your registers,' says Mrs Parker. I can't help but smile to myself. I love the way she says 'your registers' to him, for once it isn't the teacher's fault when something has gone wrong.

Daisy! I think, looking up at the clock and I begin to run – with difficulty (pencil skirts weren't designed for this) – to the nursery.

Chapter 15

Eye stitch, also known as eyelet stitch, is made using the same construction principle as Algerian stitch. It is made up of stitches arranged in a square. As a filling stitch it creates a regular geometric pattern of blocks. It is an Icelandic speciality.

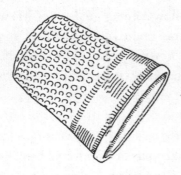

I'm feeling triumphant, I've passed my lesson observation. Before I can unlock the caravan and fetch a bag of pasta for tea, Robbie the builder rushes up to me.

'We have to start the painting in the morning. We can't leave it any longer. We're all on bonuses if we finish on schedule,' says Robbie bouncing up and down in excitement. Just watching Robbie makes me feel tired!

'I'll definitely sort it out tonight. I promise,' I say, never having met builders who were so hard-working. I still haven't got used to them being parked outside our house at 7.30 in the morning and still there when I get back from work. I'm amazed that Adi has left all the dealing with the builders to me, when he knows so much more about it all.

'Here's my number. Ring me tonight with your final choice,' says Robbie scribbling his details down. I take the piece of paper and slip it in my bag.

'Adi, I passed the observation,' I announce as I attempt to cook in our half-decorated kitchen. I'm warming to the pale pink plaster colour and thinking that pale pink might be a good choice for the kitchen. I try not to think about my effort to white-wash the kitchen and how it ended in disaster. My attempt at turning the cottage into our home seems like ages ago now.

'That's great news,' he says in a monotone. 'At least you're not sat on your backside in an office all day. So are they going to keep you on then?'

'Of course they're going to keep me on! Ye of little faith. They can't exactly sack people for failing a lesson observation, but they can make your life a misery,' I say, expecting perhaps a hug or a kiss. 'But he wasn't on for paying for the sewing class,' I add, realising that sadly, Adi isn't even going to give me so much as a pat on the back.

'I'm not really surprised. If I asked the partners to pay for me to do a bit of wattle 'n' daubing or thatching I'd be laughed out of the office,' says Adi, without even a hint of sympathy in his voice.

'But that's not right.'

'Get real, Laura,' says Adi, huffily.

'I am real. Anyway they paid for you to do that website design course. And don't forget the outward bound course.

Weren't you making rafts in the middle of a London park? How *real* was that?'

'I did enjoy the raft making,' says Adi, his khaki eyes sparkling for the first time in days. 'And you never know when my web design skills might come in handy,' he adds, enigmatically.

'We've got to decide on the paint colours.'

'I know. I know. I don't think there's a lot to discuss. Simplicity is the key,' says Adi cryptically.

'Why don't we eat tea in the yurt,' I say. 'Neutral territory. It will help us think colour.'

'Whatever you say.'

I carry a very heavy tray out into the garden, turning to push open the louvre doors with my back. Adi follows me, holding the paint charts. I can't help but think there's some male/female role reversal going on.

'What are all those bits of fabric still doing out? I don't mind you sewing in here but you could tidy up. You're making a real mess of the place. I'm always tidying up after all of you.'

I can't believe what I'm hearing. It's as if all my work around the house goes completely unnoticed.

'They've been there for ages and it hasn't bothered you. It wastes time putting things away. I've only got to get them out again.'

'The reason they've been there for ages and I haven't said anything was that I knew you had your inspection coming up. I was *trying* to support you.'

As I pop our plates of pasta on the floor I wonder if eating in the yurt is a good idea. Adi and the girls sit cross-legged and look like they're eating with Bedouin.

'I should have cooked something Middle Eastern, like couscous or lamb kebabs,' I say struggling to sit cross-legged in my 1940s pencil skirt.

'Pasta is fine. But you do need to sit up straight. You've got to keep an eye on your posture. None of us are as young as we used to be.'

Nothing I do seems right any more, in Adi's eyes that is. What has got into him? For a moment I wonder if his grumpy behaviour is because he's having an affair. He never used to be so mean. He doesn't mention anyone at work, apart from David. Is that because there's a woman there he's seeing?

Luckily it's Lilly who changes the subject. 'I want my room orange.'

'Mine's going to be pink,' Daisy butts in. 'Pink with gold stars.'

'I'm not sure if Robbie is up to that.'

'We'll discuss it when I get back,' says Adi.

'Back from where?'

'I'm going to yoga with Mark Randall. He says they run a really good class down at the Buddhist centre.'

'What a good idea,' I say, holding back from the fact that it was my idea in the first place. 'I'm sure you'll be the star pupil. You've got such good posture already.' I know that I'm being childish and sarcastic, but I can't help myself.

I clear away the tea things and leave Adi lovingly fondling the yurt trellis. I refuse to tidy up any of my sewing stuff. According to Hannelore, up to forty people may sleep in the same yurt; so there's plenty of room for one man and some fabric.

I tuck the girls up in the caravan. I finally get to sit down and think how strange it'll feel when we move back into the house. I've got used to sharing a space with just me and the girls. I wonder why Adi wants to wait until he gets back to discuss the decorating? Is there something else he wants to tell me, but not in front of the girls? I'm beginning to think that I don't know him, that I don't know what he's thinking any more.

I hear a car draw up and then footsteps in the garden. I quickly turn out the light. Why am I pretending that I'm asleep? Why am I avoiding speaking to my husband? I don't want to think about any of that.

I slowly move the net curtains to one side; with just one eye up against the glass I watch Adi through the window. He bumps his head on the louvre door, curses (so much for the stress-relieving yoga class!) and goes into the tent. He was too tall for the cottage. Now he's too tall for this yurt. They obviously didn't make the yurt or the cottage to a tall Englishman's proportions, I think, remembering Hannelore's yurt construction lesson.

He thinks he's some kind of Ray Mears, an SAS survival expert off on an outward bound course to the jungle. Except, as I look out through my little window and see his torchlight up the white canvas, to me he looks more like a boy scout.

I want to toss and turn but am constrained by a mattress made for a much slimmer and shorter person. I remember the paint charts. It's too late to ring Robbie. Anyway he'll be parked out the front in not too many hours from now. I'm secretly pleased that Adi's forgotten about the paint charts. So much for a joint colour scheme! He can't complain if he doesn't like my choice. He had his chance.

Half asleep I peep through the caravan nets. It's going to be a sunny day. Adi's Audi has gone already. When I finally got to sleep I must have slept like a log, as I didn't hear the car leave. I'm amazed how he manages to get up in time for work now we're in Reedby. In London, that's ever since we've been together, it's always been me who's forced him out of bed, especially in the winter, made the packed lunches (sometimes) and got him out of the house; only to then replay the whole getting up routine with Lilly. Daisy of course is usually up before me.

I think he likes this bachelor life of his in the tent; he only has to think of getting himself ready for the day. But when I come to think of it it's always been like that. If I was being really mean I'd say that the only thing he has to sort out for himself in the morning is going to the loo.

The builders are waiting, like undercover agents, in their vans. I can't go out in my dressing gown to let them in again! They must think I'm a complete slob. Oh, what the hell. I put on my quilted pink 1970s dressing gown – a little present from Liz after the fire. She knew that I'd enjoy the kitschness of it. I love it. It reminds me of being around ten years old again.

Robbie spots me and leaps out of the van.

'Morning Mrs Stark,' he winks. 'I've brought Raymond as we're making such good progress.' A man, half Robbie's size, waves meekly from the van. I swear that Robbie has Attention Deficit Disorder; the way he rushes about it's either ADHD or he has incredibly strong coffee for breakfast! I can only admire the way he tackles the rebuild, this man could move mountains – and he must be in his fifties. A thought crosses my mind. Why don't those ADHD boys, like Leon, come and work with Robbie, rather than making their teachers' lives (my life) a misery? Laura, you should be a politician. As if reading my mind, he says, 'I tell you, Mrs Stark, I was no use at school, but look at this wall.'

'It looks great. And you've built it so quickly,' I say, praising this middle-aged man as if I'm admiring one of Lilly's drawings.

'A cuppa would go down well,' he says. 'Raymond takes two sugars.'

'Just the two of you today?'

'The Polskis will be here when I've got all the paint. Got your colour scheme sorted?'

I nod excitedly and say smugly 'You bet I have.'

'Look, Mummy, Daddy's left us a letter on the caravan door,' says Lilly, already dressed for school.

For a moment my heart misses a beat. Adi has left me – left us. He is having an affair. These scenarios flash through my mind. 'Don't touch! Don't read it! Give it to Mummy without looking.'

I look at the note.

L Didn't want to wake you up, as we just need to paint the whole house Traditional English White. A

'How could he?' I shriek. 'He doesn't even trust me to choose white paint. It has to be a specific white!' I say, out loud.

For the first time in my life I have a team of decorators at my beck and call and Adi wants to paint the cottage white. 'Anyone can choose white, it's safe, it shows a lack of imagination,' I mutter to myself.

'Daisy, why are you still in your pyjamas?' I yell. 'You need to get ready.'

'It's pyjama week at playgroup.'

'Really?'

'I thought you knew Mummy, you've got your dressing gown on. The teachers are wearing their pyjamas too.'

'OK,' I say and go into the cottage and put the kettle on, while hunting out my old fur mules. If it's pyjama week I need the complete look. I then hunt in my dressing gown pockets for the list, my definitive colour list which I know is hiding somewhere among the used tissues. I take Robbie and Raymond their mugs of tea and hand them the list.

Robbie slowly reads, 'Man-dar-in Or-ange,' sounding out the letters, just like Lilly did when she was learning to read. For an uncomfortable moment I realise that Robbie is probably at the same reading level as Lilly, aged seven. 'Duck Egg. Sum-mer Pud-ding. Isn't that something you eat?' asks Robbie.

'It's a really dusky pinky-red,' I reply.

'You'd best give us the paint chart. So there's no misunderstanding,' says Raymond.

We walk up to school, Daisy and I both in our nightwear. Thank God pyjama week is in the spring. There are crowds of children walking up the Green. This is typical, I think. The one day I walk to school in my dressing gown and the whole world comes to look.

'It's very busy today,' I say.

'It's walk to school week,' Lilly huffs. 'Didn't you know?'

'I can't keep up with everything at the moment.'

'We ought to be walking Prada too,' adds Lilly.

'I'll take her later. Perhaps Daddy took her this morning. He was up very early,' I say, with just a little hint of bitterness.

'Can't they walk every week?' It's certainly a relief not to have four by fours speeding past us. Usually it's only us and a few families from the council houses on the edge of Reedby who take the ten-minute walk to school. Here in the countryside walking seems to be reserved for the poor, the young mothers who never had a professional life or rich parents to fund their driving lessons. In Ealing the middle classes wanted to be seen walking to school as much as they enjoyed discussing the whys and wherefores of installing solar heating panels in the suburbs.

We hurry past the other parents and children loitering at the school gate and I deliver Lilly into her classroom. I'm glad that I'm in a rush, it almost makes it less painful that none of the other parents, Liz excepted, ever says anything to me beyond a polite 'hello'. And as I seem to be the only parent in nightwear I'm glad nobody is speaking to me.

Daisy and I run home and I quickly change. I'm not going on my sewing outing in my dressing gown. There are limits!

Chapter 16

*A **French knot** is a little tricky but with practice it can be mastered. Some people find it better to work the knot with the fabric stretched in an embroidery hoop using a chenille or straw needle.*

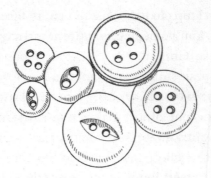

I sprint across the car park and see that the ladies are already congregated by the big wooden door of the Textile Study Centre.

'How are you, Laura?' asks René. Today she looks like one of those ageless French women: svelte figure, classic fitted wool jacket and immaculately bobbed hair.

'I've been sewing every free moment I've had,' I answer breathlessly and as usual feeling decidedly unchic.

'Sewing gets you like that.'

I'm really excited to be out of Reedby and on a trip. And what's more I haven't had to organise any of it. I've got big hopes that the study centre will give me that push and inspiration to see how I can develop my sewing project.

I see the ladies waving to a tall man in a dark overcoat and stripy scarf who's crossing the road.

'There's our token man,' whispers René.

'Just like fashion and textiles everywhere.'

'It does seem that when men go into fashion and textiles they become overnight successes. Often they're just doing what women have always done,' pronounces René.

'Laura,' calls Chris.

The ladies stop chatting and all turn to face me.

'Hi, Chris. You've been let out from the monastery, then?' I say, playfully. Chris doesn't look too pleased. 'Sorry, just joking. I like your scarf.'

'It's Merino wool,' he says, in that deceptively camp tone of his. Chris was one of the most heterosexual males I knew at college. He smiles. Is the smile for me or the ladies?

'How are you young man?' says Joyce, moving towards us and wedging herself between me and Chris. I look at Joyce and love the way she stubbornly ignores her age and fashion dictates. Right now she is wearing a pink floral skirt with white ankle socks and trainers.

'Good, thank you. It's Joyce isn't it?' says Chris. 'I wasn't sure with the pink rinse. It matches your skirt.'

Joyce beams from ear to ear. 'It was green last time. But once met I'm never forgotten,' she chortles.

René edges closer. 'No introductions necessary. You two know each other already, I take it,' she says.

'I'm still waiting for an invite to your flash new studio,' says Chris, smiling at René and trying to avoid catching Joyce's eye again. 'I'm still working in a shed. I want to see how the other half live.'

'No need for an appointment. I'm there pretty much all the time,' says René. 'You know where we are, just down Cut Loke past the church.' René looks around. 'Where's our *Führer*? We're all here.'

Chris gives me a lopsided grin.

'The *Führer*,' says Hannelore loudly and clearly, 'is arrived.' She's wearing a short beige macintosh and knee-high tan boots. I couldn't get away with an outfit like that, but on her it looks great.

'Eight, nine, ten, that's everyone,' says Hannelore doing a quick head count. 'They hate it if a group arrives in bits 'n' pieces.' She pulls down the wrought-iron handle and rings the bell.

A pretty, young blonde girl opens the door and ushers us in.

'The house belonged to the Colman family,' she explains, pointing to the portraits and moving us along into the dining room.

'Oh, I love a bit of English mustard on my sausages,' says Joyce.

'The Colmans made mustard,' René whispers to me. 'They were one of the richest families in Norwich.'

We sit down at what must once have been a dining room table for twelve. I almost have to beat off Joyce to sit next to Chris. This is unbelievable. Joyce is one of the most senior ladies in what is a very senior group. She must be in her eighties. The ladies keep giving him big friendly smiles. This doesn't faze Chris at all. He's always been comfortable in all-female groups. At college he was the only male in my Indian Art seminar group.

If Adi were here, he'd be decidedly uncomfortable with all these women and would probably have made an excuse to leave by now. Momentarily I'm feeling jealous and am tempted to tell the group that Chris was once my boyfriend.

The young curator in a black shirt and drainpipes sits down next to Hannelore. Close up I see that she's clearly a good few years younger than me. And with Chris here it really bothers me. Where has my confidence gone?

What a lovely place to work, I think. Hannelore and the girls talk in hushed whispers for a few minutes. We all gaze at the table. It is covered with an enormous red cloth and under it are strange lumps and bumps. By the looks of the opulent wood panelled room I wouldn't be surprised if there was a boar's head with an apple stuffed in its mouth under the cloth.

'Hi, I'm Emma Sinclair and one of the curators here at the study centre. A warm welcome to you all. It's a treat for us to have such eminent visitors here today,' she says looking at Hannelore and Chris. What has Chris done to deserve this praise?

'Well done for not peeking, ladies and gentleman,' she laughs nervously. And then, like a magician she whisks the cloth off.

I'm mesmerised by the neatly folded clothes and carefully arranged accessories: swimsuits (made of thick elasticated and rouched fabrics), a corset, red buttons sewn onto a card, a trilby hat.

'Have a good look and then choose an object. See what memories it conjures up.'

175

'She probably thinks we've all got Alzheimer's,' says René in a stage whisper. For the second time today mine and Chris' eyes meet and we share a smile.

'Don't take anything away!' says the curator, laughing nervously. 'Now I'm going to leave you in Hannelore's capable hands. I've got to oversee my volunteers.'

For an indecisive person, who often spends longer perusing a menu than eating the food, I'm feeling surprisingly decisive. I know immediately what I'm going to choose. Or perhaps the object has almost chosen me? Everyone begins to move things around and chatter. The table soon looks like a jumble sale.

'Ladies and gentleman!' calls Hannelore. 'Would anyone like to begin talking about their chosen object?'

'I'll begin,' says René, picking up an orange and pale blue swimsuit. 'Mum and Aunty Joan always wore swimsuits like these when we went to the beach. They never went in the sea. That was what Dad and Uncle Ken were there for.'

'Look at the support for the bosom,' says Joyce, grabbing the swimsuit from René and pulling the beige lining apart from the swimsuit. 'They don't make swimsuits like this nowadays.' Everyone gives a knowing nod.

I'm desperate to go next, but like my teenage students I don't want to seem too keen! I let some of the others have their turn.

Juneko holds up a trilby hat and talks of her grandad, a quiet man who always wore his trilby when eating miso soup. The ladies listen intently, trying to make out her softly spoken words.

'Excellent,' says Hannelore. 'It would seem that grandads

all over the world like to wear the same thing, especially when eating soup. You see, the history of our world can be told in these objects. Norwich's history can be told best in textile objects. From the sixteenth century Norwich's prosperity was based on textiles. Wool was shipped along the river to Great Yarmouth and across to Antwerp and Bruges. Fifteen days later the ships returned with spices and other luxuries.'

'It was England's second city,' butts in René. 'Weavers were also invited from the Low Countries and settled in Norfolk.'

The young curator drifts past and says, 'Most of the items donated here are from families descended from the Flemish "Strangers".'

'My mother donated a Norwich shawl,' says René. 'I wish she'd have left it to me, I'd be a lot better off,' she laughs.

Hannelore eyes me fiddling with the faded card with stitched on red buttons.

'Laura, you want to tell us about your object?'

I hold up the card. 'My mum used to have loads of these cards. I've inherited them,' I say, with a quick glance and smile at René. 'We also had jars of buttons. They were big, old sweetie jars,' I say, thinking that you still get proper sweet jars in Phyllis' shop. I feel my voice waver. I continue with tears now starting to fall. 'I used to tip them on the cold kitchen floor and make animal shapes out of them.'

Before I know it, the ladies are all up and crowding around me. I'm feeling very embarrassed and exposed.

'Thank you Laura. OK, ladies, time to split up and go into the library,' says Hannelore, thankfully moving the others on. René gets up, squeezes me on the arm and follows the others.

Chris comes over and sits next to me. His sky blue eyes have also welled up with tears.

'You didn't say anything about the objects,' I say, slightly accusatorily.

'I couldn't even begin,' says Chris. 'You know it was me and Dad and my two brothers, before single fathers were really heard of. Most of the things here weren't my past. And if I'd started to tell the ladies and Hannelore that, I'd have been sobbing on the floor.' He strokes my arm.

'Why are you really here?' I ask.

'Fine art textiles has been good to me. That's why Emma,' he says, looking over towards the office, 'has a bit of a crush on me. I made a good living out of exhibiting my constructed installations. My work was a hybrid of sculpture and textiles. Catching up on a motherless past was what my father used to tell his golfing buddies about his wayward son. You haven't googled me?' he asks.

'No, I haven't googled you,' I say, feeling thrown back into the past. I'd forgotten how much Chris thought of himself, even when we were students.

'But that's not me any more,' he says. 'I'm looking much more at the meaning of things. Let's go in the library. You'll love it,' he says, taking my hand and leading me there.

I pull my hand away before anyone sees, and sit at the round wooden window table. Chris browses through the bookcases while I flick through the Freemans catalogues. Some of the earlier ones have illustrated covers. I remember spending hours of my childhood looking through these. We lived on the edge of a market town with very few shops to excite an eight-year-old girl. Mum was known at the butcher's, baker's, ironmonger's, haberdasher's and wool shop. But with no clothes shops for miles around catalogues were my secret pleasure. I'd draw up my wish list of clothes and toys (winter catalogue – aimed at Christmas presents) and garden toys (summer catalogue). I also gazed at the lingerie pages. I was fascinated and scared of these pages: they showed me what it would be like to be a real woman. This room isn't a library, it's a time machine, I think.

Chris comes over and sits down next to me. 'It's come full circle,' I say. 'Catalogue shopping is back in fashion. A lot of the mums in Ealing used to buy the family's clothes from upmarket online catalogues. Now there's the *Annika* catalogue from Sweden. It's printed on beautiful paper, with just a few choice garments, each one costing a month's wages and yours with just a click of the mouse. Mum used to buy on HP, paying a bit each week or month. The big difference was *Freemans* sold hundreds of things. You could spend a week looking at it.'

'You were always so good at thinking outside the box and making these historical links. Laura, I was wondering,' says Chris, 'and say no if you don't want to. But there's something I'd like you to look at here.'

What is he going to ask? Part of me hopes it's something I should say no to.

'Ask away.'

Part 2

Chapter 17

Feather stitch is also known as single coral stitch and briar stitch. Feather stitch is found extensively on traditional English smocks and on antique crazy quilts.

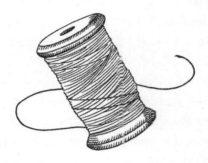

I can't believe that we're back in the cottage. It looks nothing like its former dowdy self. It's amazing what a dedicated team of builders and decorators can do – they've given the house a facelift!

What's really incredible is that it was only the kitchen and bedrooms that suffered structural damage; but the insurance company insisted on re-painting the whole cottage. The girls got their wishes: Lilly has an orange bedroom which looks like a showroom for Mexican Pueblo style, Daisy has a pink room with gold stars – thanks to Robbie taking pity on her. And what's really fantastic is that the girls spend hours happily playing in their new-look rooms.

I got my wish too, I think, as I go into the study and admire the fuchsia pink walls. I just love it! I love the boldness of it. Especially the single wall of chinoiserie wallpaper, with white willow trees on a fuchsia background. It makes me feel happy. The colour also, contrary to popular belief (or Adi's belief in this instance), makes the smallest room in our cottage look spacious.

I boot up the PC and check my e-mails. I'm looking to see if there's anything from Gill about the men's floral range (that's what I tell myself). There's nothing from Gill or anyone else. I have a bad feeling about my designs. It's unlike Gill to go quiet unless there's something she's avoiding telling me. Then again my designs are all speculative and it occurs to me that the tidy sum promised for the pick 'n' mix range and the men's florals may never materialise in this economic climate.

I gaze out of the window and calculate how nil sales will fit into the family budget and decide not to think too much about it. It's not as if I'm a big spender. But I do have a weakness for beautiful things: a punnet of strawberries, an art deco cake stand, a Staffordshire coffee pot or even a vintage dress. It's hard to admit such thoughts these days. However, the thought that's hardest of all to admit is the real reason I checked my e-mails, that is, the guilty hope that Chris will have contacted me.

Life isn't certain. Nothing's for ever. There's no job for life. I don't know how long I've been staring out of the window at the almost dayglo green buds in the garden. Spring has sprung in Reedby. It's strange how much I think about the weather here. There's more weather in Reedby than in Ealing. In London we didn't have seasons, the year merged into one.

The only time I noticed the seasons were the shop window displays at Harvey Nichols. I still remember one spring, stopping in the middle of Knightsbridge and joining the crowd outside Harvey Nicks' window. The whole crowd, me included, marvelled at the exaggerated cut-out origami cherry blossoms. In Reedby spring is real.

I check my e-mails again – just in case something has popped into my inbox. No new messages. I wouldn't be obsessing over whether or not I had an e-mail from Chris if it wasn't for him asking me to help him with his project, I try to tell myself. I want to send Chris my latest thoughts about Lorina's sampler, the embroidered scroll he invited me to look at at the Textile Study Centre; but to do that I need to sit and transpose those tiny intricately stitched words.

I take out the zoomed-in photos of the first section and reread the tiny, upper case letters from the transposition I sent Chris last week: I MISS LORINA BULWER WAS EXAMINED BY DR PINCHING OF WALTHAMSTOW AND FOUND TO BE A PROPERLY SHAPED FEMALE. This text on it still makes me go cold. It's so odd, I begin to wonder if the sampler's real. But then why would someone fake it when it must've taken hundreds of hours to complete?

Lorina Bulwer's patchwork of fabric with every single word hand-stitched on it is nothing short of remarkable – and the fact that Chris has asked me to help transpose the text makes me feel like an Indiana Jones of the textile world.

It all started back at the Textile Study Centre when Chris and I put on the special white gloves and began to read the intricate stitched words. Emma, the curator, hovered about saying things like 'These stitches tell a bitter tale.'

'These stitches don't talk, they shout,' I said to Chris.

'What's really remarkable is that she made it in the lunatic ward of Great Yarmouth workhouse,' said Emma.

For years I've taught snapshots of art and textile history and asked students if the objects were talking to them. Usually the objects didn't talk to them or me. But this is different. As I read on, I note each and every one of Lorina's words from a hundred years ago. She's speaking to me as clearly as if she's in the room with me.

I love the way she stitches her honest, open thoughts: BOTH OF THESE DISGUSTING LOOKING OLD WOMEN AWKWARD /SHAPES AND HORRID NAMES IN CAMBS ... KISSING HIS WIFE'S TOES AND TELLING HER WHAT A BARGAIN HE HAD. So much for sewing being all about polite, upper-class ladies keeping themselves busy embroidering cushion covers before marriage! Lorina's stream of consciousness shows a true gutsy, grumpy old woman. And perhaps the answer to what it's all about is simply that it doesn't tie up and make sense.

I type up my notes and click, sending the section to Chris. Immediately I receive a reply. It's a depressing out of office reply, which anonymously tells me he's away and will contact me on his return. Where is Chris? Where has he gone?

I can hear the growling sounds of a truck pulling up outside the house. There's a knock on the door. I'm not expecting anything. I'm sure the builders are well and truly finished and on to their next project. Robbie was chuffed with my evaluation of his work. I couldn't give anything less than ten out of ten to someone who'd gone beyond the course of duty and painted gold stars on to my daughter's wall.

'Mrs Stark,' says the man. He looks familiar but I can't quite place him.

'Hi,' I say.

'I've got a delivery for you.' I'm sure I haven't ordered anything. Maybe it's a present from Adi, something nice for the new-look cottage. For a moment I even wonder if it's something from Chris, but stop myself.

'Where do you want it?' says the man in wellies and tweed jacket.

'Excuse me?'

'Where shall I leave the manure?'

I begin to laugh, thinking that this must be some sort of joke. A new version of the kissogram. 'We didn't order any manure. Perhaps you've got the wrong house?'

'Your husband, Adrian, isn't it? He's already paid for it. It'll go down a treat at the allotment.'

Manure is going to be our only treat from now on, I think.

'So where's the best place for now?'

I point to the far corner of the garden, thinking that he wouldn't mind carrying it over there.

'Could you move your car out onto the verge. I'll see what I can do.'

I reverse the Micra on to the verge and see the clock. I need to go to school NOW.

'Leave it wherever you think best,' I say.

I rush back inside and call Daisy

'I'm busy in my room!'

'We won't be long,' I say, forcibly moving her from the starry room into the hall. I pop on my red PVC mac and we set off (determinedly on foot) for school. The mac feels so light,

187

and it's as if I'm not wearing anything. Until I move and then I crackle like a load of plastic bags. At least mine is authentic 1970s. A strange sensation comes over me, as I remember wearing a similar red plastic mac as a toddler. It's probably one of my earliest memories. I hear my mum's voice, 'What goes round comes back again.' How right Mum was. Maybe we'll have power cuts like when I was little. I can still remember Mum heating up baked beans on her fondue set.

'Mummy, there's a tractor outside our house. It's Farmer Mackie.'

'Yes, I know,' I say, finally realising who it is and as though having a tractor outside the house is an everyday event.

'How do you know Farmer Mackie?'

'Daddy took us round on Saturday, when you were busy sewing.'

'He showed Dad this big metal cutter, it looked like the moon.'

'Really? What did Daddy want that for?' I say, thinking, how dangerous. Men have no idea of risk.

'He's going to cut down all the weeds with it. And he got loads of woodwork tools.'

'I don't know when he's going to have time to do woodwork,' I say, breaking out in a sweat pushing Daisy up the Green. I stop to take off the mac.

'Daisy, you don't really need the buggy any more. You'll be going to school in September.'

'My legs are tired,' she moans. I feel like whingeing and saying, 'My legs are tired,' in fact I'm tired most of the time. But there's no one to moan to.

'Lovely day for gardening. These daffodils are in their

prime,' calls Kurt Weatherall. 'Lots of work for Adi to do in the garden and on the allotment. It'll take more than a scythe to clear everything.'

That's what Daisy's on about. I should have just asked Kurt to tell me everything about my husband and my life!

'Mrs Jones always had her lawn scarified and cut by Mother's Day,' he adds, looking back at our wild garden.

In Ealing neighbours were just pleased if you kept your garden free from rubbish. We did use to talk about our latest interior design ideas. I enjoyed my art deco stained glass door being the talk of the street. Here, it's all about your garden. Here, the stakes have been raised and there's nowhere to hide.

'Your Adi, would he like some of these?'

'What are they?' I ask, peering into the little pots with things sprouting.

'Tomato plants,' he sighs.

'Thank you very much,' I say, over enthusiastically.

'And I'll be round this evening to take Harriet home? Adi asked if we could take her asap, so he can get on with planting some salad where she is.'

'The girls will miss her.'

'Your dress,' says Kurt, 'it reminds me of being a boy. The blancmange, the plates of radishes, ham and artichokes, and not forgetting the lovely red tomatoes,' he says, touching one of the tomatoes printed on my dress. I start, rather too abruptly, and wish I'd left my mac on. 'We had cloth napkins in rings with pictures just like that,' he continues, looking at the dress rather than meeting my eyes. 'People just don't do things properly any more.'

'No, they don't,' I agree, not completely sure what I am agreeing with, but keen to get up to the school and glad I'm not wearing my lobster print dress. Apparently Dalí used lobsters as sexual symbols – what would Kurt have made of that? I then remember that I don't have that sundress any more. It was completely ruined in the fire. I compose myself, grab the flowerpots and place them under the buggy.

'They'll need to go in that conservatory of yours. Can't go outside till the frosts are over,' he calls to me down the path. Daisy and I wave.

'By the way', he says, rushing up the path as ever in his blue overalls, 'you need to make sure you don't leave your bag on the phone table when you go out. Someone could get hold of it with a fishing rod and pull it out through the letterbox.'

I smile and nod, feeling my face flush and unable to speak. Am I being spied on? Is Adi talking about me to Kurt? Perhaps Adi has paid him to keep an eye on me – his scatty wife.

I stand in the playground with Daisy. You must make an effort. It'll pay off in the end, I tell myself, forcing a smile for all the parents. I feel invisible to these people. Perhaps I should put my red PVC mac back on? It's hard to be invisible in that.

'Laura, how's the cottage? I heard it's finished,' says Liz.

I nod and smile at Liz, admiring her daring dress – not the cleavage! – but the colours. The bright scarlet, sunshine yellow and orange concentric circle patterns are lovely and look good against her black curls. I'd love to wear such bold colours. Even with her pale skin she looks Spanish and exotic, a bit like a Joan Miró abstract painting.

'So does that mean that you're actually back in the cottage?' she asks.

I relax and breathe a sigh of relief. 'Yep, and what's more I'm receiving visitors,' I say in a jaunty voice. 'Do you want to come back for a cuppa? The girls would love to have Kate round.'

'There's Jack as well.'

'Sorry, of course Jack is welcome too. In fact Daisy would love someone to play spaceships with in her new-look bedroom.'

'Is it all done? No more builders? No more decorators?'

'Yep. It's just us again.'

We walk back in a long convoy. I'm really excited about having someone to show off our newly decorated house to.

'What's that in the garden?' says an eagle-eyed Lilly.

I squint down the Green at what looks like a brown pyramid covering most of my front garden.

'I don't believe it! When he said he was delivering some manure I thought it would be a couple of bags or a wheelbarrow full. I know why he's doing this,' I say, looking at Liz. 'It's because we didn't see eye to eye about the colour scheme. The kitchen is the only room I allowed to be painted white. I still think it would look better in a pale plaster pink.'

'There's steam coming off the cow poo!' shouts Jack, excitedly.

'That's boys for you,' laughs Liz. 'Anyway, I want to see these exciting colour schemes and what you've been up to at that sewing class.'

'I haven't been up to anything!' I exclaim, realising I'm going almost as red as Liz's dress and am unable to mention,

191

even to Liz, my friendship with Chris. Liz looks taken aback and I quickly move things on. 'Come on, I've got a whole yurt-ful of bits 'n' bobs I've been making. I'm a woman obsessed,' I say in a slightly false jolly voice.

'A yurtful? Is that a new unit of measurement?' laughs Liz.

'Actually the yurt is my new studio. I thought I'd never get Adi back into the house, so I've really cluttered it up with all my sewing things.'

Chapter 18

Fern stitch *is easily worked as it is simply an arrangement of three straight stitches of equal length which radiate from a central point.*

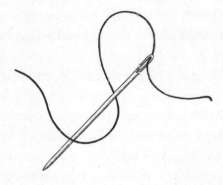

The alarm clock goes off. 'It's a fire! The house is on fire again,' I shout and sit bolt upright.

It takes me a few minutes to realise that there is no fire. For a moment I have one of those scary early morning thoughts: Am I sweating because I've started the menopause? You do hear about women starting the menopause in their thirties.

I look around my sunflower yellow bedroom and smile. It lifts your spirits having your bedroom painted in your favourite colour. The curtains (my pride and joy of yellow petals with crimson and purple appliquéd centres on a very, very pale turquoise background) are wide open and clouds race across the big sky.

Sometimes I prefer the curtains shut. Then I'm in my very own sunflower field and we're living in Provence and not in Reedby. It is morning, a bank holiday *and* Daisy isn't up. I could go back to sleep. I could try and curl up with Adi.

But where is Adi? The only thing in bed with me is a half-sewn necklace of textile pearls – my own technical term for beads made solely of fabric scraps wrapped round and round a knitting needle, pulled off the needle and held together with a bullion knot stitch. I must have fallen asleep sewing. Oh no, some of the fabric pearls are missing and probably on the floor or even in bed.

I look down at the carpet and under the bed. On the far side of the bed I see Adi on all fours stretching his bottom in the air. Either side of him are several fan heaters switched on to full blast. Am I still dreaming? I wonder.

'You look like Prada,' I say.

'I'm supposed to look like a dog. It's downward-facing dog,' says Adi very slowly as if I'm a child.

'Should you be talking while doing this?' I mutter.

'Of course not. The breath is everything. Sanjay says I'll just have to compromise with my practice as I have a family, hence my getting up at the crack of dawn and trying not to let my yoga get in anyone's way.'

'Why are you just wearing your pants?' I ask.

'It's too hot for clothes. The warmer you are the less likely you are to injure yourself.'

'Who says?' I ask, belligerently, knowing the answer.

'That's what Sanjay says. I need to hold this for five breaths,' commands Adi, already the expert.

'Come on Laura, just try it. It would be good for us to have a joint hobby.'

I'm suddenly wishing I never suggested Adi take up yoga. It was like this with jogging when we lived in London. Sometimes our whole weekend's eating seemed to revolve around the optimum times and menu for Adi's marathon runs.

Keeping my nightdress on, I get down on the carpet and copy Adi. I'm sure I don't look like a cat or dog. After only a few minutes my arms feel as if they're burning. I'm not sure that I'll have any breath left if I stay in this position any longer. Is this really what married couples should be doing on a bank holiday morning when the children (for once) are sound asleep?

'Jump back now. Ouch! Bloody pins, what are they doing on the bedroom floor?'

I keep quiet and pretend to be in the yoga zone.

We then sit cross-legged trying to empty our minds. My mind just gets fuller and fuller with sewing ideas. I have to think of something to take my mind off the pain in my hips. If I did this pose every day I don't think I'd ever be able to sit in a proper cross-legged position – or lotus position, as Adi calls it.

How am I going to survive the two week Easter holiday from my class? With the girls home all day, and Adi around for the long weekend, there won't be a free moment for a sewing 'fix'. I'm addicted. I begin to think of combinations of fabrics and party bunting, an evening bag to go with Liz's order of a textile pearl necklace – it's the least I can do to repay their kindness. I can see strappy sandals draped with fabric flowers to customise them. It dawns on me that the difference between my accessories and most other people's is that they're all one-offs.

'You know what makes my designs unique?' I say.

'Shush! You shouldn't be talking.'

'Maybe I could design yoga bags? They could be just the right shape for a rolled-up mat and be all wholesome and recycled.'

'I'll see what Sanjay thinks,' says Adi.

My mind wanders to Chris. I wonder if he'll be working on the transcript over Easter. I also think about Lorina and count my blessings. Lorina is like a nagging voice in the back of my mind telling me to stop being so spoilt. I am free to make what I want – more or less when I want!

Chapter 19

Fly stitch is also known as 'Y' stitch and open loop stitch. Fly stitch is worked easily since it is made up of a V-shaped loop which is then tied down by a vertical straight stitch.

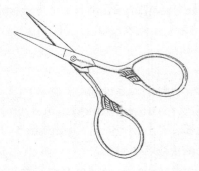

I lean on a reluctant Adi as I change from my wellies into my red strappy high heels. I love red shoes. Every spring I buy a new pair of red shoes. This year is no exception, the only difference is I've had to wait what seems like ages for their first outing. The multicoloured fabric flowers I've stitched on top are my prototype – my very own customised shoes.

The main problem is that the grassy verges and footpaths of Reedby aren't really made for high heels; they want to suck them in. I never had these kinds of problems in London. I didn't have to put my new shoes in a carrier bag until I got to my destination. I loved listening to the clack of my heels as

197

Adi and I walked to the underground station. It always signalled the beginning of our night out. I could even safely mount the escalators of Leicester Square in the thinnest of heels.

The metallic red high heels and criss-cross straps are just like the gold and silver versions Mum used to wear for dinner-dances when I was a child. I can still see her transformed into a star for an evening, showing off in her gold lamé dress and matching clutch bag. People are so dull nowadays, they always wear the same jeans and shirt for any occasion.

Adi of course doesn't have to bother with all this changing shoe business. He's already in the pub. His waxed Timberland boots were born for wading down the track to Reedby's pub – the Ferry.

I walk in and smell the chips. I'm starving. Since having the girls I'm used to eating with them at 6 p.m. I'm out of sync with the grown-up routine of eating at 8 p.m. I feel like dinner's happened already. I had to cook and clear away a meal for his mother and the girls, but at least I managed to restrain myself from eating with them as well, although I'm now so hungry that I'm starting to wish I had eaten, especially when I see the leftover soggy vegetables and anaemic-looking pie placed on the table next to us.

'I thought they were teetotal,' says Adi somewhat disappointedly, looking at the group from the Buddhist retreat propping up the bar.

'Is that Sanjay?' I whisper, discreetly pointing to a small dark Asian man at the bar.

'Of course it is. You don't exactly get a very diverse mix of people in Reedby,' says Adi, giving Sanjay a wave and a smile.

Chris Taylor is there too. He's laughing and talking with the others and knocking back a pint. I thought he must have been away. He hasn't e-mailed me for a few days. They all look so relaxed, so easygoing. Part of me wishes that we could go and sit with them rather than have our married couple night out. Adi and I used to despise couples like us, people who either have nothing to say to each other, or when they do finally speak just bicker. And I'd give anything to steal a handful of their chips.

Adi isn't smiling at me. He is all tense for some reason. I know this look – he's not great with new people or groups, and probably wishes we'd gone somewhere anonymous, like one of the Indian restaurants in Norwich. Sanjay needs to come over and do some breathing exercises with him.

I gaze up at the blackboard.

'It's a really retro menu,' I say. 'Look, prawn cocktail, mushrooms in breadcrumbs, Black Forest gateau, homemade trifle ...'

'OK Laura, I can read the menu myself,' he says huffily.

The waitress comes over and I spend some time deliberating aloud as to whether I should have stuffed mushroom or the prawn cocktail for a starter.

'Laura, I'll have the stuffed mushroom, you have the prawn cocktail and then you can try both,' says Adi. We finally place our order with the teenage waitress and sit back in silence.

My prawn cocktail arrives. 'It's like being back in the 1970s,' I say, desperate to make conversation.

'You can't remember the '70s,' he says. 'Anyway, didn't you have a dress with prawns on it?'

'Not any more. And of course I can remember the '70s. I'm sure I wore hotpants, shorts with a bib and straps attached with Velcro. I definitely ate strawberry Angel Delight, but only when friends came round for tea. I bet you don't know how they make Marie Rose sauce?'

Adi peers at my prawn cocktail.

'They mix up salad cream and tomato ketchup,' I say, expecting Adi to laugh.

Instead he says, 'I don't like all this harking back to the past. Most of it is fictitious. We should think of our future. You know the Ploughman's Lunch?'

'Oh yes, crusty bread, a hunk of cheese and a pickled onion,' I say, suddenly wishing a Ploughman's Lunch would appear in front of me.

'It's all a lie, an ad campaign dreamt up in the 1960s,' says Adi, ruining my dream dinner.

'You must remember the Smash potato men,' I say, trying to get the cosy conversation about the past going again.

Adi sits back and smiles. 'Mum used to use Smash to make our favourite tea. Did I ever tell you what our favourite tea was?'

I shake my head and am relieved to see a glimpse of the old Adi.

'Dog meat pie was mine and Tim's favourite.'

'Your mother fed you dog food!' I exclaim.

Adi bursts into uncontrollable laughter and then I join in.

'But did she really feed you dog meat?' I ask, having visions of Adi's mum bustling around my kitchen, her enormous bosoms leading the way, to cook the girls a midnight feast of Prada's dog meat.

'No, of course she didn't. It was tinned meat, but for humans, not for dogs.'

'Do you think she'll be all right tonight with the girls?'

'We're only going to be gone a few hours. The girls were so excited – an evening with Nana.'

Adi smiles.'I'll tell you what else I remember, everything on sticks.'

'Cheese and pineapple,' I say. 'I should have done those for our housewarming, instead of those crisps which most people didn't eat, thinking they were pot pourri.'

'Perhaps I should buy you a hostess trolley,' says Adi, well into the spirit of things.

'Um, I could wheel it into the yurt.'

'I'm sorry, Laura, if I've been a bit tense lately,' says Adi, uncharacteristically taking my hand. 'The new job. Then the four-day week. It really is like the 1970s. I remember Dad working a three-day week and driving Mum mad loitering around the house.'

'But – hold on – you've been going into work all week, haven't you?'

Adi flushes and I know I'm on to something.

'You're not one of those men who don their suit and bowler hat and spend the day in the park, are you?'

'You know I'm not one of those men. When did I last wear a suit voluntarily?' jokes Adi. 'But David and I are working on a little project of our own. It's our back-up plan – I don't know if it'll work out yet. I really don't want to move back to London.'

'What project? What plan?'

'Just a bit of side-stepping, architecturally. It's not very interesting.'

Now usually I'd be like a dog with a bone as I hate secrets, other people's, that is. I'd keep questioning Adi about 'the project' – but as I've got my own secret textile project with Chris I decide to change the subject.

'We haven't really talked about the fire, have we?' I say. I am still waiting for a big telling off.

'We're all safe. Nobody was injured. And I've ordered a fire extinguisher and fire blanket, Kurt gave me the name of an industrial supplier.'

I begin to laugh. 'Sorry, I know it isn't funny and of course we should have a fire extinguisher after what happened.' I see a glint in Adi's eyes, but he's loyal to Kurt and isn't going to laugh about him in public.

'If a year ago somebody had said my vintage clothes would be left in tatters, I'd have been having heart palpitations. But now ...' I shrug my shoulders. 'One door closes and another opens.'

Adi throws me a big grin. 'This sewing business has been like the phoenix rising out of the ashes, and of course we got the house all done up on the insurance. You don't have to half kill yourself trying to decorate again.'

I look up and Chris Taylor looms above us holding a full pint. Behind him in the corner I see a middle-aged group, probably holidaymakers, their cruiser moored up at the pub. They laugh and eat their fish and chips. The ladies can't help but look at Chris and I feel a tinge of jealousy. He still has all the ingredients of a model, extra-tall, bright blue eyes and dark, shiny hair – albeit these days best seen at a distance!

I shouldn't be surprised he's come over or that he's in the pub; old habits die hard. Not that there's anything wrong with having a drink, it just doesn't match up with my image of him working at a Buddhist retreat.

I'm about to say, Adi, this is Chris, he was at Chelsea, and talk about a small world when Adi gets in first and says, 'This is Chris, the man who takes the money. Sanjay's too shy.'

Instead of owning up to knowing him, for some reason I say, 'Hi I'm Laura.' Of course he knows I'm Laura. Not only did we once go out together, we now, or should I say, until recently, have been talking textiles nearly every day. I thought he was genuinely interested in our little project, in the Lorina Bulwer sampler, even if he wasn't interested in me!

Adi and I walk back along the unlit carnser, typical of the Norfolk Broads with its narrow strip of road flanked either side by the watery marsh. I wish he'd want to hold my hand again, or link arms at least. But he doesn't. He's been increasingly cold and disinterested in me since we left London; it's as though now he has the longed-for countryside he doesn't need me any more. He couldn't be more different from Chris, who always enjoyed an audience.

The cloud and rain of the afternoon has gone and it's an amazing starry night which sparkles on the water either side of us. I just wish Adi would show some small hint of being romantic in this perfect setting.

'You don't get skies like this in towns, there's so much light pollution. People weren't meant to live in cities. Mum thought we could take her up to that new museum in Great Yarmouth tomorrow, before dropping her home,' says Adi. 'After the Easter egg hunt, of course.'

'But she lives in Great Yarmouth,' I say.

'Yeah, a bit of a busman's holiday.'

I feel tears drip down my face, as if from out of nowhere.

'Laura, Laura, what is it? What's up?' says Adi. 'I know Mum's a bit odd. Dad always says she's highly strung. But she is my mum.'

I'm sure that highly strung is what neurotic dogs are called. But say nothing.

'It's nothing to do with your mum. I don't know. I'm just not sure we did the right thing moving here, leaving everything behind. And there's not much work up here. I don't mind shopping at Lidl and all that.'

'I didn't know you shopped at Lidl,' says a surprised Adi.

'You know Liz's Mark won't be seen in Lidl,' I say, thinking, What have things come to that we discuss budget supermarkets on a rare night out. 'Do you realise this is the first time we've been out together without the children since we arrived in Reedby?'

'I hadn't really thought about it,' confesses Adi. 'It's just been such a hard slog getting into the new job. I never see anything of Reedby during the week. It's been dark when I leave in the morning and dark when I get back, hence the bike. I've never hidden the fact that I get down in the winter.' You certainly haven't! I think. 'That's why I'm so excited about the allotment – a chance to be outside. And we'll have our own homegrown food. Now the clocks have changed that'll make a difference too.'

'I've had a new job, new school for the kids, new everything too,' I bluster.

'I'm sorry, Laura. I just feel so responsible for us all. If my job doesn't work out I really don't want to move back to London.'

Maybe we should. Maybe that would be better. 'I don't want to give up either. To go backwards,' I say, trying to reassure Adi. The past always seems a better, cosier place.

'Is there anything you miss about London?' I ask. Adi takes my hand in his.

'I've got everything I need here. You and the girls are everything. Look, I'll try and get back earlier in the evenings. Perhaps we should find a babysitter who lives in the village and get out more. That dinner wasn't half good. You can't beat big portions of beef and ale pie. Just what we need in this credit crunch. No more nouvelle cuisine. I never liked it anyway.' Adi takes my arm and together we walk up the Green.

This all sounds well and good, but I know this means that I will have to find and book a babysitter. And it costs money. Don't knock his suggestion, Laura. It's just it was all so easy in Ealing, with our babysitting circle.

'They're all asleep,' whispers Adi. I hear a strange whimpering noise coming from the study. Is Prada in there? I carefully open the study door and see Adi's mum snivelling on the sofa bed.

'Are you all right, Pammie?' I ask, knowing jolly well that she isn't.

'It's the colour, it's so distressing.'

'I always think of fuchsia as such a happy colour,' I say. Pam doesn't look convinced.

'Shall I move the sofa into the lounge?'

'Would you, love?'

I rummage in the fridge for the Easter eggs and carefully open one of the girls' eggs. Inside are mini chocolate eggs. I take a couple and carefully replace the wrapping.

'There you are,' I say, handing her a cup of tea and a couple of chocolate eggs. It's not enough to have a husband and two children to look after – I also have a needy mother-in-law!

Chapter 20

Carpet stitch. Short lengths of wool are cut; each length is folded into two; a crochet hook is inserted in the loop thus made at the fold, and the fold drawn through the canvas from the top surface in and out again to the top a thread or two further on. This is half the stitch. In the other half the hook catches the two loose ends and draws them through the original loop. All the loose ends thus come to the surface of the canvas where they can be fringed out to give a matted appearance

I wake up to an empty bed. It's Easter Sunday and there's no sign of Adi, not that I'd get as much as a cuddle at the moment anyway. From under the bed I pull out an old carrier bag. Inside are three little chicks. I'm very proud of their feathers. I used carpet stitch to make big loops, which when cut look amazingly soft and fluffy over their patchwork bodies.

Still wearing my nightdress and dressing gown I take the

chicks out into the garden. For a moment I wonder at the mad lengths parents go to today to get everything ready for Christmas and Easter. I carefully place Daisy's chick under the slide and Lilly's in the yurt. I look across the cold, misty garden and know exactly where I'm going to hide Adi's chick.

I go back inside and find that Pam is up and busy casting off some knitting in our new-look kitchen.

'They're for the girls,' she whispers. 'So much better for them than a load of sweets. And I'm very up to date, this knitting is recycled, I unravelled an old jumper,' she says proudly.

'Good for you, Pam,' I say, a little unsure of exactly what it is that Pam has knitted. 'I'll let you into a secret, my presents are made from the leftovers of our new bedroom curtains.'

'I love this granite worktop,' says Pam, more interested in running her hands across the sparkly black stone than my sewing ideas. 'I'll be having words with Dennis when I get home. Although trying to get Adi's dad to change anything in the house is an uphill struggle.'

I hope Adi has bought his mother an Easter egg, otherwise there's only the measly collection of mini eggs in the fridge; most of which Pam and I ate last night.

'So who's ready for the Easter hunt?' asks Adi, bringing the girls into the kitchen and looking very excited.

'Where've you been?' I mouth.

Adi taps his nose with his forefinger. I start to feel excited too. Perhaps he's been hiding some really special chocolate eggs. 'Mummy will give you her clues first.'

'I haven't written my clues yet!' I mumble. I rummage in the kitchen drawer and scrawl my clues on the back of (hopefully) unimportant letters.

'Youngest goes first,' shouts Daisy.

I hand the first clue to her.

'Lilly, Lilly, what does it say?'

'People are always sliding over my head,' reads Lilly in a disinterested monotone, more befitting a teenager than a primary school child.

We all follow Daisy out into the back garden and watch her run around in a frenzy.

'What on earth's that tent doing there!' exclaims Pam.

'Mum, I told you about the yurt,' says Adi, impatiently.

'I didn't think it would look like this. It would make a lovely marquee for a party. I always thought you should have had a marquee for your wedding party, much nicer than that restaurant in London we all had to go to.'

I can see Adi begin to stiffen. I need to step in here. 'Pam, do you think you could help Daisy?'

Pam totters after Daisy and Daisy rummages about under the slide.

'Mummy, he's lovely, all in orange, my favourite colour,' says Daisy, cuddling the chick.

'Where's my clue?' demands Lilly.

I pass her the piece of paper.

'The magisterial home of princesses of a thousand and one nights,' reads Lilly.

'Goodness,' says Pam, 'We never had clues like that when Adi and Tim were little.'

We follow Lilly into the yurt, which with all my bits of fabric really does look like something out of a thousand and one nights.

Adi inspects the trellis and fiddles with the louvre door. He opens and shuts it several times. He smiles lovingly at it. I'm starting to think that he's more interested in the yurt than me. I can see the tabloid headlines: Man leaves wife for a yurt!

Lilly runs up to pull her chick out from behind a trellis. 'It's lovely, Mummy,' she says pulling at the fluff. 'Look, underneath it's the same fabric as your bedroom curtains.'

'You're so observant,' I say, feeling all cosy watching her stroke the chick.

I hold Adi's clue in my hand and make a snap decision.

'Pam, here's your clue,' I say.

'Oh, Laura, I never expected a present.'

'Nana, read the clue!' shout the girls.

'It's very healthy, but smelly where I live,' reads Pam.

'I know, I know,' says Lilly running off to the corner of the garden. 'It's here, Nana, in Daddy's manure pile.'

'Beside, not in it,' I say.

'You bring it over for Nana,' says Pam.

'Look, Nana, you've got the biggest chick.'

'Thank you,' she says giving us all (except Adi) a kiss. 'Now it's my turn to give out pressies,' says Pam. 'Follow me to the kitchen.'

'That's good, I'm starving,' says Lilly. Oh dear, I think.

'Now girls, this is Miss Lilly,' she points to the taller one, 'and this is Miss Daisy,' says Pam, proudly pointing to the smaller of the two knitted loo roll holders with real dolly heads.

'It's like voodoo,' whispers Adi in my ear.

'Shush!'

'Nana, they're just like the knitted dollies in your bathroom.' Pam smiles and is really pleased.

'Except mine is called Miss Amanda Jane,' adds Pam.

'Now it's my turn for surprises,' says Adi. 'I've got just one clue.'

What does he mean one clue? I'm really looking forward to a nice cup of coffee and some chocolate. Perhaps he's got us one big Easter egg?'

'So what's the clue, then?' I ask.

'Where does a man take refuge in a house full of girls?'

I'm about to say, the yurt, when Pam butts in and says, 'If he's anything like his father we should go to the shed.'

As if on cue, Prada wakes up, jumps out of her basket (made from fabric, the girls' old pram cover – not wicker) and follows us outside to the shed.

Prada yaps and sniffs frantically at the shed door. 'Go on, open the door, Mum,' urges Adi. Pam slowly opens the door to five real chicks. She screams and runs back into the cottage, with Prada close at her heels. 'Catwalk queen,' says Adi, pointing to a bird with Dalmatian markings. She's yours, Laura.'

'Thank you. So I'm Cruella de Vil?' I laugh, shaking my head and looking at the white chick with little black spots.

'In *101 Dalmatians* Cruella wanted to make a coat from the puppies. Are you going to make a feather coat from the chickens?' asks Lilly, earnestly.

'Oh goodness, Lilly, I haven't thought that far – what I am thinking is how is Prada going to adjust to living with chickens?'

'Which one's mine?' squeals Daisy.

'For the girls we have *a bit of fluff*.' He points to two grey fluffy chicks.

'They look a bit like kittens,' says Lilly.

'And for you?' I enquire.

'*A good egg* or two. You might not choose these for their looks, but they deliver true blue eggs,' says Adi, looking at a black and grey mottled chicken, clearly older than the others, whose feather patterns look distinctly reptilian. I don't like reptiles – of any kind.

'Can we have our chocolates now?' asks Lilly.

So now, not only do we have an allotment, we're branching out into livestock! I really wouldn't ever have predicted this.

Chapter 21

*The **Ghiordes knot** is also known as Turkish rug knot, single knot tufting, quilt knot stitch, tufted knot stitch and single knotted Smyrna rug stitch. It is a pile stitch which has traditionally been used in canvas but is enjoying a revival as one of the textured embroidery stitches.*

I'm up bright and early. If it isn't Adi waking me up with his yoga practice, then it's the cockerel telling everyone it's time to get up. Briefly, the thought crosses my mind that I could stuff the cockerel (who didn't appear with the lovely little chicks) and turn him into a doorstop. There may be some link between sewing and taxidermy. Then again I may be turning into a woman who makes links between the oddest of things, just like poor Lorina, who, stuck in the workhouse with just her needles and fabrics, talked of all kinds of weird, wonderful and unmentionable things.

It's the first day back at school after the Easter holidays and as if on cue the sun shines for the first time in two weeks. I feel reassured that all is OK. The beginning of term and the promise of a new start still excites me. Lilly sits on the sofa ready for the summer term in her red and white gingham dress. She's well turned out, as my mum used to say. I rush around packing school bags, lunch boxes, pre-school bags and my sewing bag.

Thank God Town and Country doesn't go back until next week. I'll have some me time at last. Holidays aren't what they used to be. In London, most days of the school holidays I'd meet up with friends and the children would all entertain each other. At least I've got plenty of sewing to show for my time. And I'm not completely 'Billy-no-mates' as I've got two dates in my diary this week – one is my sewing class, today.

I'm the last to arrive, and sit down at my usual sewing table. Spring really has sprung, for once the awful blowy heaters aren't on full blast. I haven't felt this excited about my artwork since I was at art school. I don't really think of stitching as sewing, it's more like drawing (or, dare I say it, doodling) with thread. Out of my big patchwork bag (made over the holidays out of recycled dresses and curtain scraps) I pull out doorstops, table mats and purses, out of which come necklaces and flowers to customise shoes. I haven't only done my homework, I've surpassed myself. I feel like a little schoolgirl expecting to get a gold star for her hard work.

Hannelore walks over, 'Ah, they're like matryoshka dolls.'

I smile, wondering what she's talking about.

'You know the Russian dolls. Every East German girl had a collection. See one thing goes out of the other,' she says demonstrating this by putting the necklace in the purse, in the clutch bag, in the big bag.

'I think I almost have a range,' I say.

'You've got the sewing bug,' she says, pronouncing the 'bug' in her strange guttural accent.

'It must be village life,' I joke. 'My husband's as obsessed with his allotment as I am with sewing.'

'You know why?'

'It's just great fun doing things by hand,' I answer, not sure if she's asked me a rhetorical question.

'It's all about power in uncertain times.'

'Like Lorina Bulwer's sampler?' I suggest.

'Ah that,' says Hannelore. 'I've looked at it before Chris started on his project. Something to remember is that great art: painting, music, sewing, is always greater than the maker. And beware of trying to make sense of it in a hurry,' she adds, enigmatically.

René leans over and whispers, 'Don't take it personally.'

Do I really look that upset? I thought Chris and I were onto something special.

'It's better that you're in charge of your life and able to make your own clothes and furnishings, grow your own food. I ate vegetables my father grew on his little Dacha. The Dacha, with its homegrown produce was *symbolisch* of our country. East Germany was a land where everything was homemade,' says Hannelore, and before I can ask her if my giant hand-stitched buttonhole is OK she's gone across to the other side of the hall.

'Hannelore's a good teacher,' says René. 'She's just got this bee in her bonnet about sewing being political. She'll have us all marching on Downing Street if we aren't careful. At least if we are called to march on Downing Street we can make our own banners,' laughs René, flicking her enviable neat bobbed hair.

'So she should be interested in Lorina's sampler.'

René shrugs her shoulders. 'I don't know. Anyway, how are things with you? Did you get up to anything good over the holidays?'

'Well, where do I begin?' I say, so pleased that someone wants to hear what I've been up to. 'We went on a trip to Great Yarmouth. We, that is myself, the girls and Adi's mother. In fact she lives near there. I have to tell you Adi's excuse for not coming.'

'Was he off at the allotment? I tell you, being a beekeeper's wife is just as lonely. He's always off transporting bees here, there and everywhere.'

'It wasn't the lotty this time. It was all because of the chicks.'

'Chicks?!'

'Yes, we all got a chick as our Easter present. Real live chicks! I don't want to sound ungrateful, but just one little chocolate egg would have been so nice. Anyway, we were all ready to go, the car was loaded up with all his mother's suitcases for her two-night stay in Reedby, when Kurt popped round. The girls told him all about the chicks and he started on about chicken rustling.'

'Chicken rustling?' calls Joyce from across the hall.

'According to Kurt most of the meat you buy at farmers' markets is rustled, especially rare breeds. So, Adi decided to stay at home with our chicks,' I say, somewhat tongue in cheek.

'Men, any excuse not to go out,' laughs René. 'Did you get to go to Lorina's old workhouse when you were in Great Yarmouth?'

'No. By the time we got there it was pouring with rain. I took them all to that new museum and gallery, the one that's won all the prizes. It's in an old herring factory. We had lunch, potted herring, and I thought we ought look at the exhibitions. That was my big mistake.'

'Why? What happened?' asks René. 'Did the kids do something?'

'It wasn't the kids. It was Adi's mum Pam who did something.'

'Go on,' says René. I see that Joyce is all ears and has even stopped sewing and Juneko is listening too.

'All we did was go into the Great British Art Gallery. I made a beeline for the Tracey Emin piece. The big patchwork hanging with all the text.'

'She's a funny one,' says René. 'I'd have liked to have been a bit more like her if I was born a few years later.'

'That wasn't what Pammie thought. She started shouting out things that were written on the banner. I think the comments were meant for Tracey. When she shouted, "Bitch, I hate women like you," which was carefully appliquéd on the banner, I didn't know what to do. And of course I had the girls with me. The guard came over and asked if we were all right and suggested that I take the upset lady for a cup of tea. We finally left the gallery with Pammie shouting, "Rot in hell." We finished our outing watching the rain trickle down the steamed up windows in a little cafe on the seafront, and do you want to know what she said?'

At this point the whole class seems to be listening and nodding. 'She said, "Laura, I feel so much better, now. It's amazing what a cup of tea, a slice of Battenburg and a good old rant can do." So René, tell me, what was that all about? I didn't know what to say to Adi that evening. But the girls filled in the gaps.'

'I think it means that freedom of speech is only for the chosen few,' says Hannelore, creeping up behind us.

Then I have one of those lightbulb moments which creative people are supposed to have all day long (and that are supposed to come out of nowhere – which never happens). I'm going to use everyday words, thoughts, speech in my stitching. It's been staring me in the face: Lorina's sampler is talking to me as much as Tracey Emin's rants talked to Pammie. Like a fortune cookie, each of my artefacts will have a thought for the day.

Chapter 22

Tacking stitch is used to hold the fabric in position while it is being permanently stitched. It is similar to running stitch but with longer stitches. Also known as basting.

I see myself in the hall mirror as I dart by. We have lots of them – mirrors, that is. In a house with so many mirrors you can't be vain, or so I've always thought until I see the dowdy mess looking back at me. It's hard to see which bit of me is causing the biggest problem. My skin's OK. I'm finally past my acne, well, acne is an exaggeration, but I was prone to more than the odd spot. It's my hair. The split ends seem to have arrived overnight. I need a haircut now! And what's this, a grey hair? Help!

Why am I fussing so much for the school run? The truth is, I'm dressing for after the school run. I'm not planning to spend the morning by myself. I can't go to meet Chris looking like this. I run upstairs and rummage through the almost bare rails.

'It looks like a shop,' Liz had said to me at the house-warming party, when I first showed her my vintage clothes collection. Now it looks like a closing down sale! Liz had gone on to explain her system of having a small wardrobe, an heirloom which housed all her clothes. If she wanted to get something new, something has to go. It was as simple as that. Some people are strange, I think.

Since moving to Reedby I haven't once been out for a coffee with a friend. In London I'd meet someone or other, most weeks. Lotte and I would go to the deli-cum-cafe in Ealing or I'd whizz up to town with Daisy and meet old work colleagues for lunch and a natter. I keep telling myself that's the reason I'm so excited about meeting Chris this morning. There's nothing in it, he's a substitute girlfriend! We've got a perfect morning planned: coffee and discussing Lorina's sampler and then hitting the charity shops – just like we used to when we were students.

I walk along the old part of the city searching for our rendezvous point. I pass the timber framed Maddermarket Theatre, I must be close now. I look across the narrow street and spot the Maddermarket Cafe sign with its trendy red and black graphics. What's this obsession with the colour red – with madder? I wonder. The last time I used rose madder oil paint I was at art school. I hug my Americano coffee and look out the long glass windows of the coffee shop. I see an orange Volkswagen camper van negotiate the tight corner of the old city wall and park on the double yellow lines. I'm mildly disappointed when nothing happens. I then feel bad. Am I some vacuous thrillseeker?

A few moments later a tall, handsome figure enters the cafe. There's a silent acknowledgement that someone very good-looking has just come in. In the same way a pretty dress warms your heart and soul.

'I couldn't find anywhere to park the van,' says Chris.

'You're driving?' I ask, remembering that Chris is the most unnatural driver I've ever met.

'I only drive when I have to. Sorry I'm late, by the way.'

'No problem,' I say, thinking of the endless little jobs I had to complete in order to get here on time. 'I've only got till 11.30 before I go and collect Daisy, though,' I say.

'So we won't have time for a picnic,' he says, looking at my wicker basket.

'Oh, it's not a hamper,' I laugh. 'It's my shopping bag.'

'So have you decided on some more sections from the sampler?' asks Chris.

'I thought you wanted to get it all transcribed?'

'Emma is doing the full transcription,' says Chris casually. 'You do remember her, the curator at the textile centre?'

'Of course I remember her. So what's my involvement? You haven't really told me what this project is.'

'If I knew, I'd be a happy man. Of course I filled in all the Arts Council blurb about looking at Norwich's textile heritage, how it played an important role in the textile world, its wool and linen industries,' says Chris, now doing a fake yawn a bit like one of my students. 'What I need you for, Laura, is to discuss my ideas with me. And for you to select the best, most quotable, pieces from Lorina's sampler.'

'How about this then?' I begin, feeling excited that I'm in the midst of something happening in the world outside Reedby. 'Lorina seemed to reserve some of her harshest words for her family, especially her sister.' I take a plastic sleeve out of my basket and read out loud. 'I MISS LORINA BULWER WONDER ... THE SLOPS OF THIS NOTORIOUS BUG LICE AND FLEA TRIBE, AS HIS SOCIALIST ANN FAGGOT WIFE DIED AND WENT TO HELL.' I have a déjà vu moment of Pammie on Easter Sunday at the museum. But here nobody seems bothered in the slightest. The other customers just carry on reading their newspapers. 'How about that for a good quote?'

'Um, I think we might be on to something. Anyway do you fancy a bit of shopping, proper charity shopping?' says Chris, moving on to the next thing; he's so like Leon, my ADHD student.

We head off around town. It's a perfect sunny morning.

'I like your skirt,' says Chris, touching the fabric, following the outline of the Eiffel Tower print, not in a sensual way, but more like ladies of a certain age examine seams and hems before purchasing a suit.

'My Paris skirt,' I say, proudly. 'Got it on the Portobello Market, I don't think I'll find anything like this in Norwich,' I add, 'although you never know.'

'But that is what excites me. You never really do know what you'll find.'

I smile, knowing exactly what he means.

'You're a man after my own heart,' I say. He blushes.

There's something special, decadent about being in town on a weekday, while the rest of the world works. I know it's naughty but I feel all the more important being accompanied by this man who isn't my husband.

'Reedby doesn't have many charity shops,' says Chris. I'm about to say that Reedby doesn't have any charity shops and Norwich is the nearest charity shop paradise, when I realise he's joking. Something about his face is like a game hunter, stalking his prey. Rather than reminding me of some macho hunter, images of normally well mannered ladies who push and shove me out of the way at jumble sales come to mind.

He walks quickly and I clunk along in my clogs struggling to keep up, outpaced by his very long legs. He's definitely taller than Adi. There's something automatically impressive about tall men. I could never have married someone shorter than me, it just wouldn't have been right. So am I a shortist? Will I be legislated against? Can you legislate against personal taste?

'I know what I wanted to ask you. What's all this about madder? The Madder Market and so on?'

'It's a fabric dye.'

'I do know *that* much,' I taunt Chris.

'The weaving and dyeing of cloth was the basis of Norwich's economy for more than 600 years.' I put all that in my grant proposal,' says Chris with a wink. 'I even met an elderly man at the Textile Centre who remembered his mother telling him that in Norwich the "river always ran red".'

'Red?' I say, imagining some bloody crime scene.

'Red with dye,' he says, winking at me again.

We slow down and wait for the red man at the crossing to change. 'Come on, let's run,' says Chris, grabbing my arm. We run across the road and I feel great. Chris still has hold of my arm as we go into the charity shop. I hope no one is looking, as to tell the truth it feels like being out shopping with a girl-friend.

'They're all overpriced in here,' I whisper to him. 'They have central sorters. Anything vintage goes to a special shop to be sold for a fortune, then the upmarket shops like Cambridge, then the bargain shops in places like Biggleswade, then for rags.'

'You never know, something might have escaped, got through. You know so much about this, Laura.'

It feels good to have someone interested in what I have to say. Adi would have changed the subject or wandered off to browse in music shops by now. I'm determined to find something – just a little something, after all my hard earned money going to pay off old bills.

Chris is a man on a mission; instinctively he seems to know just what he's looking for. He picks up a fake leopardskin bag.

'It just wants to be stroked,' he says.

He then puts on a blazer and a hand-knitted stripy scarf and parades around the shop. The old lady at the till smiles indulgently at him, as if he's a naughty but sweet little boy.

'Do I look like an art teacher?'

'Of the old school,' I say. 'Chris, do you wonder who wore these clothes? Why they were given away?'

'It makes new clothes seem really soulless, doesn't it, when you look at these,' says Chris, thoughtfully.

He suddenly stops by the rack of curtains and beckons me over.

Between a pair of brown Dralon and some rather grey-looking nets is gold dust. Or should I say a length of taupe cotton with little semi-circles of orange and yellow with black outlines dancing like musical notes from the 1950s.

'I'm sure it's Lucienne Day,' I whisper.

I hear the chimes of the city hall clock and feel like Cinderella leaving the ball.

'Look, I've got to go now. Have a good time,' I say curtly, immediately wishing I'd said it in a more friendly way.

'Remember to break a few rules. It's part of the creative process. Don't play safe!'

When Chris says things like that, I realise what a narrow little creative world the college is. I'd love Curtis to meet Chris, to see what he'd make of a real artist.

I wave back at Chris through the shop window. He mouths, 'Laura, do you want it?' I nod frantically, hoping he gets my answer as I run, with a real spring in my step, down the road to the car park.

Chapter 23

Herringbone is an old stitch which has many variations. In the fourteenth century the Italian painter Giotto illustrated herringbone worked with great precision on the borders of garments. Herringbone creates a regular crossed zigzag line. It is a versatile stitch that can be used to couch ribbon, cord and heavier threads or can be laced with contrasting threads.

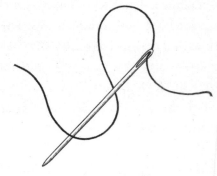

'Mummy! Mummy!' calls Lilly. 'Your fabric designs are on TV.'

'I thought you were watching *In the Night Garden*,' I shout back.

'No, we're not. You left the breakfast show on. That pretty presenter with the white trouser suit is talking about fashion.'

I feel slightly giddy at the thought of my work finally getting there. *I was wrong. I've managed to do something right!* All those years as an anonymous textile designer with an agent who only occasionally sells one of my print designs – and now my work is on television. Why didn't Gill tell me the agency's work would be on television? Maybe this is why she's being so quiet, she's been negotiating with television companies, I think.

I run into the lounge. Lilly is sitting on the sofa with Prada on her lap. For once I don't say, 'The dog's not supposed to be on the sofa', because like Lilly (and Prada!) I am transfixed by the television screen. I see the glamorous young reporter with an exaggerated look of concern as the cameras follow her around a clothing factory.

'They used to have factories like that in England,' I say. 'Did you know Norwich was an important textile centre? They even used to export things to Europe and the Far East,' I say, trying to remember all the facts and figures.

'My mum, your nan, the one you never met, once had a big industrial sewing machine at home. I wasn't allowed anywhere near it – not even in the same room. She made curtains for the big department store in the next town.'

'In Norwich?'

'No. It was quite a long way away from here. I remember Mum used to make up lots of curtains for a month or two to save up for a holiday, or a new sofa, one of her gold lamé dresses, then she'd tell the shop she was busy and not work for months. She was their best seamstress so they never complained.' Maybe Mum had it sussed? She played the job game far better than I do, I think.

'There's your rose trellis and your rainforest,' says Lilly, still staring at the television and probably not having heard a word I've said. I'm frustrated, yet I understand that as she never met my mum it's as if I'm talking about a stranger. I'm amazed that Lilly has taken so much notice of my designs.

'You did those in the old house,' she says.

'Shush!' I say, trying to hear the reporter. I wait for the light tones of the fashion reporter, but instead I hear angry words boom out from the television.

'These girls work seven days a week, twelve-hour shifts, for less than a dollar a month. It's outrageous that women in this country are prepared to exploit women from the third world. It's the twenty-first century equivalent of slavery!' she exclaims, rather excitedly. 'Just so young girls can buy throw-away clothes from these large chain stores.'

'Mummy, how could you?' shouts Lilly. 'That is so mean, making those poor girls work in that horrid locked-up factory just to sew your designs.'

'It isn't quite like that,' I try to explain. Lilly storms off.

I listen to the presenter. 'Why spend more on clothes when every penny counts in a recession? Because cheap fashion can mean that garment workers, dumb animals and the planet pay the price.'

'And how much did you pay for your trouser suit? It looks designer to me, which means it was still probably made in China. How much did the poor seamstress get paid for making *your* trouser suit. I bet *you* didn't make it!' I rant.

I drop Lilly at school and Daisy at the playgroup and arrive home feeling guilty. Maybe my textile work should be more political like Tracey Emin's? Maybe I shouldn't just be designing and making pretty things? The sun is shining and at last I can feel its warmth on my face. Images of those poor girls shut up in factories swarm around my head. I think about the cheap T-shirts Adi bought after the fire. I think about the lovely bargain hand-embroidered top I bought Daisy from one of the chain stores. I was so excited at how cheap it was.

Reedby is another world. The Green looks like a picture postcard, gardens coming to life with dayglo forget-me-nots. I should feel like I've got it all. Yet I don't.

The only thing I enjoy at the moment is my sewing and of course the girls, but that's a given. I spend half the week dreading going to teach, not because I don't like the teaching, I love all my class projects. But I'm forever on tenterhooks about saying or doing the wrong thing. Curtis is playing cat and mouse with me. He hasn't taken out a disciplinary procedure – yet. I'm sure I've broken a whole host of health and safety rules, so it's forever looming. I escape into daydreams of how my life might have been with Chris. And I avoid thinking about the fact that I don't really have a love life – my marriage is a sensible business partnership.

Sometimes it just takes so much energy to be good. Yesterday I couldn't be bothered to wash out the empty peanut butter jar. Nervously I put it in the bin, when it should have stood sparkling with the other bottles ready for the car journey to the bottle bank, because we don't have a bottle collection, or bottle bank, in Reedby. I could drive to the supermarket with the bottles and use their bottle bank, but then I'm trying to shop locally, at the farm shop, which doesn't have one.

Maybe I should opt out? I might end up like one of those bag ladies, like Glamour Tramp, as Lilly calls the fully made-up and bleached blonde woman who wheels a pram around

Norwich with all her worldly goods inside. She's not a strain on resources.

At least I don't have an enormous credit card bill. The usual reasons for buying from charity shops, that it's cheap, it's green, aren't my reasons, but it's the thrill of the hunt that I love, and I think Chris loves it too.

Part of me already knows what I want to do. Can I really turn my sewing hobby into paid work?

Chapter 24

Couching is also known as convent stitch and kloster stitch. Medieval embroiderers made full use of couching to be economical with expensive threads, such as gold thread, on the surface of the work. It is used, to this day, to attach threads which are too thick or textured to pass through the foundation fabric. The term is from the French word coucher, *which means to lie down.*

Daisy runs round and round the playground. Prada chases after her. I give up chasing both of them and stand with the other mums as the children stream out. As usual they nod, even smile at me, but nobody actually says anything.

Liz joins me. I didn't quite recognise her at first, dressed in a black suit and with her curly hair swept back in a French pleat. 'Had a good day?' she asks, wearily.

'I think so. You look smart,' I say, noting her dangerous-looking pointy shoes.

'I don't feel myself dressed like this,' says Liz, pulling on the pinstripe lapel. 'But I've just come from a meeting with the bank.'

'Did it go OK?'

'I think so. The bottom line is I need to write more articles and get them out there – sold. But everything is so competitive at the moment. Anyway, been up to anything crafty today?'

'Of course, I've been sewing frantically,' I say, proudly pointing to today's creation.

'Where did you get that necklace from?' says a very smiley big strawberry-blonde woman, touching the little fabric shapes.

'One of Laura's creations,' says Liz. 'Laura, meet Hattie.'

'You wouldn't be able to make one for me, would you? Well, for my sister actually. It's her birthday soon. And what do you get for the sister who has everything?' chortles Hattie.

'I could, but it wouldn't be the same as this one. They're all one-offs you see, not like the usual textile pieces you buy on the internet,' I say, proud of my sales patter.

'All the better,' says Hattie.

'What sort of colours does she like?'

'Just like me really,' she laughs, in a jolly hockey sticks kind of way. 'Honestly, Laura. I'm not joking. She's my twin.'

I look at Hattie, dressed in pale pinks and blue, the English rose type. I've got just the fabric in mind.

'That was a pretty good sales pitch,' whispers Liz.

'But I don't know what to charge her,' I whisper back.

Suddenly Mrs Jones, the headteacher, is right in front of me. 'Dogs aren't allowed in the playground,' she says sternly, as if I'm one of the children.

'I'm sorry. I'll tie her to the gate,' I say, thinking, She's only little – does it really matter?

Liz, Daisy and I finally catch Prada and decide it's simpler to wait just outside the gate. As usual Lilly's class is out last. And Lilly and Kate trail behind the others, too busy gossiping to notice Liz and me.

'Mum, you wouldn't believe it, we talked about your textile designs in our assembly,' says Lilly.

'What? Why?' I say.

'Reverend Matthew came to the assembly with people from Fairtrade. It's fairtrade week,' she says excitedly.

'Did you know that the children of cocoa growers in Africa never get to eat chocolate?!' shouts Kate to Liz and me.

I now feel even more guilty about stealing the girls' Easter chocolates.

'Can we stop at the shop to get some sweets?' whines Daisy.

'Probably not,' snaps Lilly. 'I doubt Phyllis sells fairtrade chocolate.'

'Actually, there's one well-known chocolate bar which is fairtrade *and* Phyllis does sell it. Come on,' says Liz, taking Kate and Jack's hands, 'I'll treat you all. You too, Lilly, Daisy. Laura,' she calls. 'Laura, you'd best wait outside the shop with Prada,' laughs Liz.

We wander down the Green munching on KitKats. 'These aren't like they used to be,' I say. 'I don't mean the chocolate, because it's fairly traded, it's the wrappers. What I mean is, I loved the foil wrapping inside the paper cover.'

'Oh, I remember rubbing my fingers over it to spell KitKat,' says Liz, with a look of longing.

We stop at the corner.

'Oh, we're like old ladies, aren't we?' I giggle.

'No. We have a sense of memorabilia,' says Liz. 'I'm going to try and write some articles on that theme. I think I might start with chocolate. You know those campaigns to bring back old favourites.'

'And you'll need to do some taste tests,' I say, in my most authoritative voice.

'Mummy, are we going home or not? You're always gossiping.' I pull a face. I wish I was always chatting. It's how it used to be after school in Ealing. We say our farewells to Liz, Kate and Jack.

'Are you sure Lilly doesn't want to play today?' asks Liz.

'Can we make it next week?' I say, failing to admit my true reasons for wanting Lilly to myself.

'Why not today, Mummy?'

'Next week,' I promise.

'I'm thirsty,' says Lilly, as soon as we're in the door.

'Me too,' chips in Daisy.

I sit the girls up at the dining room table. 'So, Lilly, what's this about you looking at my textile work in assembly?'

'Reverend John played us snippets of this documentary, it had the nice presenter,' she says. 'It's going to be on television tonight. That's why it was on the breakfast show this morning. I told everyone how they were your designs!'

'Thanks, Lilly,' I say.

'What's wrong, Mum? Why are you cross with me?'

'I'm not cross!' I snap.

When the girls have finished their drinks they run off to play and I sip my mug of Earl Grey. Reedby is too small a

234

village to make enemies, I think. It's unlikely they'll even mention my name, or Gill, my agent's, name. They'll probably talk about the company she sold them to. I'm so far down the food chain only my daughter recognises my work.

It's dark when Adi comes back from the allotment and slams the secateurs down, almost leaving a dent on the new granite worktop that I am just getting to like.

'What's it got to do with Kurt?' he exclaims.

'What? You're not making sense.'

'Kurt Weatherall is talking about you as if you're a criminal. He said, "Sorry to hear about Laura's involvement with all those poor girls in the sweatshop. I'd never have thought that she'd be involved with something like that – seeing as you've got two young girls of your own."'

'How on earth does he know? He must have us all bugged!' I'm almost seeing the funny side of it.

'Well, Heather popped her head round the hedge and said, "Kurt, you should stop listening into other people's conversations. You're not in the police any more." She said it in that dog trainer voice of hers. He did look a bit scared. I don't think he's going to tell anyone else,' laughs Adi.

'It's too late now. It's been so hard to get to know people and we'll probably be ostracised after this,' I say. It doesn't seem remotely funny any more. I burst into tears and immediately feel a complete wimp.

'You've got nothing to feel bad about,' says Adi, surprising me with a hug.

'You know Heather employs a Polish cleaner. I bet it's cash in hand.'

'So what? We had some Polish builders, if you remember?'

I feel envious and secretly wish that Mrs Lasky would clean our house too. I understand that Heather needs to concentrate on her book. You have to have a room of your own and no interruptions to be creative. You never hear about Picasso not being able to get a painting finished because he had to clean the bathroom. But what about me? I'd love to be able to concentrate on my sewing. Maybe Mrs Lasky is on the minimum wage, or less, and cash in hand; but I don't get paid anything for cleaning Marsh Cottage.

I look round into the lounge and see that the girls are happily watching *The Sound of Music* – if only real life was like the films.

This is my chance. I've got to say something. 'Adi, you know I've been doing all this sewing? Well, I'm starting to get orders. It could develop into a business.'

'Laura, be sensible, it's only pin money,' he says, flippantly.

'Was that supposed to be funny?' I say.

'Come on, Laura, I was only trying to cheer you up. You used to like my jokes,' says Adi, thoughtfully.

Before I can answer Lilly comes running up. 'Mummy! Mummy, it's Harriet's mother on the phone for you.'

'What? We don't know a Harriet,' I say.

I go into the hall and wonder if Adi's and my life is always going to be full of snatched, unfinished conversations.

'Hi, it's Laura,' I say cautiously.

'It's me!' shouts a very loud voice down the receiver. 'How's my sleeper spy?'

'Sorry, who is this? I don't understand,' I say, ready to slam the phone down to some mad saleswoman.

'It's Charlotte.'

For a moment I wonder if she's dialled the wrong number and should be talking to Kurt.

'You remember your promise to do something arty for the Fayre.' *My promise?* 'Well, the time has come to call you into action – you see the analogy – sleeper spy.'

'Ah, I get it now,' I say, tentatively.

'We're meeting at the Buddhist retreat tomorrow night, 7 p.m. prompt.'

'I'll be there,' I say, unable to stop myself wondering if Chris will be there too.

While I'm still holding the phone I then ring Liz.

'It's Laura.'

'Hiya, are you all right?'

'Not really,' I snivel. 'Everyone seems to be talking about my designs being on telly and how they're made up in sweatshops.'

'What? What are you on about?'

'Some of my designs ended up getting made in a sweatshop in the Far East,' I ramble. 'And there's going to be a programme about it on television tonight.'

'I'm afraid I won't be able to watch it. Well, it's more Mark, you see, he's got this thing about not watching television. It's a bit odd really,' she whispers, 'considering he's a journalist.'

'I've explained this all in a muddle. I don't want you or anyone to watch it. It's just I think everyone is going to disapprove of me. And Lilly told the children . . .'

'Laura, calm down. Anyway, you must have known that your designs were made up in factories in the Far East. Most of us have got clothes made there. If other people are anything like me you buy a couple of "good" things: organic cotton knickers, a bamboo dress, and then you just can't resist the T-shirt for a pound when you take a shortcut through one of these bargain shops.'

'You're right, Liz,' I say, feeling relieved.

'These people aren't looking at the bigger picture. I've also heard that it's not necessarily the cheaper clothes that are sweatshop-made. Some of the expensive labels are the worst culprits.'

'Perhaps you could do an article, an exposé on that?' I say, excitedly.

'I'll put it on my long-term plan. Once I've got some good articles under my belt. Anyway, we can't think about these things day and night. Come on Laura, I've got some green beans in the fridge, flown in from Kenya. I know I shouldn't buy them but it's the only vegetable that Kate'll eat.'

'Well if Adi has anything to do with it, she'll be eating Reedby green beans by the summer,' I say, laughing. 'And guess what? I'm going to be on the fayre committee.'

'Good luck, Laura. You'll need it,' says Liz. What does she mean by that? 'I've got to go now, Kate and Jack sound like they're killing each other in the lounge. Be strong!'

'Thank you.'

I put the phone down and vow that I am going to think about things a bit differently from now on. I'm going to prioritise, just like Liz. I'll make a short-term and a long-term plan. But before that, a cup of tea and a chocolate digestive are my top priority!

Chapter 25

Loop stitch is worked from left to right. Loops in the first row are free at the top. They are caught down by a second row worked above them, and so on.

I stand at the grand Georgian door of Trishna – otherwise known as the Buddhist retreat. I'm quite excited really, I have a bona fide opportunity to go in and explore. I've always been a bit nosy about other people's houses. I used to love the television programme *Through the Keyhole*, where the panellists had to guess, 'Who would live in a house like this?' I've even accepted dinner party dates and coffee morning invites just to see what was behind closed doors. Oh my God, I sound worse than Kurt Weatherall!

I'm about to lift the knocker when the door opens.

'Come in, I'm John,' says a very fair man with a Kiwi accent.

'What a beautiful house and garden!' I exclaim. 'People must feel that they've found heaven when they come here.'

John smiles at me and I realise that of course Buddhists don't do heaven.

Soon we're sitting on cosy sofas around a beautiful, wrought-iron fireplace. Heather Weatherall is already here. She looks practical and slightly sporty in her brown velour tracksuit bottoms and white polo shirt – just like the tops the girls wear for school! She pats the ethnic cushions, a cue for me to sit next to her. John takes our drinks order.

'He's the chief Buddhist. I'm not sure if the Buddhists call him an abbot . . . or is that just for Catholics?' whispers Heather.

'I'm not sure. How's your book going?' I ask.

'Nearly there. It's been an uphill struggle. I haven't had a moment's peace since Kurt took early retirement. But then again I won't know what to do with myself when it's finished,' she laughs.

John returns with a chrome cafetière and a multicoloured spotted teapot. I help myself to a chocolate digestive and it begins to feel a bit like a mother and toddler coffee morning (albeit without the toddlers), with John as our token dad.

Then the men arrive.

'That's Roger Payne,' whispers Heather, discreetly pointing to a small sandy-haired late-middle-aged man. 'Self-made businessman,' she says, admiringly.

Roger is followed in by a jolly couple who I know live up by the church, near René. The man from the smiling couple introduces himself as Steve.

'But we all know him as Father Christmas,' says Roger, slapping him on the back.

'And this is Laura,' says John.

'Hi,' I say.

'We all heard about the fire,' says Roger, rather than saying hello.

John says, 'We were very sorry to hear about the fire. But there's always a seed of hope in the most difficult of circumstances. We just have to open our eyes to it.'

Everybody nods and mutters in agreement. The fire seems so long ago now that I don't know what to say.

'If it hadn't have been for Kurt, it could have been much worse,' says Heather. 'He really saved the day.' Everybody nods politely again. 'Perhaps he could help you boys here?' says Heather, giving me a wink.

'I'll make a note of it,' says John earnestly.

There's the roar of a car engine and then screeching brakes. A few moments later we hear: 'Sorry I'm late, luvvies!'

'Evening, Charlotte,' says the group in unison.

For a moment there is something about her which reminds me of Toad from *Wind in the Willows*. Maybe it's her love of speed, her excitement, and despite the good country clothes, she's stately rather than beautiful. 'Edward's feeling a bit rough. He looks like he's coming down with something nasty,' she says. 'Had to put him to bed.'

Chris hovers at the door.

'You're very welcome to join us,' says John. I move up on the sofa and Chris comes in and sits down between me and Heather. I watch Heather flush slightly. Why do his good looks always have this effect on women?

'Do you like the throws?' he whispers, pointing to the thin, striped voile fabric.

'They're gorgeous. Where did you get them?'

'Sanjay brought them back from India. You just don't get these rich spice greens and saffron yellows here. There's the man himself,' says Chris, pointing to the doorway.

It's Adi's guru from the pub, I think.

'Hi Sanjay,' calls John to the lithe dark man who is now peeping around the door. 'Are you joining us?'

'Busy. But I have two contributions. I can make some Indian snacks – bhajis, pakhoras.'

'Yes please,' says John.

'You're making us all hungry!' laughs Charlotte. 'You could rustle some up for the next committee meeting.'

Sanjay doesn't rise to the bait.

'And the other contribution?' asks Roger, with notepad in hand.

'I can do a yoga demonstration.'

'I'll tell Adi,' I say. I then feel uncomfortable mentioning him when Chris is sitting next to me.

We all begin chatting and the meeting goes into freefall.

'Sorry I haven't been in touch,' says Chris.

'That's OK,' I say, thinking, I wish you were in touch.

'The thing is, the Lorina sampler is making me think about how to get your voice across in art – radical textiles for the twenty-first century.'

'I've been radical,' I say, and quietly tell Chris all about the not-fairtrade incident. All the time I'm talking Chris' eyes light up. I know him, he's incubating an idea.

'Hu hum!' says Roger, in a theatrical cough. 'I think we need to draw the meeting to a close and put together our "to-do" list.'

I sneak a look at Chris' watch. How on earth have we been talking for the last hour and a half?

'Shall I make some more coffees?' offers Chris.

'I'll have another one,' I say. I then hear the others all make excuses to leave and to not have another drink. I sip my refill and don't care that I'll be caffeined out and unable to sleep.

Heather whispers, 'It was worse before Roger was Chair. At least he runs it like one of his many businesses.'

'I don't mind. It's actually great to be out in the evening in adult company,' I laugh and smile.

I'm about to go with Chris and look at the Buddha wall-hanging in the hall when Charlotte insists on offering Heather and me a lift for the half mile back up the Green. I really want to stay and chat but instead feel like I'm fourteen again at a school disco with Dad hovering in the doorway.

'I'm walking,' says Heather, leaving me no choice but to accept Charlotte's lift home. Why am I always so polite?

'I just need to ask you one more favour,' she says the moment I sit in the passenger seat. 'Will you join the Reedby Ladies' Book Club?'

'Liz Randall did mention it a while back. She didn't say anything else, so I didn't like to pester.'

'We haven't met for a while. That's why I'm calling a meeting.'

'I'd love to come, but I'm not a very fast reader,' I mutter.

'That's fine by me. I'll drop off the details,' she says, screeching to a halt outside Marsh Cottage.

The girls are fast asleep and on the kitchen table is a magazine, *Grow Your Own Organic Vegetables*, but there's no sign of Adi.

'I've been thinking how we could be self-sufficient,' he says, in a strange choked voice from the lounge.

I'm more horrified than surprised by the idea of 'the good life'. The only outdoorsy thing Adi did in Ealing was to light the barbecue and refill the garden bucket (not with manure!) with ice and beer.

My head is full of lists of things to do. Why did I agree to organise a craft fayre? Why did I offer all my cake stands plus fabric cakes for the WI cake stall? It all seemed such a good idea at the time. Now I've got to make something that people will want to buy. I've still not started Hattie's necklace and I'm going to have to read a book. Help! I must prioritise! But the wonderful thing is this: none of these things are to do with teaching.

I walk into the lounge. Where's Adi? I look at the Wedgwood green walls and know that I made the right decision. Then I spot Adi hanging backwards over the sofa.

'Adi, what are you doing?' I say, sounding like a primary school teacher.

'Sanjay said I need to loosen up my upper back.'

'You'll be able to show everyone this in the yoga demonstration.'

'What demonstration?'

Chapter 26

Outline stitch is, as its name suggests, mainly used for outlining shapes and it is an extremely versatile stitch. It can be worked in single or multiple rows and follows complex linear details and curves well. It was used during the Middle Ages and is one of the stitches found on the Bayeux Tapestry.

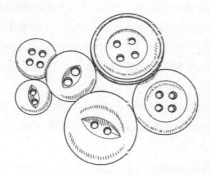

It's Adi's yoga night and technically my free night (once the girls are in bed). Although he's also been spending an increasing number of the light spring evenings nipping off to the allotment. Why doesn't he want to be at home with us? And is he really at the allotment? I begin to wonder. And what do I do with my free nights in? I don't buy a bottle of wine, rent a DVD and invite girlfriends round; nor do I buy myself a Flake and a glossy magazine.

I sit in bed and sew; and I am happy! I'm more lost in my sewing than any blockbuster movie. All I need now is an audio version of *The Importance of Being Earnest* and I can get to the end of the book club book. What's more, at the end of the evening I've got something to show for my time. Perhaps when I'm a bit more proficient I'll sew and watch a film too. Will I become as good at multi-tasking as my mother-in-law? She seems to be able to knit at great speed and still follow every detail of the latest soaps without dropping a stitch.

I'm still surprised how happy my golden yellow bedroom makes me. Apparently yellow stimulates your creative thoughts. I think of Van Gogh's sunflowers as I sit in bed making my own fabric flowers in rosette chain stitch – which is the perfect choice for sunflower petals. On the back of each one I stitch different phrases: sunny days, open fields ... now I can actually do decorative knots such as bullion knots, coral stitch and scroll stitch, rather than trying to sew and my sample ending up in a tangle.

I hear the slam of the front door. 'I didn't think you'd be back so soon. Had a good workout?' I say, watching Adi hobble into the bedroom.

'I'm not early, in fact I'm late.'

'The time's just flown by.'

'You mean sewn by,' says Adi, looking at all the bits of fabric and thread around me. 'Sorry about the pun. I did have a good session. I do love that house. Maybe we should have gone for a Georgian house, it's got lovely proportions and is so light and airy.'

'We couldn't afford a Georgian house in the country.'

'I know, I know, just daydreaming. But you won't believe this. Because the class is now two hours long Shona managed to take up ten minutes, not five – I timed her, you know –

going on about her fallen arches and sore shoulder before we could start. I know Sanjay has to check for injuries as a condition of his insurance, but there are limits.'

'What have you done to your leg?'

'Just a little strain.'

'You're like the others now. You'll be able to give weekly updates on your injury and delay the class. Perhaps they should employ a yoga physio?'

'It's not funny,' snaps Adi.

'Well sewing is far less dangerous,' I say with a smirk.

'Really! Yesterday morning just as I was about to do the cat I put my hand straight down on a pin.'

'What, in here? Or in the yurt?' I ask, trying to make up for not taking Adi seriously.

'Not only has my yurt been taken over as a sewing studio, so has my bedroom. I want a yoga room,' says Adi, impersonating one of Daisy's *I wants*. 'Do you think there's some self-help group for the sewing class's husbands?'

'And yoga wives.' I can't help myself and burst out laughing. Thank goodness Adi laughs too.

'What's this? Laura reading a book?' says Adi.

'I've got to read this by Thursday. We're meeting at Charlotte's.'

'So not only has she roped you in to organising the Midsummer Fayre, you've got to read a book as well? And I'm babysitting every Thursday, presumably?' says Adi, pulling a face.

'No we don't read a book a week. At this rate I can't read a book a year. Anyway you can practise your yoga in privacy when I'm out,' I say, unable to help myself from sounding just a bit pleased with myself. 'Just joking.' He grabs me and we sneak a few minutes laughing and rollicking in bed. What's going on? Am I suddenly attractive again? Or is he feeling guilty about something?

'Ouch!' shouts Adi.

'Sorry, sorry. It's my chenille needle.' I don't add how brilliant a chenille needle is with such a sharp point, but not too wide. My knowledge of stitching is verging on the serious. It would be a hard choice now between vintage dresses and hand-stitching for my *Mastermind* specialist subject, I think.

The moment passes and I drift in and out of reading *The Importance of Being Earnest*; which wasn't what I expected to be reading in Reedby Ladies' Book Club. When I told Liz how I thought we'd be reading something new and contentious, she explained that with Charlotte in charge they always ended up reading her English course books, and *voilà*, she has ready-made discussion topics and the notes she uses for teaching her English literature classes.

I'm several pages into the book and can't remember a thing about the last couple of pages. Will I have anything intelligent to say about it? If I don't finish this, I'm going to have to stitch an opinion together from some Amazon reviews. Would Charlotte or anyone ever guess? Or would I end up getting expelled?

Chapter 27

Oyster stitch is a member of the chain stitch family and although it looks complex is not difficult to work.

I drop the girls at school and playgroup. I'm not supposed to call it playgroup. According to Linda, who's in charge, it's a 'pre-school' – with learning outcomes and records for each child. I don't see the point. Especially when students come to college and are unable to 'play' and develop creative ideas and solutions. If I were running things . . .

I arrive home. I'm still dwelling on a playground conversation I heard this morning. I know that I shouldn't eavesdrop, but the fact that some of the mums met for coffee and cake yesterday, and I wasn't invited, really got to me. What have I said or done to deserve this? Or is it simply that they don't like me? It's as though I'm still the new girl and being excluded. I now know how the kids feel in class when no one wants them to join in their games, or invites them back home for tea. I know I wasn't the only mum not invited. It's just so different to Ealing where I had my little support group of other mums and old friends. It's those little things that get you through the day – and through life.

I've got to focus on the positive. I've got the sewing class ladies. René is lovely and Hannelore awe-inspiring and I have an old friend, Chris. I suddenly feel foolish, like a child of Lilly's age. What have things come to when I spend my time counting up the number of friends I've got?

Feeling like a child again, my eyes well up with tears and I wish once more that I hadn't had to move house and that I was back in London. Today, life seems one step forward and two steps back. Well, it's just me and my textiles, I think. I'm feeling creative. I'm going to make something, not for Gill, or for a college mock up, but for me. Then a little voice says, Laura, you should be reading the *Importance of Being Earnest* (at least I've been invited to the book club!). You should be cleaning the house. You should be tidying up.

Yet in the great history of things, do any of these little tasks really matter? I wonder. Help! Am I beginning to think like Hannelore!

Although I want to make something I can't settle and stay in the house. I go back outside into the damp, grey spring morning. I walk. I think back to that awful lesson when I first started at Town and Country and their mean comments about my clothes. Not from anyone in the art department, but little jibes from the ever-changing temps in the admin office. I think of all the little comments about my fabric designs and sweat-shops. I really do care what other people think of me, but I know I've got to stop worrying about that. I know all of this is trivial. It's certainly too trivial to tell anyone. I find myself walking down the muddy track and towards the Buddhist retreat.

'Laura,' calls a familiar voice.

I stare down the track and recognise the figure with the neat bobbed hair. 'Morning René,' I call.

'What are you up to?' she says, now up close.

'Nothing,' I say, too quickly.

'I'm searching for motivation,' says René.

'You? Unmotivated?'

'I always have a little walk to summon up the creative spirits. Do you want to come and see my studio? Only if you've got time.'

'I'd love to.'

We change direction and head past the church and down to René's. In the grounds of the old rectory is a beautiful flint and brick building with skylights in the roof.

'This is it. It's new but made using reclaimed bricks and local flint,' says René proudly, as she unlocks the big wooden door.

We go inside. The ground floor is taken up with several looms and in the corner I spot a spinning wheel. I can't take my eyes off it.

'You can touch it! I'm not the wicked fairy, and you won't fall asleep for a hundred years,' laughs René. 'Although this,' says René, touching the loom, 'is considerably older and hopefully worth a fortune.'

'Where did you get all this equipment?'

'You remember when we were at the textile centre I complained that Mother gave away all our old family textile pieces – I'm still reeling about the shawls. But luckily these have survived,' she says, stroking the loom. 'Except of course I'm not weaving the traditional colour fabrics, known as Norwich Stuffs. I'm a contemporary maker,' says René proudly, 'a direct descendant from the weavers or Strangers from the Low Countries.'

'Is that where the name René came from?'

'Probably not, but before I married I was a Delf. We think Delf is an Anglicism of the Dutch town Delft.'

'Where all the blue and white pottery came from?'

'Exactly. Potters and weavers are in my blood. Sometimes I wish I'd kept the name, like you younger people do.'

'You could use it as your artist nom de plume,' I suggest.

'I'm too old for that.'

'What *is* that you're weaving with?' I ask, touching the hard, semi-transparent surface of the piece.

'My secret ingredient – fishing wire. Do you like it? It's a commission for a gallery in Edinburgh and at the moment I don't think I'll ever finish it.'

'I love it. Have you thought of stitching into it with more wire?'

'I'm really a weaver. The stitch class is a change of scene and to get out. But I might just build up some surfaces that way,' she says with a wink. 'But you, young lady, could stitch with wire. Here, take a reel,' says René handing me what looks like an industrial reel of wire. 'I've got a good deal with a little fishing tackle shop in Great Yarmouth,' she laughs.

'I'll have to make sure Kurt doesn't see me. He's got a thing about burglars using fishing rods to pull things out of let-terboxes.'

'There's someone with too much time on their hands. The devil makes work for idle hands,' tuts René. 'Come and have a look at the upstairs.'

We go upstairs and she shows me a single bed with a beautiful patchwork cover.

'This studio is my bolthole. Sometimes I just keep weaving all night.'

'René, I'm going to have to go now. I'm really inspired,' I confess. 'I want to go and start . . .' I say, holding the fishing wire.

'Of course you do. I really *do* understand.'

I walk back in the grey, wet mist which seems often to come to Reedby. I make a coffee, switch on the radio and begin to make Hattie's fabric pearls. I cut up an old pink chiffon scarf and tiny pieces of coarse silk from my never-to-be-worn-again 1960s cocktail dress.

There's a ring at the door. No, no, not now, go away, I think. Moments like this I wish I had a little spy-hole like we had in Ealing. I peek through the window and see the back of the thick, grey, shaggy head of hair which is Heather Weatherall's. I bob down again just before she turns to face the door. I don't think she's seen me. So I lay down under the window and hide in the drapes. My midnight blue and black velvet skirt merges really well with the navy curtains.

I feel like the girls playing hide and seek and begin to think, What's she doing? She's probably got a place for Prada on her dog training course. If I let her in I'm never going to finish my sewing. So I lie on the floor wrapped in the drapes of our sitting room curtains. I smell and then see that mould is growing on the curtain linings. I can't believe it! I made them specially out of a 1950s sheet and they match perfectly with my Wedgwood green walls.

I'm a bad housewife. Maybe, like Heather Weatherall, I should employ Mrs Lasky who could be a proper housewife instead of me. Does she clean curtains? Do other women try to gain time to work by hiding between mouldy curtains? I wonder.

There's more banging on the door. Prada starts to bark and now she's peeping through the window.

'Laura, Laura!' she shouts. 'Are you all right? Can you hear me? Look, I'm going to call an ambulance. Don't move!'

What am I going to do? I'll have to get up.

I go to the door. 'I think I must have fainted,' I lie. 'A spot of low blood pressure,' I find myself saying, rather convincingly.

Heather looks at me suspiciously. There's no fooling a dog trainer!

Prada immediately runs to Heather and looks up at her as if she's some goddess of the canine world. I'm sure Prada prefers Heather to me. And after all I do for that dog!

'Kurt said you were just back home,' she says, giving Prada a cursory stroke. 'Have you got a minute?' Oh God, is she going to ask me why I've got so much fishing wire? Where is it? I look at my hand and see that I'm still holding the reel of wire.

Before I know it she's sitting on the sofa with a cup of tea. 'You see, it's our fortieth wedding anniversary next month and I wanted to get Kurt something special. And I've heard that you're making these special one-off designs.' She pulls out an amazingly glamorous 1960s mini-dress from her dark green nylon rucksack. 'I wore this the day I met him. Couldn't fit in it now, though.'

'So what is it you want me to do?' I ask, suddenly worried that she wants me to wear the dress for Kurt's enjoyment.

'Would you be able to make him a couple of ties from it and maybe embroider our initials on them?'

I'm really moved by this and say, 'Of course I can. Do you want me to stitch a little message, a word or a phrase into it too? That would make it even more of a one-off, extra special.'

'"Best friends." Can you write that on one of them?'

'Ah! That's lovely,' I say.

'He is my best friend. Even if he thinks that I prefer dogs.'

I finally sit down on the chaise, exhausted from talking to Heather. I look at the clock. It's mother's rush hour, as I call it. It's time to collect everyone, prepare the girls' tea, clear away tea, run baths, prepare mine and Adi's dinner, clear away, have my bath, and only then will I be able to get ready for the book club. My God! I haven't quite finished Hattie's necklace! But I've got an idea, a bit of fishing wire rather than thread will link the beads together rather nicely. This is how creativity works, always having thoughts lurking about ready for that eureka moment when they can turn into something real.

Chapter 28

***Oversewing,** or overcasting stitch, is a way to neaten a raw edge to prevent heavyweight fabrics from fraying. Relate the length of the stitch to the fabric and how badly it will fray.*

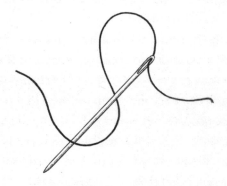

I notice my reflection in the long glass doors of River Cottage. I never thought that Charlotte lived anywhere quite this grand. How does she make her windows and doors sparkle like that? Perhaps Mrs Lasky 'does' River Cottage as well. Rather than seeing myself in a green kaftan, I see my mother look back at me. Laura, you're not only dressing exactly the same as your mother – you're the same age now as she was when she wore it. A grown up! The thought sends a shiver down my spine.

I remember Mum's fashion catchphrase: 'I don't have to think like everyone else, therefore I do not have to dress like everyone else.' She'd once read it in *Vogue* (although she wasn't the rich, sophisticated woman you'd think of as the typical *Vogue* reader). I'm sure she was once wearing this very kaftan when she said it, probably sitting at her industrial sewing machine (which terrified me as a child – it was like some rickety metal beast). It's spooky how clothes are like a smell which takes you back to another time and place, especially when you are wearing someone else's.

Mum's life revolved around fabric. People were always turning up at our bungalow with reams of material, wanting her to make them curtains and home furnishings. She earned a pittance but didn't mind the poor pay because she loved fabric – the colours and its tactile quality. And she could work from home, no big boss, so she sang life to her own tune.

My attention drifts back to the present. I'm not sure where to knock. It's so minimalist that there's no knocker or doorbell. This is the sort of architecture Adi was always into. But lately all he can talk about is traditional materials and sustainability or the allotment. I don't want to smear the glass. Throwing a stone at the window is definitely out. This is no cottage. In fact there's nothing old to be seen. I do hear laughter through the window, though. I clutch my bottle of chilled Sauvignon Blanc tightly. Have I got the wrong time and place? For a paranoid moment I think they're all playing a cruel joke on me and there's no Reedby Ladies' Book Club at all. I'm about to knock on the glass of what is possibly the front door, when: 'Have you been waiting long? Do come in!' booms Charlotte. 'We're always so pleased to have new blood for our little book club.'

I hand her the wine. 'How sweet. Did nobody tell you it's

down to the hostess to provide refreshments? Just one of our little rules,' she says in an exaggerated high pitched voice.

'I'm not very good at rules,' I mutter under my breath as I step down into the lounge. The oak floor is impressive and doesn't compare favourably with our grubby lounge carpet. I feel as if I'm on board a boat, or rather an ocean liner, as I look through the window straight onto the river Yare.

'Everybody, this is Laura Lovegrove, or should I say, Cecily. I'm Lady Bracknell,' she grins at me. 'And of course you know Hattie and Liz.'

'I thought you were Charlotte,' I say.

She ignores me and adds, 'Ladies, we now have a full cast.'

I've made some terrible mistake. Quickly I move towards Liz.

'I thought this was a book group,' I whisper. 'What's this about a cast?'

'It's a little surprise of Charlotte's, she thought we should read some extracts from *The Importance of Being Earnest*. Don't worry, it's one of Charlotte's little whims.'

'The thing is, I haven't finished it. Something important came up *and* I can't act,' I say to Liz with a grimace.

'Don't worry, we'll probably be doing a read through of it,' says Liz, nudging me. This doesn't help. I'm absolutely terrified. I hate acting.

'Cecily,' says a voice out of nowhere. 'Red, white, or I've got orange juice or cranberry. I don't normally stock cranberry, I just keep getting bouts of cystitis. I'm sure it's the damp here at River Cottage.'

Until I moved to Reedby I'd never heard so much talk of damp and people's waterworks!

'White, white wine will be lovely,' I say, almost envious of Charlotte, or should I say Lady Bracknell's, openness. She doesn't seem to care what anyone else thinks. You wouldn't catch me discussing cystitis with party guests I've never met – well at least not when I was sober!

We begin to read. Phyllis from the village shop makes for a strange Miss Prism. She's still acting really coolly towards me. Ever since Lilly told her (unbeknown to me at the time) about my sweatshop connections and the TV programme, she's stopped asking after the girls when I'm in the shop. I want to tell her that I hardly ever sell any designs and how unfortunate it was that a couple I did sell went to the Far East to be made up. But I don't, instead I sit upright and pay attention as she calls me Cecily in her broad Norfolk accent and sounds distinctly unlike a governess, my governess. Nervously, at first, I read out my lines.

'But I don't like German . . .'

'Louder, I can't hear you,' says Charlotte in her Lady Bracknell voice. I begin to think that Lady Bracknell's and Charlotte's upper-class voices are interchangeable.

'It isn't at all a becoming language. I know perfectly well that I look quite plain after my German lesson,' I read out loud. For a moment I think, Is this some kind of stitch up? All this talk of German makes me think of Hannelore, although she's teaching me stitching rather than German. Is the joke on me? If it is nobody is laughing. Maybe my part as Cecily is pure chance. Just like the way Chris Taylor turned up in Reedby.

By Act III we are all laughing and slurring. I have no trouble speaking up and Liz is a born actress, mastering her male role.

'Is the book club strictly ladies only?' I venture, thinking of Chris.

'You bet it is,' replies Charlotte.

'Hear, hear!' says Hattie.

'Wonderful! Wonderful! I think us "gals" could think about the book club branching out into amateur dramatics. The Reedby Players slips off the tongue very easily,' announces Charlotte. Liz is the only one who doesn't look completely stunned.

'Laura, not all our meetings are like this,' whispers Liz. 'You will come again, won't you?' she asks. 'And when we come to you we could meet in the yurt.'

'Of course,' I answer very loudly, unable to control the volume of my voice. I'm sure I haven't drunk that much. The wine was to steady my nerves.

'Well that's great, then,' says Charlotte. 'One person signed up for the Reedby Players.'

'What?' I say, feeling like a naughty school kid.

'Laura, you could always do the costumes, if you didn't want to act,' says Charlotte. Was my acting really that bad?

'Laura, have you got the necklace?' asks Hattie, the school mum I think of as the English rose. In fact this evening she's wearing a red rose print dress which flatters her full figure and contrasts with her strawberry blonde hair.

'I have. Well, what I've done,' I say, trying to fudge the issue that it's unfinished, 'is to do most of it, but I wasn't sure whether you wanted them on fishing wire or fabric. Also, I've started stitching little messages; words, phrases, into my work.'

'Wow! What a lovely idea. Your pieces really are bespoke one-offs. Could you write, I mean stitch, "doppelgänger"?'

'That's a bit weird,' says Phyllis.

'Not at all,' says Hattie. 'The necklace is for my twin sister. And when we were kids a great aunt called us "doppel-gängers",' says Hattie, slurring her words. 'Gosh! How much wine have I drunk?' she laughs. 'Anyway, we loved it, the odd word – toppelgänger.'

'Don't worry, I know what you're trying to say. Doppelgänger it is. I could add a tiny letter to each bead. What do you think?'

'That's a lot of extra work.'

'It's all about putting in time to get it right.'

Suddenly everyone gathers round us and is admiring my handiwork. I find myself telling them about Heather and the ties.

'What a wonderful idea,' says Charlotte. 'I know Heather is my sister, but I never thought she'd come up with such an imaginative present,' she continues, in a theatrical voice, still sounding very much like Lady Bracknell.

'Kurt's present is top secret,' I say to the group.

'Mum's the word,' says Charlotte.

We say our farewells, Charlotte kisses everybody four or five times on each cheek and promises to e-mail us with the next title.

I'm about to leave, when she says, 'Hang on a minute.' Charlotte returns flamboyantly wrapping a multicoloured scarf around her neck. 'This was our mum's special scarf. It's full of moth holes,' she says fingering it. 'I can't bear to throw it away. Do you think you could make something for Heather and Kurt?'

'But these rainbow colours would look fabulous with your red hair.'

'I know, it would match my freckles too,' snorts Charlotte. 'But I've made my mind up, I want something for their anniversary.'

'Something for both of them? That will be a challenge. I'll have to have a think.'

I walk back up the Green and finally feel that I am settling into Reedby life, and realise that I haven't laughed and had such a good time since I was in London. Although I now love being alone with my sewing, I realise just how much I still need to have a laugh with the girls.

Chapter 29

Renaissance stitch is also known as queen stitch and is a variation on Romanian stitch which creates a beautiful regular pattern. This hand embroidery stitch produces a series of diamond shapes that can be arranged in patterns or worked solidly to produce a filling.

As soon as the light comes in through my appliqué curtains I sit bolt upright and am wide awake. I really do need blackout curtains, just like the girls. My appliquéd sunflowers on muslin may look pretty, but they aren't functional.

As slowly and quietly as possible I roll over and pick up my sewing bag. Adi is sound asleep and doesn't need to get up for work for a couple of hours. I prop myself up on my pillow and notice that some of the appliquéd sunflower leaves are curling up at the edges. I ought to take the curtains down and add a few stitches, perhaps I should outline them in leaf stitch?

I must sleep in fits and starts more than I know. I do a line of yellow running stitch around a purse. Am I 'sleep-stitching'? Before I know it the purse is sewn. I really like the yellow stitches against the 1960s purple crushed velvet and pull it shut with the little drawstring.

Something clicks in my brain and I suddenly remember the drawstring plimsoll bag that Mum made me. I can still see the green and black geometric pattern. I wonder where that bag is now, my vintage 1970s plimsoll bag. It was far nicer than Lilly's ghastly red plastic PE bag. My bag was special, it had my name stitched on it. We all had bags our mums had made for us. In my opinion making bags is a far better way of meditating than yoga: not only do you clear your mind, you end up with something to show for it!

I now need a wee and am desperate for a cup of tea. I pop to the loo and as I put the kettle on, from the kitchen window I see a procession of people in white making their way down the Green. Who are they? Am I seeing things? I know I'm not fully awake. Who, other than me, would be up at 5 a.m. in the morning?

It's cool and even my long white Victorian nightie isn't enough to keep me warm at this hour. I pick up the multi-coloured crocheted shawl from Daisy's buggy and wrap it around myself and tag along onto the procession as if following the Pied Piper. What I'd give for a pair of binoculars – the men are still little pin pricks on the horizon. Everything seems quite unreal as though I'm in a picture postcard. The bluebells and tulips are the most beautiful shapes and look like a Persian rug.

I give up on joining the procession and sit down on the

bench near the village pond. I realise that I've brought my sewing bag with me, as if it's some appendage that I can't live without. I take out a couple of pieces of fabric. I never know which stitch I am going to choose, each fabric dictates the stitch I'll use; one to complement the marks and surface texture, to balance the whole composition, as if I am painting.

Hand stitching is like handwriting (even when you're not stitching words), it's personal, like writing a letter. Machine stitching is quick and impersonal like typing an e-mail. After all you wouldn't type a birthday card, would you? My little sampler is neither quilting nor embroidery, but beneath the fabric, it anchors it. Sometimes the stitch appears on the surface. It is a kind of braille – inviting the eye, if not the hand, to touch. I surprise myself, thinking such poetic thoughts so early in the morning.

Sewing is the perfect artistic occupation for those who juggle their lives. You can start and stop it anywhere. It's not like making a watercolour or a screen print, where you spend more time clearing away than painting or printing.

I get up and walk back to Marsh Cottage. I'm already halfway through making Lilly a proper PE bag. I just need to choose the colours for the last L and Y.

I walk into the kitchen and see a bombsite of breakfast cereals, milk and toast crusts sprinkled across the kitchen table.

'Where were you?' snaps Adi.

'I just went for a walk. It's a beautiful morning. Look! I even did a bit of sewing,' I say, rummaging in my bag. Why do I have to produce an alibi? I haven't done anything wrong.

'Just don't do that again,' says Adi on his way out.

Does he suspect me of something? I feel guilty, have an urge to confess. But I haven't done anything.

'I needed to be gone by now,' he says, waving his arms around. This means he's really annoyed.

'Why didn't you tell me?'

'I worry that you're not happy here,' says Adi, avoiding answering my question.

'I am. Now it's spring it's different.'

Adi kisses me on the cheek, which is very worrying as he's hardly shown me any affection for weeks. Maybe he was off for a secret early rendezvous? And that was why he was so agitated.

'Come on girls, get ready for school,' I say.

'It's May Day,' announces Lilly. 'We're going to be dancing around the Maypole today.'

I switch on the radio and make over the kitchen like some cleaning guru. If I can clean up before school and playgroup my whole day can be devoted to sewing. The newsreader's voice takes on a particularly sombre tone.

'Last night's earthquake in Mexico ... thousands are suspected dead.' I switch the radio off. Hearing about these life and death situations I now feel I was being petty getting annoyed with Adi earlier.

I drop the girls off and take my bike out of the garage. I brush off the cobwebs, fill the basket with all my sewing bits and set off for Kirby St Mary village hall. If I cycle to my class I'm going to get fit as well as being green. My 1950s plain blue skirt billows out and it looks like I'm wearing knickerbockers. I cycle past the bluebell-filled woods and hedgerows full of Queen Anne's lace. It doesn't feel real, it's too pretty, more like a set for a Merchant Ivory film. My skirt perfectly matches the cloudless blue sky.

I then remember the news report, with details of those who are suffering after the Mexican earthquake – that doesn't feel real either. I can't join all the bits of my life together. Soon my thoughts wander to the real and present fact that Norfolk isn't flat when you're on a bicycle. I stop, get off my bike and walk the last five minutes to Kirby St Mary.

I'm sweating and windswept when I walk in. I'm even later than usual, but proud of myself for cycling.

'You OK, Laura?' calls René. 'You look rather flushed.'

'Do I? I touch my face and it feels as hot as Lilly or Daisy's when they're coming down with a bug.

I sit down and take out all my bits 'n' pieces. The ladies are talking about their gardens, the beautiful weather.

Then Joyce says in a voice loud enough for all of us to hear, 'Isn't it awful about the earthquake I'll be sending a cheque off to Save the Children.'

'I might rally the WI ladies to do a cake stall up at the hall on Saturday,' suggests René. They carry on sewing and talk about planting salad and visiting the foxglove woods.

Hannelore comes over. 'You're a fast learner,' she says. 'Been practising at home?'

'Of course. I was up at the crack of dawn sewing,' I say, stitching on the final Y and completing Lilly's bag. 'Do you ever wonder how important all this is? You know in the grand scheme of things? Especially when you listen to the news.'

'The philosophy of the sewing,' says Hannelore, pulling up a chair. 'Wherever I have travelled I have found that what we wear and how we furnish our homes are two of the great preoccupations which unite us all. What unites us is important. And sometimes our preoccupations can have unexpected results. As you know, Peter has spent his life doing the most important scientific research, which has introduced us both to nomadic cultures across the world. We collected yurts as we travelled. And so a few years ago he worked with Unicef building emergency tents, because he has a scientific passion for finding solutions to problems, he has the knowledge – not because he's some good-doer.'

'Do-gooder,' I mutter, embarrassed to correct Hannelore's nearly, but not quite, perfect English.

'You can't always have a defined outcome for your life's work. It will come knocking at your door. Once I was lazing on the beach in Turkey, soaking up the sun ...' I find it very hard to imagine Hannelore sunbathing on a beach, 'while Peter was at some conference. As usual I was doing a little embroidery – and an American woman started up conversation. It soon became clear she had great problems. She seemed on the verge of a breakdown. We talked about stitching and before long she was back on the beach with some fabric, a needle and some thread. From that point on, whenever I saw her she was absorbed in her embroidery. At the end of the week, she checked out of the hotel and the manager handed me an envelope. Inside was a gold ring,' Hannelore holds up her right middle finger, displaying a thin band of white gold, 'and a note which said: You saved my life.'

And then like some fairy godmother Hannelore is up and off round the class. I feel a lump in my throat. It's strange how we never really know the effect we have on others.

'A penny for your thoughts,' says Joyce. I look at Joyce in

her Liquorice Allsorts dress (I want that fabric!) and white ankle socks and trainers, which seem to be her trademark, and smile. I love being in this room surrounded by all this creative energy.

Chapter 30

Rice stitch is also known as crossed corners and William and Mary stitch. Rice stitch produces a rather dense texture.

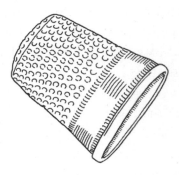

I've been so busy with my sewing projects that I haven't had time to think about, let alone do, what's usually a whole day of unpaid teaching paperwork. And I feel a whole lot better for it.

Lately, if I haven't been able to sleep or if I wake early, it's been because I'm preoccupied with a sewing idea, rather than putting finishing touches to a lesson plan. I wrote my lesson plan for this college trip on the back of an envelope. I'm excited about my subject again – that has to be a good thing – educationally, doesn't it?

Then again, I don't skimp on getting all the health and safety documents together. I can't give Curtis any excuses to fire me. The wad of papers I left on his desk made it look like we were planning to go abseiling in the Himalayas; rather than on a drawing trip to a museum in Great Yarmouth. All the students have had to sign a disclaimer that they won't go in the sea. I know Great Yarmouth is on the coast – but the museum is over a mile from the sea, far too far for a teenager to walk!

My students crowd the pavement outside the college. Where is Jim? There has to be a male and female member of staff. If he doesn't turn up soon I'm going to have to cancel the trip.

Leon is visibly excited about the trip and performs a somersault to the open-mouthed surprise of passersby. Help! I haven't included parkour, the urban acrobatics which Leon focuses so beautifully on, as part of my risk assessment.

'Stay on the pavement! Don't walk on the kerb,' I call as I block the entrance to the bus, allowing only those with their names ticked off on to the bus. I watch from the door, there's a mad rush for the back seats and lots of jumping up and down. It's hard to believe these students are sixteen rather than six. Their excited body language is entirely out of step with their earlier moans and groans of: 'Museums are boring.' 'Do we have to do any work at the museum?' 'Why are we going to Great Yarmouth? We've all been there before, anyway.'

I'm about to go up the steps when I spot Curtis waddling down the road, holding up a wad of papers. Following him is a late-middle-aged, red-haired man wearing a blue and sunshine yellow Hawaiian shirt. Jim's got his beachwear on!

'You haven't signed this page,' Curtis says, thrusting the piece of paper and a pen into my face. I obediently scrawl my signature.

'Do you need my autograph too?' asks Jim, breathlessly.

'You're just in time to catch the surf,' I say, looking Jim up and down.

Curtis turns to us both and says, 'You know this trip takes us over budget. I shouldn't really let you go at all.'

'I checked with the finance department. This group paid their trip levy in September and nobody's taken them any-where. They actually deserve more than one trip,' I say, thinking, What is it about me and Curtis? Why can't I keep my mouth shut? The normal Laura hates confrontations, but I just can't keep quiet when he's around.

'If you really want to know about the budget, I'm saving as much as possible for the end of year exhibition. It's our show-case to the rest of Norfolk.'

'Are we going to Great Yarmouth or not?' calls the bus driver.

'I'm off now,' announces Curtis, 'I was double booked for two meetings five minutes ago. Just don't pull any more stunts like this.'

'Oh, aren't you Mr Important,' whispers Jim. 'All this stuff about the show, he doesn't really care about the students. He's just waiting for the great and good of Norfolk to give him a pat on the back.'

'You're sounding a bit militant,' I laugh, as we take our seats.

Finally we're off. I'm squashed between conversations. In one ear Leon is discussing the best amusement arcades in Great Yarmouth and how they're really educational and the students ought to have some time to visit them. In the other ear, Amy tells them all that Blackpool Pleasure Beach has school visits which cover the national curriculum so we really should be going to the pleasure beach.

Talking loudly and directly in my face is Jim, recounting

his latest role in his local amateur dramatics group. He's starring in *The Importance of Being Earnest*. My book club book! I reel off a stream of comments, mostly repeating Charlotte's words, not my own. Yet I fail to impress him.

My comments pass him by and before I know it he's down at the front chatting to, or should I say distracting, our driver. There's a deafening noise and it is Jim testing the microphone. He points out all the safety features of the coach and commands the students not to leave any litter. Unaware of the laughter coming from the back of the bus he continues his address to anyone who will listen with the history of Great Yarmouth. There's no stopping him as he talks of herring fleets and holiday camps.

At least my phone will get a signal here! I switch it on and immediately there's that tell-tale ringtone of a message and the illuminated envelope. A message from Chris. I'm so excited. I know text-talk is minimal, but this really is odd. I think, reading, 'drawn threads, lashed, prick, pounce'. Before I know it, Jim is standing close enough in front of me for me to see his matching freckles. Just like a naughty student I surreptitiously switch my phone off.

The bus drives along the Golden Mile, but the beach is decidedly un-golden. It looks more like mud than gold in the light drizzle of an overcast English summer.

'Oh, I do like to be beside the seaside,' is now booming out, mainly from Jim. Thank God we've arrived!

We gather under the sail awning – the museum's prize-winning entrance. A very dishevelled woman hurries through the glass doors. 'Welcome to the museum,' she says. 'I'm Nicole, the director. Your students look really excited.'

'Um, they are,' I say. I don't say that they're excited about being out of college, not by the prospect of the museum. And that it's only me that really wants to see the Great British Art exhibition, especially after my last trip with Pammie ended so abruptly.

'OK guys,' I say. 'In a moment we're going to go into the galleries.'

'I'm afraid that the objects cannot be touched or moved – and there's no flash photography,' Nicole mouths almost apologetically.

'You'll have to draw,' I say, rather meanly.

Amy is twitching with excitement. Leon is moving from one foot to another and unable to stand still. Jim, I note, has moved near the entrance like someone queuing for the January sales.

Jim makes it into the gallery first. He fiddles with and then picks up an assortment of disparate household objects. The attendant stands up and gives me a second look. Please don't recognise me! Please don't remember the rainy Easter Monday when I brought Pammie here and she had one of her turns. Luckily Nicole swoops over to explain again that the exhibits – in this case an installation – cannot be touched or moved.

The morning flies by. The students are happy. I'm happy. Maybe because I'm not looking over my shoulder and expecting criticism by Curtis Lampard. I'm excited that I have no idea whatsoever as to the outcome of the students' work. Sometimes learning should be like making art, where you just try things out, without a tick box of outcomes. Isn't that true inventiveness?

After spending some time looking at the Tracey Emin piece my head is buzzing with ideas of how I too could stitch larger words into my textile pieces. Although I'm not quite brave enough to use her range of expletives.

I sneak off to the cafe and treat myself. This is the life! I think, eating my roast vegetable panini and drinking a latte. I don't mind that the panini doesn't resemble the tempting picture on the menu. I pick up a museum flyer, stuffed in with the menu. I glance through the list of evening lectures – how civilised, I think. I see Hannelore's name as a guest speaker, here in Great Yarmouth. She'll be signing her new book, *The Material World*. I don't remember her telling the class about it.

Some of the students wander in. I keep a low profile, they must be old enough to buy some lunch and eat it without needing me.

After lunch we gather under the awning with Nicole. Before I look at everyone's drawings I fill in the register and do a head count. Amy is missing.

'Does anyone know where Amy's gone?' I ask.

There are mutterings of: she wasn't well, tattoo parlours. Why didn't I get everyone's mobile number?

'I'll put out a tannoy announcement,' says Nicole. I agree, knowing that Amy won't be in the building, but that we have to go through these formalities.

I convince Leon to ring Amy.

I grab the phone off him. 'Can't talk now, the needle's hurting a bit,' she says, all too blatantly.

'Which tattooist are you at? You're supposed to be at the museum. Either I come and get you or I ring your mum to come and collect you,' I say, assertively. 'It's your call.'

'The Golden Dragon,' she says.

'The Golden Dragon,' I repeat.

'It's down in the rows,' explains Nicole. 'Around the corner and easy enough to find. They're just like the life-size reconstructions at the museum, but instead of housing fishermen and sail makers, they are full of tattoo parlours and discount shops.'

'Jim, you do whatever you think best with the afternoon session,' I say.

'Aye, aye, Laura,' says Jim, in a mock military salute. 'I'll hold the fort.'

I head off down the rows of narrow terraced houses, which in a strange way remind me of the kasbah in Tangiers. I wonder which house Lorina Bulwer lived in before she was sent to the Great Yarmouth workhouse. It should have a blue plaque, saying Lorina Bulwer, subversive stitcher, lived here.

The Golden Dragon looks so seedy, with ripped posters of snake, mermaid and flower tattoos pasted onto the window. I don't like the fact that I've become old and scared of anything out of my comfort zone. I missed the tattoo generation. Every other student I interview for college wants to be a tattoo artist. In my day we all wanted to be album cover designers. I brace myself and walk inside.

'It's nearly finished,' says Amy, her right bra strap pulled down so that the young man can access her shoulder.

'Is that your mum?' says the man, whose hair is so short and his body so covered in tattoos that he's almost in disguise.

'No, but I wish she was my mum,' says Amy. For a moment I feel a connection with her. The few things she's said about home, the lack of interest in anything she does, the days she's left to look after herself, make me think it's a miracle she's doing so well at college.

We wander back together and Amy and I stand for a moment outside the gallery. I can hear what sounds like singing and shouting. What on earth is going on?

'What are they doing in there?' says Amy, looking worried.

'Let's see, shall we?' We walk into what seems like a scene from *High School Musical*.

Nicole is standing at the back. She's nodding and smiling. On the make believe stage the students are acting out some story about being an art hero. They wear a bizarre mixture of dressing-up clothes: fishermen's smocks, shopkeepers' aprons, a Second World War gas mask, items normally kept for primary school visits.

'This is really good,' she whispers. 'I'd like to get Jim to do this with some other groups.'

I suddenly see Jim in a new light. It makes me think that you've got to do what you really love, otherwise your work is just going through the motions. In Jim's case it's the grease-paint that is beckoning.

'You should give him some work,' I say, really meaning it. But what I should say is: Do you have any work for me? After the news gets back to Curtis that one of the students ended up in a tattoo parlour, and now has a ship's anchor permanently etched onto her shoulder, he's bound to fire me.

Chapter 31

Rosette chain stitch *can be worked on all types of fabric. As a decorative stitch it is also known as bead edging stitch and simply Rosette stitch.*

On my doormat is a large white envelope with my name written in a black calligraphic script. For a moment I think it might be from Chris, something I partly know is a ridiculous thought – but I can't help longing for another outing with him, another face to face chat. These days, he hardly ever answers my e-mails, and if he does it's with elusive comments such as 'I'm busy with a new focus on our textile project.' He seems to have lost interest in my transcription of Lorina Bulwer's sampler.

He does send me texts, which I only ever pick up when I'm out of Reedby. When I'm working at the college I get messages that are lists and part-sentences, saying things like: 'a model, a pattern. Pinned down. Hooks. For gathering; fullness, squeezed, bound, lashed, herringbone. Part of me tries to read too hard between the words, another part hopes that no one's looking over my shoulder – is this what is meant by sex-texts? We didn't even have mobile phones when Adi and I were dating! That makes me feel very old. I always feel that these brief texts must mean something more. They're so open to interpretation.

I open the envelope half expecting to see one of Chris' words jump out at me, and instead pull out a thick glossy invitation. I read the very well designed pale grey letters, the words cleverly made out of 'fake' stitches.

'You are cordially invited to the launch of *The Material World*. Hannelore's book launch, the one I read about at the museum,' I mutter to myself. I can't remember the last time I was invited to anything in the art world. I ring her immediately.

'Hannelore Lawrence.'

'It's Laura. I'd love to come to *The Material World* launch.'

'Wonderful. Sorry it's such short notice. There was some delay with printing the invites.'

'The invite's beautiful,' I say.

'Thank you.'

I then find myself saying out loud to Hannelore, 'I don't have anything to wear for such a posh event. All my party dress scraps are now being turned into coorstops and neckties.'

'Don't worry. I'll sort something out for you.'

I ring Adi.

'I have to go to Hannelore's book launch. It's tonight. Will you be back by 6.30?' I ask.

'OK, I'll cycle back extra quickly. I know you only want me for my babysitting services,' laughs Adi. He seems really happy today. Instead of being pleased, I can't help but wonder what the reason for his cheerfulness might be.

I look in the mirror and don't think I look too bad, considering that I've just been slaving over a hot stove. I hear Adi wheeling his bike round the back across the gravel. He's just in time. I can see a car pulling up in our drive. It must be Hannelore.

I open the door. 'You're a size ten like me, aren't you?' says Hannelore, looking me up and down. Her compact figure is dressed all in black and she looks fabulous. I know I'm not that compact and have never been a size ten, although apparently all the labels changed a couple of years ago. Today's size ten used to be a size twelve, all of which is very confusing. I know I'm getting bigger but the shops say I'm getting smaller!

'I don't really know what size I am,' I say. It occurs to me that maybe one of the key advantages to buying vintage clothes is that anything pre-1960s doesn't have a size label. Up until the '60s pretty much everything was either home- or dressmaker-made. Bespoke fashion for all.

'But I got you a twelve, just in case,' says Hannelore handing me a pair of trousers wrapped in swathes of clear plastic. I am speechless. I wasn't quite expecting her to really bring me clothes. I don't know Hannelore well enough to refuse the trousers. And to make it worse Adi is standing there, grinning.

I squeeze into the khaki trousers. I take them off and check the label. I knew it – an eight! Why did she have to bring a smaller size? Is this deliberate? Or was it a genuine mistake? I know that I do have some size fourteens and sixteens in my

1970s wardrobe, but that is because the sizes were one or two sizes smaller than today. These trousers are so tight around my belly. There's no other option, I find myself lying on my back on the bedroom floor pulling up the zip. Hannelore paces about outside alternating between smoking and throwing cigarettes into our still-sizeable pile of manure.

'I'm ready,' I announce.

Adi winks at me. 'I can hardly tell the two of you apart in that outfit.'

'Mummy!' shouts Lilly. 'You've got something on your bum.' Adi slaps off fluff and other carpet debris.

'Just an excuse to grope your bottom,' he laughs. 'You'd better go, she's revving up the engine.'

'I need to tie my hair up. It looks a complete mess.' There's no time to wash it. I scrape it back and realise I've got no hair ties. They could be anywhere. What else has elastic in it? Without anyone noticing I take a pair of black knickers from the clean laundry pile and twirl them round my ponytail.

'Your hair looks nice,' says Adi.

Instead of saying thank you or goodbye, I shout back, 'They'll both need a bath tonight.' The off the peg clothes make me feel as if I'm in fancy dress I never wear brown; the colour depresses me. I hardly ever wear clothes without a print on them: florals, spots, stripes, teapots, the lot. I'm no longer Laura Lovegrove. I feel as if I should be some kind of slick businesswoman. Is that what Hannelore wants? I wonder. Except my hair isn't at all slick.

We speed along to Great Yarmouth 'I thought Peter would be with you.'

'He's a bit over the weather.'

'Under.'

'Of course it's under the weather. I've got my mind on my talk. Did you know this is the straightest road in England?' she says, changing the subject from both the talk and her husband.

'Really? I didn't know that.' The sooner we arrive the better. Being trapped in a smoke-filled car isn't my idea of a fun night out. Oh, I'm sounding so old fashioned. So middle aged. I never even noticed if someone smoked when I was at art school, but since having the girls I can't stand it. I wind down the window and immediately regret it as my fine hair begins to escape from my knickers and weave into even more of a mess than it usually is. I try to close the window and at first press the wrong button and let more of a gale in.

'You OK?' asks Hannelore.

'Just some grit in my eyes,' I lie. 'So, who will be there tonight?' I say.

'Who knows?' she replies, in a really secretive sort of voice. The kind of tone I usually save for half-telling the girls about a surprise.

'Will the other sewing ladies be there?'

'Probably not, they're only interested in making pretty trifles,' she says. A shiver goes through me. Am I only interested in making pretty trifles too? 'Of course René will be there. She's a pro. A pro like you, Laura,' she says, making my day.

We park just around the corner from the tattoo parlour. The lights are still on. I feel myself blush at the memory of collecting Amy.

'Can I see your ticket, please?' asks a nervous girl on reception duty. Hannelore just stands there. I stand there too, wondering if I should say something.

'It's because of health and safety,' says the girl, breaking the silence, 'we can only have a hundred people, I have to keep a tally. We've almost got a full house,' she says, nervously. 'There are even some men here,' she adds with a blush.

'I *am* the author,' says Hannelore.

The girl goes even redder and makes a phone call. She hands us our badges. A security man arrives and we follow him up the stairs and into the auditorium. The guard keeps turning around and squinting at me, as if he recognises me from somewhere. I certainly recognise him from my outing with Pam. Everybody is already seated when we go inside. Except that is for Liz, I didn't expect to see her here. She's pacing about at the front, followed by a man in a leather jacket and carrying a supersize camera.

'What are you doing here?' I say.

'That's a nice greeting!' jokes Liz.

'Sorry, I didn't mean it like that,' I apologise. 'I just didn't expect to see you tonight.'

'I'm getting quite a bit of freelance stuff now. And you'll find Norfolk is a small world!'

'You need to sit there, Laura,' says Hannelore, pointing at a reserved seat in the front row. I am enjoying tonight already. I feel like a VIP. Do we all dress for a part? I wonder, looking down at my linen trouser suit. I don't quite feel like Laura Lovegrove. My students would think I've aged a decade, and joined the grown-up world. I'd give anything to nip to the loo and re-tie my hair. I can hardly take the knickers off and redo it in the auditorium.

I look round and spot some of the sewing ladies. René is there and so are Juneko and Joyce. They smile and wave. It looks as if Joyce has had a purple rinse especially for the occasion. At least they like me. They'll all see me in this hideous suit. I feel completely exposed and shallow for making all this fuss about my clothes, but it's very hard to relax dressed like this.

The director of the museum, Nicole, is on stage. I wave to her, feeling that I really am fitting into Norfolk life now. It was only last week that I met her.

Hannelore sighs and shifts in her seat. Nicole smiles her big, generous smile. I don't think Hannelore sees it.

'Look at her,' whispers Hannelore. 'She's not taking her job seriously; a man wouldn't get away with being dressed like that.'

I think her badly bleached hair, baggy shirt and three-quarter length army trousers kind of suit her.

Tonight I've crossed the divide into seriously grown-up clothes. *I'm too young for what I'm wearing! I'd readily swap with Nicole.* Good for her, I think, looking at Nicole. It's what she does that counts. Although part of me doesn't quite believe it. Whatever we wear says something. It can't be avoided. I remember listening to the great traveller Rory Stewart on *Desert Island Discs*. He always dressed to fit in, national dress in Afghanistan, including a rucksack which looked like a rice bag, and then a Savile Row suit for visiting Kirsty Young at the BBC. I fell in love with the voice of this man who reminded me of Mr Benn, my *Watch with Mother* hero. Each day he'd put on a different costume and stop being his plain self and became whoever he wanted. Perhaps I should see if I can get Mr Benn on video. I'm sure Daisy would love it.

There's no hiding, with whatever you wear – unless you go to a nudist colony. Now there's a thought!

'*The Material World*,' says Hannelore into the microphone.

'Each stitch we make tells our social history. It's a link in the chain, a connection through time,' Hannelore says from the stage. 'The only real history is our stories and the objects we use to tell them with.'

Hannelore looks amazing in her tight black dress and pearls. It's hard to believe that she is over sixty. Will I look this good at sixty? What is her secret of eternal youth?

'I've been asked to talk about *The Material World*. Hannelore sips on her water. 'Sewing. How is stitch important?' she says. 'Some people will say it is trivia, we should be looking at important things: the environment, education, the health service, rather than spending all this money on promoting books.'

A few people begin to nod. I wonder where this speech is going.

'Some of you may say that fashion and interiors are silly, transitory and vain. A hem line up or down. Black is in. Brown is the new black.' People chuckle to this. 'What we wear and how we furnish our homes are two of the great preoccupations that unite us all.'

I smile to myself. I think I've heard these words before. Hannelore was trying out her speech on me at the sewing class. Or better still, maybe our chat inspired her speech.

'I recently returned to my home city for the first time in forty years. A lot has changed. But some things remain. I visited Berlin's Jewish Museum. It's won as many awards as this fabulous new building has.'

Again the audience let out an uncertain laugh. 'But inside I saw an important object of our shared history: a sewing machine. It belonged to a Jewish tailor from the 1930s. He probably inherited it from his father, and his father before. That was when professions ran through families.'

For a moment I think of Chris Taylor. Is he descended from an actual tailor? It would certainly explain his interest in fashion!

'The history of fashion, of inside architecture ...'

Does she mean interior design? Perhaps Germans call it inside-architecture. I like the term! It sounds much grander and more important than interior design.

'Our social history is the people's history, a history or in the majority of cases her-story.'

There is a delayed laugh as the great and the good finally get the play on words. There's some jostling at the back of the room. Hannelore continues, 'Stories of the life of the little person are the zeitgeist.'

It takes me a moment to remember how I explain the term zeitgeist to my students. I usually call it the sign of the times.

'It's not just her-story!' shouts a familiar voice from the back row. I look round and spot Chris in his infamous paisley shirt, which, interestingly, he has now customised with stitched and appliquéd bits 'n' bobs.

'I'm stitching with knicker elastic!' he proclaims. 'You can stretch it, distort it, manipulate it. It is all very exciting. Stitching is the zeitgeist.' Is this the moment for me to confess that my hair is tied up with a pair of black knickers? Is there synchronicity between Chris and myself?

The security guard is moving towards him.

'Would you like to do some sewing?' asks Chris, politely.

'You should have a wife to do that!' proclaims the guard.

Hannelore lets out a theatrical cough. 'To have something physical that generates ideas is more interesting than just an idea that might generate something physical,' says Hannelore. 'And of course, my countryman, the philosopher Nietzsche, writes of ecstatic states, of singing and dancing, and how someone becomes a work of art in themselves, rather than just an observer. If Nietzsche had had the opportunity to sew, like this gentleman here, sewing would have been on his list.'

The audience applaud her. I look around; some people are nodding their heads, others just look baffled. I am feeling a real buzz of excitement. Norfolk, not London, seems to be where it's happening.

I'm starting to feel that sewing, including my sewing, is important. For a moment I wonder if Chris' outburst was all some elaborate publicity stunt to generate book sales and for Chris to get his name back in the press.

'Nostalgia is rife,' says Hannelore, her voice commanding our attention. We're hanging tightly onto the past. Last Christmas a big supermarket chain, which will remain nameless, sold thousands of shepherd costumes which aped the homemade look – you know, with a tea towel for the headdress.' I see Liz scribbling furiously in her notebook.

'So are these purchases a time-saving device for busy working mums? I don't think so. It's about buying a piece of their past, their childhood memories, yet circuiting it short the making process ...' Perhaps with all these complicated words Hannelore should have read this from a script? '... and rushing in for the end result. The instant fix. So, if a child's shepherd's outfit can tell us so much we should start to value our sewing projects.'

'Hear! Hear!' shouts René from the audience.

'Sewing is part of the Slow Movement.' Hannelore looks at Nicole, who gets up and walks over to join her.

'Thank you so much, Hannelore. Could I ask everybody to put their hands together for what was an enlightening talk?'

I spot Liz looking pale. I think Hannelore's touched a sore point.

I make my way along the row of seats to Liz.

'You look very official in your outfit,' says Liz, eyeing me quizzically.

'Oh, it's the new me,' I joke.

'I prefer the old one,' she says. I feel myself begin to flush.

'So do I,' I say. 'What are you going to write about this?' I say.

'By the look of Declan's photos we're going to have a good article for the local paper. I might sell it on to the nationals. You know the sort of thing, headers like: All stitched up.'

'Or, Man points the needle,' I say.

'No longer pin money. Sewing's good for puns. I'm going to have to go and write this up. Think of me sitting in the car and typing away on my laptop. I can e-mail it off straightaway. You know this is a whole new ball game, in the few years I was a stay-at-home mum technology has gone mad.'

I don't think I've got the patience to join the queue for a signed copy. But by the look of this queue Hannelore will be on the WI speaker circuit for years to come. Then I see groups of women, girls really. They're younger than me, in their

288

twenties. She really has tapped into something we all want to be part of.

Hannelore and I are the last to leave. As if making up for lost time we speed along inland towards the sunset.

'I think it went well, don't you?' I say.

'Yes, it was good. But enough of me. What about you, Laura? What will you do with your sewing?'

'I'm at a bit of a crossroads at the moment,' I find myself saying. There's something about Hannelore's smoke-filled car and the evening's event which has reminded me of being young again. It's brought to mind the bars and clubs of my art school years, which today are all sanitised and strictly non-smoking. Life has become all proper and goody-goody. The sparkle's gone.

'Why are you at a crossroads?'

'I don't want to do any more agented work. I churn out loads of pieces and if I'm lucky I might sell one of them. And then it'll be made up in a sweatshop somewhere. Some people in the village still give me funny looks after that television programme. The teaching is my bread and butter, but I really love sewing – making my own creations.'

'You teachers are under the control of the state.'

'No, it's not that bad,' I laugh. 'Nobody arrests us – not yet.' I then recount the whole Big Brother incident of us being forced to photograph each other's studios.

'Don't get me on that subject. I spent three months in an East German prison before I got to England.'

'Sorry, I didn't mean ...' I've really put my foot in it here.

'I used to teach at the Humboldt University in Berlin.

They watched you. Just like they watch teachers here now. The only difference is you fail to complain. Aren't you going to have CCTV cameras in the classrooms soon?'

I'm starting to think that Hannelore is a bit paranoid, but the scary thing is, it's true how monitored our everyday lives are.

'These school inspectors write lengthy reports which cover every detail. It's a well known and much used method. Because if you do well, you're happy to go along with the system. You and your family benefit. If you do badly you're demoralised and live in fear of the next inspection. There's no collaboration. It's all competition between different schools and colleges to get the most students and the best results, which equals more money.'

'I have to say it is a bit like that,' I find myself agreeing.

'But Laura, the really important thing is while you're caught up in all this, you've lost the bigger picture. When you reach my age you know that life is short. I never thought I'd be old.'

'You're not old!'

'You know there used to be a lecturer at the Royal College of Art, back in the '70s, he lived in a hole on Hampstead Heath.' I'm desperate to laugh, and would love Chris to listen to this. 'When he did turn up he was the best teacher ever, he had a gift for it.'

'I know what you mean. If they did get CCTV I think that would be the final straw.'

We drive past the wrought-iron sail – Reedby's village sign – and pull up at Marsh Cottage.

'Thanks for inviting me, and for the talk,' I say.

'Thank you for coming. I never like to go to these things on my own.'

I walk up the path and realise that Hannelore invited me as some sort of chaperone or partner, instead of poor old Peter. And the thing is I really don't mind. It's great to be out there in the world.

Chapter 32

Running stitch is the simplest and most basic of all stitches and can be used for straight and curved lines and outlines as well as to build up patterns and texture. It is often the foundation for more complex stitches and it is also used for hand quilting.

It's five to seven and I'm going out for the second night in a row. A book launch one night, the Summer Fayre meeting the next. What a socialite I've finally become! I pace about the kitchen and there's still no sign of Adi. Has he got a puncture? Why does he have to insist on cycling to work *every* day? I know his answer: it saves petrol, keeps him fit, outside, and absorbing copious amounts of vitamin D. My answer is: You don't have to prepare tea, sort out the girls' activities, walk the dog or wash the clothes because you're either at work, cycling or on the allotment!

The phone rings. 'Lilly, can you get it?' I call from the kitchen. 'Who is it?'

'It was Daddy. He's at Nana's. Nana's got an emergency.'

'Did he say what's happened? Has she had one of her turns? Where's Grandad?'

'I don't know.'

'Sorry Lilly, I didn't mean to interrogate you. There's only one thing for it – I'll have to take you both with me.'

'Yeah!' they shout. 'A late night!'

I can't let Charlotte down, after she's made me so welcome in the village – and offered to pay me a fortune for Kurt and Heather's anniversary present. If I could find more customers like her I wouldn't need to work at the college.

I fill up my beach bag with a selection of Daisy's books and we head off down the Green. I am really pleased with my beach bag design – old curtains with pictures of sailing boats made six super-size bags.

We arrive at the Buddhist retreat and I am full of very un-Buddhist envy for the Georgian country house; its windows are the size of our cottage's front door.

'Come in,' says Sanjay. 'How's Ad? Is he practising every day?'

'You bet he is,' I say, with a tinge of unavoidable sarcasm. We follow him into the lounge and sit down by the wrought-iron fireplace. For once, as if model children, Lilly begins to quietly read to an attentive Daisy.

'Tea or coffee?' asks John, the head Buddhist – there's something calm and informal about his Kiwi accent. 'Or juice?' he adds, smiling at the girls, who are already tucking into the plate of chocolate digestives on the coffee table.

'Girls, don't get crumbs everywhere,' I whisper, signalling to the stack of white plates.

'Shall we introduce ourselves again, as we have some new people?' suggests John. 'I'm John and I coordinate the activities here at the retreat.'

He looks at Charlotte.

'Charlotte, I'm the village dogsbody,' she chortles.

'René, I'm here on behalf of the WI,' she says, giving me a big smile.

'Steve, also general dogsbody,' he says, looking at Charlotte, 'and school Father Christmas.' The girls' ears prick up. 'The wife can't make it tonight. So just give her any of the jobs nobody wants,' he laughs.

'Roger. Roger Payne. I live up at Piglet Manor and have agreed to chair the committee. 'And apologies from Heather, she's going to be there on the day, but is opting off the committee. She said something about making the finishing touches to her book,' he adds dismissively.

Suddenly it's my turn. 'I'm Laura. Laura Lovegrove. From Marsh Cottage – on the Green,' I say. 'I'm working on ideas for a craft fayre, within the main fayre,' I add.

Roger Payne says, 'You could incorporate a school art project?' He says it in such a businesslike way that it's not really a question.

'What did you have in mind?' I venture.

'Well that's for you arty people to decide,' he says, dismissively.

'Ask a busy person if you want something done,' says Charlotte. I really want to say no. But what can I do with so many witnesses present? This means that I'll not only have to

294

make more things, I'll also have to speak to Mrs Jones, the headteacher. I really don't think I've got time to be going round all the classes at Reedby Primary delivering an art project – what about my sewing? And I'll have to display the work. I need to learn to say no – but I just don't seem to be able to.

'Will we have enough space for arts and crafts and a children's project?' asks Charlotte.

'Um,' says John, contemplatively. Say no!

'I've got it!' exclaims Charlotte. 'We could put your yurt up in the garden, here at Trishna. It would look fabulous filled with arts and crafts.'

It already looks fabulous full of my things as a studio, I think. 'I'm sure we could move it. That's the whole point of yurts,' I say, 'they're portable. Put Adi's name down for that, he'd love to help.' Roger then proceeds to ask René and Steve about delivering leaflets.

This is my opportunity to find out where Chris is. 'John, is Chris joining us tonight?' I say, quietly. 'It's only that he didn't send apologies or anything.'

'He's not formally on the committee. He likes to have his fingers in lots of pies, so to speak. He's got quite carried away with this new project of his.'

'I know, I was helping him with the transcription of an old textile piece,' I say.

John smiles politely and says, 'He's nearly finished his project.' He sighs. 'He bent my ear too about the words on that sampler. Sorry, I don't mean to sound, you know.'

'Used?' I venture.

'I spent ages talking to him about it and what he might make and then – nothing. I've hardly seen him since. Between you and me I don't think he'll stay here much longer. But he gave me this,' says John, passing me a note from his file – with my name on it!

I'm desperate to read it immediately, but decide to savour the moment. I slip the note into my bag and then, before long, I use the oldest trick in the book for escaping. 'I'm sorry everyone, but we have to go now. The girls are going to be tired for school tomorrow if we stay any later,' I say, assertively packing their books up.

'Jolly useful-sized bag,' says Roger. This is my moment to do a Roger on him, that is, to think business first and foremost.

'I'll pop one round to you, I've got an extra one or two,' I say, really pleased at my sales technique. I could be on *The Apprentice.*

Then Roger, the real businessman, says, 'I'll expect it at cost price.'

I'm such a novice businesswoman that my brain ticks along thinking, Is cost price materials plus labour, but no profit? Then that's no good. 'Roger,' I say, as forthright as possible, 'I'll give you a discount, three for the price of two.' Which I'm hoping is a better deal for me.

Roger looks at me quizzically and then says, 'It's a deal.' He shakes my hand. I feel really proud of myself and hope that I'm not blushing.

We walk back up the Green. The lights are on at home. And I hope it's Adi and not one of Kurt's much talked about burglars.

The girls rush into the living room. 'Daddy, we went to the meeting with Mummy,' says Lilly. 'We're going to do an art project at school – for the fayre.'

'Possibly,' I say.

'Definitely,' says Lilly.

'You haven't asked me about Mum and Dad,' says Adi, as though he's desperate to tell us something. I can tell by the still-startled look on his face that all is not well.

'How's Nana?' says Daisy on cue. 'She isn't dead is she? I thought we were going to have a Daddy night.'

'They've been burgled, sweetheart.'

'What?' I say.

'Burgled. The worst part is, it was all avoidable, all Mum's fault, as it turned out. She left her bag on the stair rail and, listen to this: the burglar apparently pushed a fishing rod through the letterbox and hooked the bag and her keys.'

'Well, I can tell you who did it,' I say. 'Kurt.'

'You shouldn't make fun of him,' says Adi defensively.

'He told me about fishing rod burglaries not that long ago. I thought it was his vivid imagination and he was having me on.'

'We'd all be better off if we listened to him. But there is something funny,' says Adi. 'Girls, go and get your pyjamas on.'

'What? What is it? How can you find something funny when your parents have been burgled?' I say, immediately remembering the time when Lotte, my old neighbour, and I had been out up the West End. It was the middle of a heatwave, and as we came back home on the tube she went redder and redder. She realised she'd taken her full dose of antihistamines, before we'd shared a bottle of wine. Today I'd probably call the emergency services, but that night we both collapsed in a fit of giggles to the amusement of the other passengers.

'Sometimes if you don't see the funny side there isn't much hope. They took pretty much everything portable in the lounge; television, CD player etc., except Mum's knitted dolls.'

'Adi, you're awful,' I say, now smiling as well. 'How did you get there and back, anyway? Weren't you on your bike today?'

'I borrowed a pool car from the office. Also I said you'd pop over. You're only working part-time. I can't take any time off work.'

'But you're supposed to be working four days a week. If they've got enough money for pool cars, why can't they pay you for the hours you work?'

'I'm working five days a week and being paid for four. But they're letting David and I work up some business ideas on the day I'm not officially there.'

'OK,' I say, none the wiser as to what Adi and David are cooking up between them.

I go into the bathroom with my handbag and the note. I'm half expecting another enigmatic list of sewing related words – just like in the handful of texts, which now seem to have come to a standstill. Perhaps he expected a response to: 'fingers join, prick, bound, lashed'. Maybe I should have replied.

I open the note and it says something I never expected.

Chapter 33

Satin stitch is also known as damask stitch. As one of the oldest embroidery stitches satin stitch is worked on traditional embroideries in practically every country. The traditional embroiderers of China and Japan excelled in the use of this stitch. It is formed by working straight stitches close together.

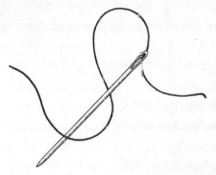

The ladies all look up briefly from their embroidery, smile and wave and look back down. I'm always the last to arrive and first to leave. Today I need to leave even earlier than normal. Their punctuality makes me look like the black sheep of the group. It is still a few minutes to ten. If anything today I am early!

'Ladies,' says Hannelore, in her authoritative girl-guide voice. 'I've brought some signed copies of my book for those of you who couldn't make it to the launch.' She looks at René and I as her fellow conspirators.

'And my favourite handsome man was there,' says Joyce,

excitedly. 'Seeing him was the highlight of the evening,' adds Joyce, with her usual lack of tact.

I decide not to tell them that Chris has given me a note asking if any of the ladies are up for an interview – about the importance of sewing in their lives. He's booked a room at the library in Norwich. I know I shouldn't be disappointed that he didn't want to talk to just me. But I am. What I do have to ask is about help with the fayre.

'Um, I have something to ask everyone. The Midsummer Fayre will be with us very soon and I've been asked to organise a craft tent. Would anyone like to submit any work?' My words fall on a stony silence. René, please say something! You are on the committee as well, and your work is sought after.

'Nobody would want to buy one of my embroideries,' says Joyce, breaking the ice.

'Of course they would! They're – they're so well made,' I say. Which is absolutely true – they just lack a bit of design finesse.

'I'm probably on the most wanted list,' says Joyce.

'The most wanted list for your embroideries?' I venture.

Joyce grins and shakes her purple hair.

'Sorry, Joyce,' I say, not sure whether Joyce has lost the plot completely. 'Tell us all.'

'I was flying out to Ireland last week, to see my niece, Róisín. And do you know what those silly men at customs did?'

'What happened?' I ask.

'They wouldn't let me on board with my sewing box. Said it could be a dangerous weapon, all those pins and needles.

Can you believe it? He made a note of all my details,' she says, still smiling.

Great, I think. I'm going to have to produce enough items for a whole stall. Then before thinking it through I say, 'Would anyone be interested in using some of my scrap fabrics to make some little bags for my necklaces?'

I show them my attempt at patchwork and explain the shape and how the template is really important.

'If you sort the design we'll make them. Shan't we gals?' commands Joyce. There is a resounding 'yes'.

'I'll do a few, but I've got my weave to finish – gallery deadlines,' grimaces René.

'Thank you,' I say.

Hannelore takes me aside at the tea break and says, 'You're not upset that they didn't want to sell any of their work, are you?'

'Well, I see an awful lot of grot being sold for a fortune,' I say, sipping strong tea out of those Wedgwood green teacups that every village hall in England seems to have.

'Ah. You see my ladies love to embroider, yet they don't want to play with ideas. They copy and they love to copy. They're not innovators. When I wove rugs with women in the desert it was the continuation of the ideas, passing designs down, almost without words and certainly with no written instructions.'

'But we all have ideas,' I say, sounding like some novice teacher.

'Sometimes we have to accept things. I've tried very hard to politicise them. I can tell you they are all excited about making these bags and purses if you supply the kit.'

'OK.'

'I've been thinking about your progress. You're a slow burner – I learnt that phrase from Peter. When you first came, I thought you'd give up after a few sessions. But now you're my star.'

I can't tell anyone how elated I feel finally getting some praise for my work. They'd think I was boasting. Contrary to what people think, as an artist you can't be fragile, you have to be so motivated and so thick-skinned to keep on making work. I spend my life praising my daughters and my students but rarely do I get any praise, even from Adi.

I don't think he'd notice any difference if I wore a sack. And, put on the spot, I don't think he would know my eye colour. I know I'm being really mean here, as Adi is colour blind. Apparently colour blindness is more common among architects than other professions. It's not surprising really, especially when you see the hideous colours some of them use, almost childish in colour: primary blue, kiddies' paint-palette green. But returning to the point, Chris would know my eye colour, and he always noticed what I wore, I find myself thinking.

'Time to get back to work, ladies,' calls Hannelore.

This is my moment to ask. 'Hannelore, I've got to leave early today, Adi's mum is in a bit of a stew.'

'A stew? I haven't heard that one before. What does it mean?'

'She's upset, not well.'

I sit in the car and think about the literally forking road before me. Do I turn left and go into Norwich and discuss sewing with Chris? Or do I turn right and drive over to Pammie's and be the good daughter-in-law?

*

Daisy comes rushing out of the playgroup. She seems to have more energy than when she went in. What do they give them for snacks? I suddenly notice that she's wearing trainers. She's wearing brand new trainers which I certainly didn't send her to playgroup in.

'I hope you're not offended,' says Linda, the playgroup leader. I saw them yesterday when I was getting my son some shoes. You'd never believe it, he came out of school with just one shoe on and he's fourteen,' she gabbles. 'She can keep them for as long as you like,' she adds. I'm too stunned to be offended and quietly leave.

'Daisy, why did Linda buy you trainers? Daddy said you had your new sandals fitted at John Lewis and I sewed those lovely sunflowers on.'

'Linda says they're too big and the flowers aren't practical as they get wet when we go out to play.' I hate trainers, you wouldn't see me dead in a pair and they make your feet sweaty. What do I do? Do I send Daisy to playgroup in trainers all through the summer and then give them back when she's finished?

I return home and it looks like the burglars have been in. There just isn't time for cleaning, washing up, tidying-up when I've got a sewing project. I feel a real pang of guilt at the word burglar, because Adi and I were so childish laughing about his parents' burglary.

I sit making the finishing touches to Kurt's neckties. In my more fanciful moments I compare myself to the pioneering Amish women, early North American settlers who made beautiful quilts in difficult conditions. Of course now everyone's talking about the credit crunch, about making do and mending. I feel virtuous, as if my new business idea is like the war effort.

Daisy rushes in from the garden and exclaims, 'They look like Elmer the Elephant.'

'They're neckties, not elephants,' I snap, thinking of the multicoloured elephant that Lilly and Daisy both loved; they used to call out the different colours to a story where nothing much happened.

'But Mummy, they're all little jewel colours, just like Elmer's patches.'

'You're right, Daisy. Quite right.' Sometimes it amazes me how an almost-four-year-old uses far more exciting descriptions than I read in my students' essays.

'You know Daisy, this sewing business takes forever,' I confide, looking at the two neckties. 'Thank God the sewing ladies are helping with the Midsummer Fayre.'

With that I decide to abandon sewing to sort and cut shapes and pack them in bags labelled René, Joyce, Wendy, all those names which denote women of a certain age. Then I add Juneko and Trishna – I'm scared to write Chris, but it's time he did something useful.

I have to admit I enjoy the selecting of the colours and shapes most. Perhaps I'm still a designer, rather than a craftsman or craftswoman, at heart.

'Daisy, we're off on our deliveries.'

I drop a bag off at Trishna. My inclination is to leave the fabrics on the doorstep and run, but behind me coming up the path is Chris.

'Where were you today? Lots of people turned up for the sewing seminar.'

'That's good,' I say, clearly without conviction.

'I put a notice up in the village post office,' says Chris. I don't remember seeing a notice. 'It just drew all the closet sewers out of the woodwork.'

'I was actually sewing – at home.' How grand, to call his interviews a seminar, typical Chris. 'But I've left some bits 'n' pieces to make up, if you're interested. It's for the village fayre, community spirit and all that.'

'So was my seminar,' says Chris, taking me by the arm. 'I thought you were really into all this textile stuff. I partly set it up for you. I thought it would give you ideas.'

I want to believe this. I do believe it. I don't believe it. I do believe him. 'Sorry,' I say. 'Daisy and I have to get going now.'

We return home with Daisy carrying a bag of goodies, a chocolate bar or two from each of the ladies. 'You look like you've been trick or treating. You'll have to share some of these with Lilly,' I say, looking at her sweetie stash.

'Mummy, who was that man at the Buddhist place? He kept looking at you in a funny way.'

'Just one of the people who works there. Buddhists look at everyone that way.'

Chapter 34

*Slanting Slav stitch can be worked in diagonal or
horizontal alignment.*

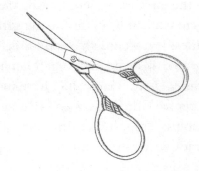

The sun is going down behind the garden. A perfect setting.
It's 10.30 p.m. I look at my stitching, a patch of psychedelic
purple and orange next to eggshell blue and red stripes, and
decide to add a little bit of emerald green in leaf stitch. It's
going to make a lovely hairband.

I feel great as I've done my good deed for the day and visited Pammie, who to my surprise seemed very upbeat about the
burglary. Although Dennis, Adi's dad, did take me aside and say
that if her knitting had gone it would have been a different story.
I stood up for Pam and explained that CD players and televi-
sions can be easily replaced. Pam's knitting is a labour of love.

As it turned out we did each other a good deed. I told her
all about the craft tent at the Midsummer Fayre and she

offered to knit a whole range of items: egg cosies, tea cosies, and pencil cases – all from unravelled jumpers. I didn't even need to ask, or persuade her. She's even going to start on a winter range of mittens and Christmas tree decorations. I just hope that Reedby will have a Christmas Fayre; otherwise I know what we'll all be getting for Christmas.

The girls are sleeping peacefully. I feel as if I'm living in a time warp and back in my own childhood. Television is definitely out once the girls are asleep. I sit and sew. The whole necklace seems to vibrate. I'm glad I didn't give these fabrics to one of the ladies. I remember Mum cooking shepherd's pie in the blue and red striped apron. I remember her wearing the purple and orange polyester tunic to collect me from infant school – this is probably one of my earliest memories – what would a psychologist make of that? I wonder. They're all special, kind of forget-me-nots. That would be a good name for my range at the Midsummer Fayre.

Where is Adi? This is a rhetorical question and one I know the answer to. He's turned into an adult and is spending all his time at the allotment – or so he says, as there hasn't been much produce to show for the amount of time he spends there. At least he's taken the chickens to the allotment. Does working on the allotment really take up that much time? I wonder. Or is he up to something else down there? Perhaps I should pay a surprise visit?

Our garden is beautiful, the perfect English country garden. But it's not quite as beautiful sitting here on my own. I've just thought up a really good name for my sewing project, and there's no one to share the news with. I could e-mail Chris. He'd have something to say about the name.

It's almost dark, Adi must be back soon, unless he's going to sleep with the chickens. Perhaps he prefers them to me? Am I really so uninteresting, so unattractive? Is there something wrong with me? I look down at my denim smock. It's practical, but oh so unexciting. In London one of my favourite things was to dress up in my vintage clothes, put on a Doris Day or Frank Sinatra CD and become another Laura. I think Adi used to like that. It always used to bring a smile to his face!

I go inside and rummage through my very limited wardrobe. There's not an awful lot left since the fire. I pull out a 1950s blue and white striped dress. I look at the waistline and decide that to fit into this I probably need a corset! I could wear an apron and slippers with it and stand at the door with a tray of Horlicks and Nice biscuits, ready for the moment Adi returns home. I move through the rails and feel the satin of my 1930s evening dress. I run my fingers along the diamanté neckline. I have to wear it. I change into the dress. The fabric feels so soft and feminine against my skin. I parade down the stairs as if I'm a Hollywood movie star from the old musicals. All I need now is one of Hannelore's fur stoles.

I saunter into the garden and I see some lights coming down the Green and hear a whirring noise. Maybe it's Adi turning his wind-up torch? How our London friends laughed when I told them about it back in February.

Before I can make up my mind as how to present myself, I feel something circling my head. 'Ouch!' It's pulling at my hair, like a dog with a bone. My apology for a bun is being tugged and pulled.

'Help!' I scream. Then I freeze. Adi runs up the road

pushing a wheelbarrow full of salad and shines the torch into my hair.

I'm shaking.

'Laura, breathe,' he shouts.

'Help!' I try to scream, yet it comes out in a pitifully quiet voice which in no way resembles how scared I am. I feel like a damsel in distress straight out of a 1930s movie.

'What is it?' I ask, gasping, still rooted to the spot.

'A bat.'

'A what?'

'There's usually several whirring around the garden as soon as the sun goes down. It's gone now.'

We stand and look around the garden in the wonderful almost luminous semi-darkness. There's still some light in the sky at the top of the Green.

'I think I should set up the allotment wives' club,' I joke, feeling guilty for my suspicions as I look at Adi's fully laden wheelbarrow.

'Look what I've got for you.' From under the rocket Adi pulls out an enormous box of strawberries and a bunch of lavender.

'My favourite!' I say, 'How did you know?'

'Of course I know. I'm your husband!' laughs Adi.

I parade around, eating the strawberries and smelling the lavender. I give Adi a great big spontaneous hug. 'I could dry this and make Norfolk lavender bags!'

'Laura, I do love you. You know that, don't you?'

I dance around the garden and Adi stands speechless.

'You know sometimes the world isn't big enough for you.' Adi smiles his beautiful grin and I follow him towards the bedroom.

'I've been making things from people's memorabilia,' I say as Adi feeds me a strawberry.

'Memorabilia or just clutter?' asks Adi.

'Memorabilia. Special things, their forget-me-nots. Mum and Grandma's old dresses. Or even a never worn again wedding dress – like my one. Then you can carry it around every day.'

Adi looks at me intently, as though I've said something in a foreign language.

'Do you really want to carry your dead relatives' old clothes around?'

'You don't get it, do you?' I snap and ruin the moment.

But sometimes we really do seem to be speaking a different language.

Chapter 35

Slipstitch is used for holding a folded edge, such as a double hem, to a flat piece of fabric.

I pull up in the drive with a boot laden with Pammie's creations. I can't believe how many pencil cases and tea cosies she's made in such a short time. She even took me up on the idea of making oddly shaped cafetière cosies – with a little hole in the top for the plunger.

Through the kitchen window I spy Hannelore. She's dashing around my kitchen without a blonde hair out of place *and* laughing and chatting with Adi. What on earth do they have to talk about?

'I told her she could make a start,' says Adi, smiling, coming out of the kitchen with a pair of secateurs. He makes his way over to the herb patch – our little kitchen garden.

'I forgot all about Hannelore coming to show me how to bake "proper" cakes for the fayre.'

'I think she's ready and waiting,' says Adi, with a lopsided grin, tilting his head in the direction of the kitchen.

I watch Adi continue to weed the raised bed. He looks different. His face is no longer pale and tired. He's bronzed and weather-beaten. He looks earthy, all real man. For a moment my stomach sinks. Don't men start to look different, get their sparkle back, when they're having an affair? Maybe he hasn't been at the allotment these past evenings after all? He's been so vague about how many days he's at work, too . . .

'Aren't you going to ask about your mum?'

'How is she?' sighs Adi.

'She's been very busy knitting,' I say, half looking through my kitchen window and seeing my kitchen being taken to task. 'Your dad says if it wasn't for the knitting he wouldn't have known what to do with her.'

I see Hannelore is wearing my yellow rubber gloves and wiping down the surfaces. She bangs on the kitchen window.

'I won't be a minute,' I mouth. I don't know what to make of her. On the one hand she seems really independent – I guess she has to be, with Peter always off on one of his trips. Apparently, before he dies (which is a bit of a morbid way to view this) he wants to complete making his survey of soil types around the world. But on the other hand, sometimes I think she's quite lonely. Apparently Peter's going to be in Quirgizstan until September, then on to northern India.

'What were you two talking about?'

Adi ignores me and makes himself very busy piling up the weeds into the wheelbarrow.

'Lovely to see you, Hannelore,' I say, opening the stable door into the kitchen.

Hannelore looks set for an operation in her white apron and gloves, her cook's tools laid out at the ready.

I like to think of myself as a woman who prefers to cook rather than clean. There's just one thing holding that statement back from being entirely true. I don't do cakes. Well that's not exactly true, I do make cakes, they're just very 'free range' – and by that I don't mean just the eggs.

There's a tap on the kitchen door. 'Ladies,' says Adi. 'Egg delivery.'

'Wonderful,' says Hannelore, closing the door on him after taking a carton of eggs.

I wave at Adi through the window; he smiles and gives me a thumbs-up sign.

'Precision, Laura. That's what you need to remember when baking,' says Hannelore. Now I'm going to bake a cake, a proper grown-up cake. Help!

'I've brought a thermometer,' she says.

'Oh, I know, it's so hot,' I say, 'a heatwave is predicted for the fayre.'

'Laura, it's to measure the temperature of the melted chocolate,' she huffs. 'You know, being careful may save your life one day.' What on earth is she talking about? This is very intense for cake making. I thought it would be a laugh getting together to make some cakes for the Midsummer Fayre, I'm not so sure now. I stuff a chocolate square in my mouth while her back's turned.

'Cooking is alchemical. It isn't until you have exactly the right measure and combination of ingredients that it will work.' I nod in agreement, thinking how it sounds rather like witchcraft. What I'm now thinking about are my cupcakes. I always use plenty of baking powder as I never measure any of the ingredients; I just throw them all in. Thank God for icing sugar! A quick dusting of icing sugar and a few rainbow hundreds and thousands always cover up any imperfections.

Hannelore goes into my fridge and takes out a cling film-wrapped ball of pastry.

'When did you make this?' I ask her, looking around the clear and clean kitchen.

'I brought it with me,' she laughs, handing me the heavy ball.

I follow her instructions and stretch pastry over the kitchen table. This is good upper arm work; an alternative to the gym. I just hope Prada hasn't sneaked up on it again. I'll never live it down if the villagers of Reedby find white hairs in their *apfelstrudel*. Or more likely drops of my sweat. It's too hot to bake! And why isn't Hannelore showing the slightest sign of being hot, yet alone perspiring?

'I don't know why people are complaining about this temperate weather. In Quirgizstan it's over forty degrees at the moment and in winter you can freeze to death,' says Hannelore holding a piping hot tin.

'Wait!' I shout at Hannelore. For a moment I think she's going to drop the *Sachertorte* on my new floor tiles. I run and put a rack on the new granite.

'What a useless design! A kitchen needs to be functional. England is full of the grandest kitchens in Europe producing little more than reheated ready meals!'

'Um,' I say. 'Yes, I think you're right.'

I seem to be relegated to washer-up in my own kitchen. I break a glass in the butler sink. It's the third thing I've broken in the last few days.

'You need stainless steel. You won't keep breaking things then,' says Hannelore while slicing the apples with a chef's precision.

It dawns on me that if I can bake a *Sachertorte* and strudel, and now that I am sewing, I will make somebody a perfect wife. Although I don't think Adi would think so – he'd also want me to bring in a wage.

'I'm hungry,' says Daisy, appearing at the kitchen door. 'I want a cake.'

How am I going to pacify her?

'These are for the fayre,' I say.

'The strudel will be some time. It'll be worth waiting for,' says Hannelore, clearly out of touch with the needs of young children – who only live in the now.

Daisy forces herself to burst into tears.

'Come and help Mummy then.' I say.

I grab the food processor, flour, sugar, butter, a couple of eggs and my little pot of baking powder. I whizz away in the utility room. In twenty minutes we have a warm tray of cakes. Life is too short to spend all day making strudel pastry when you've got a hungry child!

Hannelore takes off her apron, 'I'm done here,' she announces, revealing a fine knitted cotton jumper with lots of little misshaped buttons stitched all around the neckline. Down the front are several outsize buttons covered in patterned fabrics with more mini buttons stitched on top. 'Just cook the strudels like your apple pies.'

'Where did you get your top? It's lovely, mixing knitted with fabric and stitch.'

'David bought it at some little boutique in London. Sons do buy things for their mothers sometimes. You know he's so busy, he's taken over our barn. I'm not allowed in. He's the only person who is,' she says pointing at Adi through the kitchen window. 'It's mine and Peter's fault. His childhood was so nomadic. He missed years of proper schooling, until Peter insisted we sent him to boarding school. I felt so guilty that when he was home for the holidays I indulged him with all his little obsessions. Anyway, I must be off now, work to be done.'

I wave Hannelore off and am desperate to be alone with Pam's goody bag of knitted bits 'n' bobs. I've got lots of buttons and little scraps which are calling me.

Then what she just said suddenly clicks. What have Adi and David been up to in Hannelore's barn? When we lived in London Adi was far more predictable. Then, if given an empty barn to play around with, he'd have either installed a gym, or tried out some strange combinations of steel and glass. Now, though, with his new interests, the list is endless. A mushroom farm, a giant chicken coop, a yoga studio ... Perhaps my brain's on overdrive and they're just doing some surprise renovation for her? But why all the secrecy?

Chapter 36

Stem stitch is also known as crewel stitch, stalk stitch and South Kensington stitch. Stem stitch is often worked to outline a shape.

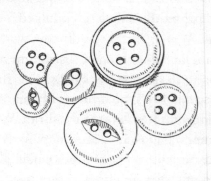

It's Saturday morning and after an almost-all-nighter customising Pammie's knitting I wake bleary eyed and with a cloudy head. I look at Adi sleeping peacefully and I'm sure that I do still love him. Am I being overly sentimental after only a couple of hours' sleep? I don't think so. I just wish he'd notice me more. I wish he wouldn't blow hot and cold towards me. I wish he wouldn't spend all his free time with David, if that really is where he's been going.

'Mummy! Daddy!' say the girls, jumping on our bed and returning me to the real world. 'It's the Midsummer Fayre,' they say in unison.

Lilly opens our curtains and says, 'Another hot day is

predicted,' impersonating her favourite weathergirl. She really is a good mimic.

Daisy ignores all of us and simply runs around the room.

'Don't go near the sewing!' I shout as they both end up in a bundle on top of my heap of goodies for the fayre.

'Laura, you need a proper studio,' says Adi. 'Perhaps I should draw up some plans?' he says with a twinkle in his eye. It's probably to stop me complaining, as I'm like the plumber's wife who is forced to live for years with a dripping tap. Perhaps that's what he's up to at Hannelore's barn? He's turning it into a studio for me.

'I need to make some money first before we can afford one,' I say, trying to conceal my suspicions. 'But we haven't done badly.' Maybe this is the time to tell him the sewing plan I've been toying with – to become a full-time maker of accessories and homeware using beautiful vintage fabrics. But before I can say anything, the girls get wilder and wilder.

'Mummy, that's your old dress,' says Daisy, looking at the purple and orange swirl that now makes up most of a handbag.

'Are they Nana's tea cosies?' asks Lilly, picking up the stripy cosy by the big fabric-covered button stitched on the top.

'They almost look "designery" rather than "Pammie",' says Adi.

'Is that a compliment for your mum or me?' I ask, wanting him to make concrete his compliments – they have never been very forthcoming!

'You didn't have to wear a blue and white striped knitted swimsuit which sagged as soon as you went into the water,' complains Adi. 'I bet that's what she's been unravelling.'

'Don't give me ideas.'

'There's the dress you wore for the housewarming,' says Lilly, pretending to eat the fruit. I look at my favourite party dress which is now a posh kitchen apron.

'You all right, Laura?' asks Adi.

'Yeah,' I say, trying desperately to hold back the tears.

'Think of it this way,' says Adi, 'You've given them a whole new life.'

I manage to sniff a 'Yes, I guess so.'

'In fact why don't you keep the tropical fruit bag? You ought to be seen wearing your creations. It's a shame I couldn't dismantle the yurt in time for the fayre,' mumbles Adi, without sounding as if he means it. It is a shame you didn't make time.

What am I going to wear? How do I look like a maker of fashion and textile accessories? There's little left in one piece from my former collection of dresses, skirts and blouses. I can't wear my 1930s evening dress in public, during the day. Then I spot one thing, it will both keep me cool and keep the sun off me. I can't resist it.

My red silk kimono is perfect, I think, I hope. I try to convince myself of this. My idea is to wear something eye-catching, memorable – it's part of my PR plan. I know that a kimono is in another league compared to simply wearing my usual vintage clothes. Although like my vintage clothes there aren't any size labels, so I'm feeling slim. I would have worn a 1950s illustrated dress, perhaps one with pineapples or teapots. But they've been turned into evening bags, belts and necklaces.

I step out onto the Green. The heatwave, as the villagers

are calling the hot weather, began only a few days ago. Yet already the Green looks positively Mediterranean as I walk down the road with a wheelbarrow filled to the brim. I imagine I'm an Italian fashion designer sauntering along the tree-lined paths of Tuscany.

'What do you need the girls and me to do?' asks Adi, calling down the Green. 'You know you need a licence to operate one of those,' he says, eyeing his wheelbarrow and completely breaking my Tuscan daydream.

'You just need to come and spend lots of money. And help Hannelore load up her cakes. And you may need to bring some extra cake stands. And, oh yes, the girls need to bring their miniature gardens,' I shout up the Green.

'What miniature gardens?' calls Adi. I then hear Lilly pipe up, 'Daddy, I know where they are. Daisy and I made them for the competition. Leave it to me.'

This morning I can see why Reedby features in the Norfolk tourist guides. It's early, the air is hot and sweet already. Under the cloudless blue sky I am walking through a picture postcard. I stop and laugh at myself, I'm wearing a kimono with flip-flops decorated with my own big fabric flowers, and I'm pushing a wheelbarrow full of accessories. How and why did I ever take my clothes so seriously? I wonder. I'm out of mourning for my vintage collection and am playing a different role: the country wife! Well, maybe Japanese-style.

Suddenly my wheelbarrow is churning up something. I look underneath it and see that bunting is now wrapped around the wheel and more of it is strewn down to the bottom of the Green. I'll never live this down. I am unable to drive a wheelbarrow, maybe I'm not so much the country wife after all!

'Laura, let me help you,' calls Chris, coming up the Green in flip-flops. He's smiling with that look which tells me I'm still all right and I haven't joined the unnoticed group of women. I remember Charlotte telling me, 'At twenty, you care what everyone thinks; at forty, you no longer care what they think; and at sixty, you realise nobody is thinking of you – and you're free at last.'

'I'm sorry, I wasn't looking where I was going. I was all distracted by the trees and plants,' I add, hoping that he will understand. Aren't Buddhists nature loving?

'Well, it's Madame Monet, isn't it,' he says, kissing me on the cheek.

I smile and frown all at once; not sure what Chris is talking about.

'You look just like her, Madame Monet, in that daring red kimono. You must have seen the painting. Don't you remember our lectures with Naomi Green, the Impressionist expert? You know Japonisme was all the rage in nineteenth-century Paris. Although some were shocked, they thought she looked like a courtesan in the shocking red.'

It's one of those situations when I know I should say something clever in response. But I can't think of anything other than the fact that it's nice to talk to someone who knows about art.

'We should have been out earlier,' he says, changing the subject. 'There was an oil tanker that couldn't get under the bunting. How often do oil tankers go down the Green?' he laughs, 'A couple of times a year? But bad timing for us.'

I look at the bunting as we carefully unwrap my barrow. 'You've used cut-up carrier bags to make it,' I say.

'They look good, don't they? See, all that art education wasn't completely wasted on me. Charlotte came round with a bag of mouldy bunting,' says Chris, in a voice of mock outrage. 'I've been thinking about being green, and Hey Presto, re-used carrier bag bunting.'

'You should patent it,' I say, slightly put out that Charlotte didn't ask me to make some bunting. But all this gives me an idea for fabric leftovers – one-off bunting. It would be completely different to the pretty, samey, bunting they sell in John Lewis. Why didn't I think of it before?

'I'd no idea that it would look this good,' says Chris.

'It must have taken ages cutting up and stitching bags into bunting.'

'Actually I only had the idea. We ran it as a little workshop on a retreat weekend. Well, John did actually.'

'I like the way bits of words and colours are all chopped up and at a distance it all looks so festive,' I say. Chris looks really proud of himself.

'We finished it off – stapling the last few bits on last night at the beach. It nearly took off, like a kite! Me and some of the guys from the retreat headed out in the old van. You should have come. We sat on the beach and watched the sun come up.' Does Chris really mean that? Is he asking me out in reverse?

'I'd have loved to come, but I was up all night working as well,' I say, proudly.

'When the boys arrive we'll get the bunting back up,' he says. 'Unless there's another oil tanker. The yurt looks good.'

'You've seen our yurt?' I say.

'Not your one, well, it is your one.'

'Chris, what are you talking about? You've lost me.'

'Your husband and his blonde friend were here the night before last. I offered to help, being a designer and all that, but your husband didn't seem to want my help erecting it,' says Chris, stroking me on the shoulder.

'I've got to go,' I say, wishing we were somewhere else less public. The whole of Reedby is probably watching us.

I turn the corner, pushing my wheelbarrow along, and see the large, looming figure of Charlotte. She's a big woman, her silhouette made even taller by her lacquered bouffant hair. She's facing Roger Payne; he's looking up at her. I can hear her clipped voice booming up the road. My God, if I was in one of her English lessons I'd be scared stiff. She'd know how to handle Curtis. The thought gives me great pleasure. But I'm not going to start thinking about college work today.

'Laura, Laura! What wonderful artwork!' she says. 'You could have a display in your wheelbarrow. It would be like a window display for the yurt. It would save on a trestle table, we never have enough tables.'

'What a good idea,' I say, ungratefully wondering why I'm the last to know that I have a yurt to display my wares in. I want to say, what yurt? Where's the yurt?

I'm soon out of the limelight, as Hannelore steps out of her shiny Polo, carrying my cake stands piled high with *strudels* and *sachertorte*.

'These are top quality cakes,' she says to our little group. We all stand mesmerised, with our mouths watering. 'I'm going to need a clean table, with a white cloth, and out of the sun.' I see some of the Buddhists rush away, ready to carry out her orders. Why can't I be more assertive?

I wheel my barrow around the back of the building and on the neatly mown lawn is a round sunshine-yellow cloth structure. There's an envelope pinned onto the canvas. I open it and unfold the piece of A4 printer paper on which is written in tell-tale capitals: LAURA'S STUDIO. There's only one person I know who doesn't do 'joined-up' writing, but prefers using capitals – maybe it's a designer thing? I want to run home and fling my arms around Adi (which would probably embarrass him); instead I do him proud and start to set up shop.

There's a real buzz in the air as everyone is getting ready. The old hands, like Heather Weatherall on the 'White Elephant', have thought ahead and are now opening Tupperware boxes of sandwiches. *Why didn't I think to bring a packed lunch?*

'No time to go home,' she says, excitedly munching on her ham sandwich. Perhaps Hannelore will let me have a cake, as of course I haven't brought any money either. I leave Heather in charge of my stall and wander over to the WI stand.

Hannelore is in full swing chatting to these ladies.

'We loved her talk at the museum,' says René. 'She's such a mine of information about fabric,' she confides and I smile and decide to leave them to it. This must be what it's like when she travels round the country to these National Trust sewing weeks, where she is the centre of attention and of course a mine of information.

I'm ready, I think, as I display the last of my necklaces on a mannequin head I stole, or should I say borrowed, from work. I like arranging the display, it brings back memories of

Saturday jobs and always being the one asked to arrange shop windows.

I see David Edwards coming up the drive with the girls. Why isn't Adi with the girls?

'Are you responsible for this?' I say, smiling and pointing to the yurt.

David nods his now very sun-bleached blonde head.

'Thank you,' I say.

'We thought you needed a little treat. And Mother needs me around with Dad off in Quirgizstan.'

'Your mum's been busy baking,' I say. 'Where's Adi by the way?'

'They wouldn't let him in with Prada. The man on the gate said, "No dogs allowed." It's not fair,' says Lilly.

'He's just walking her home,' says David.

'Mummy, I need some more money,' says Lilly. 'Kate and I are going to look round on our own. Daddy said we could.'

'Well Daddy's not actually here, is he?'

'Yes he is,' announces a breathless Adi, creeping up behind us. 'They won a five pound note in the raffle. That's enough to keep you and Kate occupied all day.'

'Is Kate here on her own? Where's Liz?'

'She dropped her off at ours. They'll be along later. Apparently Lilly and Kate arranged by themselves to come to the fair together. They're only seven, going on thirteen,' whispers Adi. I laugh.

'No more pestering for money,' I say.

'Adi, the yurt, you never said,' I say, catching his khaki eyes.

'It was a secret! Do you like it?' says Adi, expectantly.

'Of course I like it!' I fling my arms around him.

'Shall we go to the beer tent?' David asks Adi. 'If I'm not interrupting?' noting his mother making her way towards us.

'Do you mind?' asks Adi.

'Go on. Since when did you need my permission? I've got to get back to the yurt. And the girls will know where to find us.'

I stand by the yurt's louvre doors. 'I'm sold out already! Mine are the most popular cakes here!' gloats Hannelore. I suddenly notice that I've been running on adrenalin and am now starving hungry.

'I bought you my last piece of *sachertorte*. 'Be careful not to get any of the chocolate on your sewing!' she commands before moving on to another stall.

'Laura, can I buy all the evening purses?' enquires Liz.

'How many bags does a girl need?' I ask, laughing.

'I know it's ages until Christmas but I've vowed to buy things when I see them. It saves all the last minute hassle. These are great!'

'You don't need any more bags,' says Mark, trailing us and looking hot in his leather jacket.

'Is that what husbands are for?' I ask. 'To stop you buying? Your wife is supporting the economy, getting it out of a rut,' I say, trying to sound serious.

Liz raises her black eyebrows and looks knowingly at me. 'Tell me Laura, do you buy all the presents? For all the birthdays and Christmas – and then get criticised for shopping?'

'Come to think of it, yes!' I exclaim.

'Mark, why don't you take the children down to the bouncy castle?' says Liz.

'Or join Adi and David in the beer tent?' I suggest.

Finally it's just Liz and I at the stall. 'I think I will have one of these for me now!' says Liz.

'I think the purple is best, it goes with your pale skin. Not that there's anything wrong with your pale skin,' I quickly add.

'I never tan, you know. It's the Irish blood in me. Pale skin, black hair and blue eyes,' she says with a sigh.

'What about this one?' I say, teaming the indigo bag with little strips of sky blue corduroy.

'What makes these bags or purses so special is the variety of textures, not just the colours and patterns,' says Liz.

It's funny how once you're busy the crowds roll in. Until Liz's visit I'd only sold a yoga mat, bag and a belt. Now the school mums are competing for the last few purses and hand-bags.

'I can take orders,' I say. 'But remember, each bag is a one-off,' I warn them.

'Bespoke design,' chips in Liz, who I realise is serving and selling as much as I am.

'Where did you learn such good sales patter?' I ask, when the crowds die down.

'Saturday jobs in clothes stores since I was fourteen,' answers Liz.

'Me too,' I say. 'And all through the Christmas holidays when I was at college. You know part of me misses those jobs. I was on commission, you know, selling Fendi handbags and perfumes. People used to smell me a mile off when I got on the Tube!'

Chris delivers cups of tea and mini samosas. 'Sanjay baked these this morning.'

'Would you like one of these tea cosies?' I ask, holding up one of my hybrid Pammie/Laura creations.

'I'll buy a tea *and* cafetière cosy for the retreat. Can I pay you later?' says Chris, musing over the different colour schemes. 'In fact I'll take some over to René at the tea stall. I'll bet they could sell some while people queue up for tea,' he says, walking off and catching his head in one of the low lying branches.

Liz and I giggle like a couple of teenagers. 'How tall is he?' she asks.

'Must be six foot six,' I say, nonchalantly, all the time knowing that he is exactly six foot six.

'I needed that,' I say, licking my lips after polishing off a samosa. Liz looks at me thoughtfully. 'If you wanted to make a go of this, making these things for a living, I could do a little article, try and get it in some of the Sunday supplements or fashion magazines.'

'I've been thinking the very same thing,' I say, excitedly.

'Leave it with me,' says Liz, nodding her head thoughtfully.

'Time for the raffle, everyone out on the lawn,' commands Charlotte through an enormous black megaphone.

Chris comes back and says, 'I sold them all. Do I get commission? Just joking,' he adds nudging up close to me. Please don't do this! This is a public place. And Adi's here.

'When are we going to talk sewing?'

'I'd love to,' I say, brusquely. 'I'm really busy with work, the end of year show and stuff, but after that, yes. I must go and see if I've won the raffle.'

Charlotte and Roger hand out prizes like some disagreeable married couple.

'Five-three-zero,' calls Roger. There's a hush as everyone rustles in their wallets. Out of the crowd steps Hannelore. 'It's the queen of the chocolate cakes,' he shouts. She thrusts her ticket at Roger and walks away with a pink bear almost as tall as she is.

I look at Adi, his face drops as she passes the bear onto the girls. More clutter, I know that's what he's thinking.

'And last but not least, the results of the miniature garden design competition.' Roger Payne takes over and waxes lyrically, as if he's Alan Titchmarsh and hosting the Chelsea Flower Show. 'But firstly I must thank Kurt Weatherall for all his help up at the school encouraging the children to get "green fingers".' Kurt comes forward and waves. He's wearing the tie I made. I'm so proud. It really suits him.

'Can I also thank Laura Lovegrove for having the idea of a garden design competition for the children. And can I just thank you, Kurt, for single-handedly taking up the baton and getting on with it.

'Mummy, can we put Bimba in the wheelbarrow?' shouts Lilly.

'Bimba, what are you talking about?' Suddenly a great cuddly toy is thrust into my face.

Is this family life? I wonder as we take turns pushing an overgrown pink bear up the Green.

'So did you make a killing?' asks Adi.

'I sold everything, I can't believe it,' I say, thinking that it may be time to buy myself a little treat.

It's almost dark by the time we've cleared away and start to make our way back from the fayre. I hear footsteps behind us. They're getting closer. There's a tap on my back. I spin round.

'John! You gave me a fright,' I exclaim.

'I've been trying to catch you guys up. To get in first. I've been talking to the boys at the retreat. Is the yurt for sale?'

Adi and I look at each other. Is a studio of my own going to be so short-lived?

'I'll need to talk it over with Laura,' says Adi, grinning proudly.

Chapter 37

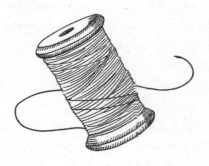

I look forward to a quiet day at college marking final project work. There's already that end of term feeling in the air. No students, no interruptions. Bliss. Slowly, but surely, I carry two cups of coffee and a packet of chocolate chip cookies wedged under my arm into a room which still smells of dust and emulsion paint, but otherwise is transformed into a white-washed gallery space. At least we've been moved out of the crummy mobile studio for the end of year show. At home the reverse has happened, I have relinquished my first ever studio of my own, and am back using the big yurt, which David says I can have until September.

It's a real treat being allowed to drink coffee and eat biscuits while working; just like Adi and all those other office workers do. I enjoy flaunting Curtis' so-called health and safety rules of the art rooms. My health and sanity depend on little things like a mid morning cup of coffee and a chocolate bar. Curtis Lampard certainly doesn't look like he goes short of a packet of biscuits or two, I think. Maybe he's got a secret sweetie stash in his office.

But there aren't any tables to put the coffees on and what's more there's no sign of Sue.

'I'm here behind the screen,' she calls, almost causing me to drop the coffees over somebody's finished work – now that would be a disciplinary offence.

I peer over and see the diminutive Sue wearing an outsize hat. 'You shouldn't be wearing his artwork,' I laugh, the coffee still wobbling in my hands.

'It's a hat!' she exclaims. She nods and the birds bob up and down like on one of those Australian bush hats with corks or whatever hanging around the rim.

'Take it off!' I command, trying not to laugh. 'I can't mark this with you wearing it.'

'Don't worry, I'm not staying long. I just need to moderate the top, bottom and middle students. You've done a good job here,' she says, her dark eyes peeping out under her fringe and eyeing Amy's winged bag and hat.

'I think this one is a borderline pass?' she grimaces, taking off the bird hat. 'Oh bless, he even bought these,' she says, eyeing some toy birds glue-gunned into his sketch book.

'It was his first fashion and textile project. I don't think he actually made much of this at all,' I say. 'But he does try. I think he just bought this hat and stuck the birds on.'

Sue puts the hat on again. 'You know ever since Jon came to college every project he's done has revolved around birds.'

'It's his first experience of mainstream education after being at a special boarding school. I like teaching autistic students.'

Sue looks at me quizzically, as if to say, why?

'I like the way autistic students can become completely focused on something. Completely in the zone.'

'These days you need to be obsessive to get anywhere in the art world,' sighs Sue.

'You like that hat, don't you?' I say, looking at Sue's incongruous outfit of a red polka dot dress, probably from H&M's children's wear, and the bird hat. 'You could offer to buy it off him at the end of year show.'

'More likely to buy this,' she says, pointing to Lizzy's vampiric underwear collection. I look at the strange combination of black lace and strips of bin liners plaited together on the college mannequin. 'Except it makes me feel old, looking at all these ideas, all this energy.'

'Tell me about it,' I say. 'All this Young Designer and Brit Art stuff makes me feel as if I've missed the boat.

'You know I would have considered wearing some sexy underwear a few years ago, but it's big knickers for me now. I don't make anything half as interesting or unusual, I spend all my time filling in paperwork and organising other people's exhibitions. Which reminds me. Are you putting any of the students' work in the show? Or your work for that matter? It's a good showcase for the college.'

'Do you mean the end of year show, or the fashion show?'

'It's all one big publicity event now. They're still trying to get some celebrity to open it. Curtis was fuming all last week that Great Yarmouth college has got Alexis Evans to open their show.'

'Who's Alexis Evans?'

'You don't know who Alexis Evans is?' says Sue in mock horror. 'She's off *EastEnders*.'

'I don't have time for soaps. I'll tell my mother-in-law. She'll want to be there. In fact, I know someone who could, perhaps, open our show.'

'Tell me more,' says Sue. 'I don't think we should have a soap star. We should get an artist or designer to open the show.'

'She's not exactly an artist or designer. But she has written loads of books on textiles and is a good speaker.'

'Is she famous? You know, mainstream?' asks Sue, hopefully.

'In her subject, yes. But she's not on television.'

'I'd love us to have someone like that. A proper old fashioned academic. But I know that Curtis wants someone who's out there in the media. Does she Tweet? Are there clips of her on YouTube? That's the sort of high profile person he wants.'

'Well, no, but what she doesn't know about textiles probably isn't worth knowing,' I say, feeling very defensive of Hannelore.

'At least the weather forecast is brilliant for Thursday. We'll be able to stage it outside,' says Sue, changing the subject. 'So what do you think? Will you be on stage?'

'Adi's working away, but I could bring the girls. In fact I can't think of anything Lilly would rather do than model some hats and handbags.'

'Could get a couple of the students to model your jewellery and things as well,' says Sue.

'Maybe Amy'd be up for modelling my fabric beaded necklaces. Let me think about it,' I say.

There's a tap on the door. 'I'm sorry I'm late,' Leon says, 'It's just my work's at a mate's house. It fell out of my bag on the bike and now it's wet. I skidded on a puddle,' he says, pulling up his trousers and showing me a long, bloody graze.

'Put your trousers down,' I say, feeling quite squeamish and realising that I'd never make it as a nurse.

'I took it to my mate's house and I'll bring it in tomorrow. Promise.'

'Have you been to the college nurse?' says Sue as she leaves. 'You ought to, really.'

'Makes a change to homework being eaten by the dog,' I say, straining to keep a straight face.

'You've got a dog, haven't you, miss?' I'm careful not to get distracted and drawn into any of Leon's rambling conversations.

'I'll tell you what, Leon. If I mark it tomorrow, will you model my neckties in the fashion show? Is that a deal?' To my surprise, Leon nods and gives me the thumbs-up sign.

'Off you go then,' I say, pinning a no entry sign onto the door and remembering that one of Leon's career ambitions is to be a stunt man.

I switch on the radio, something else Curtis has banned. Maybe he has been in a design studio and heard the fraught debates over which radio channel is going to be played. I'm showing my age now – I bet all the young designers are plugged into their iPods.

I enjoy looking through the fruits of their labours. Oh, that sounds very grand, doesn't it? But looking through their work I feel really proud. They've made fantastic progress, from Jon's bird hat to a really 'groovy' (Lizzy's word, not mine) collection of underwear, so as Curtis would say, they're great examples of 'value added'. I'll stick to progress. It's a term the students and I understand.

I'm the only person in the studio. It seems eerily empty of students as I look at all their final projects. Back in February I'd never have thought that everything would come together like this for such an exciting and diverse end of year show. I'm really proud of them.

Chapter 38

Ray stitch is also known as fan stitch because of the way the threads fan out from a single point, forming a small square stitch unit.

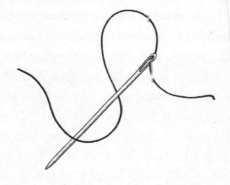

We're late for our own fashion show. If we were really models we'd be driven to the entrance in a limousine; instead, we run through the rain into the drama hall.

'Mum, why can't we have our hair done?' moans Lilly. 'You promised. You said if we modelled your things you'd get the students to do our hair and make-up – like proper models.'

'We're modelling in the show!' I proclaim to one of the security men loitering self-importantly in his dayglo jacket by the stage entrance.

'You need to go this side. Mr Lampard and the VIPs only on the other side.'

'I'm sorry, sweetie. But with Daddy away and having to

bring Prada, Mummy just ran out of time,' I tell the girls as we huddle with students, parents, friends – all of whom have been roped into modelling.

Lilly marches around in circles; her long, gangly legs look just like a mini-model's. Don't do this! To everyone else she looks like a spoilt prima donna. Where is my lovely Lilly? This really isn't how I bring up my children, honestly, I want to say.

I peep round the edge of the curtains and see Curtis take centre stage. 'Ladies and gentlemen, learners, colleagues welcome to Town and Country College's end of year show. To open this year's show, I would like to introduce you to our guest who is a leading light in the *contemporary art* world.' Curtis makes such an emphasis on the words *contemporary art*, it's as if he's still secretly writhing from not having a soap star to open his show. 'His interdisciplinary practice of art, design and writing is an inspiration to us all. Here at Town and Country we are very proud to be leading the way forward in the twenty-first century creative industries. See our Facebook page if you want to be my friend.'

'No, thank you,' mutter several of us off-stage.

'Tonight I'd like to introduce you to someone who is taking our Norfolk textile heritage in a new direction.'

'Just get on with it,' says Sue, all dressed up and ready to compère the fashion show.

'With no further ado,' as if introducing a pop star, 'may I present Chris Taylor.'

At this point the projector screen, no expenses spared and the size of a cinema screen, is filled with quotes that look as if they've been embroidered.

Curtis attempts to hand Chris, who is head and shoulders above him, the microphone. Chris stoops towards it.

'Tonight is going to be a spectacular show of inventiveness … digital media, I believe, is the way forward,' he continues.

That is so two-faced! What about the future being hand-made?

At this point there's a great round of applause and my heart sinks.

The music starts up. Jon adjusts his bird hat. Perhaps it won't look so bad from a distance, I hope. I shouldn't have allowed him to do this, I think. Jon leaps across the stage. The make-up girls have done a fantastic job. His pale face and dark eyes look positively vampiresque. And then he rips open his coat to reveal the black lacy corset and suspenders. Oh my God, he's modelling Lizzy's outfit! He's jumping so vigorously, the bird hat almost falls off onto a member of the audience. The spotlight makes him look really creepy. He reminds me of Gollum in *Lord of the Rings*. Daisy must be thinking the same. In fact she is cowering in the wings behind Lilly.

I don't really know how or why I am standing here about to walk across a stage with Lilly, Daisy and Prada. Did someone say never work with children or animals? So much for Leon's promise to model for me! I'm feeling somewhat overdressed in my 1930s diamanté dress and strappy silver high-heeled sandals. But it shows off my silver beads, made from an old Lurex jacket, very well. And I do think it's important to rise to the occasion.

The girls certainly have made an effort and are wearing more eye make-up than I'd ever dream of putting on. They are carrying matching bags – one of my favourite new discoveries: handkerchief bags. Not bags for keeping your hankies in, but ones made from vintage silk handkerchiefs. They make fabulous bag fronts. The girls are carrying ones with seaside scenes. Prada shows no sign of nerves and at the speed she leads us across the stage I'm wishing I was wearing flat shoes!

'Here we have Laura Lovegrove and her accessories collection,' says Sue, our compère. 'This is the first time they have been seen in a fashion show.' And the last, if I'm anything to do with the modelling of my creations. Amazingly, we reach the other end of the stage with no accidents. I hear the big round of applause. It must be the cute or the sympathy vote. Or maybe a combination of the two. The girls do look cute in their purple sundresses and carrying their own mini-vintage bags. Of course Prada looks cute too. It's not every day you see a poodle walk along a cat walk, or maybe it should be renamed dog walk …

It's almost over. Prada shows no signs of wanting to leave the stage. I tug on her lead and realise she isn't moving. The music for the next model begins. Sue continues with the commentary.

'Here we have our lovely Jim, or should I say Jemima, about to take flight.'

I've given up pulling on Prada, there's nothing for it. I pick her up, only to look back and suddenly see a drag queen waft across the stage in fishnets and Amy's angel wings. He's wearing very little else, other than some black underpants, and has a red hairy chest, so hairy that it could be stuck on. He is unashamedly waving to the audience and really lapping up his fifteen minutes of fame. He waves to me and I shout, 'It's

Jim!' Thinking, of course it's Jim. Who else do I know that likes dressing up as much as I do?

It's a good job he has the audience's attention as my flip-flops catch on the steps and Prada makes a leap for freedom. Thank you, Jim, I think. I'm so relieved that nobody has noticed mine and Prada's antics. I look back at Jim and have to admit with his hair – *oh, it's actually a wig!* – and the make-up very professionally done by the beauty school, he looks like a drag queen extraordinaire. Then he pulls off his wings and throws them to Curtis, to shrieks of excitement from the audience. He bounds off the stage.

I breathe a sigh of relief and hear a familiar voice, 'Laura, that was my swansong. Nicole's given me a job at the museum,' gasps Jim.

'Good one,' I say, then the selfish part of me thinks: But what about me?

As if reading my mind Jim says, 'I could put in a good word for you. I'm sure the museum needs good people to run art workshops.'

Chapter 39

Tent stitch is a small, diagonal embroidery stitch that crosses over the intersection of one horizontal and one vertical thread of needlepoint canvas, forming a slanted stitch at a 45 degree angle.

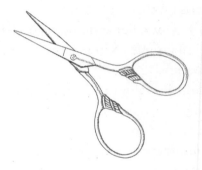

I walk into the village hall. I'm late, again. Nobody seems to notice me as I quietly make my way to what is now *my* desk. My sewing space, where I feel at home. I don't have a proper workroom at home any more, I still sew in the yurt; the conservatory is littered up with endless seed trays as if Adi is growing enough food for the whole village.

The truth is I don't dare sit anywhere else, our places in the class are truly set in stone. I feel back in the real world after my exploits at the fashion show. I'm glad Adi was away for all that. Far too much showbiz and glitz for my husband! It was bad enough the girls relaying the events to him.

Hannelore continues with her sewing notices of what's happening where and when in the world of the stitch. It reminds me of being back at school in assembly.

'I only have four tickets for the private view,' she says, reading from her list of notes. My ears prick up; I'm a real sucker for a private view.

Everyone is then talking at once and flicking through their diaries. Of course I don't have my diary. It's enough to get myself here with all my sewing things after having made packed lunches, sorted book bags, and taken Prada for her romp around the village.

I think my love of private views started when I graduated from Chelsea School of Art. It was my big end of year show and my friend Louise, who studied history, was busy ordering her cap and gown when I, the art student, was busy scouring vintage shops for just the right dress for a private view – a party, an exhibition and a chance to dress up in something far more exciting than a black cap and gown, all rolled into one. I can still remember the tight-boned bodice and how it stuck into my ribs while I chatted to the great and good, including being spotted by Gill Davison, textile agent extraordinaire (well, she was then).

'It's this Saturday 2 July. I know it's really short notice,' says Hannelore. This reminds me of her last invite. I'm glad I'm not the only person who lives at short notice.

'I'm down at the RSPB reserve for the dawn chorus, had my ticket booked for ages,' says Joyce.

'I've got my grandchildren staying that weekend,' says René. 'And there's the Safari Supper to organise. Laura, you haven't bought your tickets yet, have you?' she asks me in front of everyone.

It's a funny thing, this Safari Supper, I keep thinking of Meryl Streep in *Out of Africa* and watching herds of antelopes rush past. It doesn't seem to fit with summer in Reedby.

'Not yet,' I say. 'But can I order a family ticket?'

These ladies of a certain age have a busier social life than I have. These days I don't even care what's on in my diary.

'I'll come, Hannelore,' I shout over the top of all this discussion.

'I would like to come too,' says Juneko.

Then a thought, a naughty thought, starts to go through my mind. Chris could have the spare ticket, he'd love to come. Before I know it, I say, 'Hannelore, we could always ask Chris, who came to the study centre with us.' I look around, rather too pleadingly.

'Oh, that lovely young man. If only I wasn't down at the RSPB reserve,' says Joyce, giving me a wink. Am I that transparent? I can feel myself blushing.

'Yes, that's a possibility. He could join us,' says Hannelore, flatly.

Chapter 40

Kensington stitch is an old stitch and has been used for centuries. Its original name was opus plumarium which means plumage or feather work. That name derived from the stitch's resemblance to the plumage of a bird in its smoothly overlapping effect and its soft graduation of shades. It was revived by the Kensington School of Art Embroidery, and given the name 'Kensington stitch' by which it is now so widely known.

I can't believe how much preparation has gone into popping down to London for a few hours. It feels like I'm going on a momentous expedition to Antarctica.

I leave Adi with a list:

1. Take Lilly to gymnastics, drop off at 10 a.m. and pick up 11.30 (she'll need a drink and a snack).

2. Daisy's library books need renewing, you'll need to do that while Lilly is at gymnastics as Loddon library closes at 11 a.m.

3. When you're in Loddon can you pick up Hannelore's jacket from the dry cleaners, she's fallen out with the man there, so I took it, it's actually in my name as she thought he might damage it – one of her paranoias.

4. Daisy will need lunch by 12, if not she won't have a nap; I know she's a bit old for a nap, but you'll have an easier afternoon if she has a nap. And as we're going to the Safari Supper we don't want her being too tired.

5. Then Lilly has this school project about the Egyptians. But don't let her go on the internet on her own, unless of course you put the filter on you promised to do ages ago. I'll be back around seven, don't worry about picking us up from the station – we'll get a taxi back and join you at Charlotte's house, she's doing starters.

Laura

X

'Follow me, I've got the tickets,' commands Hannelore. The four of us walk down the platform and finally find carriage H – it's in the first class. I'm still waiting for Chris to tell me how he got the private view gig.

'Laura, I've got it,' says Chris, opening the carriage door to let me, Hannelore and Juneko on board.

'Got what?' I say, coolly. I'm still cross with him about the 'digital' speech at the college end of year show.

'I've got the Lucienne Day. Not just that piece you saw in the charity shop, but there was another one of her pieces with a leaf motif. You do remember when we went shopping?' says Chris, sitting down next to me.

'Of course I remember,' I say quietly, not sure now that I want everyone else to know about our little shopping trip. I'm beginning to think inviting Chris to London may not have been such a good idea.

'You don't mind me having the aisle seat, do you? I'm too tall for public transport.'

'Or too good, now that you're a celebrity,' I say, jokingly. 'Go ahead. I prefer the window seat.' I hug my latte and watch the train pull out of the station. It's the first time I've been on a train, or any public transport, or visited anywhere beyond Great Yarmouth since I moved to Norfolk.

The ticket collector makes his way down the aisle. 'You're in the wrong carriage,' he says. 'This is first class.'

Hannelore slowly puts on her glasses and points to the reservation on our group ticket. 'We are in the right carriage. This is carriage H.'

'H for Hannelore,' whispers Chris, as if we're naughty school kids.

'What she means is we couldn't find ...' I say, trying to smooth things over. Before I can finish, the conductor says, 'Am I talking to you? I don't want to get into an argument here.'

'But she only said ...' says Chris, coming to my defence.

This goes on for some time and Hannelore looks as if she's going to explode or more likely hit the conductor.

So much for a peaceful, grown-up day out! I watch the conductor back away.

'I think he's met his nemesis and we're staying here,' whispers Chris. 'Anyway, this is for you – Queen of the Vintage. I'm sorry it's so late.'

I peek in the bag, but manage to restrain myself and not take the whole pieces of fabric out to examine. I don't really want Hannelore to see them. In my head I'm calculating how many bags and ties I'll be able to make and what's more this time I'll be able to sell them for more than pin money.

'He's like the Prussians,' says Hannelore. 'I thought I left all that behind.'

'Who's like the Prussians?' I ask, a little unsure of my school geography as to who the Prussians were or still are. I'm enjoying these snippets of adult conversation as I half listen and half look at the big Suffolk skies rolling by.

'Constable painted these very views,' says Chris. 'I prefer it to the completely flat Norfolk landscape. In fact I think I've had enough of flat old Norfolk.'

'How can you say that? You can see for ever out on the marsh,' I reply, realising that I'm feeling very defensive of my adopted home.

'The guard. They love any opportunity to wear a uniform and a badge,' says Hannelore.

'Sorry, what?' I say.

'We were talking about Prussians, until he butted in.'

'You can't make such generalisations,' says Chris.

'Of course I can. Do you think armies would win a war without a uniform?'

Chris caves in immediately and says, 'You're probably right. Perhaps you could write a book about it.'

'Uniforms aren't just about war. You can like them for their style.' Juneko gives me a suspicious look. I try to explain myself. 'I once bought this grey/blue winter coat from an army surplus shop. I just loved the tight fit, the lapels, the shiny buttons,' I say. 'But I'm a pacifist really.'

Juneko, who has been quiet until now, is looking a little worried, and says, 'In Japan we like to be part of a group, a community. To think of others first.'

I smile and nod and then Chris whispers, 'They're like the Borg collective in Star Trek.' And says to Juneko, 'I know, we try to do our little bit at Trishna. Living as a community. Working together for the cause.' He smiles, his elusive smile.

'Like coming to open the end of year show,' I say.

'Oh yes, that. I became Curtis' friend on Facebook. He read my blog on sewing in the digital age. My photo was in the paper after Hannelore's book launch.'

'So you've become a celebrity A piece of Brit Art,' I say with equal tinges of jealousy and annoyance.

'No, you've got it all wrong. I had to create a profile, be seen. It doesn't matter any more. It was all transient in passing, as the Buddhists say.'

'How Zen,' says Juneko.

'So he didn't pay you for your guest spot?' I ask.

'Laura, how did you know?'

'I'm a woman of the world, not an apprentice monk.'

'But you don't wear a uniform like monks in the East?' quizzes Hannelore, having ignored all the college talk, or perhaps, as I sometimes suspect, not quite understanding everything. This disjointed stream of consciousness continues until we pull into Liverpool Street Station. I feel excited and charged up after our conversation. This is amplified by the buzz of the station, people coming and going and trains to different destinations.

The excitement of London soon wears off once we're packed into the Tube and going halfway round the Circle Line to South Kensington. We make our way through the subways of Cromwell Road; my red silk kimono billows in the breeze. The blasts of warm stale air give only the faintest hint that outside (in the real world) it's a beautiful summer's day.

I like the bright print against the plainness of my denim jacket. I've had a jean jacket in my wardrobe ever since I was fifteen – they go with almost anything. I don't care that I also wore the kimono for the Midsummer Fayre. I try to convince myself that nobody in the security queue is wearing anything like me. It seemed a really good idea to wear something which may well be in the Victoria and Albert's own Japanese collection: the Toshiba gallery. I'm then struck by the obvious. What does Juneko think? Does she think I'm making fun of Japanese style and her people?

'Let's get in the left-hand queue. It's going quicker,' says Hannelore.

'Your bag, madam.' I place it on the table, feeling as if I'm passing through an airport frontier rather than going to look at some work in a gallery. The men have the same muscle-bound look of night-club bouncers, the same jovial banter, except these men are in a proper military uniform of steel-blue, with lapels and shiny buttons. And just like when I travel I feel as if I am guilty.

'My old mum had a dress in a fabric like that,' chuckles one of the guards, looking at the pineapple print on my bag. I used to have a dress like that, I almost say. Now it is a handbag.

'If the likes of us dressed like that we'd be carted away to the nearest loony bin!' says one of the guards, in a stage whisper, 'They live a different life to us,' replies his mate.

'Probably see a man in a kimono in a minute,' he laughs. For a moment I feel awkward and embarrassed and wish I'd worn something less noticeable.

'They should not employ people who don't understand the collections,' says Hannelore, defensively.

We've passed the first hurdle and are ushered to the next barrier. I think this is passport control. I rummage in my handbag for my ticket. I can't believe it, it's not there! I feel like one of my disorganised students.

'Your name, madam,' says the most well turned out man I've seen in ages. I'm dumbstruck and simply smile at him.

'Laura Stark,' says Hannelore. 'She's with me.'

'And who might you be?'

'I'm Hannelore Lawrence.'

I have a sense of déjà vu and wonder if Hannelore really should be getting herself seen on television and in Sunday supplements. She's certainly got 'presence' and I could see her becoming an unexpected celebrity. She'd definitely be a formidable opponent on *Big Brother* and the surefire winner of *I'm a Celebrity, Get Me Out of Here!* The guard goes through his list, ticks our names and hands us each a badge.

'Through the shop and turn left. Have a good afternoon, ladies and gentleman,' he says, making a half bow.

I'm still having doubts about the kimono. I wipe away the droplets of sweat with my long winged sleeve.

'Ladies, shall we start with the shop?' suggests Chris. 'I won't be a minute,' I say to the others and rush downstairs to the loo. I feel a complete mess, especially compared to Hannelore, who in her oatmeal linens never seems to have a hair out of place.

I'm stunned by my own transformation when an oriental woman smiles back at me. I apply another coat of lipstick and am ready for anything. My hands are still feeling clammy after a quick rinse in the strangely beautiful, but impractical, sinks that can only be filled an inch deep. I notice the Dyson hand dryers; they look terrifying. I slot my hands between the two plastic sides, the shape has a certain urinal look to it. Oh my God, James Dyson, the design guru of Adi's much-loved vacuum cleaner – he's actually done the vacuuming since we bought a Dyson. My sleeves are billowing out like enormous balloons. I freeze and eventually the contraption switches itself off. So much for male design gurus! I pop my jacket back on. I'm pleased with my little handmade brooch – in a mini-patchwork style, it's my prototype and I couldn't resist wearing it today. I just need to get on and make a whole batch of them now. I wonder if people will look at my accessories and home-ware and call them *Lovegroves*?

I look up at the vast glass hanging. I'm mesmerised by the green tentaclelike shapes. I think it's almost too gaudy for the V&A. It looks like green roots which might grow some exotic vegetable. I suddenly remember the fruit and vegetables for the Safari Supper. I haven't put them on the 'to-do' list. I'd promised René that Adi would take her raspberries and carrots first thing. Charlotte will be having kittens about her carrot and coriander soup. And René's pavlova will just be a swirl of meringue and cream. Laura, they're all adults. They'll have to sort it out between them.

Refreshed, I feel as if I'm sailing along to the shop in my kimono. I can't see Hannelore or Juneko anywhere. Chris is completely absorbed by the display of replicas of old Eastern European design.

'We ought to go and see the real things in the gallery, don't you think? These replicas were probably made in China,' I say.

He smiles really mischievously. 'The whole world is made in China.'

I really do like Chris. I don't know why. I've forgiven him already for his appearance at college – and his vanity. He's such fun to be with and he thinks about things the same way I do. I stop and admire a beautiful scarlet crocheted cardigan.

'That would really suit you,' says Chris. 'In fact it would actually complement that kimono and make it into something new.'

'I should have made a separate zip pocket. It's a design fault I need to address in my bags,' I mumble, fishing for my purse and then having second thoughts. I can't afford, or justify, buying designer clothes.

I look up and see Hannelore signalling frantically from the other side of the shop. Obediently, stood next to her is Juneko. I sometimes wonder what Juneko thinks of us all. But I don't think she'll ever tell me – she's always so polite. Unlike Hannelore, who if asked what she thought of us would enjoy telling the truth, warts and all.

'Laura, I think we naughty children are being summonsed,' giggles Chris.

We follow Hannelore to a cordoned-off restaurant. I'm

353

desperate for a drink and a sit down. Then I realise that, like the temporary exhibition 'The Fabric of Society', the Gamble and Poynter rooms are cordoned off for us: the guests.

'I think we should steal this motto down at the Buddhist retreat,' says Chris, looking up at the William Morris tile frieze. He reads,

'There is nothing better for a man than that he should eat and drink and that he should make his soul enjoy good in his labours.'

There are no seats. Perhaps I am showing my age, needing to sit at a drinks party. Instead we stand around with the great and the good. I smile at one of the handsome waiters. His white uniform blends seamlessly into the antiseptic white and chrome of the cafe. I especially like the long starch white apron; it reminds me of Parisian cafes and professional waiters, rather than odd-jobbing students and overqualified migrant workers.

With one hand behind his back he stretches out his lanky arm and refills my champagne flute. God, it feels a long time since I've been anywhere like this! My eyes meet his name badge of indecipherable Polish Ws, Ys and Zs. Before I can thank him, he spreads out his long white arms and takes off. He could have at least smiled. Am I looking like an old has-been? Men used to smile, or at least let their glance linger. Sometimes you just need a second look from a stranger to confirm you're still all right. I haven't joined the unnoticed group of women, have I?

There's a banging of glasses and the signal to be quiet. Everyone is looking at a man at the end of the room. 'I would like to take this opportunity to welcome you all to the V&A

this afternoon. We have a fantastic new and extremely eclectic exhibition, which will I'm sure give everybody food for thought. I don't want to turn this into a drawn-out Oscar-style speech.' There's a chuckling from the audience. 'But I would like to thank everybody who was involved in the putting together of this exhibition, especially Dr Peter Lawrence and Hannelore Lawrence who have donated just some of their truly inspiring collection of yurts to this exhibition – Unfortunately Peter is unable to be here today as he is in remotest Quirgizstan. May I officially proclaim "The Fabric of Society" open.'

I turn to look at Hannelore and she looks so proud.

'I'd like advise everyone not to just explore the galleries, but to also go out into the gardens and visit the tents from Europe, Russia and the Middle East.'

'Let's start with the galleries and save the best for last,' suggests Hannelore. Our little foursome wanders around the displays. Chris stops at an exhibit entitled, 'The Shirt off your back'.

'Do you think it would suit me?' asks Chris, bending down and standing next to a patchworked, reworked shirt. Chris still has his modelling-days good looks, his clear blue eyes matching the pinstripe and chequered blues of the shirt.

'You could commission one,' says Juneko. 'I don't think this one would be big enough for you.'

'You could make one yourself,' I say. 'Look, according to the blurb, it's made from ten old charity shop shirts.'

'I wish Peter was here,' says Hannelore, wistfully.

'Would he like one of these shirts?' asks Chris, tactlessly.

'I'm sure you'll see him soon,' I say, touching her arm.

'I think he prefers the travelling life to all this. Anyway come and see the little bit of the exhibition that I am responsible for.'

We walk into a room which resembles the corner of a living room.

'I didn't know you did installations,' says Chris.

'This isn't an installation. It's real!' she replies.

'So much brown!' I exclaim. 'I've always hated brown. There's something so depressing about it,' I say, looking at the curtains and sofa.

'You're absolutely right, Laura. According to Max Lüscher, the colour psychologist, brown is the colour of resignation. You see this is what all East German homes were like for years, not just one season. Some were resigned to this. But it's also why so many of us left for the bright lights of the West.'

I'm intrigued by the paper packets containing dress patterns next to them. And in pride of place – a sewing machine. It brings back memories of domestic science, the O Level for the numpties. The real truth was girls like me could remember an endless list of facts to cram for exams, but were too uneducated to use a sewing machine.

'How did you get to do this?' I ask Hannelore. 'I mean, help put the exhibition together?' I ask, thinking I'd love to curate an exhibition which involved collecting fabrics and furniture.

'I'm an expert on Eastern European textiles, especially stitch,' she replies sharply.

'You've been told,' whispers Chris. He stays standing very close to me and I hope I don't look as self-conscious as I feel.

'Hello, Hannelore,' says a very well dressed man, who I realise is the man who made the speech. 'Lovely to see you here today. Such a shame Peter couldn't make it.'

Chris, Juneko and I smile at him, expecting an introduction. But I guess we're not important enough.

Then, as if sweetness itself Hannelore turns to us and says, 'I used to work here with Nicholas. And my favourite job happened all but once a year. I would go around London, from suburbia, to Wimbledon, Putney High Street to Oxford Street, and photograph what everyone was wearing. Each year there's a new trend, a new fad,' she says staring at me – or should I say my kimono.

I'm so hot I take off my denim jacket and have to reveal that I am wearing totally the wrong clothes in what feels like a film set. There's something familiar about the living room, the brownness of it. The lino floor The lamp. It's Berlin circa 1975 and much of it reminds me of my own childhood.

'Shall we go outside? It's so hot in here,' I say to Chris.

'I'll stay here. I like to hear what people have to say about the exhibition,' says Hannelore, oblivious to the fact that it's Chris I've invited to go outside – not all of us.

Chris and I wander into the courtyard leaving Juneko and Hannelore together. We sit down on one of the Bukhara rugs. The champagne has made me feel relaxed. I feel as if we could fly away on this magic carpet.

'Laura, I was going to give you this later. But perhaps you should try it on before we leave,' says Chris, handing me a V&A bag. I know what's inside and as I take out the red cardigan I feel really excited as I knew I couldn't afford it myself. But there's an awful sinking feeling in my stomach. I've wanted Chris to show me that he likes me, but now he has I feel so guilty.

'Chris, it's lovely. It's really kind of you.' I give him a peck on the cheek.

'I'm bankrupt now! I'll just have to complete another Arts Council application,' he says, defusing the obvious tension.

'You certainly won't get any money out of Curtis,' I joke.

'What a Scrooge,' says Chris, his blue eyes holding my gaze for longer than they should.

The taxi drops Chris off at the retreat and heads towards Juneko's brand new bungalow.

'Are you sure you don't want to come to the Safari Supper?' I say to Juneko, but she rushes in elegant little steps down her weedless drive.

'Who's next?' says the driver.

'Drop us both down at the end of The Street,' says Hannelore. I wait on the doorstep while she rushes in to collect her *Sachertorte*. I note her immaculate garden and the infamous (yurt making) flint barn adjacent to it. There's something a bit old fashioned about her hanging baskets and flowerbeds full of nasturtiums. Perhaps it's all the orange and green. Why don't I have lots of flowers? Probably because I spend too much time making fabric ones!

Hannelore hands me the perfect chocolate cake. I'm tempted to steal one of the chocolate flowers.

'Jump in,' she says, opening the door of her glossy Polo.

'Aren't we going to walk?'

'Walk! We can't walk with a *Sachertorte*.'

'Look, I'll carry it,' I say. 'It's a lovely summer's evening.'

We head off to Charlotte's. I'm walking at a snail's pace, taking it really easy over every pothole. I wear my new cardigan; I absolutely love the crocheted crimson petals. I had a bad case of indecision about whether to keep the cardigan on. Now, carrying the cake, I've no choice.

Hannelore is talking about a new idea for a book; the power of the uniform. I keep nodding and thinking, If a girlfriend had bought me it, knowing that I couldn't afford something like that myself, I wouldn't feel guilty. Would I? This little argument, or more like an internal court case, continues to go round and round in my head all the way to Charlotte's house.

I spot Adi and the girls at a table in the garden. For a split second I don't know if I want to see them. I have a funny disconnected feeling after just one day in London. I need a few minutes to adjust. Of course I want to see them. And these thoughts begin to make me feel guilty. You haven't really done anything wrong, I tell myself. Have I? How could I? I've been chaperoned all day by Hannelore.

'Our A-listers have arrived,' announces Charlotte, giving me a peck on the cheek and shaking Hannelore's hand. 'Sit down here, and Edward will serve you with our homemade carrot and coriander soup.'

'Mummy! Mummy!' say the girls. 'We had such fun at Charlotte's house. We helped her make the soup. And then Daddy took us to René's and we made pavlova.'

'Sounds like you've had a fabulous day,' I say. 'Did anyone remember to take Prada for a walk?' I ask.

'You didn't put that on your list,' says Adi, completely seriously, as though his day at home was like a formal work day.

I look at Lilly, Prada's supposed to be her dog anyway. Poor

Lilly, she looks as if she's about to burst into tears. 'Sorry, I forgot,' she says, looking down at the table.

'It wasn't really your job to remember, sweetheart,' I say, giving her a smile.

'But I did feed her,' adds Lilly. Thank goodness somebody in our house can think for themselves!

'How was London?' says Adi, with no apologies for forgetting about Prada's walk – or feeding her. 'New brown cardigan?' quizzes Adi, raising his eyebrows.

'It was reduced,' I reply. I'm suddenly feeling too guilty to snap at him and say: the cardigan is red, not brown. Adi can't help being colour blind, he can't help being unable to see the world in the beautiful multicoloured view I have.

Luckily our conversation comes to an abrupt halt with the arrival of Liz and her family. Immediately we all swap places. Adi and Mark get involved in some deep discussion about yoga positions and the girls have someone their own age to play with.

I sit with Liz, who says, 'I'm just about there with getting Declan to come over.'

'Declan?'

'Sorry, I didn't explain. He's one of the best photographers in the business. You've seen him before, he did the pictures for Hannelore's book launch. I've persuaded him to do a photo shoot to go with an article about your handmade things. Have you got a name for it all yet? I can't call it "handmade things"!'

I shake my head. I'm working on it.

Chapter 41

Whipped running stitch is also known as cordonnet stitch. Whipped running stitch will follow intricate curves easily.

I can't believe that the interview with Liz about my textile business is really going to happen – today. I go upstairs one more time and decide to swap my black sundress for something more me, more Laura Lovegrove. Yes I do want my designs to sell, but I also want to stop trying to look like a businesswoman. I'm an artist too. I'm happy in the orange and blue polka dot dress. If it clashes with my accessories in the photo all the better.

I can't help but feel really important when the doorbell rings and Liz is standing on my step.

'I'm here from *Mercia* magazine,' she jokes. 'Laura, you look fantastic in that dress. It really suits you. I couldn't imagine anyone else being able to carry it off.' What does she mean by that I wonder?

It doesn't feel like an interview. Liz and I are just chatting about fashion, as we always have, ever since the housewarming party, which is beginning to feel like a lifetime, rather than six months, ago. We discuss which time period really suits our figures; the 1920s is for the small and slight, the 1950s for the hourglass figure, curvaceous, yet with a small waist, the 1960s for the tall and leggy.

'I don't think I fit into any of these categories,' I say.

'Nor do I,' laughs Liz. 'We're both individuals. Anyway, we must get onto YOUR creations.'

'I'm calling the label, well, the business, *Handmade and Discovered*,' I say. 'Handmade because the accessories are hand crafted, and discovered because the recycled fabrics have all been searched for. Each item is a complete one-off, never to be repeated.'

'It's a fantastic concept,' says Liz, 'but don't you think it needs a more exciting name to sell the work?'

'I spent ages thinking about it,' I laugh and frown at the same time.

'It just needs to be snappier, something like *Remember me*, *Forget-me-not*, or *Threads*,' suggests Liz.

'I can't change it, Adi's doing the website. And he doesn't like changes of plan,' I say, unable not to pull a face at Adi's rigid approach to things.

'Laura,' she says, 'something I need to warn you about, this interview may turn out to be very brief, when it's printed. You see, the deal was to source garments, accessories and home-ware for their "Most Wanted" page.'

'That's fine with me.'

We're interrupted by a knock on the door. Prada starts barking and rushes to the front door.

'It'll be Declan, the photographer,' she says, grinning at me. It is Declan, who looks like he should be the one in the photo promoting my accessories. He has an androgynous look with his long, curly blonde hair and slight, slim frame.

Prada takes a big liking to Declan and follows him around as he sets up a cosy arrangement of handbags, beach bags, purses, ties, belts, necklaces, napkins and coasters and points to the vacant spot at the front. Obediently I lounge on top of my patchworked picnic blanket with Prada and feel as embarrassed as if I were a car showroom girl. He huffs and tuts while looking at the images on his laptop.

'Is there another angle we could take? Something more dramatic, with more of a narrative?' he says. I wonder what on earth he's going to ask me to do next. I get up and look at the screen and question what all the fuss is about. These are the best photos of me since I don't know when. And I want them for my website.

'I've got it,' says Liz. 'When we had our village fayre, I saw Laura walking down the Green with a wheelbarrow full of accessories.' She saw me! 'She was wearing flip-flops and all tied up in bunting.'

'Bunting as bondage,' says Declan, thoughtfully.

'Don't frighten Laura, she's a good girl,' laughs Liz, as I obviously can't conceal the look of horror on my face. 'Don't worry, I wasn't thinking of that sort of magazine.'

They continue their discussion as if I'm not really there. *Just don't suggest Prada modelling with me again. Once was enough.* Before I know it Liz is shining and polishing the wheelbarrow.

'I think you should stand outside the yurt,' orders Declan. 'It'll look like a festival or something.'

Liz puts the Lucienne Day bags on top of the wheelbarrow. I take them off.

'Laura, what are you doing? These are fab. Real trademark designs.'

'I don't want them in,' I say, surprised at the forcefulness of my words. I guess I feel guilty about the fact that Chris got me the fabric.

I agree to stay wearing my sundress. After throwing out the Lucienne Day fabric bags I even agree to wear Liz's purple and pink spotted wellies. I can't believe that I'm allowing myself to be photographed bare-legged in wellies pushing a wheelbarrow full of accessories under an archway of my home-made bunting in front of the yurt.

'Just one thing Laura, what is the address of your website?'

'I don't actually know. I'll have to check with Adi,' I say, feeling really stupid.

'I can do that,' says Liz, as if she doesn't trust me to get it right.

'Liz, what do I owe you for this? I mean for doing the article.'

'Don't be silly. It's my contribution to keeping you in the village. I don't want you all going back to London.'

'But ...'

'Laura, let me do a bit of free PR, then if you like my service you can keep me on. You need to focus on creating more things. I'll make sure you sell them,' she says, excitedly. 'In fact, I'm going to haggle for a few of Declan's pictures to give Adi for your website,' she whispers. 'It'll be a surprise,' she winks.

I'm scared and excited about the magazine spread. It's as though once it's all in print, they'll be no going back.

Chapter 42

Ukrainian interlaced running stitch is worked under the running stitches without entering the ground fabric.

I arrive back from the school run and close the door to Marsh Cottage. It's been a good morning already. Several of the school mums stopped to chat, and one of them asked if I could make a customised changing bag for her twins; apparently you can only order them from the States. The irony of it was, I was the one who wanted to rush away and get home – to my sewing. Finally, I feel accepted.

Does busy 'ness' equate to good business? It seems to be the case with sewing. It's 9.15 a.m. and I've got the adrenalin rush of a long distance runner (and I haven't even drunk a cup of coffee yet). Well – I imagine that is how they feel, as I haven't run further than to catch a bus since primary school.

There's a real buzz in our revamped cottage. And what's more I can't believe how free I feel not having to look after rails and rails of vintage clothes. So many of the dresses had to be dry-cleaned or needed a special hand wash. I'm free of all that. If anyone had told me this six months ago I wouldn't have believed them.

Today it's just me and Prada. 'Good girl! I'll take you for a walk in a minute,' I say, as I add the last few stitches to a hand-bag handle that once had another life as a dress strap. Prada looks at me pleadingly. There's nothing for it, I snap on her lead and she's taking me for a walk down the Green. I look at the nondescript black plastic lead and a thought crosses my mind. Why can't dogs have bright, colourful, patterned leads? All those little scraps could make fantastic leads. I can see it now, 'pamper man's best friend'. My thoughts race and I can't wait to get home and make a prototype.

Wham! I should be looking where I'm going as I crash into John the Buddhist.

'Sorry,' I fluster.

'No worries,' he says. 'By the way, can I order one of your bags? I know it's a long way off but when you're sending Christmas presents to the other side of the world you have to plan ahead.'

'Oh, I didn't know you celebrated Christmas?'

'I don't really. But my sister does,' he smiles.

'Find out her favourite colours and I'll make her one,' I say. 'Or better still I could do one of my special designs.'

John gives me a curious look.

'What I mean is I could make a bag from a worn-out dress or favourite cushion cover of hers. If she can send you something, or if you're making a trip back, then I'll transform them into something new. I can even stitch a special word or two into it.'

'I like this life cycle of the bag idea. It's like people really. We're all on the wheel of life. There's no real beginning or end, although we like to think there is.'

I should answer with something equally as profound, yet all I find myself saying is, 'I'm just relieved not to have all those clothes to look after.'

'Everything is transient in passing.'

'What a lovely phrase, I could stitch that on to or into your sister's bag,' I say recognising the words.

John smiles, 'She'd certainly never forget the bag was from me! What I mean is,' says John, 'things change. Life is fluid and we need to free up the past to move on. I'll speak to my mum and get her to ship something over. I like that idea,' says John, turning into the lane.

Prada is slowing down. I wander, rather than rush, home. I don't usually go in for all that new age stuff, but John's hit a button. I'm going to make Prada a lead from one of the straps of Mum's old dresses. I know that sounds a bit brutal, turning a treasured heirloom into a dog lead. But since the fire, and the fact that I don't have the whole dress any more – it seems right somehow to turn one of her old dinner-dance dresses into a lead – something I'll see every day.

The idea of making the lead leaves my head buzzing. Back in the cottage I can't work as quickly as I can think. Hurriedly, I try out plaiting the fabric, stitching, I could even cut strips and knit fabric. I rummage in what must be the most untidy cupboard in Reedby and eventually pull out a couple of knitting needles. That is the thing I love about design – having an idea and then doing it. You can't do that with many subjects, can you, I think, as I glance up at the clock.

I'm feeling resentful as I put away the lead. I need more making time. It's a slow artwork of beauty. I like being different from the teenagers I teach, who live in a world of instant results, except they are all virtual results – seen on a screen. Their life is one step removed from real making. The problem for me at the moment is that I'm too slow to finish any of my ideas properly. I just hope my handiwork is strong enough. I'll do a test drive, or rather walk, later.

But first things first. I need to go to college. My plan is to drop *it*, my important letter, my life-changing letter, in his in-tray and avoid saying anything. I put *it* in my patchwork bag and head for town.

I creep up the stairs and hover by his office door. I hope he isn't there. Laura, you're being a coward again, I think. I often telephone people when I know they'll be out, just so I can leave a message without having to speak to them. Do other people do this? I wonder. That's probably why everyone sends texts these days (except if you live in Reedby and have no signal). It avoids interaction.

I place my letter in his pigeonhole and prepare to make my getaway. I've dreamt of this day, when I would tell Curtis exactly what I think of his vision, or lack of vision, for the arts: How he has ruined my confidence as an art teacher. How he doesn't understand anything about art. How art needs time to grow and flourish. Hannelore says that artists, craftspeople and designers are guardians of a tradition, that skills can't be short circuited. Good artwork takes time. Why do we run courses on minimum hours? How can a full-time course run for two days a week, not five days a week like when I was at art school. No wonder the students never get 'into' their work and are accused of having short attention spans. I don't expect him, rumour has it, a former travel agent, who doesn't teach himself, to understand any of this. The world's gone mad. I'm really having a Lorina Bulwer ranting moment!

Oh no! He's seen me and is waving at me through the little glass window of his office. He's performing some sort of sign language which I don't quite get.

Is this my moment to say all?

'Come,' he shouts.

I walk into the office.

'I've been wanting to speak to you for some time.'

I have a horrible sinking feeling. I can feel myself begin to shake. Please don't notice this.

'Did you get the college's permission to set up this accessories business of yours? You know you signed an exclusivity of service contract?'

'You knew I was a practising designer when you took me on,' I answer, defensively.

He then winks at me, somehow distorting his fleshy – or is it foamy? – face. My heart begins to pound – is this time for flight or fight, I wonder. Questions flit through my mind: How does he know? I may have enough orders to keep me going for a while. Is this the Norfolk rumour network? Has he seen a pre-press version of Liz's article? I certainly haven't.

Curtis doesn't wait for an answer. 'Since the fashion show we've had so many enquiries, everyone wants to come here and do textiles. You've put Town and Country College on everyone's radar.'

Why does he have to use words like radar?

'And most importantly more bums on seats, which means more money,' he says, rubbing his hands together like an out-size Fagin talking of his boys.

'Curtis, I do have to rush and pick up my daughter from the nursery before it closes, but, um, there's a letter for you in your tray, from me.' Laura, you can do better than this. Go on, tell him. I should say something creepy like, As much as I've loved working here, things have taken off so well in my craft-design business – I'll be so sad to leave, blah, blah, blah.

'It's my notice,' I say and can immediately feel my face redden, involuntarily drawing attention to me. At this point after my bravery, and putting the college on the 'radar', I am feeling confident. I almost expect him to plead with me to come back – to offer me promotion, a pay rise. Instead he says, 'It's three months' notice this time of year. You'll have to do some days at the beginning of the autumn term.'

I turn my back and leave. Does this man have no inner monologue? I really don't have anything to say. I realise that I'm a resource, probably no more loved than a table!

Chapter 43

Vandyke chain stitch is also known as zigzag stitch. It is a variation of chain stitch that is effective when sewn row upon row to build up patterns for borders or as a single row.

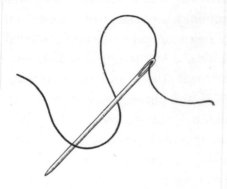

Sue had said when we were clearing out the studios to 'Bring a cake in for your last day – a nice homemade one. We could have it with coffee in the office. Just like when it's someone's birthday.'

I leave my bike unlocked outside the farm shop. It is the country after all. A sweaty and slightly breathless me looks at the display of 'homemade' cakes. They look so convincing. And surely it doesn't matter whose home the cake was made in. I'm sure Sue wouldn't know. The little label, which says *The Old Vicarage, Reedby* would easily peel off. Now Summer Cottage rings a bell. So making and selling cakes is another of

René's little hobbies, I think. Another thing she's good at. I look at the thick sponge and beautiful frosting and have a laugh out loud moment as I read the label: *may contain nuts*. I jolly well hope a coffee and walnut cake contains nuts!

I weigh up my options. I could go to the post office and buy some obvious shop cakes. Some exceedingly good Battenberg is rather appealing.

I could commission Hannelore – after her success at the Midsummer Fayre I really would impress everyone with one of her *Sachertorte* or *Marmor* cakes. No, I'm going to do it myself. There's nothing wrong with my cakes. They're just a bit inventive, a bit unpredictable. I cycle home past the allotment. Is there anything I could make a cake with? The only thing we have in abundance is courgettes. I pick a couple which look like something between a courgette and a marrow and pop them in my basket.

I dash about the kitchen and feel no different to when I'm painting or sewing, I'm in a concentrated frenzy. Still warm I pack the finished cake in the Micra and head off for my last day at Town and Country.

I've got butterflies in my stomach as I pull into Town and Country's car park for the last time. Part of me wants to leave with a bang and to have fireworks and partying into the night. The other part of me is dreading sitting with colleagues, some who I hardly know, in the drab local pub which is neither nicely old fashioned nor a glitzy wine bar. Maybe I just want to make a quick exit – nothing will happen and I'll just fade away.

I put off going into the office and pop my head into the studio. It's empty, tidy, clean and anonymous and waiting for

373

next year's intake. All evidence of our year, my time, has been erased. I go into the office and it's empty too. On my desk is a little note which says, *We're on the lawn*. The lawn is really a euphemism for the little patch of grass out through the other side of the store cupboard. I take out my courgette and chocolate cake and carry it through the cupboard, which is strangely very empty. Where are all the still-life objects? The department is like a ghost town.

I open the door onto the lawn. Our motley crew turn to face me and let out a cheer. The little green square of grass is transformed into a tea party. The still-life plates are filled with cupcakes with lemon, green, pink and lavender frosting. There are old oriental rugs and vintage cushions that I could die for. Everything looks beautiful. I take out my chocolate courgette cake and place it on an empty chipped plate.

'It looks fantastic! It looks so good with all the odd plates. Much better than a proper tea set,' I tell Sue.

I then see a figure I don't recognise. In truth all I'm looking at is the amazing fabrics. It's a mish mash of vintage. Somehow s/he is wearing very large Louboutin boots, a gold evening dress with a matching purse, a red feather boa and to finish it off a cotton apron, in a suitably foodie print of radishes, artichokes and ham slices.

There's another cheer and a round of applause.

'Oh my God, is it you, Jim?'

'Hi Laura, I thought I'd dress up for what Sue told me was a mad hatter's tea party.'

We soon abandon cups of tea for bottles of bubbly.

Finally, Sue makes an announcement. 'Laura and Jim, we're all going to miss you both. We weren't sure how much you'd miss us. So here's something to remember us by. Sue is about to unveil a large board. I feel jitters in my stomach and really rather ungratefully hope it isn't a painting, or something that Adi will banish from the house.

'*Voilà*,' says Sue, presenting two great big Fuzzy Felt boards of letters.

'We couldn't agree on a quote so we made several alphabets,' says Sue.

I start to feel all tearful reading GOODBYE in huge handmade fabric letters backed in felt.

'How did you know that Fuzzy Felt was my favourite?' I say.

'And what made you think it was *my* favourite?' asks Jim, looking at Sue.

'It's what's known as an educated guess,' smiles Sue.

After an hour everyone is going back inside to complete their mountain of paperwork before the holidays.

What was an odd tear up on the field turns into a deluge as I drive home. I am happy, yet part of me doesn't want to leave my quirky students, part of me can't imagine myself not teaching again. There's also this nagging feeling about Chris. As much as I love the red cardigan I just can't bring myself to wear it, which means it is not in the same league as a present from a girlfriend.

I pull into the drive. It's only 3 p.m. Time for a quick cuppa before the school run. Then I spot Adi's car and I can see his silhouette through the kitchen window. What's he doing home so early?

Chapter 44

Stroke stitch is a simple stitch made of single isolated stitches. It can be worked in a regular or irregular manner, in a uniform or varying size.

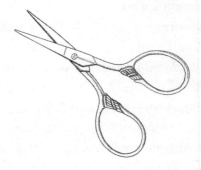

'We need to talk,' says Adi, clearing the dinner table.

My stomach sinks for the second time today. Part of me wants to hide my head in the sand. The other part of me knows that Adi and I do need to talk.

'Prada needs her walk first.' I want to add, Perhaps you should do a spot of yoga and then at least one of us will be in a fit state to talk.

I pack Prada's going out bag, as if I'm off to walk a toddler. I'd sworn no more babies! It's only a year or so ago that I stopped taking Daisy's change bag out with me – just in case of an emergency. Prada's bag was once a tablecloth, but we never used it. I attach her lead, and admire the mini-patchwork of scrap fabrics – and silver sequins (the girls' idea, not mine). You see nothing is wasted in our house!

'Mummy, I want to come too,' pleads Daisy. 'I want to take her out on her new lead.'

'You need to get an early night, sweetheart,' I tell Daisy, not revealing my real reason for wanting to go out alone.

'Go on. Take her out. I'll finish off here *and* put the girls to bed. A man's work is never done. There's a chill out there. You ought to put a coat on,' says Adi, as f he's talking to Lilly or Daisy, rather than his wife.

I put on one of my new creations: a red patchwork cape. Through the slits for armholes I take hold of Prada's lead.

'Mummy,' calls Daisy. 'You look just like Little Red Riding Hood.'

I smile. 'I'm a bit too old to look like Little Red Riding Hood.'

I step outside and sigh a breath of relief as I inhale the scented summer evening. Prada pulls me down the Green. Then she's off and I'm left holding a ripped piece of rainbow fabric covered in silver sequins. I look around and suddenly there's no sign of her whatsoever. How can such a small dog move so quickly?

I stop outside the Weatheralls'. Heather is reading in her hammock. Her hair's a bit longer than when we first met. I like it longer, there's something comforting and Old English Sheepdog about her black and white-grey mane. I wave. She waves back.

'Where do you think she is?' I call, holding up the lead.

Heather gets up and comes over to the hedge. 'Who?'

'Prada. Sorry. You're not psychic. Prada's run away.'

'As a dog psychologist, I should tell you to wait at home. She'll come back. But Charlotte's cat got locked in at the Buddhist retreat. She probably needed a little rest, a little retreat from Charlotte,' says Heather, laughing.

'I'll try there,' I say. 'Perhaps Prada has had enough of us. By the way,' I say as casually as possible. 'What do you think of this?' I hold up Prada's bag.

'What a fantastic idea. I'll certainly tell my customers about that. Have you got a website yet? That's what they'll want to know.'

'It's in progress. Well, that's what Adi says.'

'Just e-mail me the details and I'll put a link on my site. Isn't it exciting all this new technology? But it won't help you find a missing dog,' she laughs.

'No,' I say, suddenly realising the seriousness of returning home *without* Prada. My children will never forgive me.

I walk down the track towards the retreat. Reedby is so pretty in the dappled evening light. In the distance is a very tall man carrying a very small dog. It's Chris.

'We thought we'd take up your offer and have a look at your work,' I call, 'except Prada got here first,' I quickly add. Why am I saying this? Why am I flirting?

'Come to see my etchings, have you?' says Chris.

I let out a nervous laugh.

'So what have you made with the Lucienne Day?'

'This 'n' that,' I say, evasively.

'You can tell me,' says Chris. 'I'm not going to steal your design ideas.'

Before I can tell him about my Lucienne Day handbags, one of the most expensive items in my range, he looks at me with his deep blue eyes and says, 'You know you can tell me anything. Anything at all.' Is he talking about my artwork or my personal life? At this very moment I don't even know which I'd prefer him to be alluding to.

Chris nestles Prada in the crook of one arm. He takes my hand, leading me down an even narrower track and into the wood. In the distance the sun is setting and there's a flame red sky over the marsh.

'This is my humble abode,' says Chris, still carrying Prada.

'It really is a shed,' I say.

He grins back at me and with a flourish opens the padlock.

I walk inside expecting to see some pieces of constructed textiles: weird knitted organic forms of the kind Chris made after college, which more often than not bore a strong resemblance to internal organs. Instead, the shed interior is painted white and is empty, except for a closed-up laptop and a projector.

'What's happened to all your work?' I ask, for a moment thinking that perhaps Kurt is right, Reedby is a hotbed of crime and all of Chris' work has been stolen. Except Chris doesn't look in the least bit concerned.

'It's about what is seen and unseen. What is known and not known. Any designated object can be a work of art.'

'I have seen Cornelia Parker's exploded shed,' I say, enjoying a bit of name dropping. 'Although there's something quite male about the shed. I heard the other day that men have sheds and women have beach huts.'

'Or yurts. Yurts are unisex,' says Chris. 'Just like my sewing project is unisex.'

'Do you mean all the work I did transcribing Lorina's tales of woe on her sampler has gone to waste?' I ask, looking around at what is still an empty room.

'You'll see how Lorina's work fits in soon enough,' says Chris, excitedly.

He opens the laptop and switches on the projector. Am I in for a Powerpoint presentation?

'Friedrich Engels said, "Fabric made man different from primitive man. Fabric is almost like an extension of our skin,"' reads Chris from the projection on the shed wall, simultaneously stroking the back of my neck.

There's then an image of a swatch of fabric and stitched words, which as I quietly read sound so very familiar. 'PEOPLE WITH ABSURD IDEAS THESE IMPOSTERS AND PRETENDERS . . .'

Chris is smiling, 'Lorina's words are as valid today as they ever were.' I'm caught off guard in more ways than one as he begins to touch me. How can this be happening? I'm not even sure that I fancy him, not any more. I can smell curry on his breath which is a definite turn-off. Yet when he starts to stroke me, to very slowly stroke me across my breasts, it feels good. So good that I just stand there like a startled hare caught in the lights.

Then I edge away.

'You do like me, don't you? I know you do,' says Chris full of confidence.

'I've got to go. I can't do this,' I say, thinking of the girls and Adi. I want to be with Chris and I want to have my husband and family. Could I lead a double life?

'Laura, you're really beautiful,' says Chris, now stroking my hair. I want to believe him, and part of me does, yet another voice in my head is saying, He's only after one thing, you know that, Laura. And your flyaway hair isn't your best feature. Even *you* know that.

'So what do you think of my work?' he says.

Before I can say, it's fun, I like it, but it's not really your work, it's more the work of a curator, Prada begins to yap. She jumps onto the laptop keypad and in a moment Chris' artwork is gone from the wall.

'Get that dog off there!' yells Chris.

I've been saved by my poodle! What a guard dog! Thank you, Prada, my very own chaperone, I say to myself.

'This is all being exhibited! If she's deleted it! It's my whole show gone.'

'But it's not real! Not a one-off original,' I say. 'You must have a back-up copy.'

'You're just so old fashioned. You're living in the past. All your old fabrics, all your sewing, that's not art in the twenty-first century.'

'The truth's out. I really am going, now,' I say, not sounding at all assertive.

'Please don't go. Stay. I'm sorry. I didn't mean it. You know I didn't,' pleads Chris.

I grab Prada by the collar and pick her up as if she is a child. I don't really feel sorry about the damage. The work was virtual anyway. In fact I feel so powerful and excited that I'm still attractive. Is it bad to enjoy someone wanting you – when you don't really want them, or know you mustn't want them back? I'm glowing. I carry Prada home and really do feel as youthful as Little Red Riding Hood.

Heather is still swaying in her hammock. I'm not in the mood for speaking to anyone. I feel a confused mess.

Prada jumps out of my arms and goes straight to her, as if Heather's some long lost friend.

'Sit,' says Heather. I almost sit down as well, so commanding is her voice. And as if some spell has been cast, Prada obeys immediately.

'She likes you, Heather,' I say.

'You may be interested in one of these,' she says, handing me a brightly coloured flyer.

'Paws and Claws,' I say. 'Of course.'

'It's the other side of K9 Capers, if you remember,' says Heather, 'the grooming bit. Which is where you come in with those bespoke bags. I'll be telling all my clients about them.'

'Thank you.'

'You've got great names for your businesses,' I say.

'I'm sorry to hear about you and Adi,' says Heather. 'I think he confides a lot in Kurt. You never know what they're discussing down among the raspberry canes.'

'Sorry?' I stop myself and change tack. At this very moment I don't want to think about what Adi and Kurt discuss. 'Would it stop her clawing the sofa?' I ask, waving the flyer.

'Depends whether it's a psychological thing. Maybe it's her nerves.' Great, I think. What about my nerves seeing my prize throw being destroyed?

'Sometimes vets even prescribe a dog form of Valium or Prozac,' she says. 'In fact can I let you into a secret?' whispers Heather, looking around. 'I've signed up for a homeopathy course in the autumn. I could do Prada as a case study.'

'I'd be up for that.'

'Until then it's our little secret,' says Heather turning into her drive.

I loiter outside my own house. I feel like a manic depressive, as my high soon sinks to a low and then comes back again. Am I having an affair? Not really. It's just an admirer, nothing to feel guilty about. But then Adi hasn't been himself since we moved here. And nor have I. We've got to talk. We haven't talked properly since Easter, when his mother came to stay. We only seem to speak about work, decorating and the kids. Is this how it's going to be from now on? I start to think of the smell of curry on Chris' breath and feel sick. I'm desperate for a long soak in the bath – at least with Prada's antics I have an excuse for one.

I plonk Prada on the doormat and run up to the bathroom.

'Laura, you've only been for a walk, not a run. You can't need a bath,' laughs Adi. Why's he in such a good mood? I think. Is it because I was out?

'You should try getting her home without a lead,' I call back, slamming the door to the bathroom. I run the bath. The bathroom soon smells of geranium bath oil. I can't stop thinking about Chris – somehow now it all seems really stupid.

'Laura,' shouts Adi through the door. 'We need to talk.' My God, he knows already, I think. Was Kurt lurking in the bushes at the retreat? No, he can't possibly know! Oh why did we ever have to leave London and get ourselves into this awful mess? I want to go home – to Ealing. Everything was all right there.

Chapter 45

Berlin stitch is one of the oldest stitches in the history of textiles and is used worldwide today, as it was in the past. Its more common name is cross stitch and, as the name suggests, is made from two diagonal stitches which form a cross.

I walk up the path to Hannelore's cottage. I'm not sure what I want any more. I thought I'd been decisive: I've handed in my notice and I have a long list of orders. But I haven't slept all night. I try to distract myself, with the Lawrences' chocolate box English cottage. For a couple who are always travelling all over the place it's strange that they live in this Miss Marple cottage.

I ring on the wrought-iron bell. I've never been inside Rose Cottage before and have to admit I'm really curious as to how she's decorated it. Not because I'm really nosy, I just want to get a picture of what they're really like – and you can't really get that until you've been to somebody's home.

'Laura,' she says. 'What a surprise.'

I'm not sure if she's pleased to see me or not. But after a restless night I don't have anyone else to talk to who won't tell the whole village our business. I thought of talking to Chris, but that's just going to make things worse.

'You're just in time for *Kaffee und Kuchen*. I'll put the coffee maker on. Go through to the conservatory, or should I say my studio,' she says.

I walk through the lounge and marvel at all the oriental rugs, geometrics of red, black and white cover the floor and walls. I go into a proper conservatory. It's completely unlike my own 1970s uPVC-windowed and flat-roofed apology for a conservatory. I want to touch the ornate cut wood window frames and original Victorian terracotta floor. Adi would love the authenticity of materials. The only common denominator is that both our conservatories double up as studios and green-houses. The yurt has become more my warehouse.

Hannelore's is the neatest studio that I've ever seen. It's almost how I'd imagine Adi's studio to be – if he were an artist that is. On one table are textile books and magazines. Furtively I leaf through one of the catalogues. And of course there it is: a whole double page spread of Hannelore's work and she's not just listed as a textile artist, but an honorary one at that. For a moment I feel awash with jealousy. How did she become an important artist when I'm fiddling around making bits 'n' pieces from salvaged vintage dresses? After what Chris said I find it hard to believe that any of my work is important.

Hannelore hands me a fluted white porcelain plate; on it is

a wedge of plum cake, lightly dusted with icing sugar, and a cup of coffee. I love the way she does everything so properly, so beautifully. I can imagine her serving up dinner with all her fine china in a desert yurt. I daren't put my *Kaffee und Kuchen* down on the work table as it's covered with precious little piles of fabrics, like collages ready to be made.

'What are these?' I ask, pointing to the little fragments of fabric.

'My textile archaeology,' she grins. 'Don't you think it's interesting what we choose to collect, to keep. How we choose to organise and display things. Not just in museums, but at home as well.'

'Adi just calls it clutter,' I laugh.

'But look at this,' she says, handing me a piece of linen. I'm not sure what I'm looking for.

'Look at the darning, the frayed edges, the little patch. It tells us its, or should I say, our history. We didn't always live in a throwaway society. But you didn't come here to look at my studio. Did you?'

Part of me wants to say, Yes I did. And I wish I could bury myself in textiles.

'So what can I do for you?' she says.

'Everything has gone wrong,' I say. 'I just don't know where to start. Yesterday everything seemed so exciting. I handed in my notice at Town and Country. I was all ready to set myself up in a proper sewing business. Then I got home and had a bottle of bubbly ready to celebrate my news. Adi was already there. Later last night Adi told me that he's on gardening leave.'

'Oh, he loves his garden and the allotment,' says Hannelore, enthusiastically.

For the first time today, I laugh. Gardening leave means he's been made redundant,' I say, indulgently, for I do love the way that Hannelore still gets some English phrases mixed up.

'What you need is a plan,' says Hannelore, wading in and ignoring my little correction. 'You know when I decided to leave East Germany I planned my escape for years. You see the authorities didn't know what to do with artists. They tried all sorts of ideas. Sometimes they sent them to the West for five years, in the understanding that they wouldn't return. Sometimes dissidents at the Humboldt, that was my old university, were simply deported and with that any power to change East Germany was extinguished.'

I look at Hannelore and think of the sheltered, protected life I've led.

'I don't think too much about those drab times. Everything was grey or brown. You'd have hated it. But you know, things come back to, what's the word?'

'Haunt you,' I venture.

'Yes, to haunt you. René and the gang took me to an Indian restaurant for a Christmas outing. It had horrid wallpaper and a lino floor just like my old bedroom. I wanted to walk out. To run away. Memories, they're difficult.'

I know I should say something, but I don't really know what to say. So I wander over to the framed pieces of work on the wall.

'Did you dye all the fabrics yourself?'

'Of course. What do you think I used for this one?' she says, pointing at some beautiful turquoise fabric with simple little stitches.

'Um. No idea.'

'Red cabbage. Hey, us Germans don't just pickle red cabbage, we dye fabrics with it,' says Hannelore, finally smiling.

I laugh as I think it's the first time Hannelore has ever made a joke. 'You don't use all those complicated stitches you've been trying to teach me.'

'No. My stitches are just mark-making. Anything too fancy would get in the way.'

'Adi would like that,' I say.

'Anyway, enough of me. From a textile archaeologist's point of view what *you're* doing is very interesting,' she says, thoughtfully. 'It's real, unlike all the conceptual art, which in the future will be forgotten, as though it never was. Because all you'll have left of their work is a computer disk which no one will look at. Your work will leave real tracks.' *Remnants*, I think.

'What, going to charity shops and jumbles for my materials?'

'Of course! They have been donated to give them another life. The original labels, fastenings and lack of wear emphasise our throwaway society. When I first went to the West, would you believe it they were selling throwaway clothes, not just dresses but underwear.'

I burst into a fit of the giggles. Partly because Hannelore is probably the last person I could imagine wearing paper pants.

'More coffee?'

'No thanks.' My head is already buzzing and my cheeks are burning.

'What I'm trying to say is this, Laura,' says Hannelore, pouring me another cup of very strong coffee. 'If you want anything enough, if you put your mind to it you can change your life. Don't worry about what anyone else thinks. You'll never please everyone, start by pleasing yourself.'

'You've been so kind,' I say, standing up to go. 'I'd better let you get on.'

'Just one thing,' says Hannelore, 'Adi may have dreams, ideas of his own.'

I stand, stunned.

I arrive back at Marsh Cottage with a to-do list. I can hear Hannelore's voice in my head. 'Your accessories are a reassembled response to the original seamstresses of the past.' My work feels really important. 'And don't forget you need to network, that's how business works.'

I can also hear, '... dreams of his own.' What does Hannelore know about Adi's dreams? It seems that other people: Kurt, David, Hannelore, know far more about my husband than I do. Adi and I can't go on like this.

Chapter 46

Twisted chain stitch is a hand embroidery stitch which has a slightly textured appearance. It is a variation of chain stitch and can be effectively introduced in many types of needlework projects.

It is Saturday morning, early. Adi is sleeping now. The sky is still dull, more sunshine is promised. For several minutes this morning I sat up and watched him. I had to get up and leave the bedroom. I've spent most of my time in Reedby full of nostalgia, for London and my longstanding easy friendships, for a successful designer that never really was, and for some intensity of feeling, not just romantic teenage stuff, but a passion for something. I see now how Chris filled that gap, with what I thought was our passion for art and design.

'What are you doing?' asks Adi.

Startled, I look round and see him standing in the yurt doorway. He's wearing his usual black underpants. He stands with his arms folded and looks toned and muscular.

'I don't know what I'm doing. I guess I'm wondering what's going to happen next. Neither of us have a job, regular income.'

Adi nods.

'It's all right being creative, being an artist, when you've only got yourself to think about.'

Adi frowns, he doesn't speak. Is he willing to hear more? He appears to be waiting. Do I let this moment pass? I could, I could behave as if nothing out of the ordinary is happening. Nothing out of the ordinary has happened between me and Chris.

'I went to visit Chris.'

'Sorry?'

'Chris Taylor. I went to his studio the other evening.'

'Oh, did you?' His tone is neutral. He watches me, expressionless. How can he be so cool? I want him to be angry.

'And what happened?'

'I went to look at his artwork. We talk about art, you know.' My heart is now pounding. I can't look Adi in the face. 'And then ...'

'You don't have to tell me. Laura. Whatever happened, good, bad, indifferent, I don't want to hear it,' says Adi, trying to catch my eye.

'But I would like you to hear it,' I say, assertively, surprised by myself. For a moment I flash back to my Curtis rant.

'No, really,' Adi insists. He turns his back to me and gets up to leave.

'I only want you to know that nothing happened. I didn't let anything happen,' I plead.

Adi stops by the door. 'Perhaps the lady doth protest too much?' says Adi, flatly. I didn't know Adi knew Shakespeare. 'I'm always here, always dependable and now I'm jobless you don't want to know.'

His face crumples and his eyes go blurry and well up with tears. I should go and put my arm round him. Comfort him. Instead I say, 'That's not true. I want to know. I want to know what you're feeling, what your dreams are beyond the mundane, everyday.'

'I do want new things for us. I'm working on it. Just give me time.'

'Working on what? Perhaps now is the time to tell me, share it with me,' I murmur, putting a hand on his bare shoulder. He does not move and the girls have definitely woken.

Lilly runs into the garden, flapping a magazine. 'Mummy, Daddy,' she shouts, 'look at this!' she says, holding the glossy magazine against her chest and displaying the headline, 'A Handmade Life'.

'We'd agreed to call the business *Handmade and Discovered*. Everyone is going to think it's called *A Handmade Life*,' says Adi.

'I like it, *A Handmade Life*,' I say.

'Things aren't set in stone. Let's change the name,' says Adi, excitedly.

'We can remake our life. We can change things. Can't we?' I whisper.

Adi takes my hand and squeezes it. Together we read the article.

'I look at a woman across the street in a patterned dress and all I can do is calculate how many handbags, belts and necklaces I could make from it. Am I a woman obsessed?' asks Laura Lovegrove.

Adi smiles. 'This is wicked!' he says.

Laura Lovegrove has taken the world of ethical fashion to new heights. She makes beautiful accessories from recycled materials at her yurt workshop. They have a distinct English identity and are quirky and special. No two items are ever the same. She'll even stitch a special message into the piece – for no extra charge . . .

. . . All her materials are 100% recycled. The bespoke accessories: purses, handbags, belts, necklaces, picnic blankets, coasters – you name it, there's even a children's range of toys – can be made to order, either from Laura's own collection of fabrics or with her unique service. Clients arrive with a sentimental piece of clothing or fabric which is then transformed by Laura and her team into a beautiful, functional and comforting fashion accessory or piece of homeware.

She'll deliver by wheelbarrow power too! That is, if you live in Reedby, the remote Broadland village where her designs are made with the expert help of local embroiderers, the eldest of whom is 92 years of age. Here at *Mercia* magazine, we wonder if there will be a Christmas calendar of The Sewing Ladies, with a stitch for every month of the year.

Then I read the footnote:

And if you really want to embrace the material world, Laura's architect husband, Adi, will make you a bespoke yurt.

'We're like a celebrity couple, finding out about each other's plan in the media, before we speak to each other,' I joke.

'That won't happen again,' says Adi. 'You've got too many good ideas not to be involved in my design plans.' *This really is a compliment!*

'It's Liz on the phone,' calls Lilly.

I rush into the cottage and pick up the phone. 'Hey, Laura, I just can't believe our luck. You're on the front cover.'

'I know.'

'This is very unusual, you know. Covers are researched for ages and they use celebs, not models, these days,' she finally stops for breath.

'So why me?' I ask.

'I'm just guessing here, but the most likely thing is there's been a last minute problem with the real cover. Some celeb threatening litigation or whatever. And you have to admit it's a terrific picture. You're going to be inundated with orders. I hope you're ready for this. It's your fifteen minutes of fame! Sorry, that sounds a bit mean.'

'Fifteen minutes of fame is better than none,' I laugh. 'Thank you, Liz, for all you've done.'

'Laura, you didn't mind me adding the bit about Adi's yurts, do you?'

'Of course not,' I say.

As soon as I put the phone down it rings again 'Laura. Laura Lovegrove. It is you, isn't it? I always wondered what happened to you. It's Wanda. Remember me?'

'How could I forget you?' I reply.

'I saw that write up in *Mercia*. I do admire you recycling all those old fabrics,' she says, not stopping for breath. 'How do you feel about a double page spread in the *Mail on Sunday*? Something about the return to sewing in the age of austerity. And I'd like a chat with your husband about these yurts, you can't find a well-made one for love nor money. And the waiting lists are horrendous. You could even embroider some bits on them.'

Wanda finally stops for breath She then speaks really quietly as if she's revealing some state secret, 'You know a colleague of mine has just made a wedding dress from a mosquito net.'

I put the phone down and everything comes flooding back. I hadn't thought of Wanda for years. Funny though, how she didn't get back to me until she saw Liz's article.

Today is really turning out to be one of the best days of my life. That is until Adi says, 'Can we have a chat in the study?'

My heart sinks.

He switches on the computer, and the machine, as if reading my nervousness, takes ages to boot up. I start to feel physically sick.

'Liz wanted me to keep quiet about it until the article was in print. I'm so excited,' says Adi.

'You're excited?'

'Come and sit down and stop hovering.'

Adi types quickly.

'Wow! You've got a good sense of colour and composition,' I say, looking at the collaged borders of scrap fabrics, lace and rick-rack.

'Architects are designers, you know,' says Adi, taking my hand.

'When, how on earth did you do this? It's a proper website. It's so clever, each icon is something from the haberdasher's cupboard. That's the button from my pineapple dress! There's the Easter chick for the children's range. And look, a link to the yurt business.'

'You see,' says Adi, proudly, 'you thought I was busy in the conservatory with planting. Half the time I was rummaging around for things to scan and photograph. Had you fooled, didn't I?'

'Yes, you had me fooled – we've had each other fooled,' I say with a lump in my throat.

'It's a good site, isn't it?' Before I can answer Adi says, 'It's funny, quirky, individual, just like you and your accessories.'

'I do love you,' I say, flinging my arms round Adi, knowing that he feels just right and I've been such a sensation-seeking idiot. Adi only has eyes for the screen, so I let go of him and watch him as he clicks the mouse. 'We're going to make this business work, I've been thinking about it. I can do the website, orders and accounts and we'll be self-sufficient with the allotment.'

'And make yurts.'

He pulls up a list of orders.

'My God, we're going to be sewing day and night.' I give him another big hug. I want to say, I don't know if it will be that easy. But we're in this together now.

Chapter 47

Up and down buttonhole stitch is also known as mirrored buttonhole stitch. It is a variation of buttonhole stitch easily worked on all types of fabrics. The line this stitch forms is interesting as it creates a pair of vertical stitches which are crossed with a tie at the base.

It takes me over a week to get my act together and go to Trishna. This time I'm going alone and definitely dog free!

I go down the track and turn into the woods. Do I have no sense of direction? The shed isn't there. Maybe I should have brought Prada after all. Don't dogs have some kind of homing instinct? I know I didn't imagine the whole silly episode in Chris' shed. I even looked up the Engels quote. He really did say that fabric made man different from primitive man; that fabric is almost like an extension of our skin.

I leave the wood and go to the retreat house, still wondering what I'm going to say. How do you put an end to something which had barely started?

I knock on the door.

'Just the person,' says John. 'I've got a bag of my sister's old clothes. Now you can start her bag, and do keep the rest. It would be my contribution to your business venture.'

'Thank you,' I say, breathing a sigh of relief. 'Is Chris here?' I ask, trying to sound as casual as possible.

John shakes his head. 'It all happened really quickly. He's in Durham.'

'Durham?'

'So Chris won't be ...'

John shakes his head. 'He won't be back. He hasn't been expelled or anything,' says John, obviously aware of the look on my face.

'Is there another retreat in Durham?'

'No, no. Chris isn't a Buddhist. Did he not tell you? His work is all about exploring the way artworks are our way of worshipping, of paying devotion in a secular world. That's why he jumped at the chance of being Artist in Residence at Durham Cathedral.'

'But where's the shed gone?'

'Back here. We need it for storage.'

I don't say that Chris never really mentioned the god thing, or that he probably only came up with this idea to get the residency. I know this is mean spirited of me.

'He's a bit of a Salvador Dalí,' I say.

'Is that the surrealist painter? I don't think Chris paints,' muses John. 'In fact it's strange that he had nothing to clear away, no paints, canvases. He just packed his laptop in a bag and called a taxi to take him to the station.'

'Dalí was an artist *and* a showman,' I say.

'Exactly,' says John. 'Chris lives his work. I guess it's a calling – of sorts,' he concedes. 'Are you OK? You look a bit . . .'

'I'm fine. Thanks for the fabric. I need to get back.'

Perhaps it's up to Chris to decide what artwork he makes. But I can't help feeling that he doesn't really make or produce anything. Then I'm hit with a more profound, yet funny, thought. I giggle to myself, as I think how he's like one of the derided bankers, someone who doesn't actually do or produce anything. Perhaps his art days are numbered?

Postscript

Norwich stitch uses a flat square stitch unit with a woven appearance that may be worked over a square by a number of threads, suitable for medium and large areas and backgrounds, individual motifs and geometric patterns.

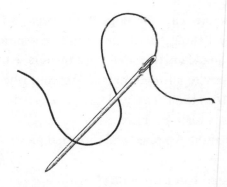

Our evenings have become a family adventure. We no longer watch television or play games, although we never did that very often. Our entertainment is this: Daisy matches fabrics, Lilly cuts out the shapes – she's actually earning her pocket money now – and Adi does Prada's evening walk, delivering fabric sets to the sewing ladies. I think they love having this 'young' man coming to drop off materials and collect their work.

Adi takes an extra delivery to Joyce. I wonder what colour hair she'll surprise him with today? Apparently her industrial sewing machine is back in action as she collaborates with her boys, Adi and David, on the yurt orders. And then like some 1950s housewife when the girls are in bed and Adi's out on his deliveries I sit in the yurt and sew, waiting for Adi to return. I don't have a pipe and slippers waiting for him, but I make the finishing touches to something much more contemporary.

I hear Adi and Prada coming back across the gravel.

'She's clean! She had a little dip in the river,' says Adi.

'She can't swim!' I scold, sounding like an over-anxious parent.

'Of course she can. All dogs swim,' says Adi, rolling his eyes. Proudly, I show Adi my latest pile of goodies, including extra strong dog leads to match their owners' handbags.

'I hope they're strong enough! We could be sued out of business with all the runaway dogs,' laughs Adi.

'Now this is for you,' I say.

Adi gazes at the wrapped and threaded pieces displayed on a card.

'I don't need hair extensions.'

'They're not hair extensions! Have a guess. What does every man or woman need?'

'Well, there's a lot I could say to that question.'

I can't stand the suspense any longer. 'They're memory stick identifiers. So if you leave yours in a different computer, if you work in a big office, or if you keep certain work on one stick – you'll know which one yours is.'

'Laura,' says Adi, putting his arm around me, 'you're a one-off, aren't you?'

'If you look really closely, can you see it says something?'

'I think I need magnifying glasses to read this,' laughs Adi, slowly reading: *A stitch in time*. 'What does that mean?'

'Whatever we want it to mean,' I say taking his hand.

We walk up the Green which is now shades of straw colour and should be called The Yellow Ochre. This morning is Daisy's taster day. I'm sure she won't remember much about her school visit come September and the day she really starts. I'm sweating and it's only ten to nine in the morning. We reach the playground and I feel as if I'm in the Mediterranean. I'm not surprised a drought is already predicted. Kurt Weatherall tells anyone who'll listen that he's using his bathwater to irrigate the vegetable patch.

'Where's your sunhat, Daisy? I told you to bring it. What will your teacher say?' I realise I'm sounding like a primary schoolteacher myself.

'It doesn't matter. I don't like t anyway. It looks like it belongs to a toddler.' I fail to add that it was hers as a toddler and she has finally grown into it. 'Anyway, we're moving up a class today and I'll have Mrs Jones. She'd never wear a hat like that. She dresses properly,' she says, while looking me up and down. Argh! This is the life, being put in your place by a not-yet reception class child!

Daisy's already running around with her pre-school chums. I'm not needed. I try to divert my thoughts. At times of crisis I've always turned to art.

Mrs Jones somehow looks fantastic in her powder blue dress and matching tailored jacket with an even paler turquoise stripe which is only visible when you're close up. I look at her in that dress and all I can do is calculate how many accessories I could make from it. Am I a woman obsessed? And anyway, why isn't she sweating like me? Is she human? I think, feeling more like one of the children.

'Mrs Stark. Mrs Stark,' says a voice, enunciating clearly. I come to, and see Mrs Jones smiling at me. 'I did like your accessories at the Midsummer Fayre. And then when I saw them in the Sunday paper, I thought I must buy something.'

Really? I almost say, somehow unable to imagine Elaine Jones wearing any of my creations.

'I'd like to order something for my niece. Do you have anything that would go with her auburn hair?'

'I'll see what I've got left. If not, I can make something to order.

'That would be lovely. And on the subject of your artwork, would you like to come and talk to the children during assembly?' This is completely unexpected. And as per usual before I know it I've said yes. I then backtrack, saying, 'I'm not sure what you want me to say.'

'You're a role model for "gals" everywhere,' she says. 'It's all about aspiration. Your training at art school, your textile designs and now your business.'

She's been reading *Mercia* magazine, I think. And I had her down as a *Horse and Hound* subscriber.

'And of course self-employment. Could you do tomorrow? We're so close to the end of term. So much to fit in with sports day. And I'd like to use the PTA money to get that lovely husband of yours to make us a yurt for the outdoor classroom project. Just send him to me to discuss it.'

'I'll pass the message on.'

'You will be doing the mums' run.' I nod, not sure whether

I've agreed to both tomorrow's assembly AND the run. I can hardly walk in this heat, let alone attempt a run.

Alone, I walk back down the Green. Soon it will be the holidays. I think it'll be a working holiday for us all. My daughters are going to be old fashioned girls, spending their summer holidays working – sewing.

The key to my business is to diversify, I tell myself. Put the dog lead episode behind you and think about the autumn term and Christmas around the corner. I think about baubles, stars and bespoke Christmas stockings filled with matching accessories for that very special person in your life. With so many ideas I'm going to need a whole army of sewing ladies. What else can I make with vintage and recycled fabrics? Perhaps I can incorporate some exotic fabrics too? I could draw upon Norfolk's old textile links with India. I know I'm getting carried away here, but I do love creative thinking!

The girls are back from school and are 'hiding' indoors. It's so hot outside. Today, Reedby reminded me of the south of France: a bright blue sky, lavender plants in flower and, not so attractive – the scorched lawn. I look out onto the patio. The sky has gone dark. I see enormous raindrops hit the burning concrete. 'It's a tropical storm,' shouts Lilly. We all run into the garden and shower in the rain. I love the smell of rain falling on the baked tarmac. It's so exotic.

I hear Adi's bike crunching across the gravel. It's strange at this time in the day. I'm not used to Adi being home so early. I haven't got completely into our new routine of all of us working from home. Adi stands in the conservatory, beckoning me in.

'Guess what! Hannelore's about to go to Quirgizstan until the spring.'

'What?' I compete to be heard against the crashing rain.

'She's packed her bags. She's off first thing in the morning.'

'She didn't tell me. How come you know?'

Adi taps his nose. I'm always the last to know things! 'I dropped a punnet of raspberries round on the way back from the allotment. She says it's time to hit the road. She also said that David and I can have the barn for six months, rent free, until we get the business up and running,' he says, excitedly. 'Then she'll be asking for rent.'

'Sounds like Hannelore. I think her and Peter are the nomads.'

'She says she's off to help Peter complete his survey of soil samples. Apparently the Victoria and Albert have been so over-whelmed by the number of visitors, just to look at the tents they donated, that they have given Hannelore a grant for more textile work. Can you believe it gives grants for the over sixties?'

'That's what we need. A grant to keep us going,' I say, still feeling guilty about leaving the college.

'Well, she did say that David and I should contact the Victoria and Albert Museum about doing yurt-making taster workshops for schools. Oh, and she gave me this. It's for you,' says Adi, handing me a large jiffy bag.

I'm always excited by presents. I have to open them imme-diately. I tear open the envelope and find two parcels wrapped in white tissue paper. One is a rectangular package, tied with blue velvet ribbon. Attached to it with blue embroidery thread is a gift tag which says Laura. The other, smaller, lumpy parcel is for Daisy and Lilly.

On top of them is a letter. My initial response is to open my parcel first. But I restrain myself and I draw out the excitement by reading the letter first. I scan the neat, italic handwriting. Then I begin to read for real.

Dear Laura,
I never did tell you how I escaped from East Berlin. I put that part of my life away – in a little box, or as you will find out, at the back of my wardrobe. I want you to know my story, because I know you will understand it. Three things helped me escape.
My false documents (that was the easy part).
A dog (a poodle! this one was black, just like the ones the ladies of Paris take shopping).
My sewing skills.

I can feel my heart beating. I'm nervous about what I'm going to read next.

This is how it happened. To leave East Berlin, pretending to be a West Berliner, the hardest part was to look exactly like one. I had to have the right clothes – a fault with my outfit would cost me my freedom. I knew I had to leave in the summer, making authentic western winter clothes would be too hard. I wouldn't be able to find cashmere or good quality wool, like the Westerners wore. That spring, the sailor dress was in fashion. I used a white cotton tablecloth to make what today looks like an outfit for Wimbledon. I carefully embroidered an anchor on the front.

I feel the tissue-wrapped bundle in my hands. I can't wait any longer, I untie the velvet ribbon and out falls a white cotton sailor dress, with an anchor as its central motif.

The border crossing took a matter of minutes. Although at the time it seemed like hours. I walked confidently in my sailor dress to the U-Bahn stop at Friedrichstrasse. I'd painted my brown platform shoes with a bright red polka dot design. Like any good West Berliner (I made a good fake West Berliner) I handed back my useless, unspent East German marks. I particularly enjoyed that part. They searched through my bag, also homemade, and soon lost interest when a loud barking sound came from one of the other cubicles.

'You cannot bring the dog without a rabies certificate,' boomed one of the guards.

'But I come every week,' said the girl, who I'd seen with a little black poodle.

In the confusion I simply stepped onto the train. It sped up and then slowed down through the dimly lit ghost stations of Unter den Linden and Potsdamer Platz. It was like passing those London underground stations in the City which close at the weekend, but are still lit and the trains still slow down. I saw soldiers up above on patrol of no man's land. Finally, after minutes that felt like hours I arrived at Yorckstrasse, the gateway to West Berlin. And I never looked back. You see I met Peter so soon afterwards. But that is another story.

I look at the sailor dress and think of Mum and her special dresses. My face feels hot and flushed as I read on.

I'm not sure when I'll be back so I have two big favours to ask you. First, I want you to make me something new from my dress. I'll never wear it again and it's wrong for it to stay at the back of my wardrobe.

I can't cut up her dress! What can I make from something white? All my designs rely on pretty fabrics. A beach bag to take to Great Yarmouth? I read on.

Second, I want you to take over my classes. I know you're not the best stitcher.

I smile, loving the way that Hannelore is so un-English and tells me exactly what she thinks, which is usually just what I need to hear.

It takes years, not months, to be as good as some of my ladies, but you can be a bridge between art, craft and design of the stitch. That's what twenty-first century stitching will be all about. David will give you the details.
H
p.s. I hope the girls like the furniture.

'Mummy! You've got a present?' says Daisy, rushing up to me. 'Mummy, why are you crying?'

'I'm not, it's the heat,' I lie, realising that my eyes have

409

completely welled up with tears. 'This is for you and Lilly,' I say, handing her the parcel.

Daisy tears it open in a matter of seconds, the contents falling on to the table.

I examine the perfect mini table and chairs made from matchsticks, an old cigarette packet, an acorn and little scraps of fabric.

'It's for your doll's house,' I say. A housewarming present for all of us I think.'

Daisy runs into the garden, shouting, 'Lilly! Look! Look!'

'We're one big, well, small, happy family, aren't we?' I say, squeezing Adi's hand, still holding on to Hannelore's dress, and following the girls into the garden.

Adi doesn't say anything. Instead he manages to lift all of us up and spin us around the garden till we fall in a heap on the wet lawn.

'Can we sleep in the big tent tonight?' squeals Daisy.

Adi's and my eyes meet. We both smile and all head into the yurt.

Appendix

Laura's Norfolk Lavender Bags

Whether you're new to sewing or an old-hand, making a lavender bag is easy. It's a wonderful gift, sew one for yourself to give your home that 'homemade' look.

Ingredients

Two 15cm squares of recycled, cotton fabric (be bold and mix 'n' match florals, checks, spots and stripes)

Two 13cm squares of wadding

A sprinkling of dried lavender flowers. 'Lavender grows very easily in a sunny garden spot, in tubs, or on windowsills and hardly needs watering,' Adi Stark.

Needles, pins, cotton and silk threads.

A recycled ribbon (from a gift box, Easter egg packaging . . .)

Recipe

Pin the right sides of fabric together (the right side is the patterned side – however it's worth checking the 'wrong' side as sometimes the pattern is more interesting) and stitch the sides and bottom of fabric together using regular cotton thread.

This is the exciting part! Turn inside out (and right way round) and fill with a lavender wadding sandwich. This is two squares of wadding with an even sprinkling of lavender in the middle.

Your last step is to sew the opening. To do this, simply turn the raw seam edges back into the hole so that nothing is hanging out and stitch along the seam. Use embroidery silks and choose a decorative stitch such as: small, even blanket, buttonhole, herringbone or zigzag stitch. *This will make your bag unique and different to mass-produced shop versions!*

Optional extras to personalise your lavender bags

Stitch a word or message on to the cotton squares before joining them together and make it special to you or for your loved ones.

Sew buttons into the centre or in a decorative pattern to add a lovely personal touch.

Use larger pieces of fabric to make a small pillow.

Adi's directions for drying lavender

Cut stems to about 15cm and tie the lavender together in bunches of about ten.

Hang the bunch upside down for 2–3 weeks until the flower heads are dry. I often hang bunches up on the walls.

When they are dry, brush all the petals off the stem and store in an airtight container.

Laura's Spring Chicks

A handmade chick adds a touch of spring to your home and makes a lovely Easter gift for young and old alike.

Ingredients

Two squares of recycled, cotton fabric (yellow gingham is my favourite spring fabric. The size of your squares is up to you, depending on how big you want your chicks, but 15cm is a good minimum.)

Contrasting fabric for the wings, beak and crown. Felt works well for this.

Wadding.

Needles, pins, cotton and silk threads.

Recipe

Using the chick template below (photocopy to your preferred size) cut two pieces of chick-shaped fabric for the body and two pieces each of contrasting fabric for the wings, crown and beak.

Pin wings and crown to the chick shape on the right side and sew round using over stitch. Make a single stitch for the eyes.

Turn right sides together and hand sew around the chick shape using running stitch. Leave a gap along the bottom edge for stuffing. Turn right sides out using scissors to push out any awkward corners. Stuff with wadding until quite full, using little clumps at a time. Sew up the opening and stitch on the beak.

Optional extras to personalise your spring chicks

You may wish to stitch a word, message, or date – such as Easter 2012 – onto the body or wing.

For adults and older children you could sew buttons on the head for eyes. You could also use star stitch or a French knot for the eyes.

And finally, if you want to be very green and use all recycled materials, you could stuff the chicks with clean, chopped up old stockings or tights!

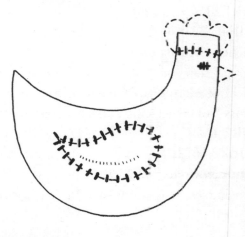

If you enjoyed this book and are
in the mood for some craft inspiration,
you may want to visit the following:

Victoria and Albert Museum
V&A South Kensington
Cromwell Road
London SW7 2RL
Tel. +44 (0)20 7942 2000
www.vam.ac.uk

Costume and Textiles Study Centre
Carrow House
301 King Street
Norwich NR1 2TS
Tel. +44 (0)1603 223870
www.norwichtextiles.org.uk

Strangers' Hall Museum, Norwich
Charing Cross
Norwich NR2 4AL
Tel. +44 (0)1603 667229
www.museums.norfolk.gov.uk

Forge Mill Needle Museum
Needle Mill Lane
Redditch, Worcestershire B98 8HY
Tel. +44 (0)1527 62509
www.forgemill.org.uk

The Women's Library
London Metropolitan University
25 Old Castle Street
London E1 7NT
Tel. +44 (0)20 7320 2222
www.londonmet.ac.uk/thewomenslibrary/

Fashion and Textile Museum
83 Bermondsey Street
London
SE1 3XF
Tel. +44 (0)20 7407 8664
www.ftmlondon.org

DDR Museum
Karl-Liebknecht-Str. 1
right on the river Spree, directly opposite the Berlin Cathedral
10178 Berlin
www.ddr-museum.de/en/

WHY DO WE HAVE TO LIVE WITH MEN?

Bernadette Strachan

'Funny, original and wise' Katie Fforde

Why do we have to live with men? As another evening with her best
friends and a few bottles of wine comes to an end, Cat O'Connor is
left pondering this very question. And, escaping from a ruined love
affair, she is about to find the answer.

When Cat joins a group of women in a huge, decaying farmhouse
deep in the countryside, she prepares to embark on six months
without men. Cat is promised a nirvana of serenity where the chores
are done without mutinous mutterings, where nourishing food
simmers on the Aga and where feelings are taken seriously. But Cat
soon discovers that women are no saints either . . .

'I really couldn't put this down, much to the annoyance
of the man I have to live with'
Chrissie Manby

'An absolute treat
Louise Candlish

Fiction
978 0 7515 4229 5

Other bestselling titles available by mail

☐ How to Lose a Husband and Gain a Life   Bernadette Strachan   £6.99
☐ Why Do We Have to Live With Men?   Bernadette Strachan   £6.99

The prices shown above are correct at time of going to press. However, the publishers reserve the right to increase prices on covers from those previously advertised, without further notice.

─────────────── sphere ───────────────

Please allow for postage and packing: **Free UK delivery.**
Europe: add 25% of retail price; Rest of World: 45% of retail price.

To order any of the above or any other Sphere titles, please call our credit card orderline or fill in this coupon and send/fax it to:

Sphere, PO Box 121, Kettering, Northants NN14 4ZQ
Fax: 01832 733076   Tel: 01832 737526
Email: aspenhouse@FSBDial.co.uk

☐ I enclose a UK bank cheque made payable to Sphere for £ . . . .
☐ Please charge £ . . . . . . to my Visa/Delta/Maestro

Expiry Date   Maestro Issue No.

NAME (BLOCK LETTERS please) . . . .
ADDRESS . . . .
. . . .
. . . .
Postcode . . . . Telephone . . . .
Signature . . . .

Please allow 28 days for delivery within the UK. Offer subject to price and availability.